THE LOST LABYR...

Will Adams has tried his ha... ...titude of careers over the years. M... ...y, he worked for a London-based ... ...mmunications consultants before ... ... to pursue his life-long dream of w... ...ion. His first novel, *The Alexander Ciph...* was a top-twenty UK bestseller in 2007, his second, *The Exodus Quest*, followed in 2008.

Also by Will Adams

The Alexander Cipher
The Exodus Quest

WILL ADAMS

The Lost Labyrinth

HARPER

Harper
An imprint of HarperCollins*Publishers*
77–85 Fulham Palace Road,
Hammersmith, London W6 8JB

www.harpercollins.co.uk

A Paperback Original 2009
1

A catalogue record for this book
is available from the British Library

ISBN: 978-0-00-728631-7

Typeset in Minion by Palimpsest Book Production Limited,
Grangemouth, Stirlingshire

Printed and bound in Great Britain by
Clays Ltd, St Ives plc

Mixed Sources
Product group from well-managed
forests and other controlled sources
www.fsc.org   Cert no. SW-COC-1806
© 1996 Forest Stewardship Council

FSC is a non-profit international organisation established
to promote the responsible management of the world's forests.
Products carrying the FSC label are independently certified
to assure consumers that they come from forests that are managed
to meet the social, economic and ecological needs
of present and future generations.

Find out more about HarperCollins and the environment at
www.harpercollins.co.uk/green

To Robert, Eleanor and Grace

ACKNOWLEDGMENTS

The Bronze Age Eastern Mediterranean, which provides the historical backdrop to this novel, is both intensely complex and endlessly fascinating. My immense gratitude, therefore, to my good friend Clive Pearson and to Dr Don Evely of the British School of Athens, Minoan experts both, for being so generous with their time and knowledge in helping me get a better grasp of it. Even more importantly, I'd like to thank them each for reading the first draft of the manuscript and making so many valuable suggestions and corrections. I have followed most, but not all, of their recommendations; so it's even truer than usual that any mistakes that remain are mine and mine alone.

Many other people helped me with my research too, both in the UK and on my travels in Greece and in Georgia. Kat Christopher, in particular, took immense trouble on my behalf in Athens, but I'd also like to thank Thanos and Angela for a delicious lunch, as well as Martin, Ioannis, Sandro, Thomas and the many others who helped out in one way or another.

Finally, and most importantly, I'd like to thank my agent Luigi Bonomi and my editor Wayne Brookes for their unfailing enthusiasm, advice and support. I owe them both a tremendous debt.

The Eleusinian Mysteries are one of the great enigmas of the ancient world. Celebrated for some two thousand years at the port of Eleusis, they were the high point of Greek religious life, until finally they were supplanted by Christianity in the early centuries A.D.

Sophocles considered thrice happy anyone initiated into the rites. Cicero called them Athens' greatest gift to man. Plato praised them as the perfect intellectual pleasure.

But the Mysteries were protected by an extraordinary cult of secrecy. People were put to death for merely hinting at their true nature. So, despite a few tantalising hints, no one today is quite sure what happened within the sanctuary's high walls; or, more to the point, what the secret was that needed such extreme measures to preserve.

PROLOGUE

Crete, 1553 B.C.

The food hadn't quite run out yet, but it would soon. And last night the snows had arrived, laying a white blanket over the plain, cutting off the pass. No relief would be coming now. Not for a month at least. More likely not until spring.

It was over.

The fire had gone out days before. There was no more wood. Not that Pijaseme needed a brand to navigate these caves. They were a natural labyrinth, yet he knew them better than any man who'd ever lived. He'd spent fifty-two summers in the service of the gods here, presiding for the last ten over the temple outside, during which time he'd led the discovery and consecration of three new galleries. But he kept his hand to the wall all the same. So much had changed these past years that it was reassuring to know that some things were immutable.

He could remember the moment still. It had emblazed upon his mind. For years, the goddess had been angry. For years, he and his fellow high priests had sought to understand their offence, the better to make reparation. But each of them had offered different solutions, and the goddess had grown unhappier. He'd been on the final descent to Knossos for the great harvest gathering when a light like sunrise had burst upon the northern horizon. For a moment he'd been euphoric: he'd prayed all his life that the goddess herself would come while he yet lived. But then he'd realised she'd come in anger.

And what anger!

Her roar had deafened him for days. Her hail of molten rock had set forests on fire all across the island. The waves she'd sent, as tall as mountains, had destroyed their fleets and ports. She'd blacked out the sky for many moons and assailed them with an extraordinary violence of storms. Ash had fallen calf deep upon their fields, killing their crops and trees and herds, blighting them with boils and deadly wasting diseases and causing this brutal, endless famine.

He reached the great gallery. It was brighter than he could ever remember, the sunlight that filtered through the thin crevice in its roof magnified by the mirrors of snow around its edges. A flake fell coldly against his temple, then ran like a tear down his cheek. He watched more arrive, fluttering slow as tiny feathers. Perhaps this was what the island needed. A purge of clean pure snow. Perhaps when it melted, it would take the ashes of the past with it, and the island would be born anew.

But Pijaseme wouldn't be there to see it.

He'd already prepared the poppy-juice. Now he poured it into the goblet. A gust of wind played the crevice like a horn as he did so. The Minotaur was roaring. He looked up at it towering above him, set there by the gods themselves as guardian of the island's oldest and most sacred labyrinth, which was why so many craftsmen and architects had made the pilgrimage here, to glean inspiration for their palaces. He poured a small libation in the basin at its feet before draining the rest in one go, grimacing against the taste. Then he walked down the corridor of axes to the great throne, where he set the bull's mask and horned crown upon his head and tried to buckle the sacred robe around his throat. But he was too weak from age and hunger to bear its weight, so he left it draped over the throne's high shoulders instead.

The poppy-juice began to ply its comforts. He felt his goddess smile, pleased by his choice of penance. He picked up the bone-handled knife and teased the wrinkled pale skin of his inner forearm with its tip.

It had been a fearful time, not knowing why the world had changed, or what to do. Survivors had converged on Knossos from every corner of the island, seeking comfort in numbers, terrified not merely by the cataclysms, but also by the knowledge that there was nothing now to prevent their one-time subjects coming here to take their revenge for all the casual cruelties they'd suffered at their hands. Nothing to stop them looting the holiest places of their sacred treasures, either.

It had been Pijaseme himself who'd suggested a solution to this latter problem – hiding all those treasures here, in the sure knowledge that no outlander would ever find them. He'd stood up before the council and given his oath that the goddess herself had visited him in a dream, and so ordered. They'd all been so eager for her forgiveness that they'd acquiesced at once. The treasures had duly arrived over the next few moons, Pijaseme giving each party in exchange a receipt for what they'd brought, along with a fired clay disc imprinted with signs so that their successors could find this labyrinth again, should none of them still be alive when finally the island recovered.

How he'd exulted as the treasures had stacked up! He'd been certain that the goddess would reward him. But her anger hadn't died. If anything, it had grown more savage, more personal. While other communities had seemed to reach and pass through the worst of this blight, his own had suffered more and more. She'd taken his surviving children, and their children and grandchildren too, until only he and his beloved grandson Eumolpos had been left of their once great family. And finally he'd acknowledged in his heart the true reason for her fury. There had been no dream. He hadn't brought these treasures here for her glory; he'd brought them for his own.

The exodus had taken place earlier that summer, when it had become clear that yet again there'd be no harvest. Eumolpos had taken charge, scavenging for wood in the mountains, dragging the timbers down to the coast, building a ship in which the few survivors had sailed north in search of a new land to settle. Their ancestors had arrived here from across the sea, after all. It seemed only fitting that they should leave that way too.

It had been a wrench to watch them go. Eumolpos had been Pijaseme's heir as high priest at the temple. But there was no temple any more: Poseidon earth-shaker had seen to that. And at least this way Eumolpos would carry with him his memories, his knowledge of the sacred objects and rituals. At least this way, the goddess would still be worshipped. Before he'd left, Eumolpos had asked Pijaseme to go with them, albeit with lowered eyes. But Pijaseme was too old and proud. Besides, he'd taken a sacred vow to look after these treasures to the death. And, to the death, he would.

Despite the poppy-juice, the pain was fierce as

he stabbed through the leathern skin of his wrist, then gashed jaggedly upwards along his forearm. He didn't let it stop him though, not with the goddess watching. He switched the blade from hand to hand, then slashed his other forearm too. Blood fell in slow waterfalls to form red lakes upon the dusty rock.

It was fitting. It was as it should be.

It had been his life to please the goddess. And he had failed.

ONE

Broward County Jail, Fort Lauderdale, Florida

'Visitor,' grunted the guard, heaving open the heavy steel door of Mikhail Nergadze's cell. 'Come with me.'

Mikhail took his time rising to his feet. It was a point of self-respect in places like these that you never gave the uniforms anything for free. Besides, he already knew who it would be. That court-appointed psychologist with her sneering upper lip and her aggressively folded arms. He'd always had an instinct for women like her. And sure enough, she was waiting impatiently for him in the dusty white-tiled interview room, dressed with her customary sharp-edged chic in a navy suit jacket and pencil skirt, her black hair cropped almost as short as his own prison crew-cut, just the faintest touches of perfume and make-up. Yet, he noted, faint though those touches of perfume and make-up might be, they were still there.

'Mister Nergadze,' she said sourly, enunciating each syllable like an insult.

'Doctor Mansfield,' he nodded. 'This is a pleasure.'

'Not for me, I assure you.' She gestured curtly for the guard to remain inside the room, then invited Mikhail to take one of two facing chairs. She waited until he was seated, then put down her briefcase by the other chair, produced a micro-cassette recorder that she placed on the floor between them, and sat opposite him. Then she brought out a set of papers on which she began to make notes on with a bulbous green fountain pen, glancing at him every few moments, like an artist working at a portrait, hoping no doubt to pique his curiosity. But Mikhail refused to bite. He folded his hands loosely in his lap and waited. It was perhaps five minutes before she sighed and rocked forward, passed two stapled pages to him, along with a blunt stub of pencil, as though he couldn't be trusted with her pen. 'Look at these for me, would you?'

'Why?'

'Do you really have so many better things to do?'

Mikhail shrugged and took the two pages, ran his eyes down the list of questions, gave her a dry cold look. But he didn't mind playing. The opposite, if anything. He knew it would tear at her all

10

the more when his family's army of lawyers finally got him out, which they would any day now; because without a body the police had nothing, and everyone knew it.

Failure to conform to social norms.

An easy starter. It never failed to astonish Mikhail that anyone should conform. Tick.

Regular bouts of irritability and aggression. Tick. *Impulsiveness.* Tick.

She had a nice figure, this shrink. He had to give her that. Terrific legs. Tan and shapely, long and smooth. Yet muscled, too. A ballerina's legs. Ideal for clasping tight around a man's waist. Making the most of them too, as far as professionalism would allow, at least, with her high heels and a slit in her skirt that showed rare flashes of thigh, and constantly drawing attention to them by folding one over the other, or allowing them to part just wide enough to offer a glimpse of the shadows beneath. Not much else to write home about, unfortunately. A face like a toad, with flared, upturned nostrils, and her complexion still raw from the ravages of teenage acne.

Disregard for the safety of others. Tick.
Irresponsible behaviour. Tick.
Multiple short-term marital relationships. Tick.

Her manner didn't do her any favours either, all snorts and squints, as if her main ambition in life was never to let anyone get the better of her. But she was young and female, when all was said and done; and Mikhail had learned long ago to take what pleasures he could in institutions like these.

Lack of regard for promises, deals and agreements. Tick.
Manipulative. Tick.
Lack of empathy.

Mikhail paused. He'd always been slightly perplexed by questions about empathy. It was like colour-blindness. People who couldn't distinguish between red and green, that was one thing; but how to know that his perception of yellow was the same as everyone else's? Empathy was like that, almost impossible to judge relatively. Over the years, a number of psychologists had shown him pictures of people's faces, as though they thought he suffered from Asperger's syndrome or something. But Mikhail had never had any difficulty distinguishing happy from sad, surprised from intrigued, angry

12

from lustful; and he understood what each of those emotions were too, having experienced them himself. Besides, people kept accusing him of being manipulative, and how could he manipulate people if he lacked empathy? He could be a bully, yes, or excessively demanding; but *manipulative*? Surely that demanded a certain level of fellow-feeling. So he'd always thought the real question was, did he give a fuck? With empathy, he reckoned you were supposed to give a fuck. He thought that was probably the whole point of it. And the answer was no. He didn't give a fuck. But here was the nub: How could he be sure that that made him unusual? How did he know that other people gave a fuck (or at least, any more of a fuck than he did)? He only had their word for it. Perhaps he was just more honest than they were. The way he saw it, no one truly gave a fuck how other people felt. Not truly. All they gave a fuck about was how other people felt *about them*. That's why they postured and pretended concern, because they thought other people would respect them or love them more. But, what the hell, he knew the answer she wanted. More to the point, it was the one that would gnaw at her most when he walked out of here a free man.

Lack of empathy. Tick.
Lack of remorse. Tick.

Though he'd never really seen what the fuss was about remorse, anyway. Such a dishonest emotion. If you couldn't live with the consequences of your actions, do something else, don't wail about it. More to the point, don't get caught. Mikhail couldn't remember the last time anyone expressed remorse *before* they got caught? No, best left to politicians and TV evangelists.

Often in trouble as a juvenile. Though it had never been his fault. Tick.

A parasitic lifestyle.

He bridled a little at the choice of word. He was no parasite; people just understood that they *owed* him, because of the kind of man he was. But fuck it, he was on a roll: Tick.

He looked up at her. 'Where do you live?' he asked. 'Somewhere around here?'

'Just finish the list.'

'Only we should get together for a drink when I get out.'

'I don't make dates fifty years in advance.'

Pathological dishonesty. He'd be lying if he said otherwise. Tick.
Cruelty to animals and other people.

'When you say cruelty,' he asked, 'do you mean physical violence? Or do you include mental cruelty as well?'

'Would it make a difference?'

Fair point. Tick.

Considers themselves outside or above the law. Tick.

He glanced up sharply enough to catch her staring at him. He smiled knowingly, and she tossed her head and looked away, haughty as a rich girl's pony, as though she thought Mikhail was so far beneath her, it was an ordeal even to be in the same room as him, as though she had to *steel* herself. But he hadn't forced her to visit. Nor had the court, not this time. No. She'd come here on her own account.

Rampant fantasies of personal prowess and triumph.

Yes, he thought. Last night I dreamed about coming after you, you bitch. Tick.

Exaggerated sexuality.

He paused again. 'Do you mean that I exaggerate my sexuality? Or that my capacity for sex is uncommonly large?'

She smiled thinly at him, reluctant to give him anything. 'The latter.'

Exaggerated sexuality. Tick.

'Is that why you've been masturbating over me?'
'Just finish the list.'
'When you masturbate over me, do you imagine me naked?'
'The list, please, Mister Nergadze.'
'Mikhail, please.'

Demands immediate and complete compliance from those around them. Tick.
Superficial charm.

He hesitated over this one, too. 'Superficial?' he asked.

She frowned, surprised he'd stumbled over such a common word. 'Superficial means, er, like, er, on the surface.'

Mikhail felt himself being lifted up by a gentle wave of anger, that his Eastern European roots and accent had yet again been mistaken for stupidity. It had happened so many times during his years of exile in England and America that perhaps he should have grown used to it, but it still had the power to catch him by surprise. On the other hand, gaol had taught him to keep his safety-catch on, to bide his time for the chance that would soon come. He waited for the wave to subside again before replying. 'I know what *it* means,' he said. 'What I'm asking is what *you* mean. Charm is, by definition, superficial, wouldn't you say? I think the word you're looking for is "false", isn't it?'

She coloured a little. 'I suppose false would . . . yes, that would be fine.'

He crossed out 'superficial', wrote in 'false' instead. Tick.

Envious of others.

He frowned. Would he really switch places with anyone else? To get out of here, maybe. But what the hell. Tick.

Often bored. Tick.

He handed her back the questionnaire. A perfect score. She took the pages with a slight smirk, as though she'd just won a bet with herself. Mikhail smiled too. He liked cocky shrinks. They thought they were so insightful, so well-armoured. It fucked them up all the more when he got inside their heads. 'You never answered my question,' he said.

'What question?'

'Do you imagine me naked? When you masturbate about me?'

'Masturbation, Mister Nergadze?' she asked dryly. 'Are you not confusing me with yourself?'

He looked into her eyes and held her gaze. She tried to stare him out; she didn't stand a chance. When finally she broke and looked away, her throat turned lovely hot confused colours, and he felt a familiar stirring in his loins that confirmed to him the true reason she'd come back, which had nothing to do with his so-called disorder. At least, it had everything to do with it, but not in a way her professional association would approve.

She composed herself again, turned back to him, flint in her eyes, wanting pay-back. 'So,' she said, 'you want to tell me what really happened that night?'

'I already told you what happened.'

'The *real* story.'

'Oh, the *real* story.'

'You want to, you know. In the end, men like you always boast about their . . . exploits.'

Mikhail nodded at the guard still standing by the door. 'And men like him send us to the chair for it.'

She turned to the guard. 'Leave us, please.'

The guard glowered at Mikhail. 'You sure about that, ma'am? This one's a mean son-of-a-bitch.'

'I asked you to leave us alone.'

They both watched him out. Mikhail could tell

she was pleased with herself; demonstrating courage and trust, just like they counselled in the textbooks. The steel shutter in the door shrieked open, and the guard put his eye to the viewing window, his face magnified and made even uglier by the glass.

'What if he can lip-read?' asked Mikhail.

'You want to trade seats?' she asked. 'So as he can't see your face?'

'I want him not to watch at all.'

She went to the door, held a murmured but intense conversation. The door closed, then the shutter over the viewing window. She sat back down. 'Well?' she asked. 'Ready to talk now?'

'With your tape recorder on?'

'This session is confidential. I assure you, nothing will be used against you.'

He snorted and raised an eyebrow. She sighed and switched off her machine. 'Okay,' he said. 'I'll tell you what you want to know. But I want something from you first.'

'What?'

'I want to know why you're so interested in me.'

She studied him a moment, as if to assess him for sincerity. It always amazed him how credulous these people were: she seemed to have forgotten her checklist already. He kept his expression impassive, knowing she wanted to tell him, her own cleverness bottled like champagne bubbles inside her, pressing for release. When she began to talk, she quickly grew excited. She stood up, began walking back and forth across the narrow room, gesturing grandly. She was working on a paper for the journals, it transpired. Her subject matter was narcissistic sociopaths. That Mikhail was one would be obvious to any first-year student, of course; but most people with narcissistic personality disorder were either cerebral or somatic, which was to say arrogant because of their intelligence or because of their physique and athletic prowess respectively. He was both. That in itself made him a curiosity. But there was more. Most narcissists were, at heart, self-loathing. It was their very hatred for themselves that drove their desperate need for adulation and worship from the people around them, their need for what she called narcissistic supply, and which she talked of as though it were a drug. When they were deprived of that supply, their fantasies about themselves collapsed, they fell into depression and despair. But he, while displaying all the signs of classic narcissism, seemed immune to depression and despair, even when his narcissistic supply was denied him, and she wanted to know why. Criminal narcissism was her thing, and she sensed in Mikhail an opportunity for a real advance, because if she could find his secret, maybe it would offer a way to palliate self-loathing in others and so break the narcissistic cycle altogether. She got all excited and earnest, wobbling a little on her heels as she walked, red patches glowing on her throat and cheeks, like a litter of kittens seen through a night-sight. Finally she stopped and gave him one of those *well, there it is* shrugs, expecting him to honour his part of the deal, tell her how he'd raped and murdered that innocent little thirteen-year-old Lolita.

Innocent! Hah!

He stood and pushed back his chair, its feet growling over the bare cement floor. Then he started walking towards her. She produced a nervous smile, her pupils flickered, and she backed away until she was up against the wall by the door. He kept advancing, slowly, fixing his best unthreatening smile in place, as though she were some lapdog yapping at him, and he didn't want to spook it, or he'd lose his chance to kick it.

She balled her fist up to pound on the door and summon the guard. She tensed her arm twice in preparation, but Mikhail kept advancing and in the end she couldn't quite bring herself to do it. Self-knowledge at last. She put both her arms down by her side, fingers splayed like sunbursts. He was standing right in front of her now, their bodies almost touching face, chest, knee, toe. He could hear her breathing patterns change until they were in synchrony with his. He rewarded her with a smile. He placed one hand on her left shoulder, the other, on her hip, began to gather up the charged fabric of her skirt. They stared each other in the eye. She neither stopped him, nor encouraged him, but when he slipped his hand beneath the skirt and up her thigh over her knickers to her pudenda, she gave an almost inaudible exhalation, like some pre-packaged grocery product being punctured, allowing that preservative air to escape. A moment of almost pure silence, except that he could hear the saliva washing around her mouth and throat, while a pulse flickered in her pussy, like some terrified rodent cowering in his palm. 'Mr Nergadze,' she croaked, in her best school-marm tone, as though to reprimand him. He waited, but she said nothing else, so he gave her a gentle encouraging squeeze and smiled more broadly at her. She smiled weakly back, a smile of complete concession, an invitation to do whatever he wanted.

He let go of her, stepped away, returned to his chair, sat back down and folded his hands once more in his lap. 'Narcissistic, am I?' he asked. 'Or is it simply that I *am* beautiful?'

TWO

I

The Kastelli Hotel, Athens, Greece, two weeks later

The three of them were laughing hard at the sheer awfulness of Knox's joke when Augustin swiped his hotel key-card through the lock outside his room and pushed his door open with his foot. But the laughter died at once.

It was the smell that did it for Knox: not that it was overpowering, just sour and ugly, but it provoked an immediate and visceral disgust, so that he knew something was badly wrong. He looked over Augustin's shoulder and saw gouts of blood and vomit on the fibrous blue carpet, and then a naked elderly man lying on his back in the narrow aisle between the double and single beds, his right arm thrown out above his head. There were stains around his waist, where his bladder and bowels had vented. There was a great gash in his forehead, too, from which copious amounts of blood had spilled, and there was a look of such stark terror on his face that Knox instantly assumed that not only was he dead, but that he'd sensed his fate in the very moment it had overtaken him.

It was a real shock, then, when the man convulsed upon the carpet, a spasm that ran up his body like a flapped-out sheet. It was Claire who moved first, trained medic that she was. She pushed past Augustin and knelt down beside him. 'Ambulance,' she said succinctly. Augustin nodded and hurried around the single bed, then knelt on it to grab the bedside phone and dial the operator.

The man opened his eyes and gave a little croak, trying to speak, blood-frothed saliva leaking from the side of his mouth. Claire wiped it away with a corner of the bedspread. He spoke again. She shook her head to indicate that he should preserve his strength, but he kept persisting, so Knox pushed aside the bed to make room for himself on his other side, then knelt down and put his ear close to his lips. But the man's voice was so weak that it was almost impossible to make out anything much more than the shape and thrust of the syllables. He frowned interrogatively at Claire. 'Elysium?' he suggested.

'Maybe,' she shrugged.

'Who the hell is he?' asked Knox, standing back up.

'Roland Petitier,' said Augustin, still waiting for the operator to answer.

Knox nodded. An old archaeology professor of Augustin's who'd vanished without trace nearly twenty years ago, only to reappear unexpectedly a few weeks before, and who was scheduled to address the conference the following afternoon. 'But what's he doing here?'

Augustin gave a very Gallic shrug, as if to disclaim responsibility. 'I hear a knock on my door earlier. I think it must be you, come to take me to the airport. But no, it's him. After twenty years. He tells me his room isn't ready yet and asks if he can stay here until it is. I tell him no. I tell him I am about to collect my fiancée Claire from the airport. He swears on his mother's life he'll be gone by the time we get back. On his mother's life!'

'You can't exactly blame him for –'

Augustin held up a finger. The operator had finally picked up. 'Emergency,' he told them curtly. 'Room five-thirteen. We need an ambulance.' He listened a moment. 'No. He's taken a blow to the head.' Another pause. He looked around the room. 'No. I don't think so.'

Claire had tilted Petitier's head backwards, and put her ear against his mouth. 'Tell them he's stopped breathing,' she said, with impressive calmness. 'Tell them to bring a defibrillator.' While

Augustin relayed the message, she moved briskly into cardiopulmonary resuscitation, using both hands to pump Petitier's chest hard. She clearly knew what she was about, so Knox stepped away to give her space, then took the opportunity to see if he could work out what had happened.

The room was virtually identical to his and Gaille's on the floor above. The medium-pile blue carpet showed signs of wear; the double and the single bed both sagged a little in the middle. There were dark spots on the mirrors of the dressing table, and on the glass of the framed prints of the Acropolis, Mycenae and Epidaurus on the walls. A splashing noise was coming from the bathroom. He pushed open the door to see the shower spraying hot water into the bathtub, trapping thick clouds of mist against the ceiling. He made to turn it off, then paused at the startling realisation that this might be a crime scene, so he went back out and closed the door behind him.

A black laptop case was leaning against the bed, bulkier than Augustin's, so presumably Petitier's. Again, he left it untouched. The white net curtain billowed over the balcony door, pregnant with breeze, revealing a few red smears upon its fabric. He pushed it carefully aside. The sliding glass door was wide open. He went out onto the balcony. The moulded plastic table and one of the two matching chairs had been overturned, as if by a storm or a fight. An overnight bag was lying on its side, the old brown leather ripped open and leaking entrails: underpants, vests, shirts and trousers. He leaned out over the railing, looked down past lower balconies to the narrow alley far beneath, congested with rusting skips filled with multicoloured bags of hotel waste. He looked left and right. The neighbouring balconies were separated from one another by spiked railings, but it would be easy enough for anyone with a head for heights to swing around them; and there was precious little chance of being seen.

Back inside, Augustin was standing by Claire, wanting to help but not sure how. 'I knew I should say no when he asks to stay,' he told Knox.

'So why didn't you?'

'He seemed so desperate. I mean he was really paranoid that someone was after him.'

'Paranoid?' asked Knox dryly.

'He made me swear not to tell anyone he was here. That's why I said nothing earlier.'

'Did he give you any idea who was after him?'

'No. But he's found something, I know that much. In Crete, apparently. Some seal-stones and maybe some other things. I think perhaps he has them with him, because he won't let go of his overnight bag, you know. I mean he hugged it against him like it was his only child.'

Lift doors opened down the corridor. There were shouts and the thud of heavy boots. Two policemen in the dark blue uniform of the *Elleniki Astynomia* appeared at the door, holding white crash helmets and truncheons in their hands, as though fresh from riot duty. The first was tall and powerful, yet his features were soft and unlined, making him look almost too young to be in the police. His partner was older, portly, wheezing from the run. He pushed past his younger colleague, sized up the situation. 'Away!' he ordered Claire. She didn't even look up, too concentrated on giving Petitier CPR. 'Away!' he barked more loudly, angered at being ignored.

'She's a doctor,' protested Augustin. 'Leave her be.'

'Away!' he shouted a third time.

The younger policeman stepped forward, nettled by this lack of respect for his partner. He reached around Claire from behind, grabbing her breast as he did so.

The colour rose instantly in Augustin's face; he punched the young policeman hard on his cheek, sending him sprawling. Then he turned to Claire. 'Are you all right?' he asked.

The young policeman got back to his feet, a look of pure fury in his eye. He lashed his baton so hard across Augustin's cheek that a fragment of tooth flew from between his lips, and he cried out and fell to his knees, hands to his bloodied mouth. Knox hurried to intervene, but the older policeman seized him by the arm and held him back. And something seemed to release in his young partner, a kind of obscene rage. His face was almost purple as he smashed his baton down on Augustin's crown, mercifully catching him only a glancing blow, yet still splitting his scalp so that the blood gushed even as he fell onto his side in the narrow gap between the bed and wall. Claire screamed and grabbed the policeman's arm, but he threw her off easily, then turned back to Augustin and hit him again. But the way Augustin had fallen made it hard for the policeman to get at his head, so he pushed the bed aside and stepped around him to give himself a better angle of attack.

Finally Knox fought his way free. He hurried across the room and grabbed the policeman's flailing wrist, twisting it sharply. The policeman yelped and dropped his baton, turning to Knox with a slightly dazed expression, as though uncertain what was going on. Then he looked down at Augustin lying unconscious at his feet, at the oily dark blood gathering in a shallow lake on the carpet, and at the red spatters of guilt already caking on his own hands, and a look of horror appeared upon his face, and he began to weep.

II

A conference room, Tbilisi, Georgia

Conflicting emotions tussled in Edouard Zdanevich's breast as he stood in front of the painting. It was executed in oils on black oil-cloth, perhaps seventy centimetres wide by a metre tall, a portrait of a voluptuous woman in a rocking chair, nursing an infant through the folds of her blue-black dress, the barest hint of breast showing. Simple colours and themes executed with intense power and humanity. A Pirosmani, without doubt, as gorgeous as any in Tbilisi. Yet Edouard had never seen it before, had not even known it existed. And while it was a thrill for him merely to be in its presence, it infuriated him that these damned Nergadzes had it hanging here on their wall, when he doubted any of them knew what it was, or why it was important, or the first thing about the great man who'd painted it. All they ever knew or cared about anything was how much it cost.

Somewhere in the building, a door opened, allowing out a billow of raucous laughter. Another of the Nergadzes' famously debauched feasts, no doubt. Edouard despised such wanton displays of gluttony, lechery and drunkenness – but it would be nice, he had to admit, to be able to despise them from the inside for a change.

A pair of glass cabinets stood against the wall, both filled with Colchian gold jewellery, vessels, ornaments and coins. The pieces were very familiar to him. They'd come from a trove discovered some decades earlier in an abandoned well in the hill-country of Turkmenistan, across the Caspian Sea, and had been on display in their national museum in Ashgabat. It had long been known that many of the pieces were Georgian, but only recently had the Turkmeni government countenanced a sale. Edouard himself had flown to Ashgabat, where he'd negotiated their purchase and repatriation. Though he'd used Nergadze money, the agreement had been clear: he'd bought the cache on behalf of the nation of Georgia, for display in her national museums. Ilya Nergadze had bathed in public admiration for days on the back of his generosity. Yet the gold pieces weren't on display at any national museum. They were on display here, where ordinary Georgians would never have the chance to see them.

Footsteps approached briskly outside, then the double doors banged open and Ilya Nergadze marched on in, followed closely by his son Sandro and one of his small army of bodyguards. He went everywhere on the march, old man Ilya, like a general on the morning of battle. He was tall and extravagantly thin, with a high brow, a flat nose and a tight line to his mouth, as though life had been unforgivably cruel to him, rather than to everyone who'd come into his orbit. His hair and eyebrows, until recently a snowy white, now glistened with black dye, while his skin had been noticeably tightened by nip-tuck surgery and botox injections, an effort at youthfulness that should have made him look ridiculous, except that people like him somehow *never* looked ridiculous, particularly not in their presence, perhaps because everyone was too afraid to snigger.

'I'm grateful you asked me here,' said Edouard, joining them at the rosewood conference table. 'We need to finalise the transfer of –'

'All in good time,' said Sandro, sitting opposite him. He was considered the diplomat of the family; which was why he'd been appointed head of his father's presidential campaign.

'But people are talking,' protested Edouard. 'My colleagues at the museum keep asking me when they'll –'

'He said all in good time,' said the bodyguard.

Edouard looked sourly at him. Nergadze bodyguards typically knew better than to talk in the presence of their superiors. But this one looked more relaxed than most, perhaps forty or so, wearing a turtleneck sweater beneath his black jacket. He was unshaven, too, perhaps the better to show off the crescent scar in his cheek, where no stubble grew. 'I'm sorry,' said Edouard stiffly. 'I don't believe we've met.'

'This is Boris Dekanosidze,' said Sandro. 'My head of security. I wanted you to meet him because you're going to be working together over the next few days.'

'I beg your pardon?'

'You're leaving for Athens tonight. Directly after this meeting, in fact.'

'I'm doing nothing of the sort,' retorted Edouard. 'I thought I'd made it clear that I won't accept any more commissions until you honour your –'

'You'll accept whatever commissions we tell you to accept,' said Ilya.

'There'll be plenty of time to complete the transfer of the cache once you return,' added Sandro, in a more emollient tone. 'But right now, we have an urgent situation, and we need your help.' He nodded to Boris, who slid a manila folder across the polished rosewood. Edouard opened it reluctantly, then read through the correspondence inside with growing bewilderment. 'This is a joke,' he said finally. 'It has to be.'

'My grandson Mikhail is going to see the item in question tomorrow morning,' said Ilya. 'You will go along with him.'

'But you don't even have a grandson called Mikhail,' protested Edouard.

'Do I not?' asked Ilya.

'Boris will be with you too,' said Sandro, into the ensuing silence. 'He'll pay for this item once you've authenticated it.'

'*If* I authenticate it, you mean,' said Edouard.

A look of profound irritation clouded Ilya's face. 'Please don't persist in telling us what we mean.'

Another silence fell. Somewhere deep in the house, a burst of uproarious laughter was timed so perfectly that Edouard couldn't help but think that Nergadze's guests were watching him on CCTV. Not for the first time, he realised how inconsequential he was to these people. Their presidential campaign was in full swing, and Ilya was making good headway in the polls. Nothing else mattered to them. 'You can't seriously expect me to authenticate a fake,' said Edouard.

'It won't be a fake,' observed Sandro. 'Not once a man of your reputation has verified it.'

'It would ruin me. I won't do it.'

'You *will* do it,' said Ilya.

Edouard forced and held a smile, aware he wouldn't get anywhere by confrontation. 'Look,' he said. 'I'd like to help. Really I would. But I can't. Not this weekend. My wife is already furious about how much I've been away recently. She issued me with an ultimatum, as it happens. We spend this weekend together, or else. You know what wives are like.'

'Don't worry about your wife,' said Ilya.

'But you don't understand. I gave her my word. If I fail to –'

'I said, don't worry about her.'

There was something in his voice. 'How do you mean?' asked Edouard.

'I mean that your wife and your daughters will be very well looked after while you're away. And that charming son of yours too.'

Edouard kept a family photograph in his wallet. He liked to take it out whenever he felt low. It came unbidden to his mind now: himself looking rather portlier than he'd like, yet undeniably grand in his chartreuse suit and yellow cravat, a quiet protest against the black worn by almost every other adult male in Tbilisi, as though their whole nation were in mourning. Nina in her gorgeous blue velvet dress. The twins Eliso and Lila in matching cream blouses and ankle-length black skirts. Kiko in the white-and-red rugby shirt signed by the Georgian national team. 'What are you talking about?' he asked.

'They are to be my guests,' said Ilya. 'Just until you return from Athens.'

Edouard dropped his hand to his pocket, felt the contour and weight of his mobile phone against his thigh. A phone call, a text message, telling Nina to put the kids in the car, take them away somewhere, anywhere.

'Don't trouble yourself,' said Ilya, reading his

35

thoughts. 'They already *are* my guests. My grandson Alexei is taking them to my Nikortsminda estate as we speak.'

'They'll be very well looked after,' Sandro assured him. 'We're having a family get-together this weekend. It will be a holiday for them. Fresh mountain air, riding, sailing, good company, delicious food. What more could anyone want?'

'And you won't have them on your mind, this way,' added Ilya. 'This way, you'll be free to concentrate all your energies on the *successful* conclusion of our project.' He leaned forward a little. 'Do I make myself clear?'

Edouard felt himself sag. Nina had begged him not to get entangled with these people. She'd *begged* him. The only time in their marriage that she'd gone down on her knees to him, taken his hands, kissed them and wept imploringly into them. But he'd gone ahead anyway. He'd known better.

'Yes,' he said. 'Perfectly clear.'

III

Omonia Police Station, Central Athens

Chief Inspector Angelos Migiakis was not in a good mood. He rarely was when forced to defer afternoon visits to his mistress because of a call of duty. Even less so when that duty was to sort out yet another mess that threatened to engulf his crisis-plagued department. 'So what did Loukas say?' he asked.

'He backed up Grigorias,' replied Theofanis. 'He says that this man Augustin Pascal attacked Grigorias for no reason, that Grigorias was only defending himself.'

'Then what's the problem?'

'Because Loukas is lying, that's what.'

'You're sure?'

'I've known him fifteen years. This is the first time he won't look me in the eye.'

'Shit,' muttered Angelos. He picked a glass tumbler up from his desk, made to hurl it against the wall opposite, checked himself just in time. Anger was a problem for him; but he was doing his best.

'I think I can get him to tell me the truth if I push him,' said Theofanis. 'But I wanted to speak to you first. I mean, the last thing we need right now is another scandal.'

'Yes,' said Angelos caustically. 'I'm aware of that.' He put the tumbler back down, then looked across at Theofanis. 'So what do you think did happen?'

'Who can say?' He nodded at the statement lying on the desk. 'But for my money it's like this guy Knox told me. Grigorias gave the woman a grope. The Frenchman saw it and got mad. She's his fiancée, after all. Then Grigorias went crazy on him.' He gave an ugly grimace. 'You should have seen what he did.'

'Not good?'

'Not good at all.' He took a long breath then added: 'And I can't even say I'm that surprised, the way Grigorias has been acting since his girl left him. I did warn you we should take him off the street.'

'So this is my fault now, is it?'

'I didn't say that.'

'You know how understaffed we are.'

'Yes.'

Angelos slapped his desk with both hands. 'That fucking imbecile! That *fucking* imbecile!' He took a deep breath, waited for the calmness to return. 'Well, we'll just have to hold the line, that's all. They're foreigners, aren't they? No one will take their word against ours.'

'They're also archaeologists. They're here for some kind of conference. So they don't exactly fit the usual profile of troublemakers, do they? And this man Knox, the one downstairs, he's the one who found the lost tomb of Alexander the Great, remember? And who brought down the Dragoumis family. He's a national bloody hero.'

'Christ!' scowled Angelos. 'I'm going to skin that *malakas* Grigorias.'

'Not until this is over.'

'No,' he agreed. 'You say this Knox is down-stairs now?'

'Yes.'

'And is he a reasonable man? Can we come to some kind of understanding?'

Theofanis considered this a moment. 'He's angry,' he said. 'But he's scared too. For himself, yes, but more so for his friend Pascal. If we could offer some kind of guarantee of good medical care . . .'

'How the hell am I supposed to do that with our fucking hospitals?'

'Then I don't know what to suggest,' shrugged Theofanis. 'Maybe you should meet him yourself.'

Angelos pushed himself to his feet. 'Maybe I should,' he agreed.

THREE

I

The Conference Pavilion, Eleusis

Nico Chavakis had learned to recognise the symptoms of an incipient attack, the accentuated heel-and-toe cadence of his heartbeat, the hot sticky flush of his cheeks and forehead, the nausea low in his gut and throat, and then, most unpleasant of all, that sudden light-headed rush that had toppled him more than once. He loosened his tie, popped his top button. 'A chair,' he said.

The girl Gaille Bonnard didn't hesitate, bless her. She hurried over to the massed ranks of wooden folding chairs in the pavilion, grabbed the two nearest and returned to place them side-by-side behind him, then helped lower him onto them, a buttock upon each. He sat there with his legs spread and his hands upon his knees and breathed as he'd been taught, deep and regular, expanding his lungs, letting time do its usual nursing.

'Are you all right?' she asked anxiously. 'Do you need anything?'

'I'll be fine,' he assured her. 'Just give me another minute.'

'I'll get you a doctor.'

'No need,' he said. It was true enough. He was still in the tunnel, yes, but the darkness was lessening, he could glimpse the other end; and the last thing he wanted was to make himself conspicuous in front of all these people, as they sipped their drinks at the back of the conference pavilion. 'Your news came as a shock, that's all.' No understatement there. Tragedies for Augustin Pascal and Roland Petitier, of course; but not so good for him either. Shameful to acknowledge such self-interest so soon after dreadful tidings, but he was only human, after all, and he had a conference to run. 'My two main speakers for tomorrow, you see.'

All sympathy instantly left Gaille's expression. 'So?' she asked tersely. 'You'll just have to cancel.'

'You don't understand.' He looked bleakly up at her. He knew all too well what would happen if he did. The delegates would sympathise with his predicament, sure, but he didn't need their sympathy, he needed their money. Those who hadn't yet coughed up never would, and everyone else

41

would demand refunds – to which, unfortunately, they'd be entitled. 'I can't,' he said. 'I just can't.'

She winced as though she'd read his mind. 'You're not bankrolling this yourself, are you?'

He closed his eyes. 'You know what things are like. My sponsors pulled out. No one else would step in. What was I supposed to do? Call it off?'

'Yes.'

'I've never had a failure,' he said. 'My reputation is all I have.'

'Look,' said Gaille. 'I'm really sorry, honestly I am, but I only came over to pass on what Claire told me, so that you can do what you have to about tomorrow. But I have to head back to Athens now. It's not just Augustin – Daniel's been arrested. Claire says they've put him in gaol, the bastards. So I really have to go.' She touched the back of his hand. 'You do understand?'

Nico was only half listening, his mind already working on contingency plans. He could take Petitier's slot himself. He'd been intending to give his talk on grain-goddess iconography anyway before Petitier had got in touch. It would be simple to resurrect. That left Augustin's talk. He looked up at Gaille, still standing there, waiting for explicit permission to leave. 'They've put Knox in gaol, you say?'

'Yes.'

'My sister-in-law's a criminal lawyer,' he said.

'The finest in Athens. All the police here are terrified of her. She's exactly who he needs right now. I'll call her if you like.'

'Would you? That would be fantastic.'

Another little thump of his heart. He held up his hand to ask her to wait it out with him, then kept it up to pre-empt the indignation to which she'd be entitled, once she'd heard what he was about to say next. 'There is one thing,' he said. 'Don't get me wrong, I'll call Charissa anyway, even if you say no . . .'

'Say no to what?'

'Augustin's speech and slides are already loaded onto the teleprompter,' he told her. 'All it really needs is someone to read it out. Someone familiar with the topic. Someone who knows Alexandria well enough to have credibility with the audience and to answer questions intelligently. Someone the delegates will accept as a suitable replacement.'

'*Me?*' asked Gaille in surprise. 'But I don't know Alexandria anything like well enough. Honestly, I don't.'

Nico stared blankly at her for a moment. The equality of women was a part of modern life he'd never quite got used to. 'I wasn't thinking about you so much,' he said carefully. 'I was thinking more about Knox.'

Her expression flickered, as though she'd read his mind; but then she nodded. 'Get him out of gaol tonight and he'll do it for you. You have my word.'

'And you can speak for him, can you?'

'Yes,' said Gaille emphatically. 'I can.'

II

There was a boiler in the top corner of the police interview room. Every so often it would click on and start heating up like a kettle, and its pipes would rattle and clank for a few moments before it abruptly switched itself off again. What with the only window painted shut, the room was unpleasantly humid and the walls were sweating like a fever. Knox, too, could feel moisture prickling all over him, disconcertingly like guilt. He rocked back in his chair and flexed his fingers together, striving to keep his memories at bay. But it was no use, they came at him like frames in a slide-show. Augustin on the hotel room floor, blood oozing from his scalp; the paramedics strapping him to their stretcher; Claire's wails and ravaged face as she'd clutched his hand.

Knox had first met Augustin ten years before. The Frenchman had arranged a drinks party in honour of Richard Mitchell, Knox's old mentor, inviting all of Alexandria's leading archaeologists and citizenry. Richard, typically, had been waylaid at Pastroudi's by a gorgeous young waiter with fluttery eyelashes and a slight lisp who'd kept bringing them pastries they hadn't ordered, so he'd sent Knox on ahead to make his excuses. Augustin's eruptions of Gallic temper were legendary, so Knox had feared for his eardrums; but it hadn't been like that at all. He and Knox had got on from the start, one of those rare friendships that arrives fully formed, which they'd both known even then would endure. Any time Knox had been in trouble since, it had been to Augustin he'd turned first; and never once had he been let down. So what did it say about him that Augustin had taken such a savage beating while he'd just stood there and watched?

The door pushed open abruptly. Theofanis, the sprightly police officer who'd taken Knox's statement earlier, walked back in. A second man followed. He was informally dressed, though from his manner and the way Theofanis deferred to him, he was obviously the boss. He came to stand in front of Knox and glared down at him. 'You speak Greek, yes?'

'I get by,' agreed Knox. He'd studied the ancient language at Cambridge before adding its modern counterpart in less happy circumstances in Thessaloniki ten years before, running a failed campaign to gain justice for his murdered parents and sister.

'I am Chief Inspector Angelos Migiakis,' he said.

He had an unhealthy, man-in-the moon kind of face, with a partial eclipse of black beard. 'I am taking personal charge of this case.' He jabbed Knox's statement at his face. 'Theofanis tells me you're the one who found Alexander's tomb. He tells me you're quite the celebrity.'

'I helped find Alexander's tomb, yes.'

'You think this entitles you and your friends to assault my officers while they're carrying out their duty?'

'Since when has it been the duty of the Greek police to grope women and put their husbands in hospital?'

'There was a dying man in the room. My officers were taking charge of the scene, as they're supposed to do.'

Knox closed his eyes. It was the first confirmation he'd had that Claire's efforts to keep Petitier alive had failed. 'He's dead, then?' he asked.

'Yes. He's dead. And I want to know why someone should want to kill him.'

'How should I know that?'

Theofanis had gone over to the boiler, looking in vain for ways to turn it off. He gave it an irritable thump and then turned around. 'You said he tried to tell you something before he died. Could it have been his killer's name?'

'I suppose,' acknowledged Knox. 'It sounded like "Elysium", but I wouldn't swear to that.'

'Elysium?' frowned Angelos.

'Where virtuous and heroic souls spent eternity in Greek myth. The Elysian Fields. They were a kind of paradise.'

'You're not trying to tell me that Petitier thought he was off to paradise, are you?' scoffed Angelos.

'I don't know,' said Knox. 'I never knew the man. But I'd say it was more likely it had something to do with his talk tomorrow.'

'His talk?'

'Yes. We're all in Athens for a conference on the Eleusinian Mysteries.' He paused to look for any sign of recognition on Angelos' face, but didn't see any. 'They were a very important religious festival that took place at the port you now know as Elefsina, but which used to be called Eleusis.' The Mysteries fully warranted their name, for the ceremonies that had taken place there had been protected by high walls, closed doors and an almost pathological insistence on secrecy that had worked so successfully that almost nothing was now known about them. It was a tantalising ignorance, not least because Sophocles, Pindar, Aristotle, Cicero, Plato and many other sophisticated, intelligent and sceptical people had considered the Mysteries to be among the greatest experiences of their lives. All the experts therefore agreed that something remarkable must have taken place there; the trouble was that no-one knew precisely what. 'Eleusis was very closely associated with Elysium by the ancient Greeks, partly because their names were so similar, but also because the Mysteries were believed to offer celebrants a glimpse of life after death.'

'And Petitier was due to give a talk to the conference tomorrow afternoon,' nodded Angelos. 'On what aspect, precisely?'

'I don't know,' said Knox. 'The organisers wouldn't say, other than vague hints about how sensational it was going to be. But I'm sure they'd tell you, under the circumstances. Or maybe the text is on that laptop of his you took.'

Angelos raised an eyebrow at Theofanis. 'Laptop?' he asked.

'I gave it to Stelios to check out.'

'Go see if he's made any progress, would you?' He waited for Theofanis to leave, then turned back to Knox. 'Your friend Augustin was also to give a talk tomorrow, yes?'

'Yes.'

'But he lives in Egypt, as I understand. A Frenchman who lives in Egypt. How precisely is he qualified to give talks on ancient Greek ports?'

'The Mysteries weren't just celebrated here in Greece,' replied Knox. 'When Alexander the Great went conquering, he set up offshoots all over the ancient world, including Egypt. There's a whole district called Eleusis in the southern part of Alexandria, and Augustin has been excavating there recently. That's what his talk was to be on. My girlfriend and I have been helping him with it, so we decided to come along too, make a holiday of it.'

'Your girlfriend?' asked Angelos.

'Gaille Bonnard,' said Knox, nodding at his statement. 'She was at the conference all afternoon.'

'So why weren't you with her?'

'I wasn't in the mood. Besides, I promised Augustin I'd drive him to the airport to pick up Claire.' He suffered a sudden memory of her emerging from the arrivals hall with Augustin, incandescent with the joy of reunion, clutching a huge bouquet of white roses against her chest, while Augustin pushed a trolley laden with luggage. 'Travelling light, huh?' Knox had grinned, kissing her cheek, catching a distinctive chemical-lemon whiff of disposable face-wipe.

'The damned shipping people!' she'd exclaimed. 'They screwed up like you wouldn't believe. I had to bring everything with me. It's cost me a fortune in freight!' She'd shaken her head and turned to the trolley. 'Pathetic, isn't it? My whole life, and that's all I've got to show for it.'

'Your life's with me now,' Augustin had said.

Her eyes had glittered; her complexion had turned a glorious glad red. 'Yes,' she'd agreed. 'It is.'

The interview room door opened and Theofanis came back in. 'I need a word,' he told Angelos.

49

'What about?'

His eyes darted to Knox. 'Not in here,' he said. They went out into the corridor, where Theofanis explained something to his boss in a voice too low for Knox to overhear. But it clearly wasn't good news, if the cry of exasperation that Angelos gave was any guide, or the sound of something glass smashing against a wall.

The door opened again a few moments later and Theofanis came in, looking a little shaken. 'I'm to take you down to the holding cells,' he told him. 'We'll pick this up again later.'

III

Olympia's arms were aching as she looked up Ayiou Konstandinou for any sign of her bus. The schoolbooks she'd borrowed from Demetria were growing heavier by the minute, but the pavement was too wet from the recent shower to set them down. She longed to take the weight off her feet, but there was only one bench nearby, and the man sitting there was watching her out of the corner of his eye, his hand in his lap, tickling himself with his thumb. And while it excited her when handsome young men stared at her that way, creeps like this merely left her feeling soiled.

The gold Ferrari caught her eye at once. It wasn't

just that it was absurdly sexy with its low deep growl and long bonnet and polished bodywork, it was the way the driver handled it, straddling lanes and dawdling like a parade lap, showing off his trophy. She watched enviously as he drew nearer, for she liked nice things, Olympia. It gave her something of a shock, then, when the car swerved across traffic and pulled up alongside her. She stooped by the window, assuming the driver wanted directions. But he got out instead, slammed closed his door, smiled pleasantly at her.

'Do I know you?' she asked.

He didn't answer directly. Instead, he walked around to join her on the pavement, his hands held unthreateningly down by his sides. He was a little taller than medium-height, burly and blessed with the kind of tough good looks that made her feel a little strange inside. Mid-to-late twenties, from the look of him, perhaps ten or twelve years older than her. A high forehead and a flat nose and a thin goatee beard, his dark hair cropped short as a soldier's – though how many soldiers could afford cars like that? Wolfish sharp canines and eyes of such dazzling pale blue that she assumed he had to be wearing contact lenses. A perfectly tailored suit over an open-throated white silk shirt, his shoes soft sheaths of calfskin-leather, his gold watch a little loose around his left wrist, so that it jangled like a bracelet. 'Let me help you with those,' he said in correct yet heavily-accented Greek, taking the top two books from her.

'What are you doing?' she protested. But she couldn't exactly stop him, not while still holding the rest of her stack. Besides, there was just something about him, the kind of man who'd do exactly as he wanted, whatever anyone said. He popped his small boot, stowed her books inside and came back for the rest. She watched as he packed those away too, then slammed the boot closed. 'What are you doing?' she asked again.

He rejoined her on the pavement, still smiling blandly, as though this was all the most natural thing in the world. But the hammering of her heart assured her that it wasn't natural at all. 'What's going on?' she asked, her voice crumbling just a little. She looked around for someone to help, someone from the world of adults. But they were all involved in their own business: even the creep on the bench was now looking the other way. 'Please give me my books back.'

'They won't come to any harm in there,' he said.

'But they aren't even mine.'

'They'll be fine,' he told her, taking her hand. 'Trust me.' His skin was faintly scratchy to the touch, like the finest imaginable sandpaper. He smiled into her eyes with a directness and self-assurance that made her feel ridiculously weak, like on those mornings when her pillow fell to the floor and she couldn't even grasp it to pick it back up. He nodded as if he understood exactly, and wanted her to know that she shouldn't worry, because it was going to be okay. Then he opened the passenger door of the Ferrari and made the tiniest gesture for her to get in. She hesitated, aware she'd have to be crazy to comply, but somehow she found herself doing so. He slammed the door emphatically, walked around to the driver's side, climbed in beside her. 'Your seat-belt,' he said, reaching across her to click it into place. 'We wouldn't want you coming to any harm, would we?'

'Who are you?' she asked.

'My name's Mikhail,' he told her. 'And yours?' She hesitated a moment. 'Olympia.'

'Charmed to meet you, Olympia,' he said. He looked at her in that unblinking way he had, reached across and brushed a strand of hair on her temple back behind her ear, then gently stroked her cheek with his thumb. Her skin tingled where he touched her, her heart twisting and dipping on a fairground ride. There was a moment of almost complete stillness as he smiled more broadly and she found herself smiling in response, unable to help herself. 'You're very beautiful, you know, Olympia,' he said. 'You're going to break a lot of hearts.'

She didn't reply to that. She didn't know what

to say. He settled in his seat, turned on the ignition. The engine made a glorious roar, like some savage beast caged at the zoo. He released the hand-brake, glanced over his shoulder for a gap in traffic. Unfamiliar sensations cramped inside her, hot and icy, sharp and sweet. Strange thoughts had been coming to her at night recently, thoughts of men just like this. But not for a moment had she imagined that one would come into her real life. A voice in her head, her mother's voice, beseeched her to get out while she could, yet she knew she wouldn't. 'Where are we going?' she asked. But really she was asking: 'What are you going to do with me?'

'You'll see,' said Mikhail, as he pulled away.

FOUR

I

A young man with flaming orange hair watched intently as Knox was led into the holding cells. He frowned and sat forward, the strangest expression on his face, as though he recognised Knox and had something of vital importance to tell him. Then he promptly vomited onto the floor.

A mop was brought, but the orange-haired youth simply lay shivering on his side on the wall-bench. None of the cell's other occupants seemed bothered, so Knox cleaned it up himself. The main door opened at regular intervals, police escorting suspects in and out of the various steel cages. A forty-something man arrived, struggling with his police handlers, accusing them of stitching him up; but, the moment they left him there, he laughed and winked as though it were only a game. A youth with a swollen lip kept testing his front tooth to see if it was loose. An elderly man in a shabby suit wiped his face with his handkerchief in an effort to hide the fact that he was crying. But then the main door opened one more time and Gaille came in, talking intently with a policeman. Knox's heart leapt, he jumped to his feet and hurried over to the cage door, waited impatiently for the policeman to open it.

'Christ!' he muttered, taking her in his arms, hugging her tight, not realising until now quite how much he'd needed to see her. 'What news of Augustin?'

She gave a little grimace. 'He's in intensive care at Evangelismos Hospital. He hadn't regained consciousness last I heard. Claire's out of her wits. I promised we'd go straight over, if that's okay?'

'I'm free to go?'

'You will be any moment. Nico called in his sister-in-law.' She glanced around, lowered her voice, wary of being overheard. 'Her name's Charissa. She's only about two foot tall, but my god! We were getting nowhere until she turned up, and suddenly the police were jumping through hoops and barking like seals.' Her brow knitted. 'It is seals that bark, isn't it?'

'Dogs have been known to, as well.'

She took his wrist. 'Listen, I had to make a promise on your behalf. I'll explain later, but I gave my word you'd stand in for Augustin tomorrow morning and give his talk. Is that okay?'

'Is that how you got the seal-trainer to come?'

'Sort of.'

'Then it's fine,' said Knox.

Nico appeared at the door, dabbing his throat with a green-and-white handkerchief. He was about the unhealthiest-looking man Knox had ever met, fat to the point of caricature, mere stubs of arms and legs, so that in his dark shirt and suit he looked like some gigantic anthropomorphic beetle, a character from a children's book brought miraculously to life. 'My dear Knox!' he exclaimed. 'I can't believe they put you in such a place!'

'Don't worry about it. And thanks for coming.'

'Of course. Of course.' He stepped to one side, revealing the woman hidden behind him. She was short, slim, stern and unmistakeably formidable. 'This is Charissa,' he said. 'My dear brother's wife.'

'Gaille just told me what you've been doing,' said Knox. 'Thanks so much.'

She waved his gratitude aside. 'I spend too much time in conference rooms. Places like this do my heart good.'

'Not mine,' said Knox. 'How soon can I get out?'

'At once,' she told him. 'It's a disgrace they brought you here at all.'

'Thank Christ!'

'I'm afraid that concludes the good news,

however. The police seem to have it in for your friend Pascal. They intend to charge him the moment he regains consciousness.'

'Those bastards!' scowled Knox. 'They started it. One of them groped Claire, I swear he did. They're just covering their arses.'

'I'm not talking about that,' said Charissa. 'I'm talking about Petitier.'

'How do you mean?' frowned Knox.

'You may not know, but he was pronounced dead on arrival at hospital. And the police are planning to charge your friend with his murder.'

II

An apartment, Tbilisi, Georgia

The thumping started again in the flat above, Rezo and his wretched home improvements. Nadya Petrova glared up at her ceiling. She kept going up to remonstrate with him, but there was something about him in his dungarees, with his dusty, paint-spattered hair and his crinkled, cheerful smile, that made her forget her indignation. Until she came back down again, at least, and he resumed his banging.

She sighed and finished her article a little more abruptly than she might otherwise have done, read it through and posted it on her blog, then turned off her laptop. That would have to do for the day.

She'd been working monstrously hard this past week, had promised herself the night off. She sat there a moment longer, staring out of her high window, contemplating the rundown yet beautiful buildings on the steep hillside beneath her, their twisted brick chimneys and sloping roofs overrun by ivy and those violet flowers that hung there like bunches of grapes: and for a moment she glimpsed a metaphor for her beloved city that she might use in one of her upcoming newspaper articles, but her mind was too tired to hold onto it, and then it was gone.

She pushed herself to her feet and made her way through to her kitchen. Her limp, the result of riding pillion with an idiot biker trying too hard to impress her, was always more pronounced after a day at her desk. She had soup left over from lunch. She turned on her gas stove to heat it up, then took a bottle of white wine from her refrigerator. She didn't open it at once, savouring the moment. Remarkably, it still gave her a mild illicit thrill to uncork the first bottle of the night. The promise of happiness, or at least of respite. She looked thoughtfully back up at her ceiling. Maybe Rezo would like a glass. At least it might keep him quiet.

Her telephone began to ring before she could decide. Her nape instantly stiffened; she hated her phone. She told herself to ignore it, let voicemail do its work. But she was a journalist at heart, and you never knew. 'Yes?' she sighed. 'Who is this?'

'It's me. Gyorgi.'

'Gyorgi?'

'From Airport Operations, remember?'

'Forgive me,' she said, reaching for her notepad and pen. 'It's been a long day.'

A mirthless laugh. 'Tell me about it. I came on at six this bloody morning. And what time is it now?'

'Is he coming home, then? Is that why you called?'

'No. But the Nergadze Gulfstream is about to leave for Athens again. I thought you'd like to know. Four passengers out, no return yet scheduled. You want details?'

Nadya uncapped her pen with her teeth. 'Please.'

'Same terms as before, right?'

'Sure,' she said. She couldn't remember what she'd paid him last time, but he sold himself cheap, she remembered that much. Gambling problems, so Petr had said. But who was she to criticise?

'Okay, then. Departing Tbilisi International 6.45 p.m. our time. Flight time ninety minutes, arriving Athens Eleftherios Venizelos private jet terminal 7.15 local, thanks to the time difference. Passenger names are Boris Dekanosidze, Edouard Zdanevich, Zaal Markizi, Davit Kipshidze. Mean anything to you?'

'No.' In fact, Nadya recognised three of the names, but she had no intention of telling that to a man this indiscreet. 'I don't suppose I can get to Athens before them, can I?'

'What am I? Your travel agent?'

'I was only wondering.'

'There aren't any direct flights from Tbilisi to Athens,' he sighed. 'You'd have to change in Istanbul or Kiev. And you won't get there tonight, not setting out this late. Maybe tomorrow morning.'

'Thanks. I'll see you get your money.' She put down the phone and sat there a minute, massaging her temples. The wine was beckoning. She was exhausted, and fully entitled to her exhaustion too. She'd earned tonight off. There was no way she could beat the plane to Athens, so what could she hope to accomplish? But then she remembered that salty look in Mikhail Nergadze's eye at the press conference, and it was like touching the shallow puddle around her kettle and jolting from the shock.

She sat up straight. Maybe she couldn't get to Athens before the Nergadze plane, but that didn't mean she couldn't have someone waiting when it landed. It was what the Internet had been invented for. With a sigh, she put her white wine back in the freezer, then limped through to her study to switch her laptop back on.

FIVE

I

There was one advantage working for the Nergadzes, reflected Edouard, as he and Boris were chauffeured out from Tbilisi International's Jet Aviation Terminal to the waiting Gulfstream 550. They knew how to look after themselves. The co-pilot welcomed them aboard and escorted them back to the luxurious main lounge, where two more Nergadze toughs were playing cards. Boris introduced them all briskly. Zaal was a short, lithe man with restless, suspicious eyes, as though he'd lived his whole life on the run. Davit, by contrast, was a smiling giant with cauliflower ears and a Zorro nose. There was something distinctly familiar about him too, though Edouard couldn't work out why.

He hesitated after shaking their hands, expecting

to be invited to join their game, as Boris was. But no invitation came, so he shrugged and sank into a white-leather seat across the aisle, stretched out his legs, watched the crew go into departure protocol. They were taxiing almost at once, no nonsense about waiting for other aircraft, before launching into the twilight skies above Tbilisi. He watched through his widescreen window the scattered bonfire of the city gradually going out beneath him, doused by a few thin wisps of cloud. Then lamb cutlets were served on silver plates by a disturbingly androgynous flight attendant, along with vintage champagne in black crystal Fabergé glasses.

His sinuses began to squeeze as they approached Athens, his ears blocking, his eyes watering: he held his nose and blew gently to equalise the pressure until they were safely down. Two immigration officers came out to the plane to process them. His ears were still plugged, he had to lean forwards and frown to make out what they were saying. A pair of Mercedes SUVs with tinted windows were waiting on the tarmac, keys already in the ignition. Boris took a folded sheet of note-paper from his pocket. 'This is Mikhail Nergadze's address,' he told Edouard. 'We'll meet you there.'

'But I don't know Athens. How will I find it?'

'The cars have SatNav,' said Boris. 'You do know how to use SatNav, I trust.'

'Yes, of course. But where are you going?'

'None of your damned business.'

Edouard flushed. It was one thing to be treated rudely by Ilya and Sandro Nergadze, another by their staff. 'I asked you a perfectly civil question,' he said. 'If you can't answer it in a manner that –'

'Your mobile and wallet,' said Boris, holding out his hand.

'I beg your pardon?'

'You heard me,' said Boris. 'Your mobile and wallet.'

'But what if I need them?' protested Edouard.

'We're here on a sensitive mission,' said Boris. 'Secure communications only. Your mobile isn't secure, so give it to me.'

'What about my wallet? Isn't that secure either?'

'Please don't make this harder than it needs to be,' said Boris. 'It won't do you any good.' He nodded to Davit, who wrapped him in the strait-jacket of his arms while Zaal rifled his pockets, pulled out his mobile and wallet, handed them to Boris.

'What if I break down?' asked Edouard feebly.

Boris reached into his back pocket for a wad of euros, peeled off two twenties that he stuffed contemptuously in Edouard's breast pocket. 'I'll want them back,' he said, 'or a receipt showing how you spent them. Understand?' He didn't wait for an answer, just climbed into the back of the

64

first Mercedes, while Davit and Zaal went up front, and then they were gone, leaving Edouard standing there, with only humiliation for company.

II

There was an awkward moment as Knox was being discharged from the police station, when Theofanis tipped up the translucent pouch into which he'd earlier placed Knox's belongings, so that they all spilled out across the varnished pine counter: his mobile, his wallet, his keys and the little red-leatherette ring box he'd been carrying around these last few days. He glanced at Gaille; she feigned distraction long enough for him to slip it away in his pocket. Then it was down the steps and out the front, wending between parked police cars and bikes.

Night had fallen. The pavements gleamed from a recent shower. A party of students engulfed them for a moment, boisterously shouting out competing plans for the evening. An elderly lottery-ticket salesman lowered his notched stick like a car park barrier across Knox's chest, promising him a great fortune for a mere five euros. Exotic birds squawked outside a pet shop, while dogs lay listlessly in small cages behind the windows, like so many Amsterdam whores. They reached a silver BMW 5-Series; a lawyer's car, not an archaeologist's. Charissa duly unlocked it and took the wheel, her seat moved as far forward as it would go, so that she could reach the pedals. Nico climbed in the passenger side, while Knox opened the back door for Gaille, then got in alongside her, taking and pressing her hand to thank her for being there.

The BMW's interior was all polished walnut and pale leather, yet it smelled of fast food and there was a colouring book half-hidden beneath the front seat, along with a few discarded sweet-wrappers. The glimpse of family life made Knox warm to Charissa even more than her getting him out of gaol had done. 'What now?' he asked.

'We go see Augustin,' said Gaille.

'I've spoken to a contact at the prosecutor's office,' said Charissa, pulling away. 'The police have been uncharacteristically active. They must want a quick result very badly. They've already reviewed the hotel's fifth floor CCTV tapes, for example, and established a provisional timeline of movements. May I run it by you?'

'Of course.'

'Thank you. A little before two this afternoon, Professor Petitier arrived outside Augustin's door. He had his laptop over his shoulder and was clutching an overnight bag, and he kept looking around as though he was worried he was being followed. He knocked. The door opened. He held

66

a brief conversation, presumably with Augustin, though he's out of view, then he disappeared inside and the door closed again. At two-fifteen you showed up and knocked on Augustin's door, then called out.'

'I told him we needed to get moving.'

'Augustin appeared a minute or so later,' nodded Charissa, looking at Knox via the rear-view mirror. 'Did he give any sign there was someone inside?'

'No.'

'Did you hear or see anything?'

'No.'

'You walked together to the lifts. A few guests came and went, but no-one left or entered Augustin's room until you and Augustin reappeared with Claire and a lot of luggage a few minutes after four. You went inside Augustin's room. The first two policemen arrived several minutes later. Does that sound accurate?'

'Pretty much. But if the police know that, how can they suspect Augustin?'

'They claim he killed Petitier *before* you left for the airport.'

'That's ridiculous!' protested Knox. 'He was alive when we came in. He had a convulsion on the floor. He even *spoke* to us, for Christ's sake!'

'Calm down. I'm only telling you the police's current working hypothesis. They think Augustin assaulted Petitier before you both left for the airport, but that his assault wasn't immediately fatal, and he was still alive when you returned.'

'No way,' protested Knox. 'No way had Augustin just done that to a man. I'd have noticed in his manner.'

'You're his best friend,' observed Charissa. 'So you would say that, wouldn't you?' She glanced up again, anticipating his indignation. 'Don't misunderstand: I'm not telling you what I believe. I'm telling you the case the police are making.'

'I know.'

'Shall I continue?'

'Please.'

'Okay. A preliminary examination suggests that Petitier was killed by a single blow with some hard, heavy blunt instrument. They found no such implement in the hotel room.'

'What about Petitier's laptop?' asked Knox.

'No traces of hair or blood on it,' said Charissa. She grunted with wry amusement. 'And you won't believe what they've done. Some idiot policeman started it up. When it asked him for a password, he typed in a few wild guesses. The damned thing only started chewing up its data.'

'Hell!' snorted Knox. That must have been what Theofanis had told Angelos outside the interview room. 'How much have they lost?'

'They don't know yet. And they may still be able to retrieve it. It's not like we don't have computer experts here in Athens. But whether they'll bother . . .' She gave an expressive shrug to suggest that they'd bother if it would serve their purposes, but not otherwise. 'Anyway, Petitier's overnight bag was ripped open, and some of its contents appear to be missing, because there's not enough to have made it look as bulky as it did on the camera. They're considering the possibility that the murder weapon came originally from Petitier's case, but that Augustin took it away with him when he left for the airport. CCTV footage apparently shows him carrying a bag. Is that right?'

Knox frowned. It *was* right. A large cream canvas bag with something bulky inside. 'What's that?' he'd asked. 'Mind your own business,' Augustin had retorted. Knox felt a first chill of anxiety. 'It didn't look heavy,' he told Charissa. 'I mean, nothing to brain a man with.'

'How do you know that? Did you take it from him?'

'This is ridiculous!'

'I'm only asking you what the police will ask. What happened to it?'

Knox sat back, striving to remember. He'd stayed with the car himself, wanting Augustin and Claire to enjoy a private reunion. 'He took it into the terminal,' he said.

'You're sure?'

Knox nodded. 'I remember him holding it aside when he met someone coming the other way.'

'What about when he came back out?'

Knox frowned and shook his head. 'He had all Claire's luggage stacked up on a cart. It may have been amongst it, but I can't remember.'

'Think,' urged Charissa.

'This is preposterous,' protested Knox. 'This whole thing is preposterous.'

'You have to understand something, Mr Knox,' said Charissa. 'Last year, our Athens police shot and killed a fifteen-year-old boy. You may remember – we had riots right across Greece. The situation here is still extremely tense. The authorities will be praying that nothing happens to exacerbate it; they'll be desperate to show that Augustin only got what he deserved. If that means being selective in their investigation, or smearing him or leaking incriminating details to their pet journalists, then that's what they'll do. Our job right now is to anticipate every move they might make, and be ready. So I ask again: did he bring this bag back out?'

'I can't remember,' said Knox. 'But isn't this all beside the point anyway? I mean, Augustin had no earthly reason to kill Petitier. Aren't murderers supposed to have a motive?'

It was a rhetorical question; he didn't expect an answer. So it was something of a shock when Nico half turned in his seat and pulled an apologetic face.

'Actually,' he said, 'I hate to say this, but I'm rather afraid your friend *did* have a motive after all.'

III

Nikortsminda Castle, Georgia

Kiko Zdanevich had never seen anything quite like it, not outside of school trips and history books, at least. A moonlit fortress of ivy-covered stone with high battlements for its archers and towering pointed turrets from which brave knights-errant like himself could rescue beautiful imprisoned princesses, all set on a small island close to the edge of an ink-black lake, surrounded by ancient forest and snow-capped mountains. He pressed his face against the window as they wound along the country lane toward the island, watched open-mouthed as the drawbridge lowered for them, and the great wooden gates creaked open. 'Is this really where we're staying, Mama?' he asked.

'I suppose it must be,' she said sternly, as though offended by his excitement. She'd been in a strange mood ever since Alexei Nergadze and the men in black suits had come for them earlier with a message from their father that they were to spend the weekend with the Nergadzes.

They passed through the outer gates into a vast

central courtyard, spotlights illuminating lawns
and interior battlements, open flights of stone steps
up to them, a chapel with a tall spire and a long
line of white-painted stables and garages, not to
mention the central keep of grey stone, outside
whose front doors they now stopped.

Liveried servants hurried down to collect their
luggage from the boot, while Alexei Nergadze led
them inside, then down a long and gloomy gallery
of stern-faced portraits to a high-stepped spiral
staircase. Kiko's heart swelled briefly at the
prospect of sleeping in one of the turret rooms,
but they headed along another corridor instead to
a rather shabby bedroom with two sagging single
beds. 'The girls will be sleeping in here,' he said,
nodding to them to stay while one of the servants
unpacked their luggage.

'What about me and Kiko?' asked his mother.

'You're further along.'

'We want to be together.'

'We have a full house this weekend. This is the
best we can do.'

'Then we'll all be fine in here, thank you.'

'Nonsense,' said Alexei. 'My grandfather would
never forgive me if I didn't make you all as comfortable as possible.'

'But I assure you we –'

'You're coming with me,' said Alexei. They
followed him and the second servant to another

set of stairs. 'I don't like this, Mama,' murmured Kiko. 'I want to go home.'

She put her hand on his shoulder. 'Everything's going to be fine, sweetheart, I promise.'

Alexei showed them next to Kiko's room. It was grander by far than his sisters'. It had its own fireplace and chairs and desks and tapestries on the wall and huge cream curtains that could be opened and closed by pulling on a rope, and a four-poster bed hung with pink silk decorated with roses. He threw his mother a pleading glance as Alexei led her off to her own room. She gave him just the hint of a wink before she left, asking him to play along for the time being, promising it would be all right.

It was another ten minutes before he heard footsteps outside and then she came back in, carrying her bag. 'You're staying with me?' he asked eagerly.

'The bed's big enough, isn't it?' she smiled.

'It's big enough for a king!' he cried, climbing up onto it, then jumping up and down.

'Careful, now,' she admonished. 'We don't want to break anything.'

Kiko nodded and went to the mullioned window, cupped his hands around his eyes, the better to see. Three black limousines with tinted windows were coming in across the drawbridge, their headlights sweeping across the castle's interior. A canvas canopy had been erected outside the keep's front steps since they'd arrived, and the cars stopped one by one beneath it. He could hear their doors opening and closing, the cheerful chatter of guests as they made their way inside.

'What's got you so riveted?' asked his mother, putting her hands upon his shoulders, laying a kiss on his crown.

'People,' said Kiko. 'Lots of them.'

'Wow!' she said. 'There *are* a lot, aren't there?'

'What do you think that canopy is for?' he asked.

'I suspect it must be to keep all these guests dry from the rain.'

'But it's not even raining.'

'Yes. But they weren't to know that when they put it up, were they?'

'I think it's to stop those cameras in the sky from seeing who they all are,' declared Kiko, who had a fondness for spy films.

His mother ruffled his hair affectionately. 'You *do* have an imagination, don't you?' she said, drawing the curtains and leading him away.

'Yes,' he smiled. 'I suppose I must.'

SIX

I

Edouard tapped Mikhail Nergadze's address into his Mercedes' SatNav, only to discover that someone had been making mischief, downloading a husky-voiced woman to deliver breathy *double-entendre* instructions. 'After eighty metres, *unnh*, turn *hard* left,' she urged, triggering in Edouard a sudden welcome memory of the one time he'd ever come even close to infidelity, tempted into a seedy Kiev escort bar by boredom and a leather-clad whore in icing-sugar make-up, then having to spend an exorbitant sum on champagne before he could negotiate his escape.

'Right turn ahead. Get ready. Yes. Yes. Yes. *Now*!'

He turned her down as low as he could, then lost himself in a brown study, brooding on Nina and the kids, how to help them. Maybe he should get in touch with Tamaz. They weren't particularly close, but they were still brothers. Tamaz had invited him over for a drink a few weeks before, had introduced him to a man called Viktor, then had left them alone together. Viktor's pitch had been simple and direct: give him Ilya Nergadze and name his price. Edouard, still believing back then the Nergadzes' own view of themselves as victims of government propaganda, had stormed angrily away and hadn't spoken to Tamaz since, but maybe –

'Left turn, *unh*, coming up.'

He shook his head. It was madness even to think of it. For all he knew, Viktor was a Nergadze mole, out to test his loyalty. He turned on the radio, punched channels until he found some music to soothe him. He drove for forty minutes, skirting eastern Athens to its northern foothills. The roads grew narrow and quiet. Through gaps in walls and fences, he caught glimpses of expensive villas. He reached a high stone wall topped with broken glass, a row of pines behind, like troops at the battlements. A private drive was flanked by 'Keep Out' signs, but the gates were open and his SatNav siren urged him on, so he crunched up the gravelled track to a whitewashed mansion lit by discreetly positioned spotlights, a gold Ferrari parked obliquely outside, its passenger door hanging open, as though someone had been in a hurry to get inside.

Edouard pulled up behind it, then sat there for a while, hoping Boris and the others would arrive. He didn't fancy going in alone. But the minutes passed and there was no sign of them, so he got out and went to the front door, which was fractionally ajar. A Nino Chkheidze love song was playing inside. A Georgian, then; this had to be the place. He knocked twice, but no one answered. The song set out on its familiar crescendo, came finally to its end. He knocked again before the next song could begin. Still nothing. He went cautiously inside, into a vast open-plan atrium two storeys high, topped by a magnificent glass dome, through which he could just about see the night sky. There was a gleaming white-and-chrome kitchen to his left, a polished mahogany dining table and chairs to his right; and, straight ahead, a semicircle of black leather sofas and armchairs facing a huge plasma TV tuned mutely to the 24-hour news. Marble staircases rose on either side of him to a first-floor landing that girdled the atrium like a belt. Numerous doors led off this landing, presumably to bedrooms and bathrooms.

'Hello!' he called out. 'Anyone here?' But he could hardly be heard above the music, so he made his way over to the music centre. A glass coffee table was covered with the debris of an impromptu celebration, two empty champagne bottles, some disposable patisserie trays, an overflowing ashtray and an enamel box of white powder that he hurriedly closed and tried to pretend he hadn't seen. A skirt was lying discarded on the floor, a torn white blouse, white knickers, a blue sport's bra. He found several remote controls, pressed mute buttons until finally there was silence. 'Hello!' he called out again. 'Anyone home?'

A door opened above and a man appeared on the landing, naked except for a saffron towel tucked around his waist. His torso and arms were lean and muscled like a middleweight boxer, and he had a crude prison tattoo on his right biceps. A Nergadze for sure, Edouard knew, partly from his characteristic broad nose and high forehead, partly from the swagger with which he held himself, but mostly from the calm yet purposeful way he was aiming a sawn-off shotgun down at Edouard's face.

II

'What the hell are you talking about?' demanded Knox angrily. 'There's no way on earth Augustin killed Petitier.'

Nico held up a palm. 'You misunderstand,' he said. 'I'm not suggesting he did. All I'm saying is that the police might be able to establish a motive.' He shifted even further around in his seat, as far as his bulk would allow, squeezed between the door and the hand-brake. 'Do you know why I offered Petitier the chance to give a talk?'

'No.'

'I was originally planning to take that slot myself, but I stood aside for him. I didn't do that lightly, I assure you. I *like* to talk.' He gave a self-deprecating chuckle. 'It's one of the reasons I organise these conferences, frankly, because no one else ever invites me. But I had a good reason to stand aside this time. You see, Petitier emailed me six weeks or so ago, demanding I let him address the conference. Very abrasive, very arrogant. I hardly even remembered him, though he used to be quite close to one of my colleagues at the university.'

'And?'

'I thanked him for his interest, but told him I'd already filled all the speaking slots. Which was true, of course; these things get finalised months in advance. I said he was welcome to speak at one of our roundtables. He insisted that wasn't good enough and assured me it would be worth my while, that he had something extraordinary to share with the world. I asked him what; he refused to say. I assumed I'd hear no more. You always get these cranks hanging around conferences, convinced they've solved all the riddles of the ancient world. But then a package arrived at my office. A note from Petitier, along with ten Linear A and Linear B seal and seal-stone fragments wrapped in cotton wool. They're not my specialty at all, so I took photos and emailed them around: because if these fragments were already in the public record, one or other of my colleagues would have been bound to recognise them. But none did. So it looked as though Petitier had at the very least found some new seals, and thus very probably an important new site too.'

'Even so,' said Knox. 'That scarcely merits a platform at a conference like this.'

'No,' agreed Nico. 'But there was something else. It slipped past me, because I'm no language expert. But one of my colleagues picked up on it at once. You see, while none of the Linear A seals were decipherable, two of the Linear B seals were. Or, at least, one word on each of them was.'

'And?'

'The first word is "gold" or "golden".'

'And the second?'

A somewhat sheepish look spread across Nico's face. 'It means "fleece",' he said.

SEVEN

I

Edouard raised his hands numbly as Mikhail Nergadze pointed his shotgun down at his face. 'Please don't shoot,' he begged.

'Give me one good reason.'

'My name's Edouard Zdanevich,' he swallowed. 'I work for your father. He sent me to –'

'The antiquities expert.'

'Yes.'

Mikhail kept his shotgun aimed at Edouard's face a moment longer, perhaps assessing the story, more likely to emphasise who was in control; but then he lowered it and held it down by his side. 'I was expecting Boris and some others.'

'They'll be here soon. They had an errand to –'

A muffled cry came unexpectedly from the room behind Mikhail. A woman, in obvious fear and distress. Edouard looked up in bewilderment. She cried out again, louder and clearer, as though she'd managed to spit out a gag. She sounded young. 'Who's that?' he asked.

'And that's your business because?'

The girl's shouting continued, anxious, beseeching, panicked, her Greek too fast for Edouard's limited grasp, but the gist all too clear. He hesitated. Mikhail smiled down at him, aware what must be going through his mind, curious how he'd respond. He couldn't just stand there, so he climbed the stairs, suppressing his fear as he walked past Mikhail, then stopped in dismay when he saw the girl lying naked on the bare mattress, all the sheets, pillows and duvet having spilled to the ground. She saw him and tried to cover herself with her right arm and by turning onto her side. Her movements were so awkward that they drew attention to her left wrist, handcuffed to the bedpost. From her modest breasts, fat hips and fluffy pubis, he guessed she must be about fifteen years old, the same age as his own twins. There were multiple livid bruises on her upper arms and chest, and what looked like a cigarette burn near her navel, and a livid redness around her throat, as though she'd been nearly asphyxiated. She would have been pretty, except for the accidental mask of hair glued by her own tears and blood to her face. There were spatters of red on the mattress too, along with other motley stains that Edouard had no desire to analyse. He turned appalled to Mikhail. 'What the hell have you been doing to her?' he demanded.

'Nothing she didn't want.'

'How can you say that? Look at her! She's begging you to let her go.'

'What a person says isn't necessarily what they want.'

Edouard shook his head. 'How old is she?'

'How would I know that?'

'Didn't you think about *asking*?'

Mikhail laughed. 'Look at you! You just want her for yourself, don't you?'

'You're sick.'

'Go ahead. She won't mind, believe me. She'll enjoy it.'

'What kind of man are you?'

'The kind you'd be, if you had any balls.'

'I'm letting her go,' said Edouard. 'Where's the key?'

'I'm not done with her yet.'

'Yes, you are.' He spoke boldly and locked gazes with Mikhail, certain that righteousness would be enough. But Mikhail's ice-blue eyes punctured his confidence, and he realised too late that this was a different kind of man to any he'd ever dealt with before, even to the other Nergadzes. His heart began to race, he felt a dryness in his throat, smelled a faintly rancid odour that he intuitively recognised as his own fear. It triggered an un-welcome memory: waiting to be seated at a Tbilisi restaurant many years before, a drunken man trip-ping over his own feet and bumping into a second man sitting on a barstool nursing a glass of malt liquor clanking with ice, making him spill a little over his hand. His apology had been too slow, too dismissive. The strangest look had passed over the seated man's face. He'd shattered his crystal tumbler on the marble bar-top, then turned and thrust its splintered base into the drunk's face before giving it a sharp leftwards twist, shredding the man's eyeball and ripping his nose and cheek apart, blood spurting and spattering across the bar and around the restaurant as he'd crashed howling into tables. Over the years since, Edouard had forgotten the victim's ravaged face, but not the chill calculating look on the assailant's face in the half-second before he'd attacked, as though rage was an army within his control, a force to be deployed at will.

The girl must have seen the shift in power; her sobs grew louder, more despairing. Her fear infected Edouard. He felt beads of sweat on his forehead, and trickles running coldly down from his armpits. 'I'm sorry,' he said, lowering his eyes submissively. 'I didn't mean anything.'

For a moment he feared his apology wouldn't work, but then the intensity of the moment seemed to slacken, and just as suddenly it was gone altogether. 'Maybe you're right,' shrugged Mikhail. 'We do have business to discuss.' He picked up his trousers, fished out a small steel key, tossed it across.

Edouard's hands were shaking as he struggled to unlock the cuffs; but finally they snapped open and the girl grabbed a sheet to cover herself, hurried sobbing to the bathroom. 'I'll get her clothes,' said Edouard, heading back out onto the landing. Boris and his men had just arrived, were taking seats around the coffee table, lighting cigarettes. He gave them a sour look, for they must have heard his confrontation with Mikhail. But you needed a thick skin to work for the Nergadzes; you needed to know who was boss. 'Maybe we should give her something,' suggested Edouard, when he went back up. 'To keep her mouth shut.'

'She won't talk,' said Mikhail.

'How can you be sure? I mean, what would your grandfather say if this got out?'

'I didn't do anything to her that she didn't agree to. Ask her if you like.'

Edouard knocked on the bathroom door. 'I've got your clothes.' The door opened a fraction, her hand shot out and grabbed them. He stood there, all too aware of Mikhail watching him, until the door opened again and she emerged, her face washed but pale, her hair brushed, holding the rip in her blouse.

Edouard put an arm around her shoulder and led her towards the bedroom door, but Mikhail stepped in front of her. He had his white jeans in his hand, and now he pulled his leather thong belt free from its loops. The girl's face crumpled at the sight. 'No,' she begged. 'Please no.'

Mikhail smiled reassuringly. 'Don't be alarmed. I just wanted to make a point to our friend Edouard here. He thinks you're going to tell people what happened tonight. But you're not, are you?'

'No. No. I swear I'm not.'

'Not even if they try to force you?'

'No.'

'Why not?'

'Because you know where I live,' she said, as if repeating lines. 'Because of what you'll do to me and my parents and my brother if I do.'

'Exactly,' said Mikhail. And he stepped out of her way.

Edouard steered her out the door, to the stairs and down. 'Where *do* you live?' he asked.

'Piraeus,' she said, her whole body shuddering wildly, as though she'd just come in from a blizzard.

'I'll get one of the guys to drive you.'

She grabbed his arm. 'Can't you take me? *Please.*'

Mikhail emerged onto the landing, now dressed in the white jeans, a maroon silk shirt and a black leather trench-coat. Boris rose to his feet. 'Great to see you again, boss,' he said. 'It's been too long.'

'Who are those two with you?'

'Davit and Zaal,' said Boris, indicating them in turn. 'They're good men. I chose them myself.'

'You brought the money?'

Boris nodded and cleared space on the coffee table, then laid a large steel case flat upon it. He entered combinations into the two locks, then opened it up and turned it around for Mikhail to see. There were fat bundles of euros within, every denomination from 50s to 500s, more cash than Edouard had ever seen. Even the girl gave a little gasp.

'How much?' grunted Mikhail.

'Four million,' said Boris.

'I asked for ten.'

'This is all we could arrange at such short notice. Besides, you know how negotiations are. If you show up with ten million, then ten million is what they'll –'

'Is that what my grandfather told you to tell me?'

'Yes.'

There was a moment of silence as Mikhail absorbed this response. It was like watching a land-mine that had just made an unexpected noise. 'Fine,' said Mikhail, finally. 'It will do.' He walked downstairs and over to the case, took out a bundle of 50-euro notes, rolled it up into a cylinder. Then he went to the girl, hooked a finger into her bra, tucked the bank-notes inside. 'Buy yourself something pretty,' he told her. 'A dress or a necklace or something. You can wear it for me when you come back tomorrow.'

'Come back?' she asked, appalled.

'You will, you know.' He turned to Edouard. 'Women always fall for their first man. It's in their genes or something.'

'I'm not coming back,' she protested. 'I'm never coming back.'

'That's what they all say,' he grinned. 'But then they come back after all. They just can't help themselves.' He turned to the others. 'Davit. I want you to drive her into town. Find her a taxi. Make sure she's well taken care of. Then come back here. We've got work to do.'

'Yes, boss.' He came across and took the girl by her elbow.

'What about my books?' she wailed. 'Can't I at least have my books back?'

'You can pick them up tomorrow.'

'But you promised. They're not even mine. They're Demetria's.'

'I said tomorrow,' said Mikhail. 'Get here around five. We'll be busy until then.'

'But tomorrow I'm going to –'

Mikhail's face darkened. 'Don't make me come looking for you, Olympia,' he warned. 'I will if I have to; but you'll regret it, I promise.' He watched Davit escort her out the door, then turned back to Edouard and the others. 'Well, then,' he said, rubbing his hands together. 'Perhaps we should get down to some business.'

II

'You're kidding,' said Knox dazedly. 'Petitier had found the golden fleece?'

'That's not what I said,' replied Nico carefully. 'And it's not what *he* said either. At most, he *implied* that he'd found it, or something to do with it. He left himself plenty of room to back away from it, if he so wished. He could have put it down to a misunderstanding. He could have claimed it was pure coincidence that those were the only two words on the seals that we could read.'

'He was a Minoan scholar. No one would have believed him.'

'No,' agreed Nico. 'Which is precisely why I agreed to step aside so that he could give his talk.'

'And Augustin knew about this?'

'I can't say for sure, but it's certainly possible. You see, I –' He broke off as the BMW bumped onto the kerb and pulled up outside an imposing-looking building.

'Evangelismos Hospital,' said Charissa economically. 'You all go on in. I'll find somewhere to park.'

Nico shook his head. 'I have to leave you, I'm afraid. I need to go to the hotel, tell all our delegates about tomorrow's revised programme.' He pulled an anxious face. 'You do understand?'

'Of course,' said Knox. 'But maybe we could meet up later? For dinner, say?'

'Excellent idea. Do you know the Island?'

'No.'

He kissed his fingertips. 'It's in Exarchia. Charissa knows where. The best seafood in Athens, and not too expensive. Not for what it is, at least. I'll book us a table, if you like.'

'Sounds perfect. What time?'

He checked his watch. 'Nine-thirty, say. That should give me enough time. If I can find a taxi, at least.'

'You two go on in ahead,' said Charissa. 'I'll drop Nico at the hotel, then come back.'

Knox and Gaille made their way through an archway into the staff car park. A TV crew and a couple of journalists were having a cigarette and a laugh together at the foot of the front steps, waiting for something to happen. In the evening gloom, it was easy enough for Knox and Gaille to slip past them and up the marble steps. The woman behind the information desk was remarkably square-looking, as though someone had thrown a rug over a washing machine. They asked her about Augustin. She directed them to ICU One, but warned that the police weren't allowing him any visitors other than his fiancée.

Bulbous lamps glowed like multiple moons in the high, wide corridors. Hard heels clacked like dominoes on the meander-patterned tiles. Monitors, gurneys, laundry baskets and other hospital paraphernalia were stacked against walls painted pastel yellows and blues, a worthy attempt at cheerfulness that had long-since faded into drabness. A wail pierced the hush: someone struggling with fear or grief. Knox flinched at a decade-old memory, walking to another ICU unit in a different Greek hospital, saying goodbye to his sister Bee on the day he'd been told she was going to die. The muffled, oppressive echoes of these places, the brutal whiteness of the equipment, that numb, dreamlike sense of wafting rather than walking, of being unable to protect the ones you love.

A policeman was sitting on a hard chair outside the ICU's double doors, reading a magazine. 'Damn,' muttered Knox. He'd hoped the police had merely issued edicts against visitors, not actually put someone on watch. A heart-monitor was on a trolley against the wall. 'Distract him,' he told Gaille, as he grabbed it.

She nodded and went to ask a question. The

policeman shook his head. She asked him something else, smiled and touched his arm. She had the most disarming smile, Gaille. It could melt glaciers. The policeman rose to his feet and walked a little way with her, then pointed her up the corridor, laughing and waving his hands, barely glancing at Knox as he ducked his head and pushed the monitor through the ICU department's double doors. He left it against the wall, washed his hands with gel at a basin, dried himself off, opened the door to the ward itself. Two nurses behind the reception desk were squabbling in hushed low voices; he caught something about missing supplies. Claire was in the far corner, sitting on the far side of one of the four beds. Even though Knox had braced himself, it was still a shock to see Augustin, the tubes and monitors of life-support, the cage over his chest to keep the bedclothes off his upper body, the white bandaging around his skull, the oxygen mask over his mouth and nose, his cheekbone swollen and tinted lurid inhuman colours.

Claire must have sensed his arrival, for she looked up, haggard, grey and harrowed, no remnant of her earlier joy. She frowned and blinked to see him standing there, as though struggling to place him. Then she touched a finger to her lips, got to her feet and came to join him outside.

'How is he?' he asked.

'How does he look?'

Knox didn't know what to say, what Claire needed from him. Situations like these rendered normal language and the conventions of human behaviour inadequate. He put his arms around her, held her against him, stroked her hair. It took a moment for the sobs to arrive, but once they'd started she couldn't stop, her shoulders shaking with grief, anxiety and fear – and not just on Augustin's account, he imagined. It was one of the crueller aspects of tragedies like this, that they made good people like Claire worry about their own futures, so that they'd later lacerate themselves for their selfish thoughts while their loved ones lay dying. He put his mouth close to her ear and murmured: 'It's going to be all right. I promise.'

She stiffened at once, so that he knew it had been a mistake. She broke away, took a step or two back, wiped her eyes. 'All right?' she asked. 'Are you an expert on traumatic brain injury, or something?'

'I didn't mean –'

'Augustin's skull has almost certainly been fractured, and his parietal and frontal lobes violently traumatised. His blood-brain barrier will have broken down. Cerebral oedemas are going to form. Do you know what they are?'

'No.'

'They occur when blood and other fluids are pumped into the brain faster than they can be removed. The whole head swells up, like a sink filling when the plughole is blocked. First it will affect his white matter, then his grey matter. It's one of the most common causes of irreversible brain damage, and it's happening to Augustin right now, and there's nothing I can do about it, except hold his hand and pray. And you're telling me it's going to be all right.'

'I'm so sorry, Claire.'

She nodded twice, wiped her eye again with the heel of her hand. 'I've worked in a hospice,' she told him. 'I've seen car-crash victims and gunshot victims and people with brain tumours. You think I haven't gone through this before? The doctors are putting Augustin into an induced coma: who knows if and when he'll come out of it? And then what? Traumatic brain injuries don't kill at once. Did you know that? They take their own sweet fucking time about it, while the body just falls apart piece-by-piece around them. And even if he should pull through, he'll be at increased risk for the rest of his life from tumours, depression, impotence, epilepsy, Alzheimer's, headaches, you name it. So please explain to me just how it's going to be all right.'

'I'm so sorry,' repeated Knox helplessly.

'What good is that? What good is being sorry? What are you going to *do* about it?'

'Everything I can.'

She nodded briskly, as though this was what she'd been working for. 'One of the nurses overheard the police earlier. They want to move Augustin out of here. They want to take him into custody. He'll *die* in custody. That's what they want, of course. They want him to die, because they think this whole incident will go away with him. So if you really want to help, do something about *that*. Stop them from moving him.'

'I'll do my best. I promise.'

'Your best? Like when that fucking monster was beating Augustin half to death?'

'What do you mean?'

'I mean you could have at least *tried* to stop him. You could at least have *tried*. He would have done, if it had been you. He'd have done *anything* for you. But you just stood there.'

Silence fell. Knox looked helplessly at her, feeling sick. 'I'm sorry,' he said again.

But she turned her back on him and didn't look round until after he'd left the ICU.

EIGHT

I

The log fire threw flickering light around the castle's great hall, tinting the stone walls orange-grey. It burned so strongly that Sandro Nergadze could feel its warmth on his back through his shirt and jacket. Yet he felt a distinct chill all the same. 'Would you care to repeat that,' he said tightly.

'You've got to understand something,' said General Iosep Khundadze. 'What you're talking about is a situation where the normal army command will break down.' He nodded at the two media magnates seated further along the oak table, who'd just outlined their plans. 'Even if these two can make their vote-rigging charges stick –'

'We can make them stick,' said the newspaper tycoon named Merab. 'If we get the exit-poll data we've been promised, at least.'

'What are you suggesting?' demanded Levan Kitesovi, head of Georgia's largest independent polling agency, angrily. 'Isn't my word good enough now?'

'Gentlemen, gentlemen,' said Sandro. 'We have to trust each other. That's why we're all here.' Everyone was a little on edge. Rumours were swirling of a new intelligence department set up specifically to investigate the Nergadze campaign. Their security arrangements had been duly tightened, because it could be awkward for their guests to explain what they were doing here this weekend. They'd swept all the rooms for bugs, had taken additional precautions against aerial surveillance, had hired more guards. But such security measures were a double-edged sword: they always made people feel more nervous.

He turned back to the general. 'Can we please assume that the first part of our plan has worked. Otherwise, there's really no point us discussing it. It's election day. The media use the exit polls to announce a come-from-behind Ilya Nergadze victory. But then the government declares victory. We flood the radios with stories of government lackeys carting off ballot boxes in mysterious vans. Our sources inside the ministries leak corroboration. Our friends across the world denounce the president as corrupt. The Supreme Court, Church and police . . .' he leaned forward to acknowledge their representatives '. . . will speak out on our behalf, or at least remain deadlocked. And so everyone will look to the ultimate arbiters of power in such situations: the army. Last month you assured us that you could bring your colleagues with you; enough of them to make the difference, at least. What's happened to change your mind?'

A faint sheen had appeared on the general's brow. When he'd made his promises, Ilya Nergadze's cause had still seemed hopeless. 'As I was saying,' he growled. 'Even if you can make all this happen, even if it looks like the president is *stealing* victory, the *whole* army won't suddenly switch sides. At best, what you'll get is factions. I can certainly help you exploit those factions.'

'I should hope so,' muttered Sandro, sitting back in his chair, looking up at the family portraits that liberally decorated the walls of the great hall, dating from the reign of Erekle II right down to the present day. All had the characteristic Nergadze features; all were shown as noble and brave and powerful; all were signed by one or other of the great masters of Georgian art. And all were fakes he'd commissioned over the past few years, to give their family a necessary patina of heritage and respectability. The whole world was a fraud; some people knew it, but most didn't.

'But that's not enough,' continued the general. 'You need to understand how the army works. When the usual chain of command breaks down, as it will in this situation, you become dependent upon other factors. In particular, you become dependent upon the will of the soldiers themselves. They'll no longer have to *obey* orders so much as *choose* which orders to obey. And they'll follow the officers they admire and trust, not the ones with the most pips and stripes. Those are the people we need on our side; and it may surprise you to know that bribes will only go so far with such men. It may surprise you to know that men like this, the soldiers that other soldiers most look up to, actually value notions like honour and courage and patriotism.'

'Spare us the sermon,' said Ilya. 'Get to the point.'

'Very well,' said the general, meeting Ilya's gaze. 'The point is this. They won't do it. Not for you, at least. They don't like you enough.'

'Why not?' asked Ilya.

'Because they think you're corrupt. And they won't risk civil war just to replace one corrupt politician with another.'

There was a shocked silence. No one spoke to or about Ilya Nergadze that way. 'How dare you?' burst out Sandro. 'My father's not corrupt.'

'Really?' replied the general dryly. 'Then why the fuck does he pay me a hundred thousand dollars every month?'

A ripple of laughter, evident admiration for such blunt talk, was quickly stifled. 'Very well,' said

Ilya, who knew when to bully and when to listen. 'What do you suggest?'

'Our country is still bleeding from the Russian fiasco,' said the general. 'People are desperate for change, but not just *any* change. They want change with hope. They want change with honour. Convince them that you're the man of destiny Georgia is crying out for, and the army will flock to you like to a saviour, I won't need to persuade anyone. At the moment you're head of a political party; you need to become head of a *movement*. You need to *inspire* people. You need to hold up a flag for them to follow. Until then . . .' He shook his head.

Silence fell around the table following this sober assessment. Everyone knew in their hearts it was true, not just for the army, but for Georgia as a whole. Ilya leaned forward. 'A flag for them to follow,' he murmured. 'There is something.'

'What?'

He glanced at Sandro. 'My son is working on it as we speak.'

Everyone looked Sandro's way. He felt his gut clench. Surely it was too early to float the idea of the golden fleece. If nothing came of it, they'd be a joke. He looked up, seeking inspiration, at the great shield on the wall opposite. It was so brightly polished that he could see the blur of his own reflection, and the orange glow of the fire like a halo behind him. It carried the Nergadze family crest, a lion rampant holding a spear. He'd commissioned that too, along with all the other weaponry and suits of armour that bedecked the walls. Curious about how convincing these fakes were, he'd taken several to Tbilisi where he'd arranged for Edouard, their tame historian, to come across them as if by accident. How the great expert had drooled! How they'd laughed at him once he'd gone! But if Gurieli could fool someone like him . . . 'I need to speak to some people before I can share this with you all,' he said. 'But, believe me, you can expect to hear some very exciting news indeed.'

The meeting broke up soon afterwards, everyone trading cheerful banter as their mouths watered in anticipation of another Nergadze banquet. Ilya tugged Sandro back by his sleeve. 'You'd better get me my damned fleece,' he said.

'Don't worry, father,' Sandro assured him. 'I'll get it for you. One way or another, I'll get it.'

II

'To success!' toasted Mikhail, as they stood around the coffee table with their shot-glasses of vodka straight from the freezer.

'To success!' they echoed.

The icy viscous liquid chilled and warmed simultaneously Edouard's throat and chest. His eyes began to water so that he had to blink. He wasn't used to such strong liquor, but refusing wasn't an option. Boris refilled their glasses, then Mikhail threw himself into an armchair and put his feet up on the coffee-table. 'So do you all know what you're doing here?' he asked.

'I do,' said Boris.

'Me, too,' said Zaal.

Edouard settled on the far arm of the sofa, the furthest he could get from Mikhail. 'I only know what your father told me,' he said.

'And that is?'

Edouard allowed himself the faintest of smiles. 'That we're here to buy the golden fleece.'

'You think this is a joke?' frowned Mikhail.

'The fleece doesn't exist,' said Edouard. 'It never existed. It was only ever a legend, that's all.'

'You're wrong,' said Mikhail. 'It existed. It exists. And we're going to buy it tomorrow.'

Edouard spread his hands. 'Look,' he said, 'your father and grandfather asked me to come here because I'm an expert in these things. And, as an expert, I'm telling you that there never was any such thing as the golden fleece. It was just a mishmash of local traditions and fanciful storytelling and –'

Mikhail's face darkened. He pushed himself to his feet and walked over to where Edouard sat on the arm of the sofa. 'I'm telling you that the golden fleece exists. Are you calling me a liar?'

'No,' said Edouard, dropping his eyes. 'Of course not. I only meant that –'

'Only meant?' scoffed Mikhail. He placed the tip of his index finger on the bridge of Edouard's nose, then gently pushed him backwards. Edouard tried to resist, but there was something inexorable about Mikhail, he felt himself tipping and then he overbalanced and went sprawling, his vodka spilling over his wrist and the floor. 'You intellectuals!' said Mikhail, coming to stand above him. 'You're all the same. You sneer at everything. But let me tell you something. I spoke to a man this morning, a professor of history as it happens, because I know such things matter to your kind. He'd *seen* this fleece for himself. He'd travelled to Crete just last week, specifically to see it, to make sure it was for real. He'd held it in his hands and he'd weighed it and felt its texture. It's for real. He swore on his life that it was for real.'

'He told you that?'

'And he had no reason to lie, I assure you.' Mikhail stared down at him, his pupils triumphant pinpricks of blackness. 'The fleece is coming here to Athens,' he said. 'It's coming because *I'm* in Athens, and it's my destiny to bring it home to Georgia. Some things are written. *This* is written. Do you understand?'

'Yes,' croaked Edouard.

'Tomorrow morning, we're going to see it.

Tomorrow morning, we're going to *buy* it. And then we're taking it home. Any more questions?'

'No.'

'Good,' said Mikhail. He turned away from Edouard, leaving him lying there feeling limp and soiled.

'So what's our plan, then, boss?' asked Boris, splashing out more vodka.

'The man who has the fleece is planning to unveil it at a talk tomorrow afternoon. So we're going to go visit him first thing in the morning, and persuade him to sell it to us.'

'He's expecting us, then?'

'Not exactly. But I know where he's staying.'

'What if he doesn't want to sell?'

Mikhail laughed. 'He'll want to by the time I'm through with him, believe me. He'll be begging us to buy it.'

'Then why pay for it at all?' grumbled Zaal. 'Why not just take it?'

'Because this isn't just about the fleece,' Mikhail told him. 'This is about the election too. It's about my grandfather *buying* the fleece on behalf of the Georgian people, *however much it costs*, because that's the kind of patriot he is.'

Edouard's heart-rate had resettled. He got to his feet, refilled his own glass with vodka, tossed it back, restoring a little courage. 'This professor you spoke to,' he said. 'The one who went to Crete to see it. If I'm to verify the fleece for you, I'll need to speak to him myself.'

'Really?' asked Mikhail. 'How?'

'Give me his address. I'll go visit him.'

'And what good will that do you?' asked Mikhail. 'Unless you take a Ouija board, of course.'

'Oh Christ!' muttered Edouard.

Mikhail laughed. 'Don't worry. I know what I'm doing.' He turned to Boris, like a doctor discussing an intriguing case with a colleague. 'I even got him to write his own note. Amazing what people will do.'

'So who's the guy with the fleece, then?' asked Zaal. 'The one we're going to see in the morning, I mean?'

'His name's Roland Petitier,' said Mikhail. He threw Edouard another disdainful glance. 'Another professor, as it happens.'

The plasma TV was still tuned mutely to the news, showing footage of a white-sheeted body on a trolley being loaded onto an ambulance, while banner headlines ran across the top of the screen. Edouard felt a touch of reckless, almost childish glee as he drew Mikhail's attention to it. 'You don't mean him, I suppose, do you?' he asked.

III

As Knox returned from the ICU, the lamps in the hospital lobby went into synchronised spasm, shuddering like lightning. Gaille was on a wooden bench, deep in conversation with Charissa. They both looked up as he approached. 'Well?' asked Gaille. 'How is he?'

Knox shook his head. 'Not so good. But at least he seems to be stable.'

'And Claire? How's she holding up?'

'She's a bit shaken, as you'd expect.'

'Any chance that she could talk to the press?' asked Charissa. 'Only we need someone sympathetic to be Augustin's spokesperson.'

'Not tonight,' replied Knox. 'She's too upset. Maybe tomorrow.'

'How about you, then?'

Knox took a step back to allow past a porter pushing an elderly woman in a wheelchair, her head tipped to the side, silently weeping. 'Isn't spokesperson a lawyer's job?'

'I'll be beside you, believe me,' said Charissa. 'But right now our most important task is to get the public on Augustin's side; and the public has a habit of making assumptions in cases like these. They assume, for example, that only guilty people need lawyers. And they further assume that lawyers will say anything for a fee.'

'Aren't you exaggerating?'

She shook her head emphatically. 'Did you know that the jury system started as a popularity contest? The party with the most supporters won the case, on the basis that good people had more friends. Public opinion still works that way. We need to demonstrate that Augustin has friends who believe in him and who'll stick by him even in terrible situations. Right now, that means you and Gaille. And, of the two of you, you've been his friend much longer.'

'Fine,' said Knox. 'What do I say?'

'Start by establishing your credentials. You're Daniel Knox, you discovered Alexander's tomb, you brought down the Dragoumises. Don't boast, just let viewers know you're a man of substance. Then tell them much what you told me: that you've been Augustin's friend for many years, and that the idea of him being responsible for anyone's death is absurd, but that you know for a fact he couldn't have been responsible for *this* death because you were with him all afternoon, collecting his fiancée – not his girlfriend, mind, his fiancée – from the airport, and Petitier was still alive when you found him. Explain that Augustin himself called the emergency services, and that none of this would have happened if a policeman hadn't groped Claire, leaving him with no choice but to defend her honour. We Greeks understand honour.'

'Okay.'

'Try to keep the blame as focused as possible for the moment. One rogue policeman, not the whole department. And, whatever you do, don't make out like it's a case of foreigners against Greeks. You'll lose all sympathy in a heartbeat.'

'Understood.'

'Good,' she nodded. 'Then let's go do it.'

NINE

I

For a moment, Edouard feared he'd made a dreadful mistake, bringing the news of Petitier's death so gleefully to Mikhail's attention. But Mikhail was too perturbed by what he saw to worry about that. He grabbed the remote, turned up the volume. A studio anchor was discussing latest developments with a reporter on location outside Evangelismos Hospital; but then the reporter broke off and turned to the front steps, down which two women and a man were now walking, their night-time faces a strobe of flashbulbs.

'That's Daniel Knox,' muttered Edouard.

'Who?' asked Mikhail.

'The Egyptologist. He found Alexander the Great and then Akhenaten. You must remember.

And that woman to his left. That's his girlfriend Gaille Bonnard.'

'She's pretty,' muttered Mikhail, his hand drifting to his crotch. 'I like a girl who makes the most of herself.'

Edouard sat back, intrigued. Knox and Bonnard had turned the world of archaeology upside down with their recent discoveries. Suddenly the prospect of the fleece being genuine seemed significantly higher.

In brisk Greek, Knox introduced his companions, gave his own background, before launching into a spirited attack on the notion that Augustin Pascal had had anything to do with Petitier's death, not least because he'd been with him all afternoon. Then he looked direct into the camera and added: 'I love Greece. I love the Greek people. I love being here in Athens. So I'd like to believe what happened to my friend was the handiwork of one rogue policeman.' He jerked his head at the hospital. 'But I heard something disturbing just now in Intensive Care. I heard that the police have been arranging the transfer of my friend into their custody, even though they have no way of looking after him properly. So I have a question for those policemen, if they're watching: why would you want to take him into custody, unless what you really want is for him to die?'

There was an audible grunt from one of the

journalists, taken aback by so direct an accusation; flashbulbs popped even faster and a clamour of questions were thrown in English and Greek. The woman lawyer threw Knox a fierce look then tried to downplay the accusation, assuring everyone that Augustin was receiving the finest medical attention Athens had to offer, and would continue to receive it. Then she thanked the press for coming and promised updates in the morning.

The camera switched back to the reporter who wrapped up and handed back to the studio, who switched instantly to another reporter who was with a Chief Inspector of police, identified as Angelos Migiakis. 'That's an outrageous slur,' he stormed, when Knox's allegation was put to him. 'Our first priority this afternoon was securing treatment for Mr Pascal. We took him to Evangelismos ourselves. We'd never do anything to put his life in danger.'

'But you must acknowledge that it was your officer who –'

'I acknowledge nothing. We're conducting a thorough investigation, and when it's finished then we'll know what happened. But I want to make two points. Pascal wasn't the only victim today. Professor Petitier was brutally murdered. Let's not forget that. We *owe* it to him to find out who killed him. And the hotel CCTV shows quite clearly that no one entered or left Augustin Pascal's room other than Pascal himself and this man Knox. So you tell me, eh. Who else should we be looking for?'

'Are you accusing Daniel Knox of being involved in Petitier's murder?'

'And let me say something else,' went on Migiakis. 'Items were taken from Petitier's overnight bag. We know that for sure. We also know that Pascal had a bag with him when he left for the airport. What was in it? No one will tell us. What happened to it? No one knows. It mysteriously disappeared while they were at the airport. So I ask again, who else should we be looking for, other than these two?'

The reporter handed back to the studio; the anchorwoman moved to the next story. Mikhail muted the volume, then turned to Edouard and pointed at the screen. 'The fleece,' he said.

'I beg your pardon?'

'That's what was in the bag. My golden fleece. Those two fucking archaeologists murdered Petitier for it. Then they stole it.'

'I suppose it's a possibility.'

'It's not a *possibility*, as you put it,' said Mikhail. 'It's what happened. Weren't you listening? They took it to the airport and then they hid it.'

'You can't know that,' said Edouard. 'Not for sure.'

'You're wrong. I *can* know it.' He touched his

chest. 'I know it in here. I'm never wrong when I know something in here.'

'Yes, but what if –'

'Are you questioning my instincts?'

Edouard dropped his eyes. 'No. No. Of course not.'

Mikhail turned to Boris. 'I want to speak to this man Knox,' he said. 'I want to speak to him *now*.'

'But we don't know where he is.'

'That press conference was outside Evangelismos Hospital, wasn't it? You've heard of phone books, haven't you? You've heard of the Internet? Your cars have SatNav, don't they? Or is it beyond you to find a single fucking hospital?'

'The press conference is over,' said Zaal. 'They'll be long gone.'

'Maybe,' acknowledged Mikhail. 'But Knox's best friend is lying in intensive care, remember. He'll be back soon enough, believe me. And we're going to be waiting for him.'

II

'What the hell was that?' scowled Charissa, once she, Knox and Gaille had walked out of the hospital grounds, and the cameras were no longer on them. 'The police are planning to take Augustin into custody?'

113

'Claire was scared they'd try something,' Knox told her.

'They wouldn't dare.'

'They certainly won't now.'

Charissa shook her head angrily. 'I can't represent you if you're going to provoke the police unnecessarily. I have to work with these people on other cases. I have to keep good lines of communication open. How am I supposed to do that if you start throwing out wild accusations?'

'I'm sorry,' said Knox. He followed Charissa down a short flight of steps into a small park, where a young woman with lank dark hair stood on an upturned beer-crate and warned that Jesus was come, He was alive. 'You're right. It was stupid of me. It won't happen again.'

'It better not,' she warned. They emerged from the park onto a main road, turned right. They walked in stony silence to Charissa's car, bumped up on the kerb behind a truck. 'I'll drop you off at your restaurant,' she said.

'Aren't you coming?'

'I like to see my children at least once a day, if I can,' she said. 'And then I've got some calls to make, to smooth down those feathers you've just ruffled.'

'I'm sorry,' said Knox again. But this time he meant it.

'It's okay,' she sighed. 'I'll sort it out. And I'll

see if I can't find out some more about what the police are up to.'

'We should talk about your fees,' said Knox. 'We need some idea of what to expect. We're only archaeologists, after all.'

'Nothing so far,' Charissa assured him. 'Nico asked me to help, so I helped. But of course if you should want me to stay on the case . . .'

'We do,' said Gaille, taking her wrist. 'Absolutely we do.'

'Then maybe you should come by my office tomorrow morning. We can talk about it then.'

'Not in the morning,' said Knox. 'I've got Augustin's talk to give.'

'The afternoon, then.' She handed him her card. 'Call ahead of time; my assistant will find a slot. And don't worry. We'll manage something. I don't charge the earth, not for cases like this. Frankly, they do my profile good. But you should be aware that it's not just my fees you have to consider. We may need expert medical opinions on Petitier's injuries, for example. We may need private investigators to shadow the police investigation. They're dealing with one of their own here, after all. At the very best, their officers will be *hoping* Augustin is guilty. It's human nature that they'll look for evidence that implicates him and exonerates their colleague. So perhaps we'd be prudent to make our own enquiries. This man Petitier, for example.

Who is he? Why did he contact Nico? Is there anything to this golden fleece business? What was on his laptop? What was taken from his bag? If we can answer such questions, we'll be in a far stronger situation.'

'Gaille and I could look into it,' suggested Knox. 'We have some experience of this kind of thing.'

'This isn't a game,' said Charissa sharply. 'Petitier was murdered earlier today. Don't forget that. And whoever did it is still running around free – unless you believe it was your friend Augustin, of course. Do you really think they'll just stand back and let you two poke your noses into their business, particularly if you start getting close?'

'No,' acknowledged Knox. 'I guess not.'

III

There was a garage beneath Omonia police station, private parking for the senior officers. But Angelos Migiakis had no intention of using his own car for this. He took the wheel of a police cruiser, put it into first gear, then nosed it against the garage wall and roared its engine furiously, his foot pressed upon the brakes, so that the tyres burned in a futile effort at forward motion, filling the air with the stench of things scorching.

Theofanis banged upon the passenger-side window, then opened the door and climbed in. 'Got to you a bit, eh, that interview?'

'Did you hear that bastard Knox?'

'I heard.'

'He suggested we'd take Pascal out of intensive care! How dare he? How *dare* he?' He revved the engine into the red to emphasise his fury. 'What kind of people does he think we are?'

'I don't know, sir.'

There was something in Theofanis's voice. Angelos relaxed his foot on the accelerator and glared at him. 'You didn't. Please tell me you didn't.'

'Didn't what, sir?'

'You know damned well what: shoot your mouth off about transferring Pascal into our custody.'

Theofanis pulled a face. 'I only asked what the procedure would be.'

'Jesus!'

'You *did* want us to put pressure on Knox to come to some kind of arrangement. I thought this would help.'

'Yes. An absolute bloody triumph!' The smell of scorched rubber that filled the car suddenly felt almost corrosive, as though it was eating into his clothes and skin. He turned off the engine and climbed out, marched back inside the station and slammed the door so hard that the officer on duty jumped. He turned to Theofanis, his temper under control again, his mind back on practicalities. 'Right,' he said, 'this is what I want. No more press conferences for Knox and his lawyer outside that fucking hospital, reminding everyone that Pascal's inside. Understand? And, while we're at it, Knox said he'd heard this *inside* Intensive Care. How the hell did he get in? I thought you had a man on the door.'

'He must have slipped by. I'll see it doesn't happen again.'

'It had better not. And I want a proper presence at that hospital. Anyone nosing around, journalists or anyone, I want people in their faces, I want to know exactly what they're doing there. We need this damned story closed down before it gets out of hand. You hear me?'

'Yes, boss. I hear you.'

TEN

I

The Island was boisterous and crowded, all the tables taken, the barstools too, with several more people milling around just inside the door, waiting to be seated. The moustached head waiter flinched a little when he saw Gaille and Knox arrive, as though this level of success was too much for him. He looked around, perhaps hoping that some miracle would create space for another table, but there seemed little chance of that. Apart from anything else, it was an awkward shape for a restaurant, all arches and alcoves and sharp corners, and every possible square inch was already pressed into service, the diners packed so close together that the larger ones had their table-edges jammed into their midriffs.

'Here!' yelled Nico, getting to his feet in the far

corner, enthusiastically waving them over. They sucked in their stomachs and wended between tables to an alcove that allowed Nico a bench-seat all to himself. 'Wine?' he asked, holding up a half-empty carafe.

'Please,' said Gaille.

'Not for me,' said Knox.

'I took the liberty of ordering,' said Nico, slopping the resinous yellow wine into all three glasses, despite Knox's answer. 'I hope you don't mind.' He put a hand upon his stomach, as if it were days since he'd last eaten.

'I'm sure you know what's best.'

'I've taken another liberty too.' He reached into his jacket pocket, produced some stapled sheets. 'Augustin's speech,' he said, passing them to Knox, the white paper smeared with sticky fingerprints. 'In case you should want to read it through later.'

'Thanks,' said Knox, folding the pages away. 'That's very thoughtful.'

'Don't mention it.' His gaze slid past Knox; his face lit up. 'Ah,' he said. 'What perfect timing.' A waiter and a waitress cleared space upon their table, then began setting down brushed steel platters of succulent seafood, baskets of warm crusty bread and a palette of dips and side-dishes. Nico rested his fingertips upon the edge of the table for a few moments, like a priest about to give a blessing, then reached with surprising grace for the fried taramasalata, scooping a good third of it straight onto his plate, garnishing it with three grilled king prawns, their blackened pink skins glistening with garlic-butter glaze. He picked one up, bit straight through its crisp shell, his lips glossing with juices. 'We have the best seafood in the world here in Greece,' he declared grandly. 'You know our secret?'

'What?'

'Salt!' he exulted, waving his hand. 'The Mediterranean is like a great marinade of salt, preparing these fish all their lives for our tables. And still there are people who don't believe in God!'

Knox smiled. 'Just a shame we're not supposed to eat salt any more.'

'Speak for yourself, my dear boy. Speak for yourself. The great privilege of a condition like mine is that you no longer have to worry about such things.'

'Condition?' asked Gaille. 'What condition?'

'Forgive me,' frowned Nico. 'I assumed you knew. Everyone does. It's hardly a secret. My heart, you see. Too many steroids as a youth. I was a weight-lifter. A good one, though I say so myself. I had the physique, of course: more wide than tall. Not quite as wide as I am now, admittedly. Useless for football, my other great love, but perfect for weights. We always had weights around the house.

A family tradition. I started lifting before I started reading. I was something of a prodigy, if you can be a prodigy at something so prosaic. I made the national squad when I was fifteen. My coach started talking about the Olympics. I began dreaming of medals. I began dreaming of *gold*. I'd have sold my soul for that. Steroids seemed an insignificant price. Now look!' He barked out a laugh. 'And of course I didn't even make it to the Games. My shoulder popped on me!'

'I'm so sorry,' said Gaille.

Nico waved away her concern. 'My own fault. I was a cheat. People keep telling me that I was just a child, too young to make such decisions for myself, that my . . . my coach must have *bullied* me into it. But I wasn't *that* young. I knew full well it was cheating. Why else all those furtive trips to our training camps in East Germany? Why else all the sworn secrecy? I didn't care a jot. In fact, I was more eager than anyone. I *insisted* on it. I thought I was destined, you see. Besides, I'm still alive, aren't I?' He spoke in short bursts, and out of one side of his mouth, leaving the other free for eating. He reached across the table with a crust of lavishly buttered bread, scooped up a scallop. 'It's my old team-mates I feel sorriest for. They all went long ago. Heart disease from those damned steroids. All but one, at least. He couldn't bear the waiting any longer, so he used painkillers instead. It can be a terrible thing, waiting.' He smiled more brightly, crunched his way through a grilled sardine. 'That's one reason I do these conferences. They give me something to think about. Having a purpose, that's the key. And it seems to work. My doctors keep assuring me I only have a few months left, but then they first told me that seven years ago. So what do they know?' He laughed and waved a hand. 'And once you accept the notion, once you get past the *dread*, it's strangely liberating. No painkillers for me, that's for sure. I plan to make the most of what I have left.' He reached across the table for the stuffed crab. 'Everyone keeps trying to put me on a *regime*. "You mustn't smoke," they tell me. "You mustn't drink. You mustn't eat so much." "Why on earth not?" I ask. "I'm doomed anyway, aren't I? Can't I at least enjoy myself while I wait?"' He laughed again, speared some octopus with his fork, chasing the oily coriander sauce around the dish until it glistened and dripped, then chewed hungrily upon it.

'You take it very well,' observed Knox. 'If that had happened to me, I'd have wanted to kill my coach.'

'Yes, well,' shrugged Nico. 'He didn't know the damage steroids would do. No one did back then.'

'You were only a child,' said Gaille angrily. 'He had a responsibility.'

'It's history now.'

'How can you say that? Is he still alive, this coach of yours?'

'Yes.'

'Do you still see him?'

He shook his head, from the look of him wishing he hadn't raised the subject. 'We had a falling out,' he said. 'When Tomas died. My friend Tomas. The one who took the painkillers. My coach . . . he gave one of the eulogies at his funeral. All those fine words. I don't know, I didn't believe them, I suppose; or perhaps I was just angry that he hadn't paid a price himself. Anyway, I stood up and accused him flat out of murdering Tomas, and of handing me a death sentence too. As you can imagine, that was the last time we spoke.'

'Good for you.'

Nico didn't look so sure. He pulled a mournful face. 'Maybe,' he said. Then he added, by way of explanation: 'He wasn't just my weightlifting coach, you see. He was my father too.'

II

They took both Mercedes into Athens, Mikhail going in the first with Boris and Davit, leaving Edouard to drive Zaal. At least this way he could turn off his SatNav and just follow the car in front.

It started to cloud over and then spit with rain as they reached the city centre, pedestrians wrapping their jackets tighter around themselves, walking closer to the buildings to take advantage of the awnings and avoid the splash of traffic.

'Boris says you've got twin daughters,' grunted Zaal.

'And a son,' said Edouard proudly.

'How old are they?' asked Zaal. 'The girls, I mean?'

Edouard slid him a sour look. 'Fifteen. Why?'

'No reason.'

They pulled up against the kerb outside Evangelismos Hospital. The place was swarming with police. They got out to confer. 'You know what Knox looks like,' Mikhail told Edouard. 'You stay here and watch for him. When he shows, call me.'

'How am I supposed to do that?' asked Edouard. 'Boris took my mobile.'

'Your father doesn't want him calling home,' said Boris, when Mikhail looked to him for an explanation.

'Fine. Zaal, you stay with him.'

'Oh, great!' Zaal shot Edouard a resentful look. 'Thanks a million.'

'Where are you guys going?' asked Edouard.

'To get something to eat,' said Mikhail. 'Why? Is that a problem?'

125

'No,' said Edouard. 'No problem.'

'Good,' said Mikhail. 'Then we'll see you later.'

III

The lights plunged out in the Island, and in the surrounding streets and buildings too, throwing the restaurant into an almost complete darkness, save for the blue flames of gas in the kitchen, and the headlights of passing traffic. A few diners laughed; others sighed. A woman struck and held up her lighter, making like she was the Statue of Liberty. The staff went smoothly into their practised drill, a waiter lighting oil lamps then hoisting them up with a bamboo pole to hang from ceiling hooks, while a waitress distributed candles among the tables, creating a cosy and romantic atmosphere. 'Ah, Greece!' smiled Nico, raising his glass in an impromptu toast. 'May she never work efficiently.'

'You said something in the car earlier,' said Knox, seizing the moment to divert him from his childhood reminiscences. 'That Augustin might have known about the golden fleece. How come?'

'I sent photographs of Petitier's seals to everyone on my speakers list, including your friend. It was a courtesy to explain the change of schedule. So plenty of people might have known about it, particularly if they knew their Linear B. And I'm not suggesting he did know about the fleece, anyway, only that the police might be able to make a case for it.' He sat back to allow the waitress to clear their plates. 'I should have just called them in at once,' he said ruefully. 'All my colleagues advised me to.'

'Really?' asked Gaille.

Nico nodded. 'Petitier had no right to those seals. He was legally obliged to notify the authorities rather than jaunting around the world giving talks on them. So, yes, technically I should have informed the police and left it to them. But no one knew where Petitier was or where he'd been living, so it wouldn't have been easy for them to track him down. And if he'd learned that the police were after him, maybe he'd have gone to ground again, and we'd never have learned what he'd found. And what was the point, after all? He was coming to us anyway, evidently intending to show us his finds and tell us all about them. It seemed unnecessarily vindictive to turn the police on him first.'

The waitress appeared again with three glasses, into which she poured generous shots of Metaxa. 'There's something I don't get,' said Gaille, once they'd clinked their glasses in a toast. 'If Petitier really had found the fleece, and wanted to announce it, why not just go to the press? Why choose an archaeological conference?'

Nico nodded, as though he'd wondered this himself. 'He must have been aware he'd acted illegally. Perhaps he wanted to legitimise himself as far as he could by dressing his announcement up in academic clothes.'

The lights flickered and came back on. Knox blinked and sat back in the sudden brightness, rather regretting the loss of intimacy. 'But why *this* conference? What has the fleece to do with Eleusis?'

'More than you might think.' He looked quizzically at them both. 'How much do you know about the fleece legend?'

'Just what you'd expect,' said Knox.

'Then let me give you a little background. For one thing, it's among the oldest of our heroic legends. It's mentioned in Homer, so it dates back at least to seven or eight hundred B.C., but almost certainly to the late bronze age or even earlier. Essentially, Phrixus and Helle, the twin children of King Athamas, were plotted against by their wicked stepmother Ino, who bribed an oracle to say they had to be sacrificed to end a famine. At the last moment, however, Poseidon sent a golden flying ram to secure their escape. The ram flew them over the sea, but Helle tragically fell off and drowned at the place we now know as the Hellespont. Phrixus made it all the way to Colchis, which is in modern-day Georgia, where he sacrificed the ram in gratitude to Poseidon and hung its fleece in a sacred grove.'

Gaille wrinkled her nose. 'I've always thought that a bit hard on the ram.'

'Never be an animal in a Greek myth,' agreed Nico. He covered his mouth with his hand, then produced a deep, long and contented belch. 'Anyway, the fleece stayed in Georgia until the time of Jason. Jason was the rightful king of Thessaly, of course, but his uncle had taken the throne, which he refused to give up unless Jason first proved himself by bringing back the fleece. Jason built himself a ship, the Argo, then gathered together the cream of Greek heroes, the Argonauts, with whom he set sail for Colchis. They endured the usual misadventures – fire-breathing oxen and dragons and metal giants and so on – but eventually Jason brought the fleece back in triumph to Thessaly, and claimed his throne. And that's pretty much it, for that fleece, at least.'

'For *that* fleece?' asked Gaille.

'Yes,' smiled Nico. 'You see, the thing is, Greek tradition mentions *another* golden fleece. It's much less well-known, but much more likely to have existed. And the fascinating thing is that it was reputedly kept at Eleusis. Did you know that, so long as they could afford it, anyone who spoke Greek could be initiated at Eleusis, even slaves. But there was *one* exception. People with blood on their hands. That is to say, murderers. Before they could participate, they had to go through a purification ceremony. The Italians very kindly lent us a vase for the conference depicting Hercules being cleansed. You may have seen it. He's sitting on a throne, and guess what's draped over it?'

'A golden fleece?' suggested Knox.

'A golden fleece,' nodded Nico. 'And of course the whole thing about Eleusis is that we know so little about what went on during the ceremony. But we do know for sure that several unknown sacred objects were shown to the congregation. Isn't it possible that the fleece was among them?'

'But I thought that Petitier made his finds in Crete,' said Knox. 'What would this fleece be doing there?'

'Again, it's more plausible than you might think. For one thing, Crete figures prominently in the Argonaut legend; it's where Jason encountered the bronze giant Talos. And more than a few scholars believe that at least parts of the fleece legend came originally from Crete. And Eleusis had its own very strong connections with Crete too. The legend of Demeter and Persephone is undoubtedly Cretan: apart from anything else, the Homeric Hymn, our best source on the Mysteries, states flatly that Demeter came from Crete. The earliest mention of Dionysus is also from Crete. His name is "Dio-Nysa" or "God of Nysa", and Nysa was most likely in Crete. Of course, he was a multifaceted god, as so many were. That is to say, he wasn't just Dionysus, he was Zeus and Poseidon too. As god of the sea, Poseidon was vitally important to the Minoans: and remember that it was Poseidon who sent the golden ram to pick up Phrixus and Helle in the first place.'

'That's a little thin, isn't it?'

'Then how about this: the families of the high priest at Eleusis were known as the Eumolpidai, from their ancestor Eumolpos, the first high priest, who came here from Crete. The high priestesses were also descended from Cretan families. I've been thinking about this a lot recently, as you might imagine. The Mysteries were celebrated all around the Mediterranean from the early Mycenaean era on; that is to say, from the end of the Minoan. The Minoan collapse seems overwhelmingly likely to have been precipitated by the eruption of Mount Thera, the greatest cataclysm in human history. It's not too far-fetched, is it, to imagine a kind of diaspora from Crete to the Mediterranean fringes, in which Minoan priests had to flee in such a hurry that they left their sacred treasures behind. Or, if you won't grant me that, we have good reason to believe that the sacred families kept up their links with Crete; so when Eleusis finally came under threat from Christianity, wouldn't it have made sense for them to seek sanctuary there?'

'Taking all their artefacts back with them. Including the golden fleece.'

'Exactly.'

'And now Petitier has found it.'

'Or so he wanted us to believe.'

'And tomorrow was to have been his great unveiling,' nodded Knox. 'But someone got to him first.'

ELEVEN

I

The sight of Knox beckoning for the bill seemed to send a jolt through Nico. 'You must excuse me,' he said, labouring to his feet. 'I have *mounds* to do before morning. Simply mounds. My speech to rehearse. Itineraries to change.' He waved vaguely. 'You can't imagine.'

'Of course,' said Knox. 'We're grateful you could spare this much time.'

'Not at all. Not at all.' He patted his pockets for his wallet, his frown growing all the time as he couldn't find it. 'Oh dear,' he said.

'Forget it,' said Gaille hurriedly. 'It's on us. The least we can do after everything you and Charissa have done for us.'

'You're too kind,' he said, a little shamefaced as he shook their hands. Then he said to Knox.

'I'll be at Eleusis from eight, if you want to see the set-up before your talk.'

'I'll see you there,' nodded Knox.

They watched him leave, smiling at how the other diners had to shimmy their tables aside to make room, then shared a wry look. 'He's really hard up,' said Gaille defensively. 'He's bankrolling the conference himself. What was I supposed to say?'

'Exactly what you did,' he assured her, covering her hand with his own. But the incident had given him a little prod. He excused himself and went to the toilets where he fished the red-leatherette box out of his pocket. Since getting it back at the police station, he hadn't had a single moment to make sure that the ring was still inside. It was, thankfully. He took it out, held it up against the strip-light above the sink. It gave him a mild thrill even to touch it, the bright cool gold, the sparkle of gemstone. More than he could afford, but that wasn't what gave it its tingle.

Three weeks before, he and Gaille had taken the tram out to Alexandria's Fort Qait Bey, the medieval fortress built on the site of the ancient Pharos lighthouse. They enjoyed evenings out there, the sense of carnival, the boys chasing each other in and out of the crowds, the young women leaning against the sea-wall as they flirted with their men, while waves crashed against the breakwaters of ancient stone, throwing spray high into the night sky, leaving dark stains on the grey tarmac. The hawkers had been out in force, selling their sickly-sweet confections and showing off their latest cheap flashy toys. A boy with bush-baby ears and a missing front tooth had pestered Knox to buy some gaudy costume jewellery for Gaille before chasing off after better prospects. But it had given Knox an opening for a question that had been much on his mind. 'Ever heard of Alexandrite?' he'd asked her.

'Alexandrite?'

'A gemstone. Polychromatic. That's to say, it changes colour according to the light, like those sunglasses.'

She'd smiled. 'You're such a nerd.'

'The most prized ones are green during the day, but then turn red by night. Two gemstones for the price of one. You know how cheap I am.' They'd laughed together at this private joke. 'The thing is, I've always had rather a fondness for them; because of Alexander, I mean. They must have something to do with him, right? Or with this city, at least.'

'You'd certainly think so.'

He'd nodded briskly, though he'd hoped for more enthusiasm. 'So when you think about it, they're really *our* gemstone, aren't they?'

She'd stopped walking, had taken his hand.

'I suppose so,' she'd replied carefully. 'And I'm sure they're just lovely. But I prefer diamonds myself.'

He smiled down at the ring. Diamonds it was. A sudden hot clutch in his chest, wanting it over and done with, Gaille as his fiancée, his wife. Not tonight, though, not with Augustin so perilously ill. He closed the box, put it away and went back out.

Gaille was on her mobile. 'Claire,' she mouthed, raising an interrogative eyebrow. He shook his head, went to the bar instead. His bill was ready: the size of it nearly gave him a seizure. No wonder Nico had patted his pockets. He put it on his card; he could worry about it when all this was over. 'The nurses are making her up a bed at the hospital,' said Gaille, appearing at his shoulder. 'I said we'd take in a bag. I hope that's okay?'

'Of course.'

'She asked if you'd said anything about your conversation earlier. What did she mean by that?'

'I don't know.'

'Yes, you do.'

'Let's get out of here,' he said. It had been raining, leaving the air fresh and bracing after the smoky warm restaurant. 'That was really good,' he said, patting his stomach. 'Nico certainly knows his restaurants.'

Gaille gave him a wry look. 'Come on, Daniel,' she said. 'What was this conversation about? Have you fallen out or something?'

'I don't think so.' He gave a little shrug. 'She just thought I might have done more to stop that policeman hitting Augustin.'

'She thinks what?' asked Gaille, stiffening with vicarious umbrage. 'But I thought his partner shoved you up against the wall.'

'He did. Claire just thinks I could have got free quicker, if I'd tried.'

'And could you have?'

He hesitated a moment before answering. 'Yes,' he admitted. 'I think I could.'

II

Kiko could sense his mother's restlessness as she lay beside him in the four-poster. She'd been on edge since dinner, which they'd eaten in the kitchens, along with those of the castle staff not needed to serve at the banquet. They'd sat at a long table of rough wood, perfect for picking fat splinters from. It had been an immensely comforting experience after such an unsettling day, what with the cheerful banter of the staff, the warmth of the ovens, the sight and smells of all that delicious food being prepared for the banquet: salmon and roast pig and venison and tiny chickens in walnut sauce and red beans with pomegranate and coriander. Not that any of that had been for them, of course, though they'd eaten heartily enough their stew of mutton with potato and onions.

Alexei Nergadze and two of his friends had come in as they'd been mopping up their plates with hunks of warm bread. While Alexei had gone to discuss the menu with the cooks, his friends had stood by the table, eyeing up Eliso and Lila, making jokes that Kiko hadn't understood, but which had made all the others blush. His mother had been unsettled ever since. Her mind, Kiko knew, was on them, not him.

Even so, he'd almost dropped off when she slipped out of the bed. Almost. He turned onto his side and saw her white nightdress flitting like a kindly ghost to the door, opening it just wide enough to make sure there was no one outside. He sat up, turned on the bedside lamp. 'Where are you going, Mama?'

'Oh,' she said. 'You're awake.'

'Yes. I'm awake.'

'I'm just going to look in on your sisters. Make sure they're okay.'

'You're coming back, aren't you?'

'Just get to sleep now, my love.'

'But I'm scared,' he told her. 'What are we even doing in this horrid place? Why can't we go home?'

'It's just for a few days.'

'Where's father? I want my father.'

'Please, my love. You have to be strong. You have to. I can't leave your sisters alone. Not here. Not tonight.'

'Let me come with you.'

'There's no bed for you in there.'

'There's no bed for you either.'

'Yes, but I'm used to sleeping in uncomfortable places. I've had to share a bed with your father after all.'

Usually, when she made jokes at his father's expense, it was a way for the two of them to bond. But Kiko wasn't having that, not tonight, not here. He pushed the corners of his mouth as far down as they would go. 'Why are you always so worried about Eliso and Lila?' he asked. 'Why aren't you worried about me?'

She sighed and came back to the bed. 'Your sisters are reaching a certain age,' she told him, taking his hand. 'Men aren't always trustworthy around girls as beautiful as your sisters. You saw those two earlier.'

'Please don't leave.'

'You'll be fine,' she said, switching off the light. 'I promise.' She kissed his forehead and then went back to the door, opened it up. 'Sweet dreams,' she murmured, before slipping out.

Sweet dreams! He trembled beneath the bedclothes, the fear of night-time monsters already growing. Noises that had meant little with his mother beside him suddenly seemed to grow louder and more malevolent. The wind rushed and creaked, flickers of rain tapped on the windows, ivy brushed the mullioned panes like an escaped convict trying to pick his way inside. An owl hooted. A door banged. Somewhere, there was a howl of laughter. He gave a violent shudder: it was much colder here than it had been in Tbilisi, and the bedclothes were thinner. He pulled them up around his throat and prayed to ancient gods to keep him safe.

III

The hotel concierge was effusively apologetic about the state of Claire's luggage, in the way that such people only ever are when someone else was to blame. He explained with unseemly relish how the police had taken her cases into an empty room, where they'd interrogated them like a mouthy suspect, flinging the contents hither and thither, slitting opening linings and vindictively squeezing out toothpaste, before finally giving hotel staff grudging permission to transfer them to the basement. He led Knox and Gaille down there, then left them to it.

Gaille crouched to pop the catches of the nearest suitcase; it sprang open like a jack-in-the-box from the chaos crammed inside. She looked wearily up at Knox. 'We'll have to repack everything,' she said. 'We can't let Claire see it like this.' They worked briskly, Gaille setting changes of clothes aside for Claire as they went, along with her washbag and towel and other essentials that she then packed into the smallest of the cases.

Knox carried it out to the car, slung it on the back seat. 'I'll park outside,' he said. 'You can run in and drop it off.'

'You're not going to start avoiding Claire, are you?'

'It's not that,' he said, pulling out. 'Parking's just a nightmare near the hospital.'

'I know. I know.' She put her hand upon his as it rested upon the gear-stick. 'But listen: what happened to Augustin happened because a policeman went berserk. It wasn't your fault.'

'I know that, but –'

'It wasn't your fault,' she insisted. 'Maybe you could have stopped one blow. *Maybe*. You'd almost certainly have got yourself put in hospital too in the process.'

'You're missing the point.'

'No, I'm not. I'm really not. You're the one missing the point. You're a brave man, Daniel. God knows how many times you've risked yourself for me. So if anything failed this afternoon, it wasn't your courage. Perhaps it was your ability to process what was going on. You were in shock, that's all, and shock numbs people. That's what it does. I don't think you realise it, but Augustin's like a big brother to you, and big brothers are *invincible*. To see him assaulted that way, it was unthinkable.'

'Maybe,' he said.

'It's the truth, Daniel. And anyway this is hardly the time to start doubting yourself. I need you too much. Augustin needs you too much. *Claire* needs you too much. She had a go at you earlier, sure, but that's because the man she loves is in grave danger, and she's terrified. Anger is one of the few ways she has of dealing with that, because she's human. So she needs you to take whatever she throws at you right now, however irrational or hurtful it may seem, and still be there for her.' She took and squeezed his wrist. 'Do you understand?'

Her words braced him, as they always did. 'Yes,' he said. 'I do.'

TWELVE

I

'So do they bring their girlfriends home, then, your daughters?' asked Zaal.

'Would you mind not smoking in the car,' said Edouard.

'Yes, I would mind,' said Zaal. He buzzed his window down as a compromise. 'So?' he asked. 'Your daughters? Do they bring their friends home? After school, and that?'

'Of course they do.'

'Any hotties?'

'For Christ's sake!'

'I always figured that would be one of the advantages of having daughters,' mused Zaal. He slid a look out of the corner of his eye, as if to assess how successfully he was getting under Edouard's skin. 'Once you get on a bit, it becomes bloody

143

hard to meet nice young girls. I mean, everyone thinks you're a pervert if you hang around outside schools, right? But when you've got daughters of your own, no problem, right? All the nice young girls come to you.'

'I don't want to have this conversation.'

'And holidays, Jesus!' He tapped ash out the window. 'Aren't you a clever bastard. All those hot young bodies oiling themselves up on the beach for you, taking showers together back at the hotel. Enough to drive a man crazy, right?'

'Fatherhood's not like that.'

'Maybe not for you. But what about when your girls go to stay with their friends. I'll bet *their* fathers will be checking them out. How does that make you feel? Doesn't it worry you, trusting your daughters to those filthy old men?'

'Will you shut up?'

'I'm just saying. You want to be careful.'

Edouard scowled and clenched a fist. Zaal had to know that his daughters were being held hostage, that anxiety for them was driving him crazy. Of course he did. That was why he was enjoying himself so much. He turned on the radio, looking for a station that might keep Zaal quiet, or at least drown him out. A car pulled up on the other side of the road. He couldn't see much through the light drizzle, but then the passenger door opened and Gaille Bonnard got out.

'Is that the girl?' asked Zaal.

Edouard hesitated, loath to bring bad things down upon this young woman, but then he imagined what Mikhail might do to him if he learned he'd shielded her. 'Yes. It's her.'

Zaal flicked away his cigarette, flapped open his mobile and called in. 'They're here,' he said. 'The girl's taking in a bag. The guy's waiting outside.' He paused to listen. 'A Citroen. Blue. Looks like a rental.' He sat forward and squinted. 'Can't read it, not from here.' The hospital doors opened again and Gaille hurried out. 'She's coming back out. She must have just dropped the bag inside.' Zaal turned to Edouard. 'Follow them,' he said.

He waited until the Citroen had passed, then pulled out. It turned onto Vasilissis Sofias, headed towards Syndagma. Zaal couldn't read the signs, so Edouard gave him directions that he relayed on so that the others could pick up the chase. Right onto Stadhiou, north towards Omonia. The square was congested; even the lightest drizzle could bring Athens to a standstill. They turned onto 3rd Septemvriou, where lines of sequined whores glittered beneath the awnings, trying to make eye-contact. The Citroen turned left down a one-way street, then into a hotel parking lot. Edouard drove on by, bumped up onto the kerb. Car doors slammed; Knox and Gaille hurried out of the car park and across the road to the hotel.

'Go stall them,' said Zaal.

'What? How?'

'I don't know. Just do it. Until the others get here.'

'Why don't you do it?'

'Because Mikhail wants you to.' He offered him the mobile. 'Unless you'd rather discuss it with him yourself.'

Edouard bit back a retort. He got out, his arm above his head to ward off the light rain, standing back to allow a blue van past, then hurrying across the road. The hotel had a glass front, but inside it was one of those places that tried to make a virtue of their heritage, its lobby rich with lush red carpeting, polished brass fittings everywhere, chandeliers hanging from ostentatiously high ceilings, its staff dressed in scarlet-and-gold livery. The bar to the right of the main door was full of prosperous-looking foreigners in comfortable chairs sipping whiskies and wines. One or two of them looked up as Knox and Gaille walked over to reception, then they drew the attention of their companions, and suddenly everyone was looking. Their appearance on the news had evidently made them minor celebrities.

There was a loud tooting on the main road; an engine roared and headlights swept down the one-way street before stopping in a slither outside the hotel. The back door opened and Mikhail stepped out, turning up the collar of his trench-coat against the rain. 'Well?' he asked.

'They're just getting their keys,' said Edouard. Mikhail nodded and reached back inside the car for his shotgun. He broke it, stuffed in two cartridges, then snapped it closed again. 'What the hell's that for?' protested Edouard.

'Your friend Knox murdered a man earlier today for my fleece,' said Mikhail. 'You think he's just going to give it back?'

'But all those people . . .'

'So?' He hid the shotgun inside his trench-coat, then led the way through the automatic glass doors into the hotel lobby just as Knox and Gaille collected their keys and headed for the lifts.

II

Kiko woke in a panic to a rush of beating wings and lights outside his window that made him think of demons with claws and sharp teeth and his heart began thundering like hooves in a horse-race. But then he saw the thing itself and recognised what it was. A helicopter. It had landed earlier that night with more Nergadze guests in its belly; now it was evidently taking them back home again.

His fears receded, leaving only a dampness of sweat in his mattress. He lay there in the growing chill, wondering for the hundredth time what they were doing in this wretched place, where their father was, how he'd allowed this to happen to them.

He was drifting back to sleep when he heard the footsteps. They seemed to stop directly outside his room. His body stiffened; he stared petrified at the blur of hallway light that marked the edges of his door, pleading for it to be imagination. But then he heard the handle squeak and he caught his breath as the door opened stealthily and close again. 'Mama?' asked Kiko, his heart palpitating violently. 'Is that you?'

'I woke you,' growled a man. 'I didn't mean to.' A lighter rasped, a blue-yellow flame sprang up to light a fat yellow candle that flickered and fluttered and then grew strong enough to reveal a thin, tall old man in blue silk pyjamas and a red dressing-gown. Ilya Nergadze.

'What are you doing here?' asked Kiko.

Ilya tried a smile to put Kiko at his ease, but it only made him feel worse. 'Do you remember me, Kiko? You had lunch last year with me in Tbilisi. You swam in my pool. You were very good.' The dim candlelight created a strange intimacy as he drew closer. 'This is my other house. This whole castle and all the land as far as the eye can see. Do you like it?'

'I suppose.'

A flash of yellow teeth that might have been a smile. 'You don't sound sure.'

'I want my father,' said Kiko. 'I want to go home.'

The old man reached the bed. 'Goodness me,' he said, when he saw Kiko's forehead damp with sweat. 'You *have* had a nightmare.' He set the candle down on the bedside table, produced a handkerchief from his sleeve and dabbed Kiko's brow.

'What are you doing?'

'You mustn't sleep in wet bedclothes,' said Ilya. 'You'll catch the devil of a cold.'

'I'm fine.'

'At least move across to where it's dry. It's a big enough bed for that. And your mother would never forgive me if you caught something.' He watched benignly as Kiko shuffled across, then sat in the gentle depression Kiko had left in the mattress, before lying down alongside him, pulling the sheets taut across Kiko's body as he did so. Ilya's hair and eyebrows had somehow turned black and shiny as shoe polish since he'd last seen him, noticed Kiko. It added to his sense of unreality.

Ilya folded his handkerchief in half and dabbed Kiko's forehead once more: his dressing-gown fell open as he did so, exposing a lozenge gap in Ilya's silk pyjamas, a glimpse of silver curls of hair and wrinkled flesh. 'Dear me,' said Ilya, righting himself, tying a new knot in his dressing-gown cord. 'That won't do.' He smiled at Kiko. 'Do you like to ride?' he asked.

'I don't know,' said Kiko miserably. 'I've never tried.'

'You've never tried?' said Ilya with feigned astonishment. His breath smelled of alcohol, and it tickled Kiko's cheek. 'We'll have to change that, won't we? Tell you what. Tomorrow we'll go riding together in the hills. Would you like that?'

'Will Mama be there?'

'Of course. Your sisters too. We'll make a party of it. And don't worry. I know just the pony for you. Gentle as cotton wool. Perfect for a young gentleman learning how to ride. I taught all my grandsons on her. Trust me. You'll be sore in the rump for a while, but you'll soon grow to love it.' He turned onto his back, cupped his hand behind the candle-flame and blew it out, so that the room fell back into darkness. The creak of springs, the tug of bedclothes, that soft sour breath again against his cheek, then Ilya's hand settling on his ribs, stroking him through the bedclothes, rhythmically down from his chest to his navel, then back up again. 'Close your eyes,' murmured Ilya, worming his other arm beneath Kiko's pillow, lifting his forearm to tilt Kiko's head against his chest. 'That's it. Try to sleep. No more nightmares now. Not while I'm here.'

III

The hotel's lifts were an extension of its retro-chic design, huge old service elevators with age-speckled mirrors and automated lattice gates. Knox had been rather charmed the first time he'd taken one, but they climbed and descended at such a ridiculously sedate pace that now his only reaction was exasperation.

'Hey, look,' said Gaille, as the gate concertinaed closed. 'You're famous.'

He smiled when he saw his name scrawled with a bold red marker pen on tomorrow's conference itinerary, taped to one of the mirrors. 'I guess Nico did have mounds to do after all,' he said. He was about to press their floor button when he saw five men approaching purposefully across the lobby. These lifts were slow, but at least they were large. 'Going up?' he asked.

'Thanks,' said the first man, his black-leather trench-coat lightly beaded with rain.

'Which floor?'

The man hesitated. 'Top floor,' he said.

Knox nodded and pressed six and seven; they began the slow ascent. It was congested with all seven of them, especially as one of the newcomers was a giant with a flattened nose and ears like pounded dough. The lattice gates meant that they could see out onto each of the floors, and that those guests waiting for a lift could see them too. They all stood facing the same way, keeping their stares neutral, observing the standard etiquette. All except the man in the trench-coat. He stared at Gaille with such open and obvious interest that Knox was about to say something. But Gaille must have realised, for she squeezed his wrist, a request to let her handle it herself. Then she turned to the man and said: 'You must give me your name and address.'

'Why's that?' he asked.

'You seem to enjoy staring at me so much, I thought maybe I could have a poster made up of myself, so that you can hang it on your wall.'

The man laughed easily. 'No need,' he assured her. 'I have a good memory for faces.'

The lift stopped abruptly at the sixth floor, jarring them all a little. The lattice gate opened automatically. Knox put himself between Gaille and the man, then followed her out. The man in the trench-coat made to come after them, and the others too, but Knox turned and blocked their way. 'You want the top floor,' he pointed out, as the gate began to close again.

'My mistake,' replied the man, blocking it with his foot. 'I thought the sixth *was* the top floor.'

There was a moment of stillness as he and Knox locked gazes. Knox didn't know what was going on, only that it wasn't good. 'Who are you?' he asked. 'Are you staying here?'

A door opened along the corridor at that moment. Two bearded men emerged, bickering good-naturedly, and walked towards the lift area. Knox seized the moment to take Gaille by her arm and hustle her to their room, swiping his electronic key through the lock and hurrying thankfully inside.

THIRTEEN

I

'Jesus!' shuddered Gaille. 'What a creep.'

'Yes,' agreed Knox. He double-locked the door then checked the corridor through the fisheye peephole.

She looked curiously at him. 'What?'

'I don't know.' He turned to face her. 'Didn't you get the sense that he had some kind of . . . *agenda*?'

'He was just a jerk, that's all,' said Gaille. 'Plenty of men think it turns a woman on to be stared at like that. You just happened to be there tonight.'

'Maybe,' said Knox.

'Seriously,' she told him. 'Don't go all paranoid on me.'

'Isn't paranoid how Augustin described Petitier?' he asked. 'And look what happened to him.'

'You're not suggesting that guy had something to do with Petitier's death, are you?' frowned Gaille.

Knox shrugged as he went over to the bed. 'Augustin said that Petitier went to see him because his own room was still being made up. But how plausible is that? I mean, the cleaning staff are pretty damned efficient here. You've got to give them that. The vacuum cleaners go in the morning, not the afternoons.'

'Maybe the previous occupant was late checking out.'

'Maybe. But maybe it was something else. I mean, the lobby here is really exposed, isn't it? Didn't you find it uncomfortable coming in just now, the way everyone stared?'

'So?'

'I'm just saying. Put yourself in Petitier's shoes. Out of the world for the best part of twenty years: crowds are bound to make him anxious. He checks in here. People stare at him. Maybe it's just because he looks a bit odd, but he fears the word's got out about the priceless treasure in his bag. He dares not go to his room now. He knows Augustin's giving one of the talks. His old student, someone he can trust. He asks what room he's in, or perhaps he glimpses his room number in the register while he's checking in. He goes up, knocks, spins his story about his room not being ready yet, and promises he won't stay long. But then Augustin heads off to the airport and Petitier makes himself at home, takes a shower.'

'In someone else's room?'

'Why not? Augustin's going to be gone for two hours at least, more like three. And haven't you ever had that feeling of being grubby and under-dressed when you turn up after a long journey somewhere as plush as this?'

'Okay. Go on.'

'Now imagine it from someone else's per-spective. Imagine you're sitting in the lobby. Nico has emailed you photos of Petitier's seals, or maybe you've just heard whispers. But suddenly you see the man himself clutching his bag and looking nervous as hell. *Jesus!* you think. *Maybe there's something to this after all*. Your whole life you've been hoping to find something extraordi-nary; or maybe you're getting on a bit and you've got nothing saved. You *want* that fleece. You *covet* it. You've *earned* it by dedicating your life to archaeology. You follow Petitier to the lifts. He tries to shake you off by going to Augustin's room, but you manage to trail him somehow, and you hear Augustin inviting him inside. Maybe you've got a nearby room. Or you know someone who does. Whatever, you're still lurking nearby when I arrive twenty minutes later and take Augustin off to the airport, leaving Petitier on his own.

And then, through the door, you hear the shower come on.'

'Not through the door,' said Gaille. 'The CCTV would have picked it up.'

'Through the wall, then.' He nodded at their own bathroom. 'I mean, we can hear everything our neighbours get up to. Presumably it's the same one floor down.'

'So I hear the shower start,' agreed Gaille. 'It's my opportunity.'

'Exactly,' said Knox. 'You may never get another. You go out onto your own balcony and see Augustin's door is open. It's a muggy afternoon, after all. It's not easy to climb across, but it's not that hard either, not with this kind of prize waiting. The shower's still running. You sneak inside and take Petitier's bag from the bed and turn to flee, but Petitier hears you and charges out of the shower. He chases you onto the balcony where you wrestle over the bag. It rips open. There's an artefact inside, solid and heavy. You pick it up and smash him over the head. He goes down hard, though he manages to crawl inside in an effort to get to the phone. But you think he's dead, so you flee back to your room, taking your prize with you.'

'A hell of a risk.'

'But plausible, right?'

'More plausible than Augustin doing it,' acknowledged Gaille. 'So one of our fellow guests, then? Maybe one of Augustin's neighbours.'

'It's possible.'

'Or what about those guys in the lift?'

'Maybe they *are* his neighbours.'

She gave an expressive little shudder. 'You think we should tell someone?'

He considered it a moment, imagined trying to explain his theory to that antagonistic Chief Inspector, the scorn he'd come in for. 'Not tonight,' he said. 'It's too late. I'll run it by Charissa tomorrow, see what she thinks.' He was sufficiently unnerved to check again that their door was locked, and the balcony too. Then he stripped down to his boxer shorts, stretched out on the bed, took out his copy of Augustin's talk, and began to read it through.

II

Any hopes Edouard had that Mikhail would give up on Knox for the night were quickly extinguished. They went to the hotel bar, took a corner table, ordered a round of firewater and discussed ways of getting Knox to open his door, despite his now being clearly on alert. 'Let's just blast his door with your shotgun,' grinned Zaal.

Edouard looked appalled at him. 'Keep your voice down,' he begged.

'Why? You really think someone here speaks Georgian?'

'You never know.'

'Why don't we start a fire?' joked Boris. 'That'll get them down.'

'Actually,' said Mikhail thoughtfully. 'That's not such a bad idea.'

'Are you crazy!' hissed Edouard. 'There must be hundreds of people staying here.'

'We don't actually have to start a fire,' said Mikhail, with exaggerated patience. 'We only need to set off the alarm. All the guests will come down and gather outside, including our two friends. We'll just grab them when they appear.'

'It won't be easy,' observed Boris. 'Lots of other people around.'

'So let's go up to their floor first,' suggested Zaal. 'We'll set the alarm off and wait for them to open their door.'

'What if we're seen?' asked Edouard.

'What if we're seen,' mimicked Zaal, earning himself a laugh.

'I only –'

'We're doing it,' said Mikhail, knocking back his drink. 'Unless you've got a better idea, of course.'

Edouard hung his head. 'No.'

'Then shut up.' He got to his feet; the others too. Only Edouard stayed seated. 'You too,' said Mikhail.

'I'm really not cut out for –'

'I said, you too.'

He rose reluctantly, followed them to the lifts. He couldn't think why Mikhail would want him along, other than it gave him pleasure to make people do the things they hated. But that was reason enough. The lattice gate closed on him like a gaol-term. The lift shuddered and began to ascend. The idea that Knox and Bonnard had anything to do with Petitier's death was patently ridiculous; only not to Mikhail. He took it for granted that everyone was as innately vicious and covetous as himself. They reached the sixth floor. The gate opened. With a sinking heart, Edouard made to follow the others out. It was only at the last moment that he noticed the amended conference itinerary taped to the mirror. He didn't have time to think things through, he simply grabbed it and thrust it at Mikhail. 'Look!' he said. 'Knox is giving a talk in the morning.'

'So?'

'So he'll be the third person associated with this damned conference to come to harm. The girl will make four. The police will go crazy.' He jabbed a finger at the CCTV cameras. 'And look at all those, for Christ's sake. We'll be caught in no time. Besides, Knox won't have the fleece here, will he? Remember what that policeman said? He and Pascal took it to the airport in a bag. I'll bet you anything they hid it out there. And he certainly won't go for it until after his talk, not while he's still a suspect.'

'What if it *is* his talk?' asked Mikhail. 'What if he unveils my fleece at this conference? What then?'

'He'd have to be mad,' replied Edouard. 'How else could he have got it, other than by murdering Petitier?'

There was silence for a few moments, as they considered this. 'He's got a point, boss,' said Boris grudgingly.

'And that's not even the main thing,' said Edouard, pressing his advantage. 'The main thing is that we know exactly where he's going to be tomorrow. We can wait for him to finish and then pick him up and do whatever we like with him. And no one will even know that he's gone.'

Mikhail frowned as he thought it through. Then his expression cleared. 'Yes,' he said, as though it had been his idea. 'We'll wait till after his talk. We know exactly where he's going to be, after all.'

'Yes, boss,' nodded Zaal. 'Good thinking.'

They turned together for the lift. A bead of sweat trickled down Edouard's flank. Catastrophe averted, for tonight at least. But what the hell was he going to do tomorrow?

III

Knox was struggling to concentrate on Augustin's talk. Gaille had begun her nightly routines in the bathroom, and she'd left the door teasingly ajar. She turned, as though aware of his attention, and wagged her toothbrush at him. 'How many times do I have to ask you to put the cap back on my toothpaste when you're finished,' she told him. 'It's grown a beard now. You know how I hate toothpaste beards.'

'Yes,' he smiled. 'I know how you hate toothpaste beards.'

She scowled good-naturedly and flicked her toothbrush at him, spraying tiny white specks his way, before turning back to the basin. He watched her fondly. She was wearing her favourite of his old T-shirts, baggy enough on him that it hung like a miniskirt down to her thighs, modest enough most of the time, except for when she leaned forwards to spit out toothpaste, and showed a little more. She was brushing her teeth with her usual rhythmic vigour, swilling water and gargling it around her mouth before spitting out the white froth, then rinsing her toothbrush out and pointedly turning to him to screw the cap back on the toothpaste before replacing them both in the tooth-glass, diligent as a schoolgirl. Then she began to brush her hair, twenty strokes with her right hand, twenty with her left. The same routine every night. These past few months, Knox had grown so used to it, he rarely even noticed any more. But every so often, like tonight, it would strike him fresh again, and he'd feel blessed.

'Come to bed,' he said.

'In a moment.'

They'd been friends and colleagues before they'd become lovers, always an awkward transition – unless lubricated by copious quantities of alcohol, at least. It had been the Akhenaten affair that had convinced Knox to do something. He'd come so close to losing her that he'd realised how much she meant to him. He'd planned to ease himself in, a romantic dinner say, edging the conversation round, a couple of loaded jokes, a flirtatious look or two, gauging her reaction, keeping his lines of retreat open. But it hadn't happened like that. The world's media had clamoured for an interview with them both until Yusuf Abbas, Secretary General of the Supreme Council, had finally buckled. He'd arranged a single press conference in the hospital's lecture hall on the morning of Gaille's discharge. She and Knox had sat side-by-side behind a trestle-table, deflecting questions as best they could, just as Yusuf had instructed them, leaving the journalists little option but to go fishing.

'So, then?' asked a Frenchman with a straggled

red goatee and beaded hair. 'Is there anything – how can I put this? – of a *romantic* nature between the two of you?'

Gaille had looked to Knox to see which of them would answer, then had leaned towards the bank of microphones. 'No,' she'd said. 'We're colleagues, that's all. Business partners.'

The opportunity had been too good for Knox to let pass. 'You see what I have to put up with,' he'd said, lounging back in his chair. 'You rescue a girl from Macedonian separatists, you save her from drowning, and what does that get you these days? Colleagues! Business bloody partners!' He'd spread his arms wide, looked to the packed ranks of journalists for support. 'I mean come on, guys. Back me up here. I mean, don't you think I've earned at least a date?'

'You've never even gone out on a date with him?' asked the Frenchman incredulously.

'He's never asked me,' Gaille had protested, throwing Knox a reproachful glance. 'Not in that way.'

'So,' he'd smiled. 'I'm asking you now.'

'Really?'

'Yes. Really.'

Her throat and cheeks had turned marvellous colours. Her eyes had sparkled. 'Then yes,' she'd told him. 'I'd like that very much.'

She came back into the bedroom now, running

her hands like combs through her hair. 'What?' she asked suspiciously, when she saw him gazing at her.

'Nothing.'

'Sure!'

'It's just that sometimes I forget how beautiful you are. And then you come in looking like that.'

She threw him a knowing look. 'Not tonight,' she said. 'I'm knackered.'

'I didn't mean it that way,' he laughed. 'I only meant that I sometimes forget how beautiful you are.'

'Oh.' Those familiar warm colours rose again on her throat and cheeks. They tugged and twisted his heart every time, like a Chinese burn. 'Then, thanks.' She pulled back her side of the duvet, clambered inelegantly, almost childishly, into bed. He got under the duvet too, stretched his foot across, ran his bare sole down her calf. 'God, you've got cold feet,' she protested.

'I could put my socks back on,' he said. 'I hear you women find that really sexy.'

'Irresistible.'

He felt a reprise of gladness for her presence, but this time it was followed by its own shadow. Happiness was a most precarious thing when you'd lost as many loved ones as he had. What with Petitier's death, and those goons in the lift, Athens felt like a perilous place right now. He didn't mind taking a little risk himself, but it was different with

Gaille. He rose up onto an elbow. 'You're okay with all this, right?' he asked. 'With helping Augustin and Claire, I mean?'

'Of course,' she frowned. 'How could you think otherwise?'

'How far would you be prepared to go?'

Her eyes narrowed, sensing something, though not sure what. 'Why do you ask?'

He put on his best guileless face. 'It's just, we've been putting all our thought into what's going on here in Athens,' he said. 'That's sensible enough, because Athens is where everything has happened so far. But maybe we're missing a trick. We know for sure that Petitier's found an important new site in Crete, thanks to those seals he sent Nico. There's every chance he was *murdered* for what he's found there. It could easily be the key to this investigation. And it isn't here in Athens. It's in Crete.'

Gaille folded her arms. 'No,' she said.

'No, what?'

'No, I'm not going.'

'I didn't say you should.'

'You were about to.'

Knox didn't bother to deny the charge. She knew him too well. 'Someone needs to,' he said. 'Surely you can see that. It can't be Claire. She'd never leave Augustin's bedside, not at a time like this. And it can't be me. I've got this bloody lecture to give, and the police made it damned clear that I'm to stay in Athens. Anyway, all we've got to go on is some Linear A and Linear B seals, and you know far more about both those scripts than I do.'

'But I don't know anything about Crete,' she protested. 'I wouldn't know where to start.'

'The British School has a major operation at Knossos,' said Knox. 'Villa Ariadne, where Sir Arthur Evans lived while he was excavating. One of the archaeologists there is called Iain Parkes. He was at Cambridge with me.'

'Then why not ask *him* to track down Petitier?'

'Come on, Gaille. It's not just a matter of finding out where Petitier's been living for the last twenty years. Someone needs to go there, poke around, see what Petitier's been up to. I can't ask Iain to do all that. It's too much. I haven't seen him in ages. But I'm sure he'd help you get started.'

'If you haven't seen him in ages, how do you know he's even there?'

'Because after we decided to come here, I got in touch with him and asked if he'd be here; but he told me no, that he'd be minding the store.'

'I don't want to go,' she said. 'I want to stay with you.'

'We need to find out what Petitier brought here,' insisted Knox. He reached for his mobile. 'Look. I'll call Iain. You check out what tickets are available.'

'*Now?*' she asked.

'It's Easter weekend, Gaille. If we leave it till

morning, who knows when you'll be able to get a flight?'

She stared into his eyes, trying to read the truth; but he held his nerve and didn't look away and finally it was she who broke. 'You really think this could help Augustin?' she asked.

'Yes. I really do.'

'Fine,' she sighed.

'Good,' he said. He leaned across to kiss her on the lips. 'I love you,' he said.

'I love you too,' she replied. But, for the first time since they'd initially made their declarations, he wasn't quite sure that her heart was in it.

FOURTEEN

I

A loud clang outside Knox's balcony door. He woke abruptly and sat up, uncertain for a moment where he was. Another clang, but now he recognised what it was, and that it was benign: dustmen collecting trash in the alley below. His heart resettled, he lay back down, listened drowsily to their good-natured banter for a moment or two before the tumult of yesterday's memories began to assail him, and then the dustcart began backing up, its reversing siren wailing. He rolled onto his side, illuminated the dial of his travel alarm clock, gave a groan.

'What time is it?' murmured Gaille.

'Four twenty. We've still got a few minutes.' He'd been right about the Easter rush for air-tickets: Gaille's choice had been flying out first thing this morning or waiting until Saturday afternoon. She hadn't been happy about it, but she'd booked the early flight all the same.

It was a little after five when they set off. The streets were empty; they made excellent time. At first, Gaille tried gamely to make conversation, but it was so obvious she was struggling that Knox turned the radio on, not wanting her to feel obliged. She rested her head against the window and dozed off, until he hit a pothole and startled her awake, her arms flailing to brace herself, her eyes gluey with tiredness. He slowed down after that, did his best to keep the ride even. He parked in short-term, woke her gently.

'There's no need to come in with me,' she said, a little stiffly, when he shouldered her overnight bag and headed towards the terminal. 'You mustn't be late for your talk.'

'Don't be angry with me,' he pleaded.

'I'm not angry with you.'

'Yes, you are.'

She bit her teeth together, as if struggling not to say something she might regret, but failing. 'This is a stupid bloody trip,' she said. 'I don't know why you're sending me on it.'

'I thought you agreed. We need to help Augustin.'

'But this isn't about Augustin, is it? Not really. It's about you getting spooked by that prick in the lift last night, and thinking up this wretched plan to get me out of harm's way.'

Knox stood there, feeling foolish. 'I don't know what I'd do if anything happened to you,' he said weakly.

'And I don't know what I'd do if anything happened to you. But that doesn't mean I'd lie to you or try to trick you or coerce you into doing things you wouldn't otherwise choose to do. It doesn't mean I think so little of your ability to help that I'd send you away when I needed you most.' She sighed and shook her head. 'Never mind. Let's discuss it when I get back. I'll do my best, I promise. And who knows? Maybe I will find something.' She nodded emphatically, as if to convince herself. 'Maybe I will.'

He gripped the steering wheel tight as he headed back into town. He felt by turns aggrieved, dispirited, foolish and lonely. The dawn sun broke behind him and threw out shadows. Traffic began picking up, not yet enough to slow him down, but enough to make it clear that he didn't have time to visit Augustin if he wanted to make Eleusis by eight; a decision he was in truth relieved to make, for he lacked the heart to face Claire.

He headed west along the old Sacred Way. It should have been infused with history, for this was the road on which, for many hundreds of years, celebrants had made their way from Athens to Eleusis. It didn't seem sacred anymore, however, just a series of shabby strips of shops and apartment blocks, interspersed with the occasional light industrial estate. He used the time to murmur his way through his talk, further familiarising himself with its themes and rhythms. Brake lights flared on the green van in front and it squealed to a stop, forcing Knox to slam on his own brakes. He leaned out his window to look, saw gridlock ahead. A minute passed without movement. Two. Drivers began to vent their frustration on their horns, late for work or leaden-eyed after a night shift. Knox took the opportunity to make some calls. He left a message for Charissa, though his speculations of the night before seemed feeble this morning. He called Iain Parkes again, for he'd only managed to get voicemail the night before. His mobile was still switched off, so he left another message with Gaille's flight number and expected time of arrival.

Away to his right, he could see the famous Rarian Plain, where the young maiden goddess Persephone had one day gone to pick crocuses. Hades, lord of the underworld, had seen her and been smitten; he'd abducted her and taken her back beneath the earth with him. Demeter, Persephone's mother and the goddess of grain, had been understandably distraught. She'd searched the

earth without success, before losing heart for a
while here in Eleusis. But then she'd sent a blight
to kill crops across the earth, causing a famine
so severe that the other gods had prevailed upon
Hades to let Persephone go. Just before she'd
left, Hades had tricked her into eating several
pomegranate seeds, thus forcing her to return to
the underworld for several months each year,
during which time the earth became barren again.
A metaphor for the seasons, of course, though
the myth was far more complex and subtle than
just that.

Traffic began to move slowly again. Three lanes
merged into two, two into one. A blue flutter of
police lights ahead, a shriek of injured car alarm, and
then the culprit, a four-vehicle shunt of crumpled
bonnets and deflated airbags, a man yelling furiously
at the sky while a woman gave her statement to the
police. And then he was through, the road at once
opening up, allowing him to put his foot down and
regain a little lost time.

To his left, the sea came incrementally into view,
the dark blue horizon and then a fishing trawler
and finally the port itself, tankers and container
ships being loaded and unloaded at the end of
their long umbilical cords of jetties; yet somehow
attractive for all that, what with the clear skies
and sunshine glinting on the rippling water.

He breathed in deep through both nostrils,

feeling surprisingly privileged to be here to give a talk.

Modern-day Elefsina. Ancient Eleusis.

II

Nina Zdanevich left her twin girls and returned to Kiko's room to find him already up and dressed, standing awkwardly by the end of the bed, as though he'd heard her coming and had wanted to look as if nothing was up – achieving, of course, exactly the opposite effect. She knew her son well enough not to approach him head on, however. 'Good morning, sweetheart,' she said.

'Good morning, Mama.'

'Did you sleep well?' she asked.

'Yes, thank you,' he said. But he wouldn't meet her eye.

She felt a lurch of dismay, she had to fight to keep her smile. She crouched and took his face between her hands, steered him gently until he met her eyes. 'Did something happen, Kiko?'

'No.'

She considered for a moment pressing him, but thought better of it. He was too imaginative and obstinate. Push him now, the lies would gloop out like cement from a mixer, and they'd soon set into stone, and she'd never get the truth. She nodded as if she believed him and smiled broadly. 'Great. Would you like to get some breakfast, then?'

'Yes, please,' he said quietly. He took her hand as they went to the door. He kept his eyes on the carpet, his voice nonchalant. 'Will you be sleeping with the girls again tonight?' he asked.

Tears pricked her eyes. She felt a moment of the most intense hatred: for herself, for her husband, for these loathsome Nergadzes, for the whole damned world. 'No,' she assured him. 'I'll be staying with you tonight.'

'You promise?'

'Yes, sweetheart. I promise.'

III

Knox drove into the town, turned left off the main road, following signs to the ancient site. Even the car park looked the part, a courtyard of haphazard cobblestones, with foundation blocks, plinths and pediments on either side, along with traces of ancient temples, stoas, altars and fountains. He couldn't see Nico at first, but then he emerged through the half-open site gates, talking earnestly with an extravagantly tall black man who carried himself with a slight stoop, as though he wanted to deemphasise his height. He couldn't have been far into his forties, yet he exuded an exaggeratedly academic air, with his shabby suit and the gold-rimmed half-moon glasses that dangled on a string around his neck.

'Sorry, I'm late,' said Knox. 'There was a pile up.'

'So we've heard,' said Nico gloomily. 'Did it look like it would be cleared soon?'

'That depends on your traffic police.'

'Then we're doomed,' said Nico, trying unsuccessfully to make light of it. He gestured towards his companion. 'Have you met Doctor Claude Franklin? A colleague from the university.'

'I don't believe so,' said Knox.

'Nor I,' said Franklin. He had elegant long thin fingers to match his frame, so that Knox was mildly surprised by the firmness of his grip.

'I mentioned him last night, I think,' said Nico. 'He knew Petitier when he worked here for the French school.'

'Ah,' said Knox, his interest growing. 'You were friends?'

'I'm not sure I'd go that far,' said Franklin carefully. He spoke slowly, articulating clearly, as though accustomed to people struggling with his residual American accent. 'We shared a house for a while, that's all.'

'You'll excuse me,' said Nico. 'I have to see this damned crash for myself. In case I need to make arrangements.'

'It'll be fine,' said Knox. 'There's plenty of time.'

But Nico only shook his head. 'A conference on Eleusis in Eleusis over Easter week. I thought it was such a good idea. I thought I was *inspired*!' He laughed savagely and kicked a stone skittering across the cobbles. 'What was I thinking?'

Knox shrugged sympathetically, then turned back to Franklin. 'So?' he asked. 'Was it just you and Petitier sharing?'

'Hardly,' smiled Franklin. 'It was a typical university house: big and old and falling apart.' He kept up his over-enunciation, turning to Knox whenever he spoke, making sure he could see his mouth at all times. 'Four bedrooms. Two of us in each, sometimes three, depending on who was sleeping with who. Everyone welcome, Greek or foreign, as long as you could pay your way and enjoyed intelligent late-night conversations. Good times. I wrote my thesis there. On the Doric Invasion, no less.'

'The Doric Invasion?' asked Knox politely, as they entered the site itself, crossing a cobbled courtyard to an ancient path of weathered grey slabs that led to the sacred hill. In the quiet morning, it was hard to imagine the furious euphoric bustle of the ancient festivals themselves, when all Athens would have been here, exuberant and exalted. He was not a religious man, Knox, but he had a strong affection for anything that celebrated the wonder and strangeness of the world.

'I know,' laughed Franklin. 'But it was in vogue at the time. Besides . . .' He gave a little wave to indicate the colour of his skin. 'I was a young black man striving to make my way in academia. In *Greek* academia. I needed to prove myself reliable. And what could be more reliable than arguing for the European origins of European culture?' He steered Knox between two of Eleusis's legendary symbols, the well beside which Demeter had mourned the loss of her daughter Persephone; and the Plutoneion, a grotto that had once led to the underworld. 'I take it that you know the broad thesis of the Doric Invasion?' he enquired.

'Aryan tribes sweeping down from northwest Greece or maybe the Balkans,' said Knox. 'Overthrowing the Mycenaeans and bringing classical Greek culture with them.'

Franklin nodded. 'A convincing scheme of history, with just one flaw.'

'No evidence,' suggested Knox.

'No evidence,' agreed Franklin. 'Of course, I knew it was thin even at the time. But I didn't think that mattered. All the minds I most admired were convinced of it, so it had to be true. After all, what reason could they possibly have had to lie? Or – more charitably – to fool themselves?'

'And then Petitier came along?' suggested Knox.

'Yes,' smiled Franklin. 'Then Petitier came along.'

IV

Edouard had woken at dawn, but he hadn't yet risen, lying enervated in bed instead as his room grew light around him. He'd suffered plenty of anxiety as a father, but nothing like this. His wife and children hostages, and no way of assuring himself that they were safe. Plumbing burbled; doors banged. He kept telling himself to get up, but still he lay there. Footsteps finally outside his door and then a perfunctory knock and Boris came in, looked with disdain down at him. 'Sandro Nergadze for you,' he said, holding out his mobile.

'For me?'

'Yes,' said Boris. 'For you.'

'Mr Nergadze,' said Edouard, sitting up anxiously. 'What is it? Has something happened to my children?'

'No.'

'You swear?'

'Of course. Your family are fine. They've just gone out riding with my father, as it happens.'

'What, then?'

A moment's hesitation. 'This fleece,' he said. 'I want you to tell me what it looks like.'

'I'm not with you,' frowned Edouard. 'We'll know what it looks like once we've seen it this morning.'

'That isn't good enough any more. I've promised my father a golden fleece by the end of this weekend, and I'm going to give him one, whatever happens at your end.'

'I don't understand.'

'Then listen. I've just ordered several kilos of gold. I've also arranged for an . . . *artisan* to come. Don't worry; we can trust him. He's done a lot of work for my family. He assures me he can make me a convincing fleece, as long as I can give him the right specifications to work from. Would it have been made exclusively of gold, for example, or would it include other materials? If so, which, and in what proportion? How heavy would it have been? What shape? What texture? What techniques did they know back then? Might they have used moulds, for example, or gold thread? How would it have handled? Could someone have worn it? What, in short, would it have looked like?'

'Oh,' said Edouard. 'No one knows. There are representations of it on ancient vases and artwork, but they're all works of imagination, and they look much as you'd expect: that is to say, they look like sheepskins, only coated with gold. And maybe that's what it actually was. Did you know that Georgians used to stretch fleeces out in wooden frames then set them in the river so that all the gold dust washing by would catch in the wool. Then they'd hang them up from branches to dry. They'd have looked exactly like the fleece was supposed to.'

'You think that's what Petitier has found? A sheepskin covered in gold dust?'

'No,' said Edouard. 'It's perfectly possible that that's where the legend originally came from, but it can't be what he's found. Sheepskin is organic. A real fleece would have disintegrated thousands of years ago. Unless it was left in an *extremely* benign environment, I suppose. Much more benign than anything Greece can offer. Perhaps in Egypt or some other desert land it might have –'

'I don't need a lecture,' said Sandro tightly.

'I'm just saying that a real sheepskin coated with gold would be a heap of dust by now. Valuable dust, yes, but dust nonetheless.'

'So if it *has* survived, what might it look like?'

Edouard hesitated. It was bad enough being asked to authenticate a fleece; it was another thing altogether to advise on forging one. 'It doesn't matter,' he improvised. 'You'll never get away with it. They can do all kinds of sophisticated tests these days. They can analyse a metal's chemical signature, for example, and pinpoint exactly where and when it was mined.' His heart was in his mouth as he said this, because while it was true that lead, silver and copper were traceable this way, gold wasn't; not yet, at least. But it had to be worth the risk.

'What if we refuse to let them test it?'

'And why would you do that, unless you knew it was a fake?'

The silence at the other end proved his argument had struck home. His relief didn't last long, however. 'I know,' said Sandro. 'We'll use your Turkmenistan cache. That's ancient Colchian gold, isn't it?'

'You can't!' protested Edouard, horrified. 'That cache is priceless.'

'Not as priceless as it's going to be,' observed Sandro dryly. 'And we'll use the gold I just ordered to make replicas of all the Turkmenistan pieces too, so that no one will ever know what we've done.'

'I won't do it. I won't help you.'

'You will do it,' insisted Sandro. 'Or have you forgotten that your wife and your children are my guests?'

The fight went instantly out of Edouard. He felt himself sag. 'I'll need some time to think about it,' he said weakly. 'And I'll want to speak to my wife too.'

'Are you *bargaining* with me?'

'I'm a father,' said Edouard wretchedly. 'I can't think about anything else until I know my wife and children are safe.'

'I already gave you my word that they're safe.'

'You abducted them from my home,' snapped Edouard. 'How can I possibly take your word for anything?' He knew he'd gone too far, but it was true, it was driving him crazy. 'Please,' he begged.

'I can't think straight. How can I help you if I can't think straight?'

Silence stretched taut on the other end of the line, like the wire of a garrotte. 'Very well,' said Sandro finally. 'You can speak to your wife when I call back. In the meantime, please work out how best to forge me a golden fleece.'

FIFTEEN

I

The ancient path took Knox and Franklin in a slow spiral up and around the natural pyramid of the sacred hill, the toppled ruins on either side covered in tall grasses ablaze with wild flowers, dandelions, buttercups and brilliant red poppies; while on the summit above them a dilapidated clock tower told the wrong time, and a Greek flag fluttered limply. 'Petitier wasn't like the rest of us,' said Franklin. 'For one thing, he was much older, and his academic career was far more advanced. He'd been teaching in Paris, as I recall, though his time there ended badly. A friend of his wangled him a job here with the French School. They had their own accommodation, of course, but he fell out with someone there and so moved in with us. That was fine, as far as we were concerned.

Another wallet to share the bills, fresh blood for our late-night debates. You know what student life is like.'

'Yes.'

'Though I don't know how he managed, if I'm honest. It was fine for the rest of us; we were all writing theses and things, so we could get away with the drunken all-nighters. But he had a day job. Not that it was particularly taxing, from what I could gather. Administrative stuff, mostly. Answering letters, that kind of thing. A waste of his mind, in truth, for he was brilliant in his own way. Take my Doric Invasion, for example. I'd soaked up the conventional wisdom without questioning a word. I'd taken it for granted that it *must* make sense, because so many people said it did, and they all had strings of letters after their names. But Petitier didn't think that way. He took it almost for granted that any established account had to be wrong. He kept asking me questions that he knew full-well had no adequate answers, and each time I stumbled over the gaps, he'd make fun of me, and my confidence would drain a little more, and I'd go to bed *brooding*. And one night as I lay there, I had what I can only describe as an epiphany, a sudden illumination of something utterly obvious yet previously unthinkable. There had been no Doric Invasion, no Aryan tribes sweeping down from the north. The whole thing was a fabrication, a work of political propaganda created not from the evidence, but in spite of it.'

'Isn't that a little strong?'

'Look at me, Mr Knox. Do I look European to you?'

'As it happens, yes.'

Franklin laughed. 'Well, I don't feel it. I never have. America was different. I felt at home there, ordinary. My father was black; my mother was Greek. So what? Mixed race families were nothing in Washington DC. But then my mother's mother fell sick and we came here to look after her. It was supposed to be for just a few weeks, but she proved a fighter. Six months passed. A year. My father hated it. Blacks were a real rarity here back then. He was a highly intelligent man, but he couldn't find work, certainly not as a teacher. And my mother refused to leave, not with her mother dying, so finally my father packed his bags and fled back to DC. I *hated* him for that. I used to *burn* with anger, though I was skilled at suppressing it. But now I realise it can't have been easy for him.' He waved a hand, to indicate the stresses that all families faced. 'It was hard enough even for me, with a Greek mother and speaking the language reasonably fluently, because my mother had always spoken it with me at home. My fellow pupils mocked me for being different, as children will. I was never an athlete or a fighter, so I had to get my own back in the only way I could: exams.' They passed several massive blocks of marble column lying by the side of the path, and the battered bust of a Roman emperor; probably Hadrian, to judge from his beard. 'I was the most conventional of students until Petitier arrived. I studied diligently and behaved myself. I tried so hard to fit in. But despite that – or perhaps because of it – I had a terrible anger burning inside me; resentment at being thought inferior just because of the colour of my skin. I think Petitier must have sensed it. He teased me with radical ideas. He suggested that Hannibal might have been black, for example. Cleopatra, too. Even *Socrates*. Think of it: that great icon of philosophy and wisdom, a black man.'

'I hadn't heard that,' said Knox politely.

'For a very good reason,' smiled Franklin. 'It's not true. Or, more accurately, there's precious little evidence to support it. But it spoke to a greater truth, one for which there's all the evidence you could want.' He paused to admire a pair of love-birds swooping and frolicking in the spring sunshine. 'We Westerners think ourselves special, don't we, Mister Knox? We have this image of ourselves as born and nurtured in the cradle of Classical Greece, heirs to its great traditions: democracy, science, philosophy, medicine, mathematics, technology, architecture, universities. Everything that's best in western culture, we credit to the miraculous flowering of genius right here two and a half millennia ago. But Petitier made me look again at this image. He made me see that all these undeniably great things, all these wonderful discoveries and inventions . . . You see, they weren't actually Greek at all. No. They were *African*.'

II

Gaille was still feeling despondent from her spat with Knox when her flight took off for Heraklion. But it was a cloudless day and she had a window seat, and she found herself growing enraptured by the brilliant green of the Aegean islands set far beneath in the astonishing blue of the Mediterranean. But then almost at once they began their descent into Crete and her spirits came back down too. She had no idea what to do on landing, particularly if Knox's friend Iain Parkes wasn't waiting. But fortunately he *was* waiting. Or, at least, a tall, cheerful and good-looking thirty-something man with short straw-coloured hair was standing outside the arrivals gate holding up a large cardboard sign with her name scrawled in red marker pen upon it. 'Doctor Parkes, I presume,' she smiled, walking up to him.

He grinned as he put away his sign. 'Always

wanted to do that, for some reason. Though I'd pictured myself in the full chauffeur's rig, you know, with the uniform and the peaked cap.'

'So much more glamorous than archaeology,' agreed Gaille.

'And better paid, too,' he laughed. He had a charming, unaffected laugh that put her instantly at ease; and she was comforted, too, that he looked more like a field archaeologist than an academic, with his deep tan, khaki photographer's trousers and short-sleeved blue shirt.

'Daniel got hold of you, then?' she asked.

'Not exactly. But he left about fifty messages on my mobile. I never keep the damned thing on, if I can avoid it. People *do* insist on calling me.'

'A terrible thing to have friends, isn't it?'

He took her bag and slung it easily over his shoulder. 'The car's this way,' he said, striding towards the exit with such natural authority that the crowds seemed to part ahead of him without him even noticing.

'It's really good of you to collect me like this,' said Gaille, breaking into a little jig as she struggled to keep up. 'I'm sure you're very busy.'

'Not a bit of it.' He must have realised he was walking too fast, for he slowed down for a few paces, though it didn't last. 'Nothing much going on at Knossos. Everything always shuts down over Easter week.'

'Really? I'd have thought it would do huge business.'

'The tourist site does, yes,' he agreed. 'I mean our excavation work. All our local staff always bunk off home anyway, so we made a virtue of necessity this year, gave everyone the week off. I'm really just keeping an eye on things; but at least it means I can give you a hand with whatever you and Knox are up to, if you'd like?'

'That would be fantastic.'

'Grand,' he grinned. 'I've been following your adventures with enormous envy. About time I joined the fun.' They passed through automatic doors out onto a sunlit concourse hazy with fumes, already hotter than Athens had been, though it was still early. It was easy to forget that Crete was almost as close to Africa as to Athens.

'Wow!' murmured Gaille, as they reached a gorgeous scarlet Mustang. 'Archaeology can't pay *that* badly here.'

'A Christmas present, sadly. My father-in-law's one of those Wall Street big swinging dicks. At least, I'm not so sure about the big or swinging, but the rest's about right.'

The passenger seat had been baking in the sunlight, leaving it uncomfortably hot on the backs of Gaille's legs through the thin cotton of her trousers, so that she had to keep shifting. 'He can't be that bad if you keep finding these beneath your Christmas tree.'

'My wife finds them, not me.' He didn't bother with seat-belts or looking around, just turned on the ignition and put it into gear. 'I always got fountain pens. His way of letting his little darling know how far beneath her she married.'

'Nothing to do with trying to make her happy.'

'You haven't met the man,' he said, moving off so abruptly that a blue van driver had to brake sharply, offering his middle finger in apology when the driver tooted angrily. 'And before you take his side too much, let me warn you that he won that particular battle. His little darling is back in the States on an extended break, and she's taken my son with her, and I'm more than a little sore about it.'

'Oh,' said Gaille. 'I'm so sorry.'

'But at least I've got the car, eh. Big swinging dick keeps asking me to sell it and send the proceeds. But fuck him, right? If his little darling wants the cash so badly, she can come back here and sell it herself. She owes me that much.'

'What went wrong?'

He let out a long breath, letting his anger go with it. 'Being an archaeologist's wife wasn't quite what she expected, I guess. Though god knows I didn't make any great promises. And Crete can be a tough place to live, especially if you don't like the heat. She kept getting rashes, she found it hard to sleep. And then she got pregnant. She couldn't find a doctor here she entirely trusted, which I suppose is fair enough, so she went back home for the delivery. And of course they made everything so damned comfortable for her there, it was easier to stay. But mostly it was the life. The lack of glamour and excitement. I reckon she thought I'd be digging up at least one new treasure a week, just like you and your man Knox.'

'You exaggerate.'

'That should have been me, you know,' he smiled. 'I was always the star student at Cambridge, not Daniel. And now look at the two of you. First Alexander, then Akhenaten.' He shook his head in mock reproof. 'Seriously, couldn't you at least move onto the Bs, give the rest of us a chance?'

Road-works had closed the carriageway opposite, forcing both directions of traffic over the same narrow stretch of tarmac. Without lights or policemen to manage it, it was bedlam, everyone driving aggressively in an effort to force oncoming cars to back off. Gaille feared they'd never get through, but then Iain spurred his Mustang through the merest blink of a gap, and they were out the other side. 'Christ!' she muttered. 'Rather you than me.'

'You get used to it.'

The traffic eased. A sign proclaimed Knossos ahead. They crested a hill to see car parks to their left, and beyond them a glimpse of the archaeological site, the palace of King Minos and reputed home of the labyrinth of legend. It was there that the half-man, half-bull Minotaur was said to have slaughtered the young men and women sent in tribute from the Greek mainland, until it had finally been bested by Theseus, thanks to the assistance of Ariadne, King Minos's own daughter. But Iain turned right down a private drive instead, past a charming small cluster of buildings set around a garden of hollyhocks and date palms, to a beautiful house set in lush gardens of acacias, hibiscus, lilies and hyacinth, along with a headless Roman statue or two. 'Villa Ariadne,' he said, somewhat redundantly. He nodded further on down the track. 'The Strat-Mus is down that way,' he said.

'The what?'

'Sorry. The Stratigraphic Museum, where we keep our finds.' A dog began barking furiously. 'Security,' said Iain, as a second dog joined in. 'Don't worry,' he added, pulling a three-point turn. 'They're chained up. I won't have the bastards running free, not when I'm here. Bloody things scare the life out of me.'

'We're not going in?' she asked.

'No. We actually do most of our work down at what we call the Taverna, those buildings we passed at the head of the drive. Much more relaxed than the Villa. Another reason the little darling headed back to the States, I suspect. She pictured herself in the grand house, you know, liveried servants bringing us mint juleps and mimosas on that lawn, that kind of thing.'

'It is beautiful,' said Gaille neutrally.

'I'll show you round later, if you like. But first let's brew up some coffee. You can tell me your plans.'

'I really don't have any plans,' confessed Gaille. 'Other than to get here, at least, then try to track down this man Petitier. But I haven't the first idea how.'

'Then why don't you put your feet up for a few minutes,' suggested Iain. 'I've got some phone-calls I can make.'

III

Knox and Franklin had reached the Telesterion, the large rectangular courtyard where the Mysteries had anciently been celebrated. The high walls that had once ensured the secrecy of its rites had long since tumbled down, leaving only their outlines, yet it was an atmospheric setting all the same. 'African?' smiled Knox. 'Isn't that rather a bold claim?'

'It is,' admitted Franklin. 'It's a very bold claim. But that doesn't necessarily make it false. It's not as cut and dried as that, of course. Nothing ever is. But I still stand by the core of it, which is that the western world has a dark secret: the golden age of Athens didn't spring fully-formed out of nothing thanks to some extraordinary flowering of Greek genius. It was simply one part of the overall evolution of thought; and much or even most of the breakthroughs that we attribute to the Greeks were actually learned in Egypt and merely *publicised* by the Greeks. And the remarkable thing is that the ancient Greeks themselves admitted as much. Not only did they explicitly credit the Egyptians with being the pioneers of religion, philosophy and thought, they also travelled in huge numbers to Egypt for their education. Thales, the father of philosophy, spent years there, as did Pythagoras, the father of mathematics, Solon, the father of law and democracy, and Herodotus, the father of history. Archimedes and Anaximander both travelled there, as did Democritus, Hipparchus, Plato and –'

'You don't need to convince me that the Greeks were influenced by the Egyptians,' said Knox, aware that the list could go on for a while yet.

'Forgive me,' said Franklin. 'I forgot that you're an Egyptologist.' He paused a moment to admire the view, down over the perimeter wall and terracotta roofs to a recreational marina, where masts swayed and clacked in the light breeze. 'But your awareness makes you the exception rather than the rule. Though that wouldn't have been the case four hundred years ago, say. Back then, educated Westerners broadly accepted the Greek's own account of Egyptian primacy.' He paused and turned to Knox. 'Europeans try their best to forget, but it wasn't just America that grew rich on slave-labour. It must have been a strange thing, don't you think, for Europe's enlightened aristocracy to own slaves? They liked to think of themselves as good, as we all do; but it must have been hard while they were shipping their fellow men in their thousands to their plantations, then whipping them to death, just for having the wrong coloured skin. The notion that Africans could be their equals or even their superiors would have been intolerable, so they did the obvious thing. They rewrote history to shut Africa out. And that's all my beloved Doric invasion ever was – another of the many theories invented by white people to rewrite the story of classical Greece as a white man's triumph.'

Knox looked curiously at him, sensing the anger burning away beneath the surface. 'Just because a theory doesn't work out,' he pointed out, 'it doesn't mean it was malicious.'

'I'm just telling you what I thought at the time,' said Franklin, somewhat unconvincingly. 'I was a young man who'd dedicated his short academic life to a theory, only to discover that it was wrong. It's not surprising that I felt a little bitter.

And there's also something indescribably heady about realising the Emperor is naked, you know. You want to point it out to everyone who'll listen, not always in the most sympathetic fashion.' He broke off as he led the way up a narrow flight of wooden steps to the forecourt of the Eleusis museum, on which the conference pavilion had been erected. 'So I took it upon myself not merely to attack these theories, but also to explain why they'd been devised in the first place, and why some of my colleagues clung to them with such tenacity, in the teeth of all the evidence.'

Knox raised his eyebrows. 'You accused them of racism?'

'Racism, colonialism, imperialism, bad scholarship.' He gave a somewhat rueful laugh. 'That was the one that really rankled, of course. Bad scholarship.'

'So how did it all pan out?' asked Knox, opening the pavilion door for him, ushering him ahead into the cool darkness within.

Franklin turned to him with a charming smile. 'Unexpectedly,' he replied.

SIXTEEN

I

Gaille poured herself a fresh cup of coffee in the Taverna kitchen, then took a little wander. The walls were covered incongruously with framed photographs of marmalade and tabby cats. A bookshelf in the dining room was filled with easy-reading material, old magazines and PG Wodehouse novels and thrillers with swollen yellow pages and bodice-rippers with their lurid covers half falling off. She picked out an old *Marie Claire* and took it outside, along with her coffee and a pack of biscuits, then up onto the roof terrace, where she moved a chair into the dappled shade of a tall conifer. Snatches of Iain's phone calls reached her on the breeze, his tone by turns cajoling, humorous and stern, but tiredness quickly caught up with her, and she fell into a light doze, only to be startled awake when

Iain appeared suddenly on the roof. '*There* you are!' he said, as though he'd spent hours searching for her.

'I'm sorry,' she said. The sun had risen above the trees, forcing her to shade her eyes with her hand as she squinted up at him. 'Not much sleep last night.'

'I'm only teasing,' he smiled. 'I saw you coming up here. I would have let you sleep, but I've made a bit of progress, and I thought you'd want to know.'

'Fantastic!'

'I'll start with the bad news. No trace of your man Petitier with the local government agencies. Mind you, it would have been a miracle if there had been, the way they are.' He grabbed a biscuit and began munching it, spraying crumbs as he talked. 'But you said he was an archaeologist, so I had an inspiration. I ran his name through our own database here, and guess what? Turns out he was one of our regulars.'

'How do you mean?'

'I mean he used to come here sometimes to do research. I even met him once or twice myself, as it turns out, though I only knew him as Roly. The thing is, we went through a security phase a few years back when we issued all our guest researchers with a picture ID; so I've got a photo of him, if that's a help?'

'That's brilliant!'

'Thought you'd be pleased,' he grinned. 'I'm running off a copy now.' He gestured vaguely towards his office, inviting her to go with him. Her legs were strangely uncoordinated on the steps, as if chiding her for waking them too soon; but it felt gloriously cool inside after the direct sunlight, with the ceiling fan on its lowest setting, breathing down upon her like a kindly angel. The printer was in the corner, the page still chunking out. 'Damned thing takes forever,' he said, going over to it. 'Never any budget for new technology: not when we can spend it on old books instead.'

It was just the kind of office Gaille loved, high shelves against every wall, packed tight with academic texts on Minoan Crete and the Mycenaeans, others on Ancient Egypt and Classical Greece, the Hittites and the Babylonians, more stacked on the desk. A letter marked a page in a bound compendium of *Journals of Egyptian Archaeology*. Curiosity got to her: she turned to it. Addressed to Iain from a small but respected London publisher, confirming the schedule for his forthcoming book. 'Hey!' she said. 'Congratulations!'

He glanced over from the printer, flushed a little when he saw her looking at the letter. 'That's private,' he said, coming over to take it from her, then folding it up and putting it away in his top drawer.

'I'm sorry,' said Gaille, rather taken aback. 'I didn't realise.'

He sighed and found a smile. 'Forgive me,' he said. 'I didn't mean to be curt. It's just, I've just been getting a bit of grief from the guys.'

'What on earth for? You're getting your book published. You should be really proud.'

'Didn't you see the title?'

'No. Why?'

He pulled a self-deprecating face. 'My book's about how we need to revise our understanding of the Eastern Med during the bronze age, using all the information we're gleaning from our excavations here in Crete, as well as in Santorini and the other islands. I originally submitted it as *The Pelasgian and Minoan Aegean: A New Paradigm*.'

'Catchy,' said Gaille.

'Exactly. Not a sniff of interest. I kept rewriting it and rewriting it, thinking the problem must be with ideas or my prose. But then one night I had a brainwave. I changed the title to *The Atlantis Connection* and got an offer within a week.' They laughed together at the ways of the world, and the moment of tension was forgotten.

The printer finished chunking out; they went over to it together. It gave Gaille a bit of a jolt to see Petitier: he'd been an abstract concept until now. His photograph did little to warm her to him, his indignation at being forced to pose for the camera evident, impatience and superiority written in the sour line of his upper lip, visible even through his tangled, tawny-grey beard. 'You don't have an address for him, I suppose?'

'We do require one for our records, as it happens,' Iain told her, 'but he only put down some hotel in Heraklion. I called them, just in case, but the woman didn't know of him, or of anyone answering his description. Maybe she was covering, but I don't think so. I've never seen him in Heraklion myself, and I certainly would have done had he been living there for the past ten years. But don't worry. I haven't told you the best bit yet.'

'The best bit?'

His eyes twinkled. 'It was just, I was struck by a thought. I mean, if he's been doing research here, then maybe he's been to other sites too, right? So I started calling around, and guess what?'

'You've had a result?'

He nodded vigorously. 'There's this Belgian dig a little east of here. One of the girls there knows Petitier quite well. The thing is, her brother came over to visit a couple of years back, and she took him on a tour of the island. And who should she see on her travels but Roland Petitier, selling several kilos of walnuts to a local shop and promising to bring more on his next visit.'

'Home turf!' exulted Gaille. 'Where was this?'

'A town called Anapoli. It's in the hills above Hora Sfakion on the south coast.'

'And how can I get there?'

His grin grew broad. 'By getting back into my car and enjoying the drive,' he told her.

II

The pavilion was deliberately windowless, to enable lighting to be controlled during the talks. Only the back third was currently lit, two matronly women setting out coffee cups and jugs of water on trestle tables. Knox felt a twinge of alarm. He'd expected the AV guys to be on hand to show him how everything worked. They must have been caught up in the traffic. He poured himself and Franklin glasses of water. They took them over to the back row of folding wooden chairs, where they sat either side of the aisle. 'You were telling me how your crusade finished,' he prompted.

'Yes,' agreed Franklin. 'It was absurd, in its own way. One of my professors – my mentor, I suppose you'd call him – had finally had enough of me. He invited me to his home, an invariable sign of trouble. I was glad, though. I was fired up, eager to hurl my young career in his teeth. He was a stickler for punctuality, so I presented myself at his front door at seven p.m. sharp. But it wasn't he who answered. It was his daughter, Maria.'

'Ah!' smiled Knox.

'Quite,' agreed Franklin. 'A man gets to know himself in such moments. One look at Maria was all it took for me to reassess my priorities in life. In a way, I'm ashamed of that. In another, I couldn't be prouder.'

'Was it reciprocated?'

'She became my wife, if that's what you mean, though it took me several years to persuade her. And her first impressions of me were not good. She teases me with it still, the way I gawped. Her father had been delayed at the university, she told me. Some idiot had let off a fire alarm.' He shook his head at the perverse tricks of fate. 'Maria sat with me as I waited. By the time her father finally made it home, I was head over heels in love, I couldn't apologise fast enough. I pledged never to embarrass him or his university again. He asked me to cut myself off immediately and completely from Petitier, who he held more to blame than me. I agreed. He was kind enough to give me another chance.'

'How did Petitier take that?'

'I don't know. I never saw him again. I moved out of the house while he was at work, and he left Athens shortly afterwards.' He gave a short laugh. 'That was a story in itself. The British School put on a series of lectures to honour the memory of Sir Arthur Evans and his excavations at Knossos. Petitier apparently stood up during a Q&A and launched into a drunken rant. It was the last straw. The French School fired him for embarrassing them, and he left soon afterwards.'

'What was his rant about?'

'He accused Evans and his successors of doing with Minoan Crete exactly what other academics had done with the Doric Invasion; that is to say, rewriting history to boost the Greeks at the expense of Egypt and the Near East.' He glanced at Knox to see if further explanation was necessary, and evidently decided that it was. 'Crete only gained independence from the Ottoman Empire in 1898, you see. But independence wasn't what the new Cretan government wanted; they wanted unification with Greece instead. They were desperate, therefore, to play up any and all historical links with Greece, while downplaying those with Egypt and Turkey. And this was almost the exact moment Evans began excavating at Knossos. Not that he needed any encouragement to make Crete more Greek. His head was stuffed so full of Greek myths and legends that within a week of breaking ground he'd found Ariadne's bathroom. Not *a* bathroom or even a *royal* bathroom. No. *Ariadne's*. After that, it was Minos' throne room, and so on. It wasn't archaeology. It was myth-making.'

Knox laughed. 'And Petitier really said all that at a commemoration of his work?'

Franklin nodded. 'And there's a lot to what he said, to be fair. Had Knossos been excavated by an Egyptologist, for example, we'd almost certainly have a completely different view of Minoan Crete. We'd think of it as the westernmost part of the Eastern Mediterranean, not as the southernmost part of Greece. But once an idea gets into the popular consciousness, it's almost impossible to get it back out.' He gave a heartfelt sigh. 'People simply don't realise how much Egyptian material has been found in Minoan contexts. Pottery, jewellery, hippopotamus ivory, seals and scarabs. Musical instruments, weapons, lamps, everything you can think of. Minoan culture is widely celebrated as unique because of its bull-leaping and distinctive artistic style; yet we've found evidence of bull-leaping all across Egypt and Asia Minor, and identical styles of artwork in Tell el-Daba and elsewhere. And that's not to mention the tantalising hints offered by language, too. The word "Minoan" derives from Crete's legendary king Minos, for example. But Minos wasn't a person's name so much as a job title. And who was Egypt's first pharaoh?'

'Menes,' answered Knox.

'Credited with uniting Upper and Lower Egypt,' nodded Franklin. 'Yet modern scholarship suggests

Menes was a job title too. Egyptian didn't have vowels, as you know, so that all we're really sure of is that it had the consonants MNS, *exactly* the same as Minos. Coincidence?'

'Probably,' said Knox. The lighting in the pavilion auditorium suddenly came on. He looked around to see that a first few delegates had gathered at the back, chatting and drinking coffee. But there was no still sign of Nico.

'The Egyptians aligned key buildings with the dawn,' continued Franklin, oblivious of Knox's distraction. 'So did the Minoans. Did you know that on certain key days of the year, the first rays of the rising sun would spear through double doorways at Knossos and bathe the throne room in light? And look at religion: Osiris and Isis are the central gods of Egyptian myth. They had a strange kind of immortality, giving birth to themselves. The same was true of the Minoan gods. Dionysus was worshipped as a young man and a bearded king. Demeter was worshipped as a maiden, a mother and a crone. A very Egyptian theology that was transformed in Crete to become the basis of Greek religion right here in Eleusis.'

'Speaking of which,' smiled Knox, getting to his feet. 'I should really read through my speech again before –'

'And that's another thing,' said Franklin, taking Knox by the sleeve to prevent him getting away before he was done. 'Eleusis was a grain cult, remember. It was all about farming.'

'Forgive me, but I really –'

'No. You'll like this. You see, Petitier was convinced that farming was the key to understanding how religion and culture had spread through the ancient world. He painted a word picture of a great golden plain of wheat and barley sweeping in from the east like sunrise, bringing socialisation, technology and enlightenment with it; and he was convinced that so beneficial a development would certainly have been memorialised in Greek legend. And because people like to credit their own, he speculated that the story would have been rewritten with Greeks as noble heroes wresting precious secrets from dastardly oriental villains, before bringing them back to Greece.'

'Don't tell me,' murmured Knox. 'Jason and the Argonauts.'

'Exactly,' smiled Franklin. 'And the crops they brought back with them, he called "the golden fleece".'

III

Nadya Petrova put on her shawl and dark glasses before emerging into the arrivals hall of Athens airport. Sokratis, the private detective she'd contacted through the Internet the night before, was waiting for her as arranged. He was a short and unpre-possessing man with sallow skin, a tired brown suit and an unattractive habit of picking the septum of his nose between his thumb and forefinger while trying to make it look as though he was merely scratching. He didn't offer to help her with her bags either, just turned and led her out to his rusting green Volvo, its front bumper patched with silver tape, its tyres as slick as a racing car's.

'Any success?' she asked, buckling herself in.

Sokratis nodded briskly. 'There were four of them, like you said. They got into two big black Mercedes with tinted windows. Three in the first, one in the second. I followed the second; less chance of being spotted. He headed to the hills north of Athens. *Very* expensive up there, *very* exclusive. If you're not a shipping billionaire or a Russian oligarch, forget about it. And the house . . .' He waved his fingers as though scalded. 'I couldn't follow him down the drive, he'd have spotted me for sure. So I went on a little way, gave him a few minutes to get inside, then made my way in on foot. There was another car already parked there, a gold Ferrari. But I figured you were interested in the Mercedes, so I was putting my transmitter on it, when guess what?'

'What?'

'The second damned Mercedes suddenly turned

up!' He gave a laugh, designed to let her know how cool he was in a crisis. 'I had to get out of there pretty damned quick, let me tell you.'

'But you got the transmitter on, yes?'

'Sure did.' He proudly patted the SatNav monitor screwed clumsily to his dashboard. 'No sign of life yet this morning, but we'll know the moment they're on the move.'

'Good job,' she said. 'You've done well.'

'All in a day's work,' he said. 'Speaking of which . . .'

She nodded and handed him a white envelope from her bag. He opened it up at and counted the notes twice, folded them away in his wallet. 'So what's this all about, then?' he asked. 'Husband being naughty, is he?'

'Something like that.'

'It always is,' he chuckled. 'That's all I ever get these days, divorces.'

'Is that a problem?'

'Not as long as I keep getting paid.'

'Good,' she said. 'Then we understand one another.'

SEVENTEEN

I

The morning was drawing on, and Mikhail still hadn't emerged from his room. 'Shall we knock?' asked Zaal.

'He took the Ferrari out again last night,' muttered Boris. 'I think he brought someone back with him.'

'Is that a yes or a no?'

'If you want to knock, don't let me stop you.'

'Maybe another ten minutes.'

It didn't take that long. His door opened suddenly and he appeared on the balcony, looking very Hollywood in shades, jeans, a white cotton T-shirt and his leather trench-coat. A waif-like young woman in a sequined dress and high heels followed him closely down the stairs, using him for cover. With her short brown hair and slight

211

frame, she had rather the look of Gaille Bonnard about her, and Edouard couldn't help but wonder if that brief encounter in the lift last night hadn't given Mikhail an itch that he'd gone out specifically to scratch. 'Knox will be starting his speech soon,' he said brusquely, as though he'd been the one kept waiting. 'We're leaving in five minutes. Be ready.'

'I'm going to have to stay behind,' said Edouard. 'Your father has asked me to work on –'

'You're coming.'

'Yes, but –'

'I said you're coming,' said Mikhail. 'Speak to my father from the car.' He turned and walked away before Edouard could protest further, over to the kitchen where he began giving instructions to Boris.

'Don't worry so much,' said Davit, with unexpected sympathy, from an armchair. 'It'll be fine.'

'I'm a historian,' shrugged Edouard, as he went over to join the big man. He felt clammy with perspiration. 'This kind of business . . .' He shook his head.

'I understand,' said Davit. 'It can take a bit of getting used to.'

Edouard sighed as he sat down. 'How come you look so familiar?' he asked. 'Have we met before?'

'I don't think so. But perhaps you watch rugby?'

'That's it!' said Edouard, snapping his fingers. 'The Tbilisi Lions! You play lock for them.'

'Used to,' grinned Davit.

'I saw you jumping against Pavel in the semis a few years back. What a game that was.'

'He was a good line-out man, Pavel. The best I ever went up against.'

'You gave him one hell of a fight.'

'We still lost.'

'Games like that, no one really loses.'

'I can tell that you've never played sports for a living.'

Edouard grinned. 'He's my son's hero, Pavel. All he wants in life is to be a lock. Poor kid takes after me, though. He'll be lucky if he's big enough to play scrum-half.'

'Best position, scrum half,' Davit assured him. 'All the glory, all the girls, none of the damage.'

'Try telling him that.'

'Maybe I will, if I see you at one of the games. I could introduce him to Pavel if you like.'

'Would you? He'd love that. Honestly, he worships you guys. I'd be his hero for a year if you –'

'Are you two going to be yapping all night?' asked Boris, standing by the door with Mikhail and his hooker.

'Coming,' said Davit, pushing to his feet.

'Hell!' muttered Edouard, feeling a little sick again. 'What if we're seen? What if someone remembers us?'

'Don't worry,' murmured Davit, nodding towards Mikhail. 'Who's going to remember you with Morpheus over there to look at?' He spoke in a low voice, yet Mikhail must have heard. He turned immediately their way and began to march towards them with such coldness in his eyes that Edouard and Davit both froze. He undid and drew out his leather whipcord belt as he advanced, feeding one end back through the buckle to make an improvised noose, wrapping the free end twice around his fist, the better to hold it. He raised it up and feinted to lasso Edouard, but at the last moment turned on Davit instead, throwing it over the big man's head and hauling it tight with such swiftness that he had no time to interpose his fingers. Then he tugged so hard that he spilled backwards over the arm of his chair, sending shudders through the polished wooden floor-boards. And now Mikhail dragged him behind him, while Davit kicked and squirmed and scrab-bled uselessly at the strangling leather, unable to prevent it tightening around his throat and cutting off his windpipe, his face bulging and turning crimson.

Edouard watched in horror. Davit was only in trouble for trying to reassure him. He felt he should be doing something to help, but he was paralysed by fear. Davit slapped the ground in submission, yet Mikhail still didn't relent. His struggles began to weaken, his eyes threatened to turn upwards, and finally Mikhail dropped the belt contemptuously onto the floor, allowing Davit to get a fingertip beneath the noose to loosen it, then to turn onto his side and suck great draughts of air into his starving lungs.

Mikhail sank down onto his haunches to gather up his belt and feed it back through his belt-loops. Then he lifted Davit's head by a hank of hair and looked him in his eyes. 'I need you alive,' he said. 'You should be glad of that.'

'I'm sorry, sir,' gasped Davit, tears streaming down his cheeks. 'I didn't mean anything.'

'If you ever say anything disrespectful about –'

'I won't! I swear I won't!'

'Don't interrupt me,' said Mikhail. 'I don't like being interrupted.'

'I'm sorry,' wept Davit. 'I'm sorry. I didn't mean anything.'

'Good. Then as I was saying, if you ever again say anything disrespectful about me again, it won't matter whether I need you alive or not. Is that clear?'

'Yes.'

'Yes, what?'

'Yes, sir.'

Mikhail let him go, then stood up and looked disdainfully down. 'Pull yourself together,' he said. 'We've got work to do.'

II

Iain and Gaille headed up into the central high-lands, quickly leaving the built-up northern coast behind. A row of wind turbines stood like Easter Island statues on a ridge, holding vigil over the seas. Away to her right, the snow-capped peaks of the White Mountains came into view. Nearby, crude stepped terraces had been cut in the hillsides, their fields full of raw young crops, while sunlight glittered on their mica-rich stone walls. Traffic clogged as the road narrowed through villages and towns. They'd been driving for less than an hour when they crossed another ridge and the southern sea came into view, the plain beneath them crawling with ugly grey polythene-clad greenhouses, like so many maggots.

Iain leaned forward and pointed away to their left. 'See that hill?' he asked. 'Phaistos.'

'Where the disc came from?' asked Gaille. The Phaistos disc was a famous fired-clay Minoan tablet stamped front and back with spirals of unfamiliar symbols. It had baffled archaeologists, historians and everyone else who'd studied it, who'd explained it away as everything from a mathematical theorem to a board-game.

'I'll take you round the palace on our way back, if we have time,' nodded Iain. 'It's a wonderful setting. And far fewer tourists than Knossos, of course, though still pretty busy, especially in season.' He glanced sideways at her. 'Crete's like Egypt that way. Tourists come for the sun and the sand, but they like a bit of culture too. Which makes the Minoans big business. Take the Phaistos disc, for example. There's a lot of controversy about its authenticity. I'm pretty sure that it's for real myself, but plenty of others reckon Luigi Pernier, the Italian archaeologist who found it, faked it himself out of jealousy for all the publicity Sir Arthur Evans was getting over at Knossos. But the point is, the dispute could be resolved one way or the other in a heartbeat if Heraklion Museum allowed a thermoluminescence test. They won't, of course. It's one of the most iconic images of Minoan Crete, so why risk it?' He shook his head. 'That's the way things work here. Profit before truth every time.'

'Says the author of *The Atlantis Connection*,' she teased.

'I guess I asked for that,' he laughed ruefully, as they came up behind a diesel-belching lorry on the switchback descent. 'But at least I'm not trying to hide anything. I honestly believe the Atlantis legend is a genuine folk-memory of the Minoans.' He slid her a glance. 'You know the gist of it, I assume?'

'Sure,' shrugged Gaille. 'In ten thousand or so B.C. there was a great empire called Atlantis

217

somewhere west of the pillars of Hercules. It was larger than Africa and incredibly powerful, yet was eventually defeated by Athens and other Greek cities before being destroyed by an extraordinary cataclysm, never to be seen again.'

'You sound sceptical,' said Iain, swinging out wide to see if there was any way to overtake the lorry, before pulling sharply back in when he saw a car approaching.

'We only have the one source for the story,' replied Gaille, 'and that's Plato, who wasn't exactly frightened of using allegory to explain his ideas. There never was any great island west of the pillars of Hercules, or geologists would have discovered it by now. And there were no civilisations to speak of in ten thousand B.C., or we'd have found evidence of them. And even if there had been, then Athens couldn't have been involved in destroying it, because it didn't exist back then. And Egyptian temples couldn't have recorded it, because they didn't exist either. So, yes. I'm a little sceptical.'

A short stretch of empty road appeared ahead. Gaille braced herself with her feet as Iain charged the Mustang recklessly into an overtake, tooting his horn to warn the lorry driver and any oncoming traffic. 'Look,' he said, swinging back in once he'd passed it, 'I know Atlantis is risky territory. All those outlandish theories about fish people from outer space with ludicrously advanced technology.

But there's nothing in Plato about fish-people or aliens. Believe me. I've looked. And the technology he describes isn't much more than irrigation systems and hot and cold running water, which we know the Minoans had.'

'Not in ten thousand B.C.'

'Of course not. You're absolutely right that a lot of Plato's account simply doesn't fit.' They came up behind a long train of traffic, and for a horrible second, Gaille feared Iain was about to try and overtake it all in one go, but then he clucked his tongue in evident frustration, and fell into line instead. 'But you've got to remember how much the story went through before it even got to Plato. For one thing, some Egyptian had to record the story in the first place. Easier said than done. They didn't have Reuters back then. They couldn't just turn on CNN. Garbled stories would have come in from across the ancient world, leaving some poor sap to try to make sense of it. And once they'd made a record, they had to keep it safe in their temple archives, even though that temple and much of northern Egypt was under foreign occupation for much of the Minoan era. And you must know better than anyone that the Egyptians weren't anything like as meticulous in their record-keeping as popular opinion would have them. They were just as lazy, deceitful, propagandistic and prone to natural disasters as anyone else. Then there's the

Egyptian High Priest who read the story in his temple records and told it to the Greek Solon. Surely there's at least the possibility that something got mangled in the translation. Solon then went back home and told it to his grandson, who later told his own grandson, who in turn told it to Socrates before Plato wrote it down. How many different people is that it had to pass through? And yet you somehow expect his account to capture the fall of the Minoan empire with perfect accuracy?'

'I don't expect anything,' said Gaille mildly.

'Take this business of dates. Plato said that Atlantis was destroyed nine thousand years before Solon's time. The Minoan empire collapsed nine *hundred* years before Solon's time. Isn't it just possible that someone somewhere got a symbol wrong?'

'What about it being west of the pillars of Hercules? Or being larger than Africa?'

'Some people back then believed that the Hercules had set his pillars at the Hellespont, not the Straits of Gibraltar. Crete was west of them. And, yes, the Egyptian high priest did indeed describe Atlantis as bigger than Africa, but he went straight on to say that it was the main island of an archipelago ruled by a confederation of kings. Plato describes this main island as a rough oblong, six hundred kilometres long by three hundred wide.

Nothing like as big as Africa, but actually pretty close to Crete. So it wasn't the *island* of Atlantis that was huge, but the area it controlled. The Minoan empire had outposts all over the Eastern Mediterranean, from Greece round to Egypt, just like Atlantis did. Add all this space together, land *and* sea, then you do indeed get a vast area, as large as Africa was believed to be back then.'

'I suppose.'

'And Plato describes Atlantis's main island in some detail. He says it was mountainous with a big plateau in its south.' He waved his hand out the window. 'We've just passed over a mountain range, in case you weren't watching, and we're currently driving through a great plain. The Atlanteans worshipped Poseidon, just as the Minoans did. They revered bulls, just like the Minoans. And Atlantis was divided into at least ten kingdoms, just like Minoan Crete. And when it finally fell, it fell to mainland Greeks, just like Minoan Crete.'

'Don't I remember something about Atlantis being formed from black, red and white rock?' asked Gaille mischievously.

'Quite right,' nodded Iain. 'Doesn't sound much like Crete, I admit, but it *is* a perfect description of Santorini, the Minoan's most important outpost. We can't be sure precisely *how* important, of course, because Santorini used to be a volcano, Mount Thera, until it blew itself up in the most

violent eruption in human history, leaving just a
semicircle of rock in the water. And that eruption
is of course another point of similarity between
the Minoans and the Atlantis legend, perhaps the
most remarkable of all. Plato says that Atlantis
vanished after a great earthquake, leaving behind
only an impassable mud shoal. Thera's eruption
would have felt like a massive earthquake, even
as far away as Egypt, and it would have left the
Aegean a thick soup of pumice and ash for decades.
And it surely inflicted a mortal wound on the
Minoan empire, leaving them at the mercy of
whoever came conquering first. The Mycenaeans,
as it happened.'

'If you say so.'

They'd reached the town of Timpaki. Iain put
on his indicator and began to brake and pull in.
For a shocked moment she feared he'd taken
umbrage at her tone, that he was about to stop
and order her out. But he merely turned into a
petrol station instead. 'Stay here,' he said, getting
out. 'I need to fill her up.'

III

The delegates suddenly started arriving at the
pavilion in a flood. The buses from the hotel had
evidently arrived. Nico entered with them, talking

animatedly with a member of his staff. Knox went to join them, and they went together up to the podium, where they talked him through the controls. He felt a sudden flutter of nerves, that coppery taste at the back of his mouth. Public speaking didn't come naturally to him.

'Fifteen minutes,' said Nico. 'Okay?'

'Okay.' He walked back and forth across the rear of the stage, keeping a lid on his nerves as he gave Augustin's text a final read-through. The lights in the main part of the pavilion went down; the stage grew brighter. He went to sit upon his appointed chair. Nico took his good time about making his way to the podium, where he tapped the microphone to make sure it was on, then cleared his throat, milking the moment. The auditorium was now packed, people standing at the back, even a few journalists, to judge from the notepads and cameras, presumably looking for new angles on Petitier's death.

'I'm sure you've all heard by now of the terrible events of yesterday afternoon,' began Nico. 'My first instinct, of course, was to cancel today's proceedings. But you good people have come so far for this conference, and it's so rare to have so many of the world's great authorities on Eleusis in one venue, that I felt we owed it to scholarship to persevere, however tragic the circumstances. And I'm glad, to judge by this excellent turnout, that so many of you agree.'

All the talks were being filmed for posterity, and the cameraman now swept the audience. It gave Knox an idea. Anyone at yesterday afternoon's talk had an ironclad alibi for Petitier's murder, with the Athens hotel a good forty minutes away. But anyone *not* there had some explaining to do, particularly if –

His name was called out suddenly. He looked up to see Nico beckoning. There was a polite smattering of applause that grew louder as he walked across and shook Nico's hand. He oriented himself at the podium, checked the controls and the teleprompter.

Over the years Knox had known Augustin, he'd come to take his friendship for granted. You did that with people like Augustin, because they never made a point of it, they never asked for anything in return. He had a sudden vision of him in the ICU, his face swollen, his skull fractured, fighting for his life; yet at the same time he had the strongest sense of his presence here in the pavilion, watching him right now, his arms sardonically folded, as though to make sure that he'd do him justice. And suddenly what Knox had seen as a chore to pay back Nico for helping get him out of gaol took on a different aspect. Augustin had talked lightly about this lecture, but it had been his chance to prove himself to the world outside Alexandria, and he'd worked his heart out on it. He'd rewritten it countless times, had rehearsed it endlessly. But now he was lying in an ICU bed, and – brutal though it was to acknowledge – this talk could yet prove his memorial. Knox owed it to him to make it fitting.

An earthquake had struck off the coast of Alexandria several months before. Not severe, as these things went, barely enough to shake dust from the plaster, rattle a roof or two, make people smile nervously at each other as they hurried out their front doors. But it had also put a crack in an old block of flats overlooking the Nouzha gardens, and a week later the facade of the building had groaned and then simply sheered away. The property had duly been condemned and destroyed. A bulldozer had revealed an underground chamber. The Supreme Council for Antiquities in Alexandria had called in Augustin, and he in turn had called in Knox and Gaille.

Now he played edited highlights on the giant screen of Gaille's footage of that first exploration, jumping and bumping as they clambered over rubble and debris, the hazy white flare of flash-lights playing over the *loculi* and detritus on the floor, human bone and the occasional fragment of pottery glowing palely against the darker dirt. He didn't speak, just let the atmosphere build. It was one of the great privileges of archaeology, exploring such sites for the first time in hundreds or even thousands of years. But finally he sensed his moment. 'Behold the Alexandrian district of Eleusis,' he began. 'They call them the Mysteries. But in Egypt, at least, thanks to my good friend Augustin Pascal, they may not be that way for very much longer.'

IV

They found Knox's Citroen parked on the cobbles outside the site entrance. Edouard backed into a nearby space, the quicker to get away, then he and Zaal went over to the other Mercedes, from which Boris and Davit were climbing out. The rear window hummed down; Mikhail beckoned from within. They all went over. Mikhail had his trousers unzipped and down around his thighs, Edouard was startled to see, and the hooker's face was buried in his lap. 'Well, boss?' asked Zaal, not skipping a beat. 'What now?'

Mikhail pointed to a nearby café, its garden overlooking the car park. 'Go wait for me in there,' he said. 'Order me coffee and an ouzo. I'll be with you in a minute.' The window hummed back up.

They took a corner table with a view of the site's entrance and the cars. Edouard watched in fascination as Mikhail's Mercedes started to rock back and forth, the shock of passers-by at the

226

shadow theatre behind the tinted windows. The sheer contempt for others, to fuck a hooker in broad daylight; how Edouard envied that. Climax arrived and passed; the Mercedes fell still. A few more moments passed and then the rear door opened and the hooker got out, her jacket slung over her shoulder, picking at her crotch and wobbling a little as she walked, her high heels unsuitable for the cobbles. Mikhail himself emerged a few moments later. He checked his reflection in the tinted glass, straightened his collar, then headed towards the café.

Boris' mobile began to ring at that moment. He answered it, then passed it to Edouard. 'For you,' he said.

'You have my answers for me?' asked Sandro bluntly.

'You have my wife for me?' responded Edouard.

'She's here now. You have thirty seconds.'

'Nina?' he asked eagerly. 'Are you okay?'

'I'm fine,' she assured him, though her tone sounded guarded. 'We went out riding this morning. Even Kiko. It was the first time he's been out since that time with Nicoloz Badridze.'

'Nicoloz Badridze?' frowned Edouard, shifting up to make room for Mikhail. 'You don't mean –'

'Yes,' she said. 'Nicoloz Badridze. But don't worry. Uncle Ilya rode beside him all the time, he kept his hand upon his arm, so there was no chance of him falling. We're all having a fine old time. Do you understand?'

'Yes,' said Edouard hollowly. 'I understand. Tell the children I'm thinking of them.'

'Of course. We'll hear from you again soon, I hope.'

'Yes,' he said. 'I'll do everything I –'

'That's thirty seconds,' said Sandro, taking back the phone. 'Now tell me about my fleece.'

It took Edouard a moment to clear his mind and focus. 'Listen,' he said. 'We'll never get away with this if people's first reaction is disbelief. I mean, once they start laughing, they never stop. So it has to be credible. Forget about a fleece that's made of gold but which handles like sheepskin. It's too improbable and too technically challenging, both for the ancient Georgians and for us. But I have another idea. It won't be as spectacular, but it'll be far more plausible.'

'Go on.'

'Metals were hugely important commodities in the ancient world. Silver, tin, bronze, copper, iron, you name it. They were all shipped around the Mediterranean in ingots, sometimes shaped like bricks but just as often in flat rectangles with small protrusions at each corner, maybe to make them easier to carry, but which look undeniably like animal skins.'

'Ah!' said Sandro.

'Exactly. Archaeologists call them ox-hide ingots: but actually they look more like sheepskins. And there's no reason at all why one of these ingots couldn't have been made of gold. And if it was made of ancient Colchian gold . . .'

Silence as Sandro considered it. 'I suppose it will do,' he said finally. 'Can you get us details?'

'We have pictures and specifications of several on the Museum Intranet. I can email them to you as soon as I get to a computer.'

'Forget that. Just give me your log-in details.'

Edouard sighed. With people like the Nergadzes, you got in ever deeper and deeper. He gave him what he wanted, handed the phone back to Boris. Their drinks had arrived: his coffee cup rattled a little as he picked it up, thinking again of his conversation with his wife, of the name she'd mentioned. Nicoloz Badridze! He'd hoped never to hear of him again. The man was a paedophile, released after twenty years in prison to be housed in an apartment block just a few doors from their Tbilisi home. The knowledge that such a monster was living so close to their twins became unbearable to them. They'd finally sold up and moved, feeling unutterably guilty because the buyers had had a daughter of their own, and they hadn't said a word. Neither he nor his wife had ever mentioned Badridze's name since.

Not until now.

He rocked forward from his waist, until the rim of the table pressed against his chest like an incipient heart attack. Ilya Nergadze out riding with Kiko, his hand upon his arm. He remembered suddenly Ilya's remark about his charming son, and that beautiful lady-boy serving champagne on the plane. *Christ!* What had he exposed his beloved son to?

More to the point, what was he going to do about it?

EIGHTEEN

I

Gaille went into the petrol station to pay while Iain filled his tank. 'You're already doing so much for me,' she said, when he came in. 'You must let me pay for this.'

'Too kind.' He got out some money anyway, to buy mints and a packet of sweets. 'I've got a bit of a throat,' he explained. 'All this talking; I'm not used to it.'

'Then they're on me too. You wouldn't be talking if I wasn't asking.'

'You'll spoil me.'

'I think that ship has sailed.'

They laughed together as they went back out to the car. Iain opened the sweets and poured them haphazardly into the coin-tray between them, then grabbed a mint for himself and squeezed it between thumb and forefinger until it squirted out of its wrapper straight into his mouth. 'Where were we?' he asked.

'You'd just proved Minoan Crete was Atlantis.'

'Ah, scepticism. An academic's best friend.'

'It's always served me well. Especially on questions that can't be answered.'

He leaned forward to make sure there was no traffic coming, pulled out onto the road. 'I wouldn't be so sure of that. I mean, all those points of correspondence I just gave you must mean something. And then there are the inadvertent clues in Plato.'

'Inadvertent clues?'

'Sure. You know the kind of thing. Like that story in Herodotus, about the pharaoh who wanted to circumnavigate Africa. He commissioned some Phoenicians to sail south down the east coast, then back up the west.' He sucked on his mint a couple of times, then switched it from cheek to cheek. 'They reappeared three years later, claiming they'd done it. But Herodotus openly mocked them, because they said the sun had been to their right when they'd rounded the cape, when everyone knew that Africa didn't extend south of the equator. But of course we now know it *does* extend south of the equator, which makes pretty compelling evidence that they did actually complete the circumnavigation properly.'

'And there are similar details in Plato's account of Atlantis, are there?'

He nodded vigorously. 'People forget that the story of Atlantis is also the story of Athens, because it was the Athenians who led the fight against Atlantis. Plato and his contemporaries didn't know much about early bronze age Athens, other than for a few anecdotes in Thucydides. Yet Plato's account of Atlantis includes remarkably accurate details about bronze age Greek cities.' He popped another mint, gestured expressively at his throat. 'And he mentions a spring in the Acropolis, for example, blocked up by an earthquake. There was no such spring in his time, yet archaeologists found one back in the 1930s. How could he have known about that? Was it really just a lucky guess?'

'It's hardly proof of Atlantis.'

'No, but it makes his account worth taking seriously. And who knows what's still out there, just waiting to be found? It's one of the reasons I love hiking in the mountains here so much; there's still every chance of discovering an important new site. And if not here, there's always Santorini. There are still whole Pompeiis to rediscover beneath the volcanic ash. What if we found something specifically mentioned by Plato? A scene from his story represented in a frieze, say. Or that golden statue of Poseidon in a chariot pulled by six winged horses. Or some of the hundred Nereids upon their dolphins? Would those be enough for you?'

'Sure. If you found them.'

'Maybe we already have. Or traces of them, at least. You'd be amazed by how many artefacts we've recovered at Knossos that we've barely even looked at, let alone studied. Who can say what treasures aren't waiting for us among them?'

'I'm surprised you could tear yourself away,' smiled Gaille.

'Hey,' he grinned. 'Who can say what treasures aren't waiting for us at Petitier's place, either?'

II

The lighting was so low in the pavilion that it was only when Knox brought up the brighter of his slides that he could see the faces in the first few rows, hushed and leaning forward in their seats. He made a joke that earned far more laughter than it deserved, and he felt the heady confidence of a speaker whose talk was going well. He didn't rely on the teleprompter anything like as much as he'd anticipated; in a strange way, it was as though he was merely a conduit, allowing his friend to speak.

It came almost as a shock to him when he reached the end and the teleprompter showed blank. He hadn't given any great thought to how to wrap it up, so he paid a short impromptu tribute to Augustin, then thanked his audience for their time and attention. There was silence for a moment or two, as though everyone else had been taken by surprise too. The silence lasted just long enough to unnerve him, make him feel that he'd misread how well it had gone. But then the applause started and began to swell, and it was like nothing Knox had ever heard before, certainly not at so formal a conference. A woman rose to her feet, and then a man, then pockets of people everywhere, and suddenly the whole auditorium was on the rise, cheering and clapping and stamping their feet, not for him, Knox knew, or even for the talk; but for Augustin, and all the unsung work he'd done in Alexandria over the years, wanting to show that they didn't for one moment believe the police slurs against him.

Nico came over to join him at the podium. 'How the hell am I supposed to follow that?' he muttered with mock gloom.

Knox laughed and nodded at the cameraman. 'You're making recordings, yes?'

'Of course. Would you like one?'

'Not for me. But I think Claire should know how well Augustin's talk went down.'

Nico nodded emphatic agreement. 'Good idea. I'll take care of it myself.'

'Thanks.' The applause still thundered on, like at a party conference. He used the moment to put to Nico his thought about checking yesterday's absentees against people who knew about the golden fleece.

'I wondered that myself,' admitted Nico. 'But everyone was here. Everyone but Augustin, at least. And Antonius, of course.'

'Antonius?'

'An old colleague from the university. An authority on early scripts, which is why I thought he might be able to help. But he was never going to show up. He's turned into a recluse, I'm afraid. He barely ever leaves his house.'

'Not even for a conference like this?'

'No.' But he looked thoughtful. 'You think I should call him?'

'It's an idea.'

'I'll do it in a moment.' He nodded at the audience, the applause finally beginning to slacken. 'You'll take a few questions first, yes?'

'A few,' agreed Knox. 'But then I really do need to get back to Athens.'

NINETEEN

I

Iain and Gaille headed back up into the highlands, passing through picturesque mountain villages and towns before turning left towards Plakias. The rocky flanks of the Kourtaliotiko gorge towered above them, giving Gaille mild tingles of vertigo as she stared upwards. A glimpse of whitewashed wall offered testimony to the Greek inability to pass a mountain ledge without building a church upon it. They soon left the gorge behind, to her relief, but within just a few more miles they'd reached a second, the narrow winding road strewn with fallen rocks and stones. 'Christ!' she muttered, as Iain slalomed casually between them, taking her uncomfortably close to the edge. 'How many of these damned gorges are there?'

'Lots,' he grinned. He pointed down at the floor

of the car. 'The African and European tectonic plates meet right beneath us. This whole island's the result; and these gorges are the places where the crust's split under all that pressure.'

'Like snapping open a baguette?' suggested Gaille.

'If you like.'

The road wound tortuously on. Clusters of houses clung grimly to steep slopes, like climbers who'd ventured beyond their competence, and frozen. The roads were narrow and in poor repair; just as well there was so little traffic. They reached a coastal plain, passed the quiet resort of Frangocastello and the cove port of Hora Sfakion, before climbing a cliff road so steep that it seemed to Gaille like a strand of spaghetti thrown against a wall. The hairpin bends grew tighter with each turn. She felt nauseous and her feet clenched with cramp. Heights didn't seem to bother Iain at all; he took the corners with lazy calm, even as their tyres skidded on the dusty tarmac, taking them perilously close to the edge. 'Please,' begged Gaille, clutching the door handle. 'I hate heights.'

'Don't worry,' he assured her. 'I drive these roads all the time.'

'Please,' she said again.

Her tone got through to him. He took his foot off the accelerator, shifted away from the edge. They were already amazingly high, the richly coloured houses and boats of Hora Sfakion like toys on the rugged, fractal coastline below, while the sea was an astonishing colour, the rich blue of a hyacinth macaw. The road degenerated into a stretch of raw bedrock. A dump-truck full of tarmac swung recklessly fast around the corner ahead, forcing them out so wide that Gaille could see nothing beneath her but drop. Hot choking dust blasted through their open windows, sending them both into coughing fits. And still they climbed higher and higher, until Gaille couldn't bear it any more, just sat back in her seat and closed her eyes.

'It's okay,' said Iain at length. 'We're past.'

She opened her eyes to see hills either side of her, removing even the possibility of falling. Her vertigo at once abated, though she still felt a little sick. They reached a small town with a tranquil square. 'Anapoli,' said Iain, pulling up outside a general store. 'I'll go in and ask about Petitier. You stay here. They're less likely to open up with a foreigner around.'

'You're a foreigner.'

'I've lived here ten years; I speak local. That makes all the difference, trust me.'

She didn't argue, still jangled from the drive. She checked herself in the mirror, wiped away the worst of the dust, patted down her hair, got out. A pleasant enough town; the kind where the same few families had been farming the same fields for hundreds of years; where the same few surnames would appear again and again in the cemetery. There was a café next to the shop, its glass doors wide open. She wandered over. A canary chirped in its cage. Goatskins were stretched out on the walls. A stuffed eagle was poised to take flight. Split logs were stacked by a potbellied stove, four men playing cards at the table next to it. Three of them glanced up at her with benign indifference, while the fourth saluted her with his glass. She smiled and retreated to the car.

It was five more minutes before Iain emerged from the shop, carrying two white plastic bags bulging with food and water. 'You had to pay for your information, then?' she said, as he stowed them in his boot.

'Worth every cent,' he assured her. 'The woman recognised Petitier's picture at once. He comes in once a month to trade supplies.'

'And? Did she tell you where he lived?'

'Yes,' he grinned. 'She did.'

II

Under different circumstances, Edouard might have enjoyed drinking his coffee in the Eleusis café. It was a pleasant morning, after all, and local families had come out in force to enjoy the fresh spring sunshine. But he was still struggling to digest the implications of his brief conversation with his wife, work out what he could possibly hope to accomplish while –

'Hey, boss,' said Zaal to Mikhail, pointing across the car park to the site gates, from which a man was now emerging. 'That's Knox, isn't it?' he asked.

'That's Knox,' agreed Mikhail. He rose to his feet but then hesitated. There were so many people milling around outside, including security guards by the site entrance, that even he must have realised that this was a wretched spot for an abduction. Besides, if Knox should spot any of them, he'd recognise them instantly from the night before. They therefore waited inside the café's grounds until he reached his car and pulled away, then they threw some banknotes on the table and hurried out to their Mercedes.

III

Knox made good time out of Eleusis and back towards Athens. Despite Nico's misgivings about the traffic police, the earlier four-car pile-up had been completely cleared away. He left the coast behind, passed through a stretch of rocky woodland, reached the top of a hill.

Nico had tried several times to telephone his

old colleague Antonius, but had got no reply. He'd grown increasingly alarmed, for apparently Antonius wasn't just reclusive; he was a genuine agoraphobic who found it hard to leave his house even to go to the shops. His anxiety had infected Knox, who'd offered to drive by his house to check up on him. Nico had assured him it would be easy to find, for it was in the shadows of the Olympic Stadium. 'You can't miss it,' he'd told him. 'Big, white and gleaming. You can see it from everywhere.'

Everywhere but here, it seemed. He reached across and popped open his glove compartment, grabbed his car-hire map of Athens and flapped it out against his steering wheel, then tried to read it as he drove, his eyes flickering back and forth between the road and –

The black Mercedes came out of nowhere and cut across his bonnet, slamming on its brakes as it did so, forcing Knox to wrench around his steering wheel even as he hit his own brakes hard, tyres screeching on the dusty surface. He hit the verge and the Mercedes' back bumper simultaneously, and his seat-belt snapped tight. A horn began blaring, he wasn't sure whose. Something jolted him from behind. He glanced around to see a second Mercedes pinning him in. Men sprang from both cars: he recognised them instantly from last night. He tried to release his seat-belt but it jammed and wouldn't let him go. He tried to lock himself in instead, but too late. His door was hauled open and the man from last night gave him a glimpse of the sawn-off shotgun beneath his leather trench-coat. Then he reached calmly inside and took the key from the ignition. 'You're coming with us,' he said.

Knox's seat-belt finally released, slinking back into its housing like a shamed dog. 'Who are you?' he asked, trying not to let his fear show. 'What do you want?'

The man nodded towards his Mercedes. 'You'll see,' he said.

TWENTY

I

Iain and Gaille drove out of Anapoli on a narrow, winding lane, deserted save for a flock of sheep that parted only reluctantly to their tooting. They crossed a deep gorge on a narrow wooden bridge, the planks rattling beneath them. There were olive groves either side of the road, black nets crowded into the claws of their branches, irrigation pipes coiled like mythic snakes around their trunks. They wended on between fields and woods and meadows to a tiny hillside hamlet called Agia Georgio where their further progress was barred by a metal gate. 'I guess this is what they mean by the end of the road,' said Iain. 'You want to open it?'

'Is it allowed?'

'Sure,' he said. 'It's only to keep their goats in.'

A Doberman was dozing on the far side of the

gate, leashed to a metal spike. It woke at once and flew into a barking frenzy that set off a dog's chorus in the village. She closed the gate hurriedly behind Iain, climbed gratefully back in. The Doberman threw itself up against her window as they drove past and raged impotently at her, leaving brown smears upon the glass.

'Christ, but I hate those beasts,' muttered Iain, looking more than a little pale. He drove through a village square to an unsealed track that deteriorated into lurching deep potholes. A tethered mule looked up briefly, then returned to munching grass. They reached an impassable row of heavy rocks placed as makeshift bollards across the track ahead, so Iain bumped off it to park in the cover of some trees, their whitewashed trunks reaching out of the ground like zombie arms. 'We'll have to walk from here,' he said, getting out.

'So how does Petitier get his supplies in?' asked Gaille, as they went around back. 'You think that was his mule back there?'

'Could be.' He popped the boot, crammed with camping gear.

'Wow. You came prepared.'

'Once a boy-scout . . .' he smiled. Then he added: 'I never know when I'm going to get the chance to go hiking.' He transferred the provisions he'd just bought to his pack, then pulled on hiking boots.

'What about me?' asked Gaille, gesturing at her flimsy plimsolls. 'I'm hardly equipped for this.'

'Let's see how it goes,' he said. 'Chances are we'll be back in a few hours. Certainly before dark.'

'And if not?'

He patted his bulging pack. 'I've got a tent, sleeping bags, food, everything we could need.' He reached into his boot for a spare day-pack. 'But you might want to take a change of clothes, just in case.'

The hillside rose with daunting steepness to a rocky ridge high above Gaille. But she was here on Augustin's behalf, and this was no time for faint hearts, so she transferred some clothes and her wash-bag into his pack, then slung it on.

'Ready?' asked Iain, heaving on his own pack.

'As I'll ever be,' she agreed.

II

The shotgun jabbed like a cattle-prod in the small of Knox's back as he was marched over to the Mercedes. The giant opened the rear door and nodded him inside. He looked longingly at the road, all those cars, trucks and motorbikes hurtling indifferently past, belching toxic fumes in his face. He contemplated making a run for it, dodging through traffic or waving someone down. But even as he tensed, the giant took his arm and his nerve failed him. He bowed his head and climbed into the –

He heard the car before he saw it, its old engine roaring, its frantic tooting. He glanced around to see a rusting, patched-up Volvo pulling up in a shriek of brakes, its driver hunched over the wheel, his forearm up to shield his face, while a woman knelt on his passenger seat and reached around to throw open the rear door. 'Get in!' she yelled.

Knox didn't hesitate, he twisted his arm free, slapped aside the shotgun, leapt head-first across the back seats. 'Go,' shouted the woman. The driver stamped on the gas. Someone grabbed Knox's leg and hauled him back. He kicked himself free but was left dangling out the side, his shoes, ankles and knees banging and scraping along the road as the Volvo picked up speed. Acceleration slapped the door against his hips as he clawed the synthetic seat fabric with his fingernails in a losing battle to hold on. The woman screamed at the driver to slow down, she grabbed Knox's forearm and gave him a precious moment to adjust his grip and then haul himself inside.

The shotgun boomed twice, pellets pinging and clattering on the Volvo's body-work, leaving circles of frost on the rear-window. Knox slammed the door, glanced back at the man standing in

the road reloading his shotgun while traffic
swerved around him and his men sprinted for
their Mercedes.

'He's got a shotgun!' wailed the driver. 'He's
got a fucking shotgun!'

'What's going on?' asked Knox. 'Who are you
people?'

'Oh, Jesus!' said the driver, checking his rear-
view. 'They're following us. I don't believe this. I
don't fucking believe this.'

'Who are you?' asked Knox again.

'I was about to ask you the same question,'
replied the woman, with impressive cool.

'Why follow me if you don't know who I am?'

'We weren't following you.' She nodded at the
SatNav monitor. 'We were following them.'

'Oh, Jesus!' muttered the driver. 'They're closing.'

Knox looked around. The first Mercedes was
still a good two hundred yards behind, but gaining
fast; the old Volvo couldn't possibly outrun them
on open roads. The driver must have realised this,
for he hauled on his steering wheel to take a sharp
right turn, tyres squealing in protest as they turned
again almost immediately left along an alley behind
a car dealership.

'Well?' asked the woman, belting herself in.
'Who are you?'

'Daniel Knox,' he told her, looking back through
the rear window. 'And you?'

'Nadya. And this is Sokratis. So why are the Nergadzes after you?'

The first Mercedes appeared into the alley behind them, then the second. Knox swore out loud. 'The Nergadzes?' he asked.

'You don't know them?'

He shook his head. 'They were at my hotel last night. But apart from that . . .' A pipe had burst ahead, water bubbling across the grey tarmac, their tyres slithering so sharply sideways when they took the next turn that Knox spilled across the back seats. 'Who are they?'

'The one with the shotgun is Mikhail Nergadze. He's the grandson of Ilya.' His blank look made her shake her head. 'You've never heard of Ilya Nergadze?' she asked.

'Who?'

'He's one of Georgia's richest oligarchs. And right now he's running to be our next president.'

'I didn't even know you had elections on.'

'Our incumbent was forced into holding them,' she nodded. 'He's been under pressure since the South Ossetia fiasco. You do remember that, at least?'

'The breakaway republic,' said Knox. 'You tried to seize it back. The Russians had other ideas.' They streaked past a furniture warehouse, employees staring open-mouthed as the Volvo left scorch-marks on their concrete apron.

'Something like that,' she agreed. A lorry hurtled across a T-junction ahead, forcing Sokratis to stamp on his brakes so hard that Knox was thrown against the back of Nadya's seat, and their engine stalled. Sokratis twisted the key frantically, but it wouldn't start. The two Mercedes closed up fast behind. At last the engine caught. Sokratis squirted through a gap in traffic that shut before either Mercedes could follow.

'But what the hell do they want with me?'

They passed an open lot filled with tractors, combines and other agricultural machinery, screeched left down a narrow alley, hit a pothole hard, bouncing them up in the air, then swung left around a corner. The main road was tantalisingly close ahead, but their access to it was blocked by a row of white-painted tubs of hyacinth and acacia. 'Hell!' yelled Sokratis, throwing up his hands in frustration.

'Let's run,' said Nadya.

'And leave them my car?' demanded Sokratis. 'No way. They'd track me in a minute.' He thrust his Volvo into reverse, but his SatNav showed a Mercedes coming up fast. 'Shit!' he wailed.

There was a mobile home dealership to their left, a parking area outside it, three broken-down caravans packed tight together, then a gap to the dealership wall occupied only by a green wheelie bin, its lid sticking up from the excess of garbage rotting inside. Knox jumped out and hauled the bin away. A black cat came screeching out of it before skipping off over the caravans. Sokratis reversed into the created gap, hitting the brick wall so hard that his rear bumper fell off with a clang, and Knox hauled the bin back across the Volvo's bonnet just as the first Mercedes appeared.

Nadya beckoned to him, wanting him back inside should they need to get away fast. He let go of the bin and tried to squeeze down the gap between caravan and car; but there was a slight slope at the front of the parking area, and gravity went to work, the wheelie bin rolling slowly down it, threatening to give them away. Knox dived full length, scraping his chest on the gravelled surface, grabbing one of the bin's wheels with his right hand, clawing it from beneath with his left, his fingernails scratching the stiff plastic.

Beneath the bottom of the bin, the under-carriage of a black Mercedes cruised past, gliding to a halt by the flower tubs. The second Mercedes came up behind it a moment later, stopping barely five feet away from Knox. The Volvo's suspension gave a little creak behind him, Sokratis or Nadya shifting in their seats. Doors opened and closed. Leather boots and shoes gathered for a heated discussion in some unfamiliar tongue. Knox was lying awkwardly on the tarmac, sharp stones pressing into his ribcage, but he didn't dare move a muscle. The wheelie-bin felt heavier and heavier. His biceps began to burn with the strain.

III

An old path snaked back and forth up the hill-side, but Iain hadn't the patience for that. He set off directly upwards with massive strides, turning and waiting rather pointedly for Gaille every few minutes. Despite that, she began enjoying herself. The freshness of the altitude kept her cool, and the walk was undeniably beautiful. Willows leaned over a small man-made lake, admiring themselves in its still waters. Lizards basked upon their trunks while bellwether sheep tinkled nearby. They reached a glade dotted with gloriously coloured hives, their mouths blurred with bees, so that the air hummed like some faulty electrical appliance. 'Good honey?' she panted, as much to slow Iain down as anything.

'The best,' nodded Iain, turning to face her, then walking on backwards. 'Always has been. They even say that Alexander the Great was embalmed in Cretan honey.' He raised an interrogative eyebrow. 'Well? You found his body.'

'What? You think I should have *licked* him?'

'I suppose not,' he laughed. 'Still, it's a shame we'll never know.'

'Alexander died in Babylon,' observed Gaille. 'What would the Babylonians have been doing with Cretan honey?'

'The best embalmers back then came from Egypt. You should know that. Alexander's generals sent for them, and they brought their supplies with them. Egyptian honey wasn't up to snuff. It's to do with the seasons, of course. Bees don't make honey for fun. Take it away from them and their hives will die, unless they can gather more pollen. So beekeeping ideally needs a land in permanent blossom.'

'Somewhere like Crete?' smiled Gaille.

'Exactly.' He swept his hand across the hillside, a kaleidoscope of grasses, anemones and irises, orchids and asphodels, poppies and other wild-flowers, all bounded by a natural fence of yellow gorse and the pink buds of Judas trees in early blossom, even a thousand metres or so above sea level. 'Heraklion used to be known as Chandia, which is where our word "candy" comes from. And the first alcoholic drink brewed here was mead. Dionysus is usually celebrated as the god of wine, but he most likely started out as the god of mead. In fact, some of the earliest myths about him may very well be brewing instructions.'

'Really?'

'Sure. Mead's a dangerous substance if you don't know what you're doing. They must have had some method for memorising and passing on their recipes. Look at the structure of the stories some-time, their use of numbers . . .'

They passed through a collar of trees, the ground a brown carpet of last year's leaves, pine needles and cones, and the soft pebbles of animal drop-pings. Giant cobwebs stretched across the path, strands glittering like attenuated silver, catching in her hands and hair. Out the other side, the land-scape changed markedly. The gradient steepened and there were fists of grey rock everywhere. She found it harder and harder to keep up. It wasn't just that Iain was fitter; his boots were much more suitable for the slippery, jagged terrain, while her plimsolls kept turning so that her ankles were soon bruised and bleeding.

She took out her bottle of water, warm from the sun, swallowed a couple of mouthfuls then splashed a little on her brow, used it to brush back her hair. Now that she'd stopped, she felt the tight-ness in her calves, a warning twinge of a hamstring. She looked longingly at a moss-covered rock.

'Fancy a breather?' asked Iain.

'I'm fine,' she assured him. 'But you have one if you like.'

He laughed, amusement and understanding mixed. 'Thanks,' he said, shrugging off his pack. 'I rather think I will.'

TWENTY-ONE

I

A convoy of army trucks rumbled past on the main road, bored soldiers staring out of the backs. Edouard glanced instinctively down at Mikhail's shotgun, but he was holding it safely out of sight. They waited patiently till the last of the trucks was gone, then Mikhail turned back to Davit, and prodded him in the chest with his finger. 'Well?' he demanded. 'I thought you said they came this way.'

'They did, sir,' muttered Davit. 'I saw them.'

'Then where the fuck are they?'

'I don't know, sir.'

'You don't know?'

'No, sir.'

'Maybe they ran for it,' suggested Edouard.

'Oh, yes,' said Mikhail. 'Carrying their Volvo with them, no doubt?' He shook his head in scorn, turned back to the others. 'And who were they anyway? Where did they come from?'

There was silence, no one daring to speak. 'Perhaps a pair of good Samaritans,' suggested Zaal finally.

'Good Samaritans!' scoffed Mikhail. 'Why would good Samaritans be following us?'

'They weren't,' said Boris. 'It was just coincidence. They were way behind us on the road.'

'They were following us,' insisted Mikhail. 'Check beneath the cars.' It was Zaal who found the transmitter, tearing it free from beneath the second Mercedes, holding it up like a tribute to Mikhail. He took it and weighed it in his hand, then turned to Edouard. 'This is your car, isn't it?'

'It's a rental,' said Edouard. 'I just picked it up at the airport.'

'You led them to me,' said Mikhail. 'You led them right to my fucking house.'

'No,' said Edouard, backing away. 'I'd have –'

Mikhail took a step towards him. 'How *could* you be so fucking stupid?' he demanded. 'You've compromised this entire operation. You've compromised *me*!'

'No,' said Edouard. His calf banged one of the flower-pots; he stepped sideways between them out towards the road. But Mikhail followed him, invading his space. He tried a submissive smile, touched his arm in an effort to establish a bond.

Mikhail looked incredulously down. 'Did you just touch me?' he asked.

'I only –'

Mikhail took another pace forward, jutting his face into Edouard's, so that Edouard instinctively stepped back and out into the road. A truck tooted as it swerved around him, clipping the rear wheel of an overtaking motorbike, sending it fishtailing down the road before the rider somehow managed to right himself. Edouard danced back onto the pavement, his heart going crazy.

'What now?' asked Boris.

'We find that Volvo,' said Mikhail, who'd already lost interest in Edouard.

'How?'

'Didn't any of you idiots get its plates?' They all shook their heads. Mikhail sighed and pointed to the transmitter Zaal was holding. 'That damned thing must belong to someone. Find out who. Then bring me their head on a fucking platter.'

'But how do we –'

'On a fucking platter,' said Mikhail. 'Or it'll be yours instead.' He checked his watch. 'You have three hours. I'd use them well if I were you.'

II

Gaille began to hear a strange rushing noise as she climbed higher, like a river in full flood. She laboured on upwards for a few more minutes, her legs burning and trembling with tiredness, before she discovered what it was – wind funnelling through a narrow pass between two high peaks. Grey clouds had gathered at the mouth, like disheartened ghosts outside the gates of purgatory, waiting to be let in.

It quickly grew chilly, all that cold air channelling through this narrow gap, the wind whipping at her back, making a mockery of her cotton blouse, flapping her trousers around her ankles. Shivers turned to shudders; she daydreamed of jerseys and thick jackets. Visibility deteriorated too; in places, the cloud was thick as a fogbank. They reached a barbed wire fence, its wooden stakes grotesquely topped by goat skulls, voodoo fetishes to warn off unwanted visitors. 'You sure we're not trespassing?' she asked.

'Don't worry about it,' Iain assured her. He trod down on the topmost strand so that the stakes either side leaned deferentially towards him, then helped her across. 'Trust me. I walk these mountains all the time. As long as you behave yourself, anyone you meet will be glad of the company. Besides, this has to be Petitier's land by now, and he's hardly going to complain, is he?'

The pass was treacherous with loose landslide cobbles, meaning Gaille had to keep her eyes down to mind her footing. She lost track of Iain in the thick mist, but assumed he was ahead of her. She'd been walking for a couple of minutes when she heard Iain shouting anxiously. 'Gaille! Where are you?'

'Here,' she replied. 'Why?'

'Be careful. I think we're near the edge of something.'

'The edge of what?' A gust of wind answered the question for her, thinning the cloud momentarily, revealing the pass falling away a few steps ahead to a sudden vertiginous drop. She stopped dead, took a step back. 'Hell!' she said. 'You must be psychic.'

He appeared out of the mist, led by her voice. 'You get a sense for these things if you do enough hiking.' He led her left, away from the centre of the pass. The wind slackened at once, and the cloud thinned and then vanished, allowing some welcome sunshine through, and also revealing what she'd briefly glimpsed: that they were on the rim of a natural amphitheatre of rock, like the caldera of some extinct volcano. There was a fertile circle at its foot far below, perhaps two or even three kilometres in diameter, divided into fields and groves, with a great yellow sea of gorse away to its north. A farmhouse stood in the approximate centre of this plateau, too distant to make out in any detail, other than for a black water tower on its roof and the glint of solar panels. And, beyond the farmhouse, two of those ugly polythene greenhouses. 'What now?' she asked, daunted by the natural stockade of escarpment walls.

'There has to a path somewhere. If Petitier can make it in and out with a mule, surely we can too.'

'I don't know,' she said.

'Trust me,' he insisted. 'It'll be fine.'

Trust me, she thought, a touch sourly. It seemed to be his answer for everything.

III

Knox was still lying on the tarmac, muscles fibrillating from the strain of holding the wheeliebin, his nose assaulted by its overheated stench. The cat he'd startled away a minute earlier now reappeared and began mewing and glaring down at him from the roof of the nearest caravan.

He could hear yelling on the road. Someone was getting an earful. A moment later, one of the Georgians appeared and got down on his hands and knees, then reached beneath the Mercedes, pulled free a transmitter, held in place by strips of black tape. If he'd just looked around, he'd have seen Knox instantly; but mercifully he didn't. There was more talking. Decisions were made. They all climbed back in their Mercedes, then reversed back up the lane and away.

Knox gave them thirty seconds or so, then got to his feet, brushed himself down, went to take a look. No sign of them. He checked around the corner. The road was clear. He pulled the wheelie-bin aside to let Sokratis out, then pushed it back into the empty slot and climbed into the rear of the Volvo. Sokratis drove cautiously off. His pale blue shirt had turned two-toned with sweat; he smelled nearly as bad as the wheelie-bin. 'I thought you said that man was your husband,' he scowled accusingly at Nadya.

'Did you?' asked Nadya innocently.

'I don't do this kind of mobster shit. I do divorces. That's all.'

'Then this is an excellent chance to expand your business.'

'You think this is funny?' he shouted. 'You lied to me.'

'I didn't lie. You made assumptions, that's all.'

'I don't work for clients who lie to me. Get out of my car. Now.'

'Don't be such an ass,' she retorted. 'You've still got my luggage. Drive me to my hotel, and then do what the hell you like, if you haven't got the balls for this kind of work.'

'I don't have *his* luggage,' said Sokratis, jabbing a thumb at Knox.

'Just drive, will you. Or give me my money back.' She turned in her seat. 'Where do you want to go?'

There wasn't much point in Knox returning to his car; Mikhail had his keys. 'How about a Metro station?' he asked.

'You heard him,' Nadya told Sokratis.

He gave her a glare, but he couldn't hope to match wills. He drove warily on. They reached the main road and he leaned forward as far as possible, his eyes almost comically peeled for black Mercedes.

'You were telling me about the Nergadzes,' Knox reminded Nadya.

'Yes,' she agreed. She glanced at Sokratis, her faith in him evidently shaken. 'Do you speak French?' she asked.

'Yes.'

'Good.' She switched language smoothly. 'Let me give you some more background on Ilya. He owns several oil and gas interests, like most of the oligarchs; but there are rumours that his first billion came from trading guns to Afghanistan in exchange for heroin.'

'Jesus.'

'The Americans put pressure on the Georgian government to go after him. But families like the Nergadzes stick together. You can't arrest just one of them without precipitating a small war.

A simultaneous mass arrest was planned, but somebody blabbed. The whole clan fled to Cyprus – they've got several houses there, not to mention a mega-yacht and much of their cash. But Ilya's not the kind for exile, however pampered. Negotiations for his return were getting nowhere, so he set up his own political party to target vulnerable government seats, and he won enough of them to make himself a real thorn in the president's side.'

'And suddenly he was allowed back, no doubt?'

'Of course. Everyone assumed he'd quit politics, having got what he'd wanted; but it seems he'd developed the taste. You have to understand something. Georgia is one of the great fault-lines of our modern world. It separates those who have oil and gas from those who need it. It separates NATO from the old Soviet Union, Islam from Christianity, drugs from their markets. Whoever controls Georgia matters.'

'And Nergadze wants it to be him?'

Nadya nodded. 'He made his first bid in the 2008 presidential elections, but he barely scraped in third. That should have been that for a few more years, except for South Ossetia. Nergadze and the other opposition leaders forced new elections. Nergadze has made himself the main challenger. Our current guy is so unpopular, he should walk it, except that he's got serious problems of his own.

He's seen as being too close to the Russians, for one thing, and we Georgians *hate* the Russians. On the other hand, we don't just hate them, we *fear* them too. So if Nergadze can convince voters he's the man to repair our relationship with Moscow without jeopardising our independence, he'll win. That's why he's been filling his speeches with nationalistic bullshit recently, and spending a fortune buying up and repatriating Georgian art and artefacts, doing everything he can to prove himself our greatest patriot.'

Knox sat back. He understood now why Mikhail Nergadze was here in Athens, though it didn't explain why he was after Knox, not unless . . . 'Oh, hell,' he muttered.

'What?' asked Nadya.

'They're after the golden fleece,' he told her bleakly. 'And they must think I've got it.'

TWENTY-TWO

I

In the end, Nina hadn't needed Kiko to tell her what had happened the night before. Their horse-riding excursion had made it obvious. The solicitude with which Ilya Nergadze had helped Kiko up onto his mount, the way he'd ridden alongside him, joshing him and tousling his hair, boasting about his wealth and lands: behaving, in short, like a smitten suitor trying to impress his love.

No way would Edouard be able to get help here before tomorrow at the earliest. He had too many troubles of his own. It was up to her, therefore, to keep Kiko and the twins safe. It shouldn't be beyond her. This was a castle, after all; and even though the drawbridge was up and there was no realistic way off the island, there were all kinds of places to hunker down. She took the children to her room, cautioned them not to leave until she returned, then set off on a search. The keep itself was too busy and too full for her purposes, so she started with the outbuildings. The stables were clean and spacious, pungent with animal smells. But the stalls were mostly occupied, and the others were empty and comfortless.

Two grooms came in laughing, but they fell silent and dropped their eyes deferentially the moment they saw her, mistaking her for someone who mattered. She turned away from them, passed through a door into an open-plan garage crowded with black SUVs and a red Lamborghini. The smell of burning was coming from an open door on the far side. Curiosity drew her on. A smithy, its forge ablaze and crackling, tongs, hammers and an axe hanging from its walls, along with horseshoes, hinges, ploughs, swords, gardening tools and other examples of the craft. Sandro and Ilya Nergadze were standing around the anvil with two other men, conferring and studying papers. Sandro crouched to pick a golden goblet from a blue plastic basket, and Nina recognised it instantly as part of her husband's Turkmeni cache.

Indignation almost provoked her into rashness, but prudence rescued her just in time. She ducked out of their line of sight, slipped off her shoes, picked them up, and tiptoed silently away.

II

'The golden fleece?' asked Nadya. 'Are you crazy?'

'I wish,' said Knox. He filled her in on Petitier and the seal-stones he'd found, then gave her a précis of the fleece's history, its connections to Eleusis and Crete.

When he was done, Nadya looked stunned. 'You think it really exists?'

'It's possible. Would it have an impact on the election?'

She gave a dry laugh. 'Are you kidding? We Georgians are incredibly proud of our heritage; and we're superstitious too, especially in times of uncertainty. If Nergadze brings the fleece back to Georgia, and it's the real thing, he'll be a national hero, he'll *walk* the election.' She shook her head, as though the prospect was too dreadful to bear.

'That bad, huh?'

'He's a drug-smuggler. He's an arms dealer.'

'So why's that your problem?'

'It's my job,' she sighed. 'I'm a journalist, a political journalist. Or a blogger, I'd guess you'd call me.'

'There's money in that?' asked Knox, surprised.

'Not exactly. But it's a good way to build your profile; and there's certainly money in having a profile. Besides, it's not like I live on caviar and champagne.'

'And you're here doing a piece on the Nergadzes?'

'Sort of.' She stared out the window for a few moments, considering what to tell him. A butcher was trimming fat from the carcass of a slaughtered lamb with practised strokes of a knife so long it looked more like a sword. 'I was at a Nergadze press conference a week or so ago,' she said finally. 'Ilya was announcing some new policy for the fiftieth time. Go to a few of these things, you soon realise all the interesting stuff happens off stage. There was a man leaning against the back wall. He was obviously a Nergadze. You recognise the look after a while. But I hadn't seen him before, which was odd, because the whole family have been out campaigning relentlessly.'

'Maybe he was a cousin,' suggested Knox.

'Not from the deference with which people treated him. But, anyway, I was curious enough to follow when he left. He was driven to the private jet terminal at Tbilisi International Airport, then got on Nergadze's plane. I called a contact in airport operations. The manifest showed only one passenger: Mikhail Nergadze. I'd never even heard of him. I tracked down his birth certificate: he's Sandro Nergadze's son, which makes him Ilya's grandson. All Sandro's boys went to the same school outside Gori. I had a friend check their records. Mikhail was there until he was fourteen, then he was suddenly sent away to an English public school.'

'So?'

'It just seemed strange, that's all. I checked the local newspapers on a hunch. Two days before Mikhail was sent abroad, a twelve-year-old girl was abducted from a nearby orphanage.'

'That's pretty thin,' said Knox.

'I contacted his English school, claiming Mikhail had applied for a job with me, and I was checking his references. He stayed there less than a year, and only two terms at his next school. I joined one of those school networking sites, asked if anyone remembered him. No one would tell me much. They sounded scared of him, even after all these years.'

Sokratis pulled in sharply at that moment, tyres screeching against the kerb. 'Your Metro station,' said Sokratis, reaching back to open Knox's door. 'Now get out.'

'One more minute.'

'No. Out. Now.'

'Be quiet,' Nadya told him, running short of patience. She turned back to Knox. 'No one was sure why Mikhail had left either of his English schools, though there were all kinds of ugly rumours. He pretty much vanished after that, except for a couple of Internet hits of him doing rich kid stuff in Cyprus, jet-set parties and night-club openings, that kind of thing. I asked my guy in airport operations to let me know if and when

Mikhail came back, but the next time he called it was to let me know that the Nergadze plane was about to set off for Athens again, carrying four Nergadze staff. I figured something big had to be going down. I couldn't get here before them, so I contacted our brave Greek friend here through his website, and asked him to pick up their trail.'

'That's it!' scowled Sokratis, as though aware he was being insulted. 'Get out.'

Knox stepped out onto the pavement, but held the door open. 'You want to meet up again later?' he asked. 'I reckon we could help each other.'

'Not tonight,' said Nadya. 'Too much to do.'

'How about breakfast, then?'

'Sure.' She pulled out her diary. 'Where?'

Knox didn't trust Sokratis an inch. He took Nadya's diary and wrote down the name of a Plaka café, scribbled directions to it. 'Eight thirty?' he suggested.

'See you then,' she agreed.

'One last thing,' he said. 'Why are you really so interested in this guy?'

'I just told you. I'm a journalist.'

'Balls. No one does what you've been doing just because a man was leaning against a wall.'

She gave a little snort; her gaze drifted past his shoulder, fixing on memories. 'I recognised him,' she admitted. 'The moment I saw him, I knew I'd seen him before.'

'When?' asked Knox.

Her gaze returned from the far distance; somehow she found a smile. 'On the night my husband was murdered,' she said.

III

Gaille gladly agreed to Iain's suggestion that he scout on ahead and search for a way down the escarpment face, not least because it gave her the chance to take the weight off her aching legs. The ground here was rocky and bare, and what little vegetation there was defended itself fiercely with thorns. She took anything that might crush from her day-pack, then sat upon it and let her body rest. A black beetle made slow progress across the dirt. She watched it until it was gone. A slab of rock jutted from the earth nearby. It looked unnaturally smooth, like an ancient monument to honour the high pass. And unless her eyes were deceiving her . . .

She grimaced as she pushed herself back to her feet, went over to it. Yes. There was a pattern in its surface, two symbols chiselled into it like ancient graffiti: a man marching and then an outstretched hand, though both so faded it was hard for her to be sure. She turned on her camera-phone and took a photograph. The signal was

271

weak and fluctuating, but at least there was one. There surely wouldn't be if they ever made down into Petitier's plain. She didn't feel comfortable that no-one knew where they were, however experienced Iain might be, so she went to the escarpment rim and took a photograph of the plain and the farmhouse, another of herself blowing a kiss to the camera. Then she sat back down and composed a text to Knox, updating him on their progress, before sending it and the photos on their way.

It was another five minutes before Iain returned. 'Good news,' he said. 'I've found a path. Of sorts, at least.'

'Of sorts?' she asked, her soles clenching with a little anticipatory vertigo. 'What if it's not Petitier's house down there?'

'It has to be. It's where that shop-woman said it was. Besides, who else would live out here? The Cretans go crazy without company: it's only us foreigners who like to be alone.'

'And if it's locked?'

'Not a problem. I've got my tent and all the supplies we could need. Besides, if we turn back now, we'll only have to come back in the morning. And didn't I kind of get the impression that speed was of the essence, what with your French friend's name to clear?'

The invocation of Augustin was the prod Gaille

needed. 'You're right,' she said, getting to her feet. 'Let's do it.'

IV

Sokratis drove in silent umbrage to the centre of Athens, wanting Nadya to know he resented the way she'd treated him. Traffic was light, they were soon at her hotel. He dropped her outside, popped his trunk so that she could take out her overnight bag and laptop, then sped off without a backward glance.

His anger was only a façade, however; he needed it to conceal his guilt. He drove around the block, parked two hundred metres up the street, then watched the hotel's front door. It wasn't long before his suspicion was vindicated. A taxi pulled up and Nadya reappeared with her bags, looking furtively around as she limped down the steps.

The bitch! He'd known she'd try something.

He gave her a healthy head-start. She was clearly on her guard. The taxi headed into Plaka, the network of narrow tourist streets at the foot of the Acropolis, then stopped outside another hotel. Sokratis pulled in behind a van to avoid being spotted. He watched as a hotel porter helped her with her bags. She paid off her driver then limped inside.

When he settled on his plan, Sokratis felt a

twinge of shame, but he stamped down hard on it. A roof for his head, food for his table, a little money to show a woman a good time, once in a while. That was all he asked. Besides, his website made it quite clear he was a divorce specialist. It was her own damned fault for putting him in such an intolerable situation. Yes. It was her own damned fault.

TWENTY-THREE

I

Knox leaned against the Metro carriage door as a woman in mourning black weaved between the passengers with her right hand outstretched, a swaddled infant cradled against her left hip, reciting a half-hearted plea, not expecting alms, nor getting them either. The tracks were elevated here, offering a view over the city. Nico was right. You could indeed see the Olympic Stadium from a distance, its gleaming white arches towering over ugly suburban housing made even uglier by graffiti and satellite dishes.

He got out at Irini, down the steps and between two shallow ornamental pools onto a windswept concourse. A brass band was somewhat unexpectedly thumping out Souza while marching on the spot, as though playing and moving simultaneously was still beyond them. A mini-cyclone fluttered the pages of a discarded phone-book like applause, while paper bags and empty sweet wrappers whirled in impressively tight circles, like gymnasts with their ribbons.

He took out the scrap of paper on which Nico had scribbled Antonius' address, then asked the people he met until one pointed him on his way. He walked through a vast parking lot, empty except for a few families visiting the swimming pool, from which he could hear splashing and squeals of delight. He hurried across a main road. A woman out walking her dog directed him to a street of plush semidetached homes with sleeping policemen and neat rows of polished cars, interspersed with occasional skips filled with ripped-out carpeting. But there was no such gentrification taking place at Antonius' house, a rotten tooth in an otherwise perfect register. His front garden was a jungle, his walls overrun by ivy. The house had withdrawn into itself, like its owner.

Knox rang the bell. No reply. He put his ear to the door, but the neighbours had the builders in, their hammers and drills making it impossible to hear. He pounded on the front door, then looked up at the first floor windows. Not a sign of life. The letter box attached to the front gate was overflowing with junk mail. His apprehension grew. Maybe Antonius had hated the noise of construction so much that he'd decamped: but with Petitier dead, and Mikhail Nergadze on the loose, it was hard not to worry.

A narrow passageway led down the side of the house. The paintwork was scarred and blistered, as though it had come second in a knife-fight. A sash window was raised a few inches, allowing the house to breathe. He tried it and it lifted easily. Surely Antonius would have locked up properly if he'd left for a few days. He glanced around to make sure that no one was looking, then clambered inside. There was a sour smell to the place, as though something was rotting. 'Hello!' he called out. 'Anyone home?'

No answer. He walked along a short corridor into the kitchen. The shades were down over the back windows; the door was blocked by stacks of crates and boxes. A half-eaten crust of sliced bread on a plate had curled up its corners and turned green.

He turned the other way. The carpet in the downstairs loo was soaked. He reached a gloomy room with a cheap pine table and chairs, their joints splashed with clumsy archipelagos of white glue. The walls were so damp that the old lining paper was peeling freely. Afternoon sunlight through the slat blinds threw a grid on the brown-cord carpet, half-covered by discarded envelopes and their onetime enclosures: bills, summonses, demands, furiously-phrased letters from small tradesmen. A life falling apart.

The hammering next door grew so violent that the walls shook, releasing motes of dust into the air that caught in Knox's throat, so that he had to cough quietly into his fist to clear it.

There was a stack of books on the table, as though Antonius had been going through them. Knox glanced down their spines. Robert Graves, Apollonius, others with equally obvious connections to the golden fleece. There was a pile of Internet print-outs too. He flipped through them. Stories of the mega-rich buying up art and history, names underlined or highlighted. He kept looking until he found a story about Ilya Nergadze celebrating the purchase of a cache of Georgian gold from Turkmenistan.

A green light was blinking on the answer-phone. He pressed play with his knuckle, wary of leaving prints. Beeps and silences mostly, people calling but not leaving messages, save for a woman who yelled abuse and a man demanding payment or else. The last messages were both from Nico, sounding anxious, asking him to call him back. The tape finished and rewound. Knox's sense of foreboding, already strong, turned to fatalism. He went out into the hall and turned towards the stairs, and found what he'd almost been expecting.

II

Back at the house, Mikhail's anger was building. For one thing, Olympia hadn't yet shown up, despite the clear instructions he'd given her the previous night. For another, his men were making little headway in tracking down the owner of the Volvo. He stood on the stairs with folded arms and watched them work their phones and the Internet, wondering who to take it out on. He'd promised consequences, after all. It was time to demonstrate that he meant what he said.

The doorbell sounded at that moment. Olympia, no doubt. He'd known she'd turn up eventually. Whores like her couldn't help themselves. He went to let her in, but found instead a teenager with lank brown hair sitting astride a moped. 'Michael Nergadze?' he asked, holding up a brown paper bag. 'I've got a delivery.'

'Who from?'

'A man.' The kid gestured vaguely over his shoulder. 'He didn't give his name. Just this bag and twenty euros.'

'I'm Nergadze,' Mikhail told him.

'If you say so,' said the kid.

The bag was stapled closed. Mikhail ripped it open and pulled out a pay-as-you-go mobile. 'You can go now,' he told the delivery boy.

'What about a tip?'

'I said you can go.' He waited until he was out of sight before turning on the mobile. It searched for and found a signal, then beeped to alert him to a message. It turned out to be a telephone number. He called it. 'You don't know me,' said a man, answering almost instantly. 'I was in that Volvo earlier.'

The fear in his voice was gratifying to Mikhail. 'You followed me,' he said.

'It was the woman. I didn't know what she was up to, I swear I didn't. She said you were her husband.'

'Who is she?'

'All she said was Nadya. She found me through my website, yesterday. She asked me to tail you guys from the airport when you arrived, so I did. It's what I do. Divorces, I mean. Not this kind of shit. And then this morning I collected her from the airport. But that's all.'

'Describe her to me.'

'I can't. I swear I can't. She wore a scarf and glasses the whole time. All I know is she's maybe forty, short, thin, pale skin. And she has a slight limp when she walks.'

'Which side?'

A pause. 'Her right, I think. But you know how it is with limps. Both legs go funny. But the thing is, I know which hotel she's staying at.'

'And?'

'You won't come after me?' pleaded the man. 'Promise you won't come after me.'

'We won't come after you,' said Mikhail. 'Not if your information is good.'

'She's at the Acropolis View. It's in Plaka.' Then he added vengefully: 'Stupid bitch thought she could switch on me.'

'What about the man you picked up?'

'I dropped him off outside Sepolia. I think she arranged to meet him again, but I can't swear to it, they were talking French.'

'Thanks,' said Mikhail. 'Now keep your mouth shut and get out of town.'

'I'm on my way.'

'If I should ever see or hear of you again . . .'

'You won't. I swear you won't.'

Mikhail ended the call then stood there brooding. He was curious about this woman in her own right, and she also seemed his best way of finding Knox. She'd seen the black Mercedes earlier, however, and his Ferrari was hardly the most discreet of vehicles. He went back inside, beckoned to Zaal. 'Get me a van,' he told him. 'Nothing flashy; just make sure it's roomy and private in the back.'

'Yes, boss,' said Zaal.

A woman called Nadya who walked with a slight limp and who'd flown all the way from Georgia to track him down. He felt, for a moment, a mild but pleasurable buzz. Life was getting interesting.

III

Antonius was hanging from a short noose tied to the base of the banisters above, his feet dangling just an inch or two from the bottom step, as though he could reach it if he just stretched out his toes. But of course he'd be doing no such thing ever again. Knox had seen death before, but nothing quite this ugly. He was an old man, and thin. Rigor mortis was already making grotesque contortions of his limbs and rucking up the sleeves of his blue jacket. There was a bulge in his grey trousers from a post-mortem erection, and his feet were so badly swollen that the laces on one of his scuffed black shoes had actually popped, while the other merely bulged like a joint of sirloin wrapped in string. A folded sheet of note-paper lay on the second bottom step. Knox lifted the flap carefully with his fingernail, just enough to read the scrawled message upon it. A simple and direct expression of regret, exactly what you'd expect. But with Petitier so recently dead, and a clear connection to Mikhail Nergadze, not entirely convincing.

Knox's heart sank, partly in sympathy for Antonius, but also – less commendably – because of the fix he now found himself in. He couldn't just leave the poor old sod hanging there, but he dared not cut him down either, in case this proved to be a crime scene. And if he notified his new friends in the Athens police, they'd doubtless use his presence here to throw more muck at him. He needed an intermediary.

The noises started up again next door, making it impossible to think. He left the way he'd come in, through the gate and a little way down the street, then called Charissa on his mobile and filled her in on his day so far, on Nergadze and Nadya and now Antonius. 'Good grief!' she muttered when he'd finished. 'Things certainly happen around you, don't they?'

'I think I'm beginning to see it,' he told her. 'Your brother-in-law emailed photographs of the seals to a lot of people, including Antonius. He must have deciphered them himself and realised the implication. He's been struggling for money. I mean *really* struggling. So he tried to find people who'd pay for the information. Unfortunately, he went to a family called the Nergadzes.'

'This man you met earlier?'

'He's one of them, yes.'

'And you think they murdered him?'

'There has to be a chance.'

'Good Christ!' muttered Charissa.

'Will you call the police for me?' he asked. 'I

don't fancy having to explain another death to them. And you'd better let Nico know too. Antonius was his friend.'

'I'll take care of it,' she promised. 'And look after yourself.'

'You know it,' he assured her.

IV

The escarpment wall was so steep that Gaille felt queasy even where the path was relatively wide and the footing secure. But it wasn't all like that. Several sections were so treacherous with shale that she had to get down onto her backside and slide across. They came across a goat lying down on its haunches. It seemed to be sleeping, except for the trickle of blood from its mouth, the flies settling on it that scattered in a cloud as they approached. It did little for her confidence that even goats could fall and kill themselves on these cliffs. She looked squeamishly away as she stepped over it. But even that was nothing like as bad as when they came across a shrub growing sideways out of a crevice in the cliff-face, blocking most of the path. Iain simply grabbed it and swung himself around, as if oblivious to the toe-curling drop yawning beneath him. 'Piece of piss,' he assured her. 'You'll be fine.'

'I can't,' she said.

'Of course you can,' he said. 'If it will take me with my pack on, it'll take you for sure.'

'There has to be another path,' she said. 'Petitier can't have brought a mule down this.'

'Well, this is the path we're on.' He reached out for her. 'Here. I won't let you fall, I promise.'

She hesitated a moment more, then reached out and took his hand. His skin was dry and rough, but his grip was strong and reassuring. She took hold of the shrub with her other hand and swung herself around to the other side.

His eyes twinkled as he let her go. 'See,' he said.

'I just don't like heights. That's all.'

'I know.' He looked at the path ahead. 'But we'd better push on. This is taking longer than I thought.'

'I'm doing my best.'

'I know you are.' He turned and marched on down. The going thankfully grew easier. The sun nuzzled the western hills as they reached the foot of the escarpment; daylight subsided into dusk. They passed through a thin fringe of walnut trees out into the fertile heart of the plateau, fields separated by tumbledown stone walls, mottled by moss and lichen: vines, barley, tomatoes, groves of orange and lemon trees with their lush green leaves and young fruit glittering like exquisite jewels. Her legs were almost done, however, so it was an immense relief when, through the gathering darkness, she glimpsed the house ahead.

The dog came out of nowhere. It must have been asleep until they were almost upon it. But then it sprang to its feet and charged, a huge black-and-tawny German shepherd hurtling across the broken ground, its eyes fixed upon her. Iain didn't hesitate, he simply turned and fled, leaving Gaille to face it all by herself. She gave a piercing shriek of terror and threw up her arms to protect her throat and face as it bunched its muscles and leapt at her with open slavering jaws.

TWENTY-FOUR

I

Night had fallen in Athens. The beautiful people had come out onto the streets. Pretty girls chattered into fashionably thin mobiles, while young men in leather jackets sat astride their fat motorbikes and roared their engines in approval, like bull moose in the rutting season.

Knox grabbed a chicken gyros at a fast-food restaurant and ate it standing up at one of their tables, hot juices trickling down his chin and forearm. What now? He dared not visit Augustin, lest the Nergadzes or the police be waiting; but he needed to let Claire know what had been going on, and find out the latest about his French friend too. He called the hospital, was put through to intensive care. 'He's still asleep,' Claire told him, when she came to the phone.

'But that's as expected. They've put him into a coma to stop the brain swelling. It's helped, I think. And his scans aren't as bad as they might have been. No fragments in his brain tissue, which is the main thing, so no immediate need for surgery.'

'That's terrific,' said Knox.

'He's not better yet,' she warned, trying to tamp down her own hopes, as well as his.

'Maybe not. But it's where getting better begins.'

'I suppose.'

'Listen, Claire,' he said. 'There's some stuff you need to know.' He told her about Gaille flying to Crete, about his talk, about Antonius, Nadya and the Nergadzes. He warned her to be vigilant, and not to leave the hospital unless she had to.

She seemed a little stunned when he was finished, as though she hadn't realised the world was still spinning outside the ICU. 'Daniel,' she said. 'I said some things last night . . .'

'Forget it.'

'I was upset. I didn't really mean anything.'

'I know that.'

'You won't tell Augustin, will you? When he recovers, I mean?'

'Of course not.'

'Only he'd never forgive me.'

'Are you kidding me, Claire? He'd forgive you anything. Besides, you were right. I should have been quicker. It was just such a blur, you know? I couldn't believe it was happening.'

'I know.'

He felt better once he'd finished the call. Energised. But to what purpose? He needed to sit down and think things through, make assessments and plans. His hotel was out. Nergadze knew he was staying there. He'd seen a 24-hour Internet café earlier, lit up like an amusement arcade, war noises pouring out, computer-gamers saving their electronic worlds. He walked back to it, took a booth in the shadows from which he could keep an eye on the door, then brought up a browser and began researching the Nergadzes. The more he learned, the more dismayed he grew. Their power, their obscene wealth, their flagrant flouting of the law. Pictures of them outside their castle and their Tbilisi mansion, boarding their private jet, arriving by helicopter upon their super-yacht.

But while Ilya and several other Nergadze men were very public figures, Nadya was right about how elusive Mikhail was. It was for a lack of better ideas that he decided to play around with alternate spellings. To his surprise, when he tried 'Michael Nergadse', he got a major pay-off, hundreds of links to Florida newspapers and blogs reporting on a recent tragedy.

Arrest in missing schoolgirl case

A 29-year-old man has been arrested in connection with the disappearance of Fort Lauderdale schoolgirl Connie Ford. The 13-year-old, who hasn't been heard from for over six weeks, was last seen waiting for a bus in Oakland Park.

The arrested man, Michael Nergadse, is a native of the Republic of Georgia. He has been studying for an MBA at Florida State University for better than two years, though fellow students claim not to have seen him for weeks. Nergadse is also being linked with a separate incident earlier on that same day, when he is believed to have tried to persuade a different schoolgirl into his car, but drove off when a passing DHL courier noticed her distress and stopped to ask if she needed help.

Missing schoolgirl case: suspect released

Michael Nergadse, the man arrested last month in connection with the disappearance of 13-year-old Fort Lauderdale native Connie Ford, has been released from Broward County Jail without charge. Frustrated officials cited lack of evidence sufficient to secure a conviction – a situation not expected to change unless missing victim Connie Ford is found.

Nergadse's lawyer has promised to vigorously fight any attempt to revoke his visa or have him deported, but confirms his client intends to leave the country voluntarily. 'I have a fourteen-year-old daughter myself,' said one assistant district attorney, when asked what he thought of Nergadse. 'I won't be letting her out of my sight until this monster's out of the country.'

Psychologist suicide

Criminal psychologist Suzanne Mansfield was found hanged in her Fort Lauderdale apartment Sunday. She was thirty-one years old. Police sources say that there are no suspicious circumstances, and they are not seeking anyone else in connection with her death.

Mansfield had apparently been in low spirits since the failed search for missing teen Connie Ford, and the collapse of the case against Michael Nergadse, the police's one-time prime suspect. 'She was sick at the thought of him walking free,' former colleague Mitch Baird told this reporter. 'She was convinced he'd strike again. She blamed herself for not getting him to confess, but we're criminal psychologists, not miracle workers.'

Not everyone believes Mansfield killed herself, however. 'She wasn't the kind,' insisted one neighbor. 'It was contrary to her faith, to everything she believed. And I saw her earlier that same afternoon. She was cheerful, not depressed. She'd just seen those gorgeous flame azaleas over on Jackson, and was really excited to plant some herself. Does that sound like someone planning to kill themselves?'

Knox sat back in his chair. Another hanging, just like Antonius. And hadn't he read somewhere that strangulation was a favoured method of serial killers, a way to express power over their victims?

'Something to drink?'

He glanced up. An attractive but sulky young woman with spilling coils of lustrous black hair was standing with her weight on her left leg, holding a tray cluttered with empty cups and ashtrays. A long day already, but plenty more yet to do. 'A coffee, please,' he told her. 'That would be great.'

II

Gaille tried instinctively to twist away from the German shepherd as it leapt at her face, but her ankle turned beneath her, and she fell hard onto her backside, screaming in terror and expecting the worst. But the dog unaccountably jerked to a sudden halt, as though some hidden hand had grabbed it by its scruff; its legs flew from under it and it fell sprawling onto its back, then it yelped and scrambled to its feet and came for her once more, riding up on its hind legs like a spooked horse, pawing the air in frustrated fury just a metre or so away, snarling and barking and showing her its fangs, while saliva frothed from its mouth and down its jowls, and its eyes glistened and raged. She scrambled on her palms and heels to a safer distance, her heart pounding wildly in her chest, still not quite sure how she'd got away with it.

'It's on a leash,' muttered Iain, returning from wherever he'd fled.

She squinted through the murky light and finally she saw it: a studded collar around the dog's throat, a length of thin black cord attached to it that disappeared in the darkness. 'Petitier must have left it here on guard,' she said in a strained voice.

'Dogs,' said Iain bleakly. 'I *hate* dogs.'

'So I'd noticed,' she said dryly. She made to get up, but pain lanced up her left leg and she promptly sat back down again. 'My ankle,' she winced. She took off her shoe, her sock. Her foot was blistered and dirty, but there was mercifully little sign of injury. She tried to stand again; again she winced and sat back down. It all felt slightly surreal, with the dog still raging impotently just a few metres away. 'I twisted it when I fell.'

Iain took off his pack, produced a first-aid kit and a roll of crepe bandage. He cut off a good length of it that he wrapped tightly around her ankle and then fixed in place with a couple of safety pins. 'How's that?' he asked.

'Better,' she told him. 'But what do we do now?'

'You wait here. I'll go explore.'

Her heart-rate gradually resettled as she sat there. The dog was still barking and lunging at her with undiminished ferocity; it dismayed her deeply that any creature could wish her such palpable ill. But even this hellhound couldn't sustain its fury forever, and finally it calmed a little, patrolling back and forth as close to her as its leash allowed, snarling and showing her its fangs.

'Hey!' called out Iain. 'Up here.'

She looked up, saw him silhouetted on the roof. 'Good news, bad news,' he said. 'I can't find a way in to the house, but the roof will do us for tonight. And there's a gate at the bottom, so that we can keep that bloody dog out, even if it should get loose.'

'What about your tent? Don't you need to bang in pegs and things?'

'It's a pop-up,' he told her. 'Couldn't be easier.

One flap and it's ready. Tell you what, I'll come and give you a hand, then I'll cook us up some pasta. God knows we've earned it. Everything else can wait till morning, when we've got some light to work with.'

III

Nadya caught up with her email and posted a couple of small items on her blog, because it didn't pay to go dark, not even for a day. She'd intended to write an update on the suspicious death of a human rights lawyer, but her heart wasn't in it, so she closed her laptop. A successful day, all in all – enough to justify yesterday's deferred reward. She checked the mini-bar, but miniatures weren't her style, so she put on some fresh clothes and went down to the lobby bar.

It was empty, however, its lights dimmed, no obvious prospect of it opening soon. She went onto the front steps, looked around. A line of cars opposite, but no black Mercedes. She put on her shawl and dark-glasses for the anonymity, then headed into Plaka, intending to walk up an appetite. Or, more accurately, a thirst.

The night was still young, huddles of gloom and shadow broken by the lights of cafés, restaurants and late-night shops; though not yet enough of them to create an atmosphere. A light drizzle started. She hunched her coat around herself and shrank into its folds, then gave a little shiver, even though it wasn't that cold, despite the gusting wind. Memories. It had been a night much like this: except that she hadn't been alone, of course, not when the evening had started.

She came to a square, where a few groups of hardy tourists were taking *al fresco* dinners. She turned and went the other way, feeling her sharpest pang yet for a drink. The sight of families often did that to her.

She'd only been at the paper three weeks, head-hunted from her style magazine by a proprietor keen to sex things up. Albert had returned from a gruelling month in Samegrelo, where he'd been covering the civil war, only to learn that his in-depth account of Gamsakhurdia's suicide was being slashed to make more room for her feature on swimwear. He and the editor had gone at it like blacksmiths. 'Sure,' he'd yelled. 'Why the fuck not? Our country is falling to fucking shit around us, so let's write about bikinis.'

She'd been mortified and angry; but mostly angry. She'd gone to his desk intending to read his copy and pick it apart, so that she could feel better about herself. It had only taken two paragraphs for her to be caught up by his story instead. She never read about war if she could help it, it was too depressing, so it had all been new to her. She'd been shocked to learn the depth of horrors going on in her own country, what Georgians were doing to other Georgians. When she'd finished, she'd sensed someone standing at her shoulder.

'So you're the one?' he'd grunted. 'The one who writes about bikinis?'

She'd turned to face him, expecting to have her head bitten off, feeling deserving of it too. But he'd noticed her eyes glistening, and had softened. It was impossible for any man to be angry at a beautiful woman who wept at what he'd written – or so he'd told her, at least, reaching over her for his cigarettes the following morning. Hero worship on her side, lust on his: not a great recipe for wedding cake. Yet despite the difference in their ages, they'd made something durable and even precious out of it.

He'd never been afraid to ask the questions others had balked at, or to write candidly about the crimes of brutal men, so they'd both always known a day of reckoning might come. A man in a tugged-down baseball cap and with a scarf wrapped around his nose and mouth had been waiting in ambush when they came home together from work. He'd waited until they were just inside before charging out of the shadows and barging Albert onto his back, then slamming the door shut, with the three of them inside.

Typically, Albert's first thought had been to get up and fight, while yelling at her to run. The man had stabbed Albert twice, first in the gut, then through his heart. He'd wiped the blade on Albert's sleeve, rummaged calmly through his pockets for his wallet, then stood and advanced upon her. She'd wanted to scream, but somehow it had caught in her throat. She'd backed against the wall instead. He'd pressed the blade against her throat with one hand while running the other down over her breast and belly to her crotch, which he'd cupped in the strangest way, as though testing a fruit for freshness. And though his face had mostly been hidden by his scarf and cap, his ice-blue eyes had burned unforgettably into her.

The police hadn't believed it had been a hit. Tbilisi was a violent place, they'd told her; muggings and burglaries happened all the time. The miscarriage had happened a week later; she hadn't even realised she was pregnant. Perhaps not surprisingly, fashion had held little interest for her since then. When the newspaper had declined to put proper resources into investigating Albert's murder, she'd thrown in her job and turned freelance so that she'd have the time to do it herself. She'd got nowhere with his murder, but she'd discovered plenty else while she'd been looking. Much of it had been too hot for any paper to publish, which was why she'd started her own blog.

Her grip on her coat had loosened, even though the drizzle had now turned into rain that the strengthening wind was spraying in her face. A few umbrellas went up, bucking and rearing like wilful horses, forcing her to shy her eyes away from their sharp spokes. Music blared from a bar ahead, an anonymous place with low lighting, frosted glass and booths set at odd angles around the wall. A place where drinkers could be alone with their vice. A tall waiter in a garish bow-tie greeted her at the door and ushered her into its shadows. 'Vodka,' she told him, for wine wasn't going to cut it tonight. He nodded sympathetically before he went, as though he could read her life, and knew it would be the first of many.

TWENTY-FIVE

I

It proved to be a gorgeous Cretan evening, the skies clear, the air lightly scented with lavender and honeysuckle. Iain and Gaille sat amid the debris of their noodles and tomato sauce and gazed up at the extraordinary canopy of stars, while grey-green geckoes made sudden short darts over the pale walls, and crickets chirped in the surrounding fields. 'Nights like these,' murmured Gaille.

'They bring the past closer, don't they?' agreed Iain. 'One of our archaeologists went to live up in the Lasithi Plateau after he retired. I heard rumours he was a bit poorly over the new year, so I headed up there to make sure he was okay. He was fine, thank goodness. But then a snow-storm hit like you wouldn't believe. It comes down fast there. Anyway, I was snowed in for the best part of a week. Fantastic stroke of luck. He tells the most extraordinary stories. More to the point, he has a telescope on his roof. We caught this amazing meteorite shower. Can you imagine what that would have been like for the Minoans? Or imagine if a meteorite actually struck! I mean, this place here, it looks almost like a vast impact crater, right?'

'I hadn't thought about it. But yes.'

'I don't suppose it was, but you never know. Of course, if Petitier *has* found something here, that might be the reason. The Minoans considered iron sacred because back then it pretty much only came from meteorites.' He stretched out his leg; his foot brushed Gaille's ankle. She pulled away, not sure whether it had been deliberate. 'There was this dig in Anemospilia,' he continued. 'They found the body of a young man sacrificed to appease the gods; though it can't have done much good, because the roof collapsed mid-ceremony and killed the priest too, as well as a couple of other attendants. *He* was wearing an iron ring. The priest, I mean, not the poor bastard he sacrificed.' He shook his head in amusement. 'Everyone thinks the Minoans were so civilised because they worshipped goddesses and decorated their palaces with charming frescoes of birds and lilies. Not so much. We've found a pit of children's bones at Knossos, and it's pretty clear from the knife-marks that they'd been butchered in just the way you'd butcher livestock for your pot.'

'Yuck.'

'They were no worse than anyone else, mind. Everyone was at it. They're a lot more like the surrounding cultures than we tend to think. That's actually the main premise of my book.'

'You mean *The Pelasgian and Minoan Aegean: A New Paradigm?*'

'That's the baby,' laughed Iain. He found a couple of stones lying loose on the roof, began to juggle them in his right hand. 'You see, we've got all these overlapping accounts of the people who lived in the pre-Mycenaean Aegean. The Greeks called them Pelasgians. Sir Arthur Evans called them Minoans. Were they the same or different? And do they have any connection with the Philistines, or the Sea People, or the *Hyksos*, and so on? And, more broadly, was the Mediterranean a series of isolated cultures with minimal links between them, or was it – as I believe and argue – far more fluid and homogeneous than most academics now allow.'

'Despite the archaeological record?'

'On the contrary. *Because* of it. There's a ton of evidence to support my view. And where there *are* differences, they're only the ones you might expect. Take Crete and Egypt, for example. Superficially, their religions and cultures look very different. Superficially, one *couldn't* have derived from, or even taken much from, the other. But we forget how much our religions are defined by our environments. I mean, imagine you live on the . . .' He dropped one of his juggling stones, muttered a soft curse, picked it up again. 'Imagine you live on the side of an active volcano. Don't you think you'd worship different gods from someone who lives in the flood-plain of a river like the Nile that inundates once a year?'

'Of course,' said Gaille.

'Egyptian priests put an awful lot of effort into calculating the annual rising of Sirius, because Sirius predicted the inundation, the natural start of the Egyptian year. But there was no reason for the Minoans to start their year with Sirius, or even to treat it as a particularly significant star. Yet they did. And Sirius didn't just make it to Crete: it became an integral part of Greek religion via the Eleusinian Mysteries.'

'What are you getting at?'

'I'm just saying, what if some enterprising Egyptians had come here, to set up a trading post, say? Crete is the hub of the Mediterranean, after all. They'd surely have brought their religion and mythology with them, because that's what people do; but how long would it have taken them to trade their river and sun gods for earthquake gods and volcano gods?' Two bats appeared as dark shadows above the roof, swirling and swooping in pursuit of flies, before vanishing as quickly as they'd come. 'Mount Thera was active long before its final blast,' continued Iain. 'The experts agree that it had regular minor eruptions. It surely had to be a major factor in Minoan cosmology. So how about this for an idea: when Persephone was abducted by Hades in the Eleusinian Mysteries, there was a blinding light and a noise like the earth being split open. Does that remind you of anything at all?'

Gaille sat up a little straighter, intrigued by the idea. 'You're not suggesting that Eleusis is a celebration of Thera erupting?'

'Why not? According to the myth, after Persephone was abducted, her mother Demeter cursed the earth and made it infertile. And this wasn't some unusually long winter: it was a famine that clearly lasted *years*. But when Persephone was finally restored to Demeter, she made the earth richer than ever.' He dropped one of his stones again, couldn't find it this time, so tossed the other irritably away. 'Volcanic ash is incredibly rich with nitrates. That's why people live near volcanoes, even though they're so dangerous. Visit Bali some time, if you don't believe me. You'll never have seen such greens. So each time Thera had one of its minor eruptions, it would have covered the surrounding islands with ash, devastating at least one year's crops, maybe even two or three. But when the fields finally started producing again, the harvests would have been magnificent. Just like in the Eleusinian myth. Until the big one, at least.'

'Can you imagine what that would have been like?' smiled Gaille, leaning her head back against the stone parapet, its edge pressing like stress against her nape. 'To have been in Crete when it went off?'

'A front-row seat on the most spectacular event in human history,' nodded Iain. 'An explosion that would literally have shaken the world. One hundred cubic kilometres of rock raining down over the next few days. Tsunamis destroying your fleets and coasts. The sun blacked out for months. The seas thick with ash. And the survivors knowing that even if they won their personal battle against starvation, their empire was doomed. It took years for the Mycenaeans to take over, but surely that was only because they'd been ravaged by Thera as well.'

'And traumatised. Think how much courage it would have taken to go back into the water after that.'

'Exactly. The whole of eastern Mediterranean civilisation smashed apart by a single catastrophic event. And though we've managed to find a great number of the jigsaw pieces it left behind, we're still not sure that they all belong to the same puzzle, or how to fit them together, basically because the picture on our box is wrong, because it's been drawn by Greek specialists, and by Egyptian specialists, and by Asia Minor specialists, not by Mediterranean specialists. But throw that box away, start out with a new picture of Crete and Santorini at the hub of a great and sophisticated empire, then everything suddenly fits. And thanks to Plato, we already have a wonderful idea of how this new picture should look.'

'*The Atlantis Connection,*' suggested caille.

'*The Atlantis Connection,*' smiled Iain.

II

It was still too early for Knox to call it a night, so he played around on the Internet for a while. He forwarded the photos Gaille had sent to his email, opened them on his screen. Agia Georgio, her message had said, near the southern coast. He tracked it down on a map of Crete, then brought up Google Earth. The connection was light-speed compared to the treacle of Egypt. He zeroed in on the Mediterranean, Crete, its southern coast. He found the port of Hora Sfakion, the town of Anapoli, then Agia Georgio.

Seen from above, the terrain looked mountainous and bleak, grey limestone covered in thin scrub, dotted with the green circles of trees. He zoomed in on remote buildings, but none of them matched Petitier's house. He broadened his search, looking for that distinctive amphitheatre of rock. It was amazingly, disturbingly voyeuristic: nowhere was private any longer. At last he found a plausible candidate, zoomed in until he was certain: a house with two polythene greenhouses nearby.

He stared at it a while, thinking fondly of Gaille, wondering how mad she still was at him, how much grovelling he'd have to do. The prospect made him smile. He wondered if she'd learn much about Petitier. If anyone could, she would. It bugged the hell out of him that so many people insisted on giving him all the credit for their Alexander and Akhenaten adventures, because the plain truth was that she deserved most of it.

He closed Google Earth, ran a search on Roland Petitier instead, not expecting much other than a few news reports about his murder. He'd dropped out of sight twenty years before, after all, well before the Internet age. But to Knox's surprise, he got a number of hits linking to the on-line index of one of the more obscure archaeological journals. Petitier, it seemed, had published an article in it, and it had evidently provoked quite a vibrant discussion. But it wasn't Petitier's name that most struck Knox, nor even the title of the piece, though that was intriguing too.

No, what really caught his eye was the name of the man who'd co-authored it.

III

Gaille was beat from her long day. She called it a night early, grabbed her wash-bag and a bottle of water then went to the edge of the roof and squeezed a worm of toothpaste onto her brush.

Iain came to stand alongside her, wearing only his boxers and a T-shirt, holding out his own brush for water. She poured it for him, the spill splashing against their feet. They stood side by side by the edge of the roof, their brisk brushing joining the sawing of the crickets. They spat in unison, toothpaste bombs making faint pale spatters on the dark ground below.

He held the flap of the tent open for her, shone in his torch. There was room enough for two, but just the one sleeping bag. She looked uncertainly around.

'All yours,' he smiled.

'Are you sure?'

'Absolutely. I've got jerseys and a jacket.'

The ground was hard and she was too tired to protest. She kicked off her shoes and socks, slipped inside the bag, unhooked her bra and removed it from beneath her T-shirt, then stripped off and folded up her trousers for a pillow. The torch went out. She could hear him fumbling around, laying out clothing to lie on, pulling on a T-shirt. She'd almost drifted to sleep when she heard him muttering, then he tapped her shoulder. 'I'm sorry,' he said. 'I didn't realise it would be this uncomfortable.'

'What?' she asked.

'Shift up. I'm coming in.'

She didn't know what to say. It was his sleeping-bag, after all. He tugged the mouth open. She felt his knee in her back, his cold foot brushing her calf, reminding her of Knox. Had it really only been last night? 'I don't know about this,' she said.

'Please,' he said. 'I won't try anything, I swear. What kind of man do you think I am?' He turned onto his side, his front against her back, pleasantly warm where they touched. She wondered what Knox would make of this; but Iain was his friend, after all. 'Good night, then,' said Iain, snuggling close, putting his arm around her waist.

She hesitated a moment longer, and then her opportunity to object was gone. She rested her head back upon her folded trousers. 'Good night,' she said.

IV

It was past midnight when finally a taxi pulled up outside Franklin's house, and the man himself emerged in his dinner jacket, and then his wife, elegant in a pale green gown and woollen shawl. They must have been at Nico's closing banquet. Knox walked towards them, slowing deliberately as he drew close, so that they'd know he had business with them. Franklin's expression clouded when he saw him. 'You!' he said. 'What are you doing here?'

'You know what I'm doing here.'

He licked his lips but said nothing. 'What is it, Claude?' asked his wife, in the nasal tone of deafness taught to speak. 'What's going on?'

Franklin turned to her with a calm smile. 'Nothing, my love,' he assured her, signing the words as well as speaking them. 'Please go inside.'

'But I –'

'Please,' he repeated. 'Go inside. Go to bed. Everything's fine. This gentleman and I just have some matters to discuss.' He watched her go in, the lights coming on downstairs and then up. 'Well?' he asked.

Knox told him. 'I just ran an Internet search on Roland Petitier. Unusual name. Did you know he'd published an article while he was at the French school. More to the point, can you take a wild guess as to who his co-author was?'

'It was a long time ago.'

'It was you, Dr Franklin. You, who told me this morning that you weren't really his friend, that you only shared a house with him for a while.'

'Everything I told you was the truth.'

'But not the whole truth,' said Knox. 'You co-authored an article with him called *The Mysteries of Eleusis Revealed*. Or didn't you think that was worth mentioning?'

Franklin looked both ways down the street, almost as though contemplating running for it. But then his shoulders slumped a little. 'Let's go inside,' he said. 'I'm going to need a drink for this.'

V

Nadya walked slowly through Psyrri on her return to her hotel. There were queues outside the nightclubs; music boomed from within. Evenings like this, loose with drink, she liked it if a brash young man made a play for her. But there were no takers tonight, not even for a little eye contact. She'd been beautiful once, lusted after; and not even that long ago. But the last few years hadn't been kind.

She reached the quieter, older streets of Plaka. Several middle-aged men were sitting in low-slung canvas chairs around a table. She walked close by them, but they didn't even look at her, so she turned around and came back and gave one of their chairs a little nudge. But all she got was laughter.

Her ankle turned on the cobbles. She went sprawling. It was always a risk to mix vodka and heels. She picked herself up, brushed off her hands and knees, aware she should be embarrassed, yet not. Her left palm began to throb. It was wet and speckled with grit and torn skin. She watched with passive curiosity as the first hints of blood arrived, the sharpness of each pulse.

'Excuse me?' asked a man, German from his accent. 'Are you okay?'

She looked hopefully around, but he already had a woman. 'I'm fine,' she told him.

She took her shoe in both hands, tested the heel. It wobbled a little, so she kicked the other one off too, then carried them as she wandered, uncertain of her way. Her feet grew cold and wet; the streets grew narrow and emptier. She reached a familiar plaza, turned left and saw the illuminated sign that ran down the front of her hotel. There were no black Mercedes outside her hotel, just a few cars and a white van. She wasn't that drunk, not to check. She paused to pull her shoes back on; her concierge was pompous, she didn't want him getting all superior with her. The echo of her footsteps made her realise how empty the streets had become.

The van door opened. A man got out. She knew at once. She turned and tried to flee, but her broken heel betrayed her and she tumbled hard onto the pavement. She opened her mouth to scream, but too late; a hand was clamped over it, holding a moistened pad of some kind. She felt its chemical burn on her lips as she breathed it in, and the strength began draining from her muscles, despite her fear. Then she was lifted bodily and carried to the van; and the last thing she saw was Mikhail Nergadze kneeling beside her, smiling down at her as though he'd just won himself a bet.

TWENTY-SIX

I

Franklin led Knox through to a dimly-lit front room with huge unframed expressionist canvases on the walls. He went to a drinks cabinet and poured himself a clouded shot-glass of firewater that he knocked straight back and refilled. 'My wife doesn't like me drinking in public,' he confided. 'I have a bad habit of not knowing when to stop, and then saying things to embarrass myself.' He turned to Knox with a meaningful look. 'She hates embarrassment, my wife, more than anything in the world. So I do all I can to avoid it: because I love her.'

'I understand.'

He found and filled a second glass that he handed to Knox. 'Do you smoke?' he asked, opening a silver case filled with cheroots.

'No, thanks.'

'You don't mind if I do?'

'Of course not.'

They sat in a pair of armchairs set obliquely near the front window, through which they could watch the few cars that passed, the occasional pedestrian. Franklin lit his cheroot; it gave off an aromatic smoke. 'I apologise for not mentioning that article earlier; you must understand that I gave my word I'd never talk about it again.'

'To your wife?'

'In part. But more so to her father.'

'Your mentor,' nodded Knox. 'When you promised to change your life, and he gave you another chance.'

'Exactly,' said Franklin.

'Still,' said Knox. 'I need to know.'

Franklin sank back into his chair, vanishing into shadow, except for a faint glow whenever he took a puff. 'It was Petitier's influence. It was greater on me than I like to admit. I already told you about his battle against Eurocentric history, but that wasn't his only fight. He hated all establishment institutions, particularly anything *smug*, anything *vested*. He was raised a Catholic, but of course he turned against them. And he couldn't just set it all aside, like most lapsed Catholics. He wanted payback.' A car pulled up a little way down the street. Its doors opened and then closed again. Knox kept an ear cocked as Franklin talked, wondering if Nergadze could somehow have tracked him here. 'He became obsessed by the *absurdity* of belief. Mocking religion was one of his favourite pastimes. That was one reason he was so fascinated by Eleusis. All these brilliant Greeks convinced they'd encountered something numinous and transcendent here: he was sure if he could find out what it was, he could take the mystique out of it, and so debunk belief.'

'And?'

'He'd originally written the paper while lecturing in France, but the journals wouldn't deal with him any more, he was simply too difficult.' He reached forward, tapped off some ash. 'But they *would* deal with me, so I submitted his paper instead. It was rather mischievous, I'm afraid, but then I was in the mood for mischief. It attributed the Greek Mysteries, indeed pretty much all established western religion, to something called ergot.'

'Ergot?' frowned Knox.

'A naturally-occurring parasitic fungus you sometimes find on grasses and grains,' explained Franklin. 'But, more pertinently for our case, a precursor of lysergic acid diethylamide.'

'You don't mean . . .'

'Yes,' smiled Franklin. 'LSD.'

II

A shock of smelling salts beneath her nose startled Nadya back to consciousness. She tried to open her eyes, but they seemed to be glued shut, leaving her reliant instead on the sensations flooding in from all across her body. She was sitting in a hard chair, her ankles tied to the legs and her wrists to the struts behind her back, the knots pulled so tight that her fingers and toes were tingling, and stress was building uncomfortably in her joints. A rope gag cut into her lips and gums. She had a crick in her neck. Panic welled suddenly in her; she began struggling and trying to kick out.

'Calm down,' grunted a man in Georgian. 'How can I loosen these damned things if you won't keep still?'

She breathed in deep through her nose, forced herself to stop fighting. There'd be time for that.

'That's better,' said the man, as he picked at the knots and then removed the gag. 'Scream if you want to. No one will hear, and I'll just put it back in.'

She licked the edges of her sore lips, worked her jaw this way and that. 'I won't scream,' she assured him.

'Good.' He picked his fingers at the tape over her eyes next, then pulled it off in one go, leaving her eyebrows raw and stinging. She blinked several times as her vision adjusted. There was no one in front of her, just a plush double bed with a red chintz cover and, on its far side, a mahogany dressing table with a triple mirror on which stood a bottle of water and two glasses, a bowl of *pot pourri*, a vase of carved and painted wooden lilies.

She glimpsed movement in one of the mirrors. A door opened and then closed behind her, leaving her with the impression she was alone. She craned her head as far as she could, saw an *en suite* bathroom to her right, French windows to her left, a gap between the curtains through which she glimpsed the iron railings of a balcony, pollarded trees and a night sky unsullied by city lights. Outside Athens, then; presumably in Mikhail Nergadze's house. She remembered Sokratis gloating about how remote it was, how *vast*.

The door opened and closed again behind her. She heard breathing. Her heart began hammering. 'Who's there?' she asked.

But she already knew.

III

Nico was sleeping on his side when the attack started, a malevolent demon reaching down his throat into his chest, taking hold of his heart and wrenching it sideways. He cried out and fell onto his back, clawing at his bedside table, searching blindly for the pills upon it, the glass of water; but the demon was too strong for him, a wrestler pinning him to the mat, pummelling at his heart. Another jolt ran through him. He arched silently. A sudden memory of his finest hour, a fifteen-year-old at the national weightlifting championships in Athens, a boy taking on men and yet not backing down; and that moment conflated with the reaction to Knox's talk earlier that day, that gratifying moment of silence before the applause started, all that glorious applause, a whole auditorium on the rise.

The vision faded. He slumped with exhaustion. One crowded hour of glorious life; that was all he'd ever wanted. What wouldn't he give now for an age without a name? Minutes passed. His sweat cooled and chilled. His heart settled back into its proper rhythm. The tunnel receded.

Not this time. Not this time. But soon.

He sighed and swung his legs to the side of the bed, sat up and buried his face in his hands. Living alone as he did, the *squalor* of death preoccupied him. The thought of being found like poor Antonius . . . it was almost worse than death itself. He needed someone in his life who loved him, someone who could check up on him, perhaps even be there when the time came. It wasn't a burden he could lay upon any of his friends or colleagues, nor even upon his brother and Charissa. Burdens like that, you could only ask of parents or spouse or children. And he was unmarried, childless.

He lay back on his bed and resolved to make the call in the morning, But it was a resolution he'd made a hundred times before, and still he was alone.

TWENTY-SEVEN

I

Mikhail Nergadze unwrapped a butterscotch as he came into Nadya's line of sight, popping it into his mouth, discarding the scrunched-up foil onto the carpet. He sucked hard twice to flood his mouth with the sweet sticky saliva, before pushing it to one side with his tongue, the better to talk. He was holding her purse, she saw, and now he opened it up, pulling the credit cards out of their sleeves one-by-one, examining them for a moment, then pushing them back in. 'Nadya Ludmilla Petrova,' he said. 'How I hoped it would be you. When I heard that a woman called Nadya was after me, a woman with a limp.'

There was no way for Nadya to know how much he knew about her. Best to assume he knew nothing, lest she give him anything for free. 'After you?' she asked. 'What are you talking about? Who are you?'

'It's a real honour for me, this. I mean that sincerely. I'm one of your biggest fans. I've been living in America these past few years, you see. They think Georgia is where the Atlanta Braves play baseball. So I've been *starved* of home news. I used to read your blog avidly.' He waved his hand. 'Everyone else, all the so-called *serious* media, they merely reprint the official press releases then go off for their long lunches. But not you. Typical, isn't it? The only Georgian with the balls to tell it as it is, and she's a woman.'

'What do you want with me?'

'You know what I want, Nadya. I want to know why you've made it your business to interfere with my business. I want to know why you hired a detective to wait outside the airport for my family plane last night, then follow my guests to my house. I want to know why you tailed us out to Eleusis earlier, and why you interfered with my effort to talk with Daniel Knox. And please don't bother to deny it. Your detective called me earlier and volunteered everything. You really should pick your help more carefully next time.'

That damned Sokratis! She should have known he'd betray her. She tried to recall how much he'd have heard and could have passed on. 'Investigating campaigns is what I do,' she said. 'You must know that, if you read my blog.'

'And what do I have to do with any campaign?'

'I'm not here because of you. I'm here because of a man called Boris Dekanosidze. He's one of Ilya Nergadze's most important advisers, you know.'

'Is he now?' laughed Mikhail. 'Very well, then. Why are you after him?'

'Because the first thing you learn in this business is that you never get scoops from following the candidates; they're too well protected. It's always the right-hand men who lead you to the real story.'

'Ah! The secret of your success!' he mocked. 'The herd trails haplessly after the leaders; but you go after the consigliore?'

'It led me to you, didn't it?'

'And why should you consider that a result? Why should you think *I* matter?'

Nadya blinked at her own impetuosity. She needed to be sharper than that if she was to get out of this. 'I'm still working on that.'

'You're lying,' said Mikhail. 'You know exactly who I am. You knew before you flew out here. In fact, you flew here looking for me.'

'I assure you I –'

'Don't lie to me, Nadya. You'll regret it if you do.'

'I'm not lying,' she said. 'It's the truth. I needed something good on Ilya Nergadze. Something juicy.

My readers were starting to accuse me of being in the tank for him.'

'It was that press conference, wasn't it?' asked Mikhail. 'The way you looked at me, I knew we must have met before. I just couldn't place you. It was only when we picked you up earlier that I was sure.' He stood tall again. 'How unlucky can a man be? Back in Georgia for two days, and I run into one of my widows.'

'One of your widows!' Despite her predicament, his callousness shocked her out of her pretence. 'What kind of monster are you? What had Albert ever done to you?'

'Don't you know?' answered Mikhail. 'He stuck his nose into our family business. We had to flee to Cyprus because of him.'

'But he had nothing to do with that,' she protested. 'It was the Americans.'

'The Americans!' said Mikhail contemptuously. 'And just who do you think told them? Unfortunately for your husband, one of the people at Justice was on our payroll.' He shook his head at the ways of the universe. 'We needed him silenced; we needed him punished. I was in Cyprus at the time, the only one of the family not under twenty-four hour surveillance, so my grandfather asked me home. I'm good at that kind of thing.'

'You shit!' she spat.

'Now, now,' he smiled. 'This is scarcely the time

to be hurling insults, is it? I don't kill unless I have to. Not people I admire, at least. And I do admire you, Nadya. So I wouldn't do anything to jeopardise that if I were you.' He walked around her, as though assessing her. 'Tell me something,' he said. 'Are you left or right-handed?'

'What?'

He produced a pair of pliers from his pocket. 'I'm asking for your own good,' he said, when she didn't answer. 'No? Very well. You're wearing your watch on your left wrist, so I'm going to assume you're right-handed. Do tell me if I'm wrong.' He took her left thumb, wrenched it away from her fingers, pinched it between the pliers' blunt jaws.

'Don't!' begged Nadya, twisting in her chair. 'Please!'

He didn't listen, he began to squeeze. She braced herself and closed her eyes, as though that could help; but she couldn't close her ears to the crunch of bone and the sickening liquid noise of crushed and twisted gristle. Then the pain came at her, spikes being hammered up her arm, making her arch and twist in the chair, shrieking and shrieking because shrieking was all she could do until finally she was over the hump of it and coasting down the other side, the pain still exquisite and intense but now at least lessening and manageable again, capable of being contained. She glanced down at her hand, she couldn't help herself. Her knuckle was a gruesome mangled pulp, already turning purple and black, the nail bulging from the pressure of blood beneath, a red crescent around its edge. She knew with certainty that she'd never be able to use it properly again.

Mikhail crouched down again in front of her, hands upon his knees, and regarded her with curiosity, a zoologist encountering some unfamiliar species. He took a handkerchief from his pocket and dabbed her eyes. He smiled almost sympathetically as he took her left index finger.

'Please,' she sobbed, as the fear engulfed her. 'I'll do anything, I swear I will. Just tell me what you want.'

Mikhail frowned, a little disappointed at her obtuseness. 'I want to hurt you,' he said.

II

'You must have heard the theories,' said Franklin. 'Why would people as sophisticated as Sophocles and Aristotle be so enraptured by the Mysteries, unless they'd experienced something truly transcendent? And what's the simplest explanation? Some ravishing *coup de theatre*? Some exquisite philosophical insight that has eluded us ever since? Or a generous dollop of acid in the drink? After all, one of the few things we know about Eleusis is that celebrants drank a barley brew called *kykeon*. Ergot grows on barley, and LSD is made from ergot. And it wouldn't be the only time that drugs were used as a way to experience the divine. The Hindu soma, for example. Peyote in Mexico. Cannabis in Germany.'

'The blue lotus in Egypt.'

'Exactly. The Aztecs called psilocybin mushrooms *teonanacatl*, which literally means flesh of the gods. The Greeks had the same conceit. Mushrooms were Zeus's plant because they so often spring up after thunderstorms. It's the rain, of course, but many people believed that they were a product of lightning strikes.' A man and a woman walked past the window at that moment, arms around each others' shoulders, looking at each other as they talked, rather than at the pavement. 'Zeus was the god of lightning,' continued Franklin, 'therefore mushrooms were his plant. And if you eat magic mushrooms, you certainly get a glimpse of extraordinary things. Petitier used to claim that the Catholic Eucharist was originally just *amanita muscaria* – those red-and-white capped mushrooms, you know.'

'The fly agaric,' said Knox.

'Exactly. There's plenty of evidence that they were held sacred by the early church. Those wonderful mushroom frescoes in Plaincourault and elsewhere, for example. Think of it: the body of Christ an hallucinogenic mushroom.'

'I begin to see why you and Petitier ran into problems,' said Knox.

'There are more serious problems with the theory than that it trod on toes, unfortunately,' said Franklin. He took a final puff of his cheroot, stubbed it out in the glass ashtray, tiny embers scattering. 'Ergot doesn't grow with any dependability, for one thing, and rarely in the kind of quantities they'd have needed. Extracting LSD is complex and precarious. Experiences would have been decidedly mixed. Some celebrants would have got sick or even died; others wouldn't have noticed anything at all. Besides, the Greeks were intimately familiar with drugs and their effects. They mixed their wine with all kinds of potent herbs. They used hemp and opiates regularly. Is it likely that so many highly intelligent and experienced people could have got stoned without realising it? And if they *had* realised it, would they truly have considered it the great numinous centrepiece of their lives?'

'Opiates and hemp give very different experiences than LSD,' said Knox.

'You sound just like Petitier,' smiled Franklin. 'He was certain he'd found the answer. As far as he was concerned, there was only one question to answer: how they prepared the potion with the technology available to them.'

Knox pushed to his feet and took both their glasses back to the drinks cabinet for a refill. 'Don't tell me,' he said, returning to the chairs. 'That's why you were really in trouble? You and Petitier searching for the secret of *kykeon*?'

Franklin shrugged acknowledgement as he took back his glass. 'We tried everything you could imagine. LSD, LSA, LSM and other such derivatives of ergot, all mixed up with opiates, marijuana, magic mushrooms and lord knows what else. We convinced ourselves it was serious and bold academic research. That we were pioneers!' He threw back his head and laughed heartily. 'We'd write up notes afterwards. Petitier insisted on that. It was utter gibberish, of course. We were kidding ourselves. The truth is, we were young men having fun. Too much fun.'

'Too much?'

He raised his glass in a wry toast. 'I began craving it every night. LSD isn't addictive; nor is hemp. But others of our ingredients were. My left hand began to tremble. I could feel my concentration wavering. I lost interest in things that had once compelled me. I was aware of all this, but I didn't know what to do about it.' He lifted his eyes to the ceiling. 'That was when I met Maria. It's one of the reasons I fell for her so hard, I suspect. Self-preservation. She was my lifeboat.' His expression softened, his gaze lengthened. 'Have

you someone like that in your life? Someone who
makes you want to do absurd things for them?'

'Yes,' said Knox.

'Keep good hold of them.'

'I intend to.' He put down his glass. 'So you
met your wife-to-be and stopped taking drugs.
What about Petitier? Presumably if your drug use
was known about, his was too.'

Franklin nodded. 'The French School couldn't
ignore it any longer, not after the scene he made
at the Evans lecture, because he was roaring
drunk at the time. And so he left. The irony is
that his ideas have since gained traction. I think
most people now accept that there was something
in the *kykeon*. For one thing, celebrants described
their experiences in such *physical* terms. They
talked about sweating, about getting the cramps.
They gave the impression that it was an *ordeal* as
much as it was an ecstasy. Take my word for it:
that's exactly like acid. It feels as though your soul
is being torn from your body. The heart of the
word intoxication is "toxic", after all; drugs are
poisons, only in smaller doses.'

'It must have been a hell of a shock for you
when Petitier reappeared,' said Knox. 'After all
that time trying to bury your misspent youth, I
mean.'

'Yes,' agreed Franklin. But there was something
in his tone that made Knox look curiously at him.

'Oh, it was a shock, all right,' insisted Franklin. 'It's just, I've been thinking a great deal about it recently, and perhaps it shouldn't have been.'

'How do you mean?'

'It's one of the hazards of being an archaeologist here in Greece that farmers and other landowners keep pestering you with the magnificent treasures they're certain are buried on their properties, which they'll happily sell you for a very reasonable sum.'

'We have them in Egypt too,' smiled Knox. 'Amazing how rarely they find anything exciting on good agricultural land.'

'Quite. It was part of Petitier's job to answer such letters. He used to bring some of them back to the house, to give us all a laugh. But he'd visit Crete quite often too, and check some of the more promising leads out. And then he came into some money, I remember. His grandmother died; he celebrated with champagne.'

'What a charmer,' said Knox. 'So you think one of these letters may have alerted him to a real Minoan site; and that he bought it with his inheritance?'

'It's possible, don't you think? After all, he'd pretty much burned his academic bridges here; no one else was likely to employ him. And it would have been just like him to sulk off into the wilderness, vowing never to return; or not until he could

331

prove himself right, at least, and all his critics wrong.'

III

Edouard paced back and forth downstairs, Nadya's screams jolting through him like electric shocks. He was a coward. He knew that for sure now. He'd always suspected it, of course, despite fond daydreams of himself as one of those quiet, understated men whose heroism only appeared at the hour of greatest need. But that hour was now, and his heroism was nowhere to be seen.

She shrieked again. His heart went out to her, as it would to any fellow human in such pain. How long could it go on? Her scream dissolved into sobs and pleas. He didn't know which was worse to listen to. But one thing was for sure: it was better to be down here listening, then up there, having it done to him.

Curiously, he'd shown a moment of boldness earlier; though of course that had been before the torture had started. After the delivery boy had brought the mobile phone, Mikhail had come inside and put it down on the arm of the settee, then forgotten about it. Edouard, frantic to do something for his family, had pocketed it and taken it to the loo, had sent his brother a text message asking for a contact number for his friend Viktor. He'd quickly grown fearful that Mikhail would notice the mobile was missing, however, so he'd hidden it down the side of the settee, where no one was likely to find it unless they looked, but where it could easily have fallen by accident.

The bedroom door opened. Zaal came out, leaned over the balcony. 'Oi!' he called out. 'Mister Nergadze wants a bottle of vodka and some glasses.'

Edouard looked at him sickly. 'You want me to go up there?'

'Unless you've got a teleporter.' The door closed again. Edouard went to the kitchen, pulled a new bottle from the freezer, found glasses in the cabinet. Another shriek pierced the air. He closed his eyes and waited for silence. *What had he become involved in?* There could be no excuse for this, no penance. It was an ineradicable stain upon his soul.

'About time,' grunted Zaal, when he took in the vodka. 'Thirsty work, this.'

'Put it on the dressing table,' said Mikhail.

He glanced at Nadya, he couldn't help himself. Her face was white, her cheeks glazed with tears, her jaw and chest with vomit. He caught the smell and saw her hand in the same moment, and the bile rose in his own throat, he dropped the glasses and the vodka and turned and sprinted back out onto the landing then to the nearest loo, but not quickly enough, the pale acidic mush spattering the floor and the seat and porcelain sides, his stomach cramping a second and then a third time. He felt it dribbling down his cheeks and chin, onto his clothes. He wiped his mouth with the back of his wrist.

There was laughter behind him. He turned to see Mikhail and Zaal in the doorway. 'Christ, that stinks,' said Mikhail.

He felt dizzy and weak, but he pushed himself up all the same. 'I'm not built for this kind of thing.'

'Clean this up. And yourself too.' He shook his head. 'You should have more self-respect.'

The vomiting had left Edouard weary, yet it had cleared his head and taken the edge off his fear too. He realised with an almost abstract curiosity that, for this moment at least, he felt unburdened by anxiety. *Was that all courage was?* he wondered. *The absence of fear?* He stood there a moment, half-expecting the sensation to pass, but it didn't. Almost as an experiment, he went downstairs to the kitchen for a bucket and mop, surreptitiously retrieved the mobile phone too. Back upstairs, he closed and locked the bathroom door, turned on both basin taps. A slight chill in his forehead, a tightness in his chest, a shiver rippling gently through him. His window was growing short. It was now or never.

He turned on the mobile, clasped it against his

chest to muffle its noises. His brother had replied
with a contact number. The mobile was pay-as-
you-go; it barely had enough credit for local calls,
let alone international ones. He knew his debit
card details by heart, however. He topped up the
account, punched in Viktor's number, ever more
aware of the risk he was taking. The Nergadzes
would find out about this eventually; and it was
a matter of pride with them that no one crossed
them and got away with it.

'This is Viktor,' said a man. 'Who's this?'

'Edouard Zdanevich,' whispered Edouard,
fearful of being overheard, despite the running taps.
'We met once at my brother Tamaz's house.'

'Yes,' said Viktor. He sounded wide awake, even
though it was well into the early hours in Georgia.
'He told me you might call. What can I do for
you?'

Edouard hesitated, uncertain how to start. 'It's
my wife and children,' he said. 'They're in danger.'

'You're calling me about your wife and children?'

'The Nergadzes have them,' murmured Edouard.
'They're using them as hostages.'

'Hostages? For what?'

Edouard could hear strange noises at the other
end of the line, clicks and humming and low
murmurs, hints of furious behind-the-scenes
activity, of people listening in, of others being

woken and briefed. He took a deep breath. 'I spoke to my wife this morning,' he began. 'She said they'd all been out horse-riding earlier with Ilya. Then she said that Kiko had been out riding before, with a man named Nicoloz Badridze.'

'I'm not with you.'

'Badridze was a child molester. My wife was trying to tell me that Ilya Nergadze is . . . doing things with my son.'

'They were out horse-riding, you say? That hardly sounds like molestation.'

'For god's sake!' he pleaded. 'You have to do something.'

'You think we can issue a warrant against a man like Nergadze on the basis of this? Are you mad?'

'You have to.'

'No we don't. We really don't.'

'But my son . . .'

'Then give me something concrete,' said Viktor. 'I know you can. You're on the inside; that's why I contacted you in the first place. With something concrete I can get a warrant. We can get your family out of there, and who knows what a search might turn up. But without anything concrete –' Nadya shrieked again, her cries loud enough for Viktor to hear, even over the running taps. 'What the hell was that?' he asked.

Edouard hesitated. Tell him what was going on

here, maybe he'd notify the Greeks and they'd send in the police. The Nergadzes would know instantly who'd blown the whistle, and his wife and children would pay dearly. 'They're watching movies downstairs,' he said.

'Oh,' said Viktor.

'You need cause for a warrant,' said Edouard. 'Fine. Then how about this. Sandro and Ilya Nergadze are right now destroying priceless artefacts that belong to the Georgian nation.' He described his earlier conversations with Sandro, the plan to melt down the Turkmeni cache to forge a golden fleece.

'And these pieces don't belong to the Nergadzes? You're sure of that?'

'They gave them to the nation in front of god-knows how many TV and press cameras. I've got the paperwork at the Museum, if you want to check.'

A click on the phone and a new voice came on. A woman. 'You'll testify to that?' she asked, a little groggy with sleep. 'Under oath?'

'Who is this?'

'Never mind that,' said Viktor. 'Just answer the question.'

'Yes,' said Edouard. 'I'll testify under oath.'

'Good,' said the woman. 'Then you can have your warrant.'

'Thank you,' said Viktor. 'Now listen to me,

Edouard. You're not to mention this to a soul, not even to your wife. You're not to do anything at all that might draw attention to yourself, or arouse suspicion. Not until we've acted. Not until you have my explicit clearance. Understood?'

'You're going in?' asked Edouard.

'Maybe.'

'When? When will you go in?'

'When we're ready.'

'What about my son? What about my –' But he was talking to a dead phone. He turned it off, put it away in his pocket. Just in time. He heard footsteps outside, then pounding on the door. He went to it, opened it a crack.

'Aren't you finished yet?' asked Zaal.

'Nearly done,' said Edouard.

'Mikhail says to get some sleep. We've an early start tomorrow.'

'Why? What's happened?'

'We broke her,' said Zaal proudly. 'You should have seen her. What a fucking mess. And it's all true. About the fleece, I mean. She just confirmed it. Knox has it, apparently. Even better, he's having breakfast with her in a few hours. Or so he thinks.' He gave a happy laugh. 'Poor sod! That's one appointment he's going to regret having made.'

TWENTY-EIGHT

I

Morning. Gaille woke to find Iain shaking her gently by her shoulder. 'Time to get up,' he murmured.

She sat up clutching the mouth of the sleeping bag, peered past him out the flap of the tent. The sun wasn't yet risen, but the surrounding hills had turned from black outlines to muted greens and greys. 'Already?' she asked.

'We need to get into the house.'

She waited until he'd gone back out, then climbed from the sleeping bag. It was cold enough that she hurried to pull on her trousers, blouse, socks and shoes. Her ankle was sore beneath the strapping, but it wasn't as bad as it might have been.

Iain was sitting with his feet dangling over the roof's edge, a coil of rope over his shoulder, a crowbar in his hand. He put a finger to his lips, then beckoned her over and pointed out the German shepherd asleep below. 'Look at its leash,' he whispered.

She rested her weight on her hands, leaned over the edge. The morning light was so milky that she had to squint. The dog's collar was attached by a black cord several metres long to a steel spike hammered into the ground near the front door, allowing it the freedom of movement to guard it as well as the sides of the house. She retreated a little way. 'So?' she murmured.

He held up the crowbar and the rope. 'I found these in an outhouse. We can use them to neutralise it.'

'It's a guard dog!' protested Gaille. 'It's only doing its job.'

'I'm not planning to brain it,' said Iain. 'Not unless I have to. The crowbar's for the front door. But first we have to get that damned hound out of the way.'

'How?' she asked.

Iain allowed himself a smile. 'That's where you come in,' he said.

II

Viktor stood in the forest fringes and stared through field-glasses down at Ilya Nergadze's castle. His mind was a little fried; he wasn't as young as he'd once been and all-nighters took their toll.

When he'd got his warrant just five hours earlier, he'd never imagined everything could be put together this quickly. But he'd underestimated the power of having a direct line to the presidential palace. He'd forgotten what special forces could do when they put their mind to it.

The castle looked impossibly romantic in the morning light, like something from a movie. Its drawbridge was up, and there was no sign of movement, except for the guards walking their rounds upon the battlements. Patches of mist lay in the little valleys in the meadows. There were wild swans on the lake and, somewhere, a hoopoe was calling. A more peaceful scene was hard to imagine.

Not for much longer.

There were techniques for taking down people as powerful as Ilya Nergadze. Humiliation was one. Film them doing something shameful, and they were politically finished. That had been his initial plan. Ilya's predilection for young boys was well-known, though getting footage was easier said than done. But Viktor's brief hadn't been merely to bring down Ilya. It had been to destroy his entire brood, their capacity for revenge. So he'd devised other approaches. They'd been ready to go for weeks. All he'd needed was the pretext.

Nikortsminda was the Nergadze's stronghold.

That made it their weakness too. They thought themselves safe here, impregnable. That was why, though the whole clan never all gathered together in Tbilisi, they often did here. And they saw themselves as above the law. The last time a policeman had come here uninvited, he'd been chased off with shotguns.

Viktor's ears had pricked up when he'd heard that.

Through his field-glasses, he could see tarpaulins on the battlements. Word was, they were gun emplacements arrayed to defend the castle from ground, lake or aerial assault. He hadn't been able to verify it, but he wouldn't put it past them. Such was the arrogance of the Nergadzes here in Nikortsminda; such was the arrogance he needed for his plan to come off. He felt flutters in his chest, exacerbated by the Kevlar vest beneath his shabby police uniform. 'Are the phones out yet?' he asked.

'On your command,' said Lev.

'And the mobile masts?'

'Like I said, on your command.'

'What about our teams?'

'They're all in place. Like they were five minutes ago.'

It was the speed with which this had been put together that worried him. In plans this rushed, it was all too easy to overlook something. In plans this rushed, you couldn't assemble overwhelming force, you had to rely on surprise – and he'd already missed the dawn. But election day was looming, and his boss was getting fretful. He took a deep breath. He'd joined the service out of a genuine desire to serve his country, not to make a career. But the life grew on you; you came to realise that nothing else would do. Fuck this up, and his career was toast. But make a success of it . . .

'Okay,' he said. 'Let's do it.'

III

Franklin had been generous enough to offer Knox a bed for the night; now he followed up by insisting on driving him to a nearby Metro station so that he could make his breakfast with Nadya. The train arrived just as he reached the platform; he had to squeeze into a crowded carriage, uncomfortably aware that he was still wearing yesterday's shirt.

He got off at Monistariki. A woman in unnecessarily high heels grabbed the escalator handrail in front of him and clung on like a first-time ice-skater. It was overcast when he emerged into the square; hawkers showed off their latest toys, while others spread out fake designer handbags and pirated DVDs on blankets. He glanced up at the white marble of the Parthenon, the camera flashes of early-bird sightseers giving off sparks like a glitter-ball. A boy blew bubbles that drifted on the light breeze, keeping Knox company as he walked along a narrow street of restaurants and shops. He found himself caught up with a Japanese tour party; they seemed to be heading towards his café, so he allowed himself to be swept along with them, fighting an urge to yawn. They emerged into a small square, most of the buildings showing patches of fresh paint: this was too important a tourist area for graffiti to be tolerated. Several mopeds were chained against the high wall to his right, the perimeter of some historic site. This whole area was studded with them. He and Gaille had already visited several during their –

He heard the man before he saw him, shouting into his mobile phone as he scanned the crowds, a hand clamped over his ear to block out the hubbub. The giant from yesterday, not a doubt of it, but he hadn't yet spotted him. Knox instinctively span on his heel and hurried away, his head ducked, his shoulders hunched, pushing his way through the tourists, praying his luck would hold. At the corner he risked a glance around. To his dismay, the giant was coming after him, bullying his way through the crowds, yelling into his phone. Knox broke instantly into a run, though it was impossible to move quickly through the narrow thronging streets.

He reached again the small square, saw two more of the Georgians from the day before converging from his right and from straight ahead. They saw him and shouted out to each other, forcing him to flee to his left, the only direction open to him, up a steep cobbled lane. A man was lopping branches from a tree with a petrol-powered chainsaw. For a mad moment, Knox considered wresting it from him and fighting a desperate rearguard until the police arrived; but the Georgians were too close behind him. And now he saw yet another of them striding purpose-fully towards him. There was a narrow alley to his right. At least it was empty of people, allowing him to break at last into a full-blooded sprint, put some distance between himself and the pursuit. The alley kinked so sharply right that his soles lost grip on the polished cobbles, and he crashed hard into the facing wall, falling onto the ground and scraping his palms, picking himself instantly up and running on.

The alley kinked again; he slowed a little to take this corner, keeping his eyes down to make sure of footing. But when he looked up again, a white van was parked immediately ahead of him, its rear doors open, blocking the full width of the alley. And then, even as he heard the Georgians running up the alley behind him, he saw Mikhail Nergadze leaning against the wall with his arms folded, looking distinctly pleased with himself at the ease with which he'd driven his lab rat here through this Athens maze.

IV

Viktor drove alone down to the castle in the battered, unmarked Lada he'd picked out from the pool. It was just the kind of car that a low-level policeman might own. He got into character as he drove: pompous, officious and stupid, just the kind of man to get under the skin of the Nergadzes. The drawbridge was up, but there was a wooden cabin this side of the moat, two guards on duty outside. One of them, his feet up on a low rattan table, was wearing a holstered handgun. The other was leaning against the cabin wall, a shotgun over his shoulder.

Viktor wound down his window. 'Police,' he said. 'I'm here to speak to Ilya Nergadze.'

'At this time of morning?' grunted the first guard, not bothering to put his feet down. 'You've got to be kidding.'

'No,' said Viktor. 'I'm not kidding.'

'Come back in a couple of hours. They had a late one last night.'

'I'm here on police business,' snapped Viktor. 'I demand to see Ilya Nergadze. Now.'

'Demand all you like,' said the guard. 'Won't make a damned bit of difference.'

Viktor got out of the Lada, slammed the door. 'Then please let him know I'm here. And that I have a warrant.'

'Fine,' sighed the guard. He got to his feet, went inside, held a brief conversation on the intercom, then came back out and sat down again.

Men appeared on the battlements, flaunting their weapons. Viktor leaned back from the waist so that his buttonhole camera could film them. You could never have too much footage. The drawbridge began to lower, evidently operated from inside. He expected the main gates to open too, but a smaller door inset in the foot of one of the turrets opened instead, and then Alexei Nergadze padded out, wearing only a pair of cut-off jeans, proudly showing off his paunch. 'Who the fuck are you?' he grunted, walking across the drawbridge.

'Police,' said Viktor.

'You're not from round here.' He'd brought a cup of coffee with him, was warming his hands around it. 'I know our local police.'

'I'm in the antiquities department,' said Viktor grandly. 'From Tbilisi.'

'Antiquities!' scoffed Alexei. 'You've got to be fucking kidding me. I didn't even know there was such a thing.'

'Well, now you do.'

'Couldn't hack it as a real cop, eh?'

'I am a real cop. What's more, I have a real warrant to search these premises.'

'Give it here, then,' said Alexei. 'We're running short of toilet paper.'

'This is not a joke, I assure you,' Viktor told him primly. 'We have reason to believe that you have valuable artefacts here; artefacts that belong to the nation of Georgia, and that are in danger of being destroyed.'

'You have to be out of your fucking mind,' said Alexei, his good humour all used up. 'Don't you know who we are?'

'You're a citizen of the Republic of Georgia, subject to its laws, just like the rest of us.'

'That's it! I've had enough of this! Get the fuck out of here.'

'I have a warrant,' said Viktor, barging past Alexei to the drawbridge. 'I'm conducting my search, whether you like it or not.'

'You're doing nothing of the fucking sort,' said Alexei, grabbing his shoulder and pulling him back. 'This is private property.'

'Assaulting an officer in the course of his duties,' said Viktor smugly. 'Alexei Nergadze, I arrest you on the –'

The head-butt caught Viktor completely by surprise. He found himself lying dazed and on his back nursing his nose, studying his hands for blood, while Alexei went over to the cabin, grabbed the shotgun from the guard, then came back to stand over Viktor. 'You were saying?' he asked, taking a sip of coffee.

There were many reasons why other careers had been spoiled for Viktor, but this was the biggest. This moment right here. In what other field would he have this kind of power over powerful men? He pressed the transmitter button on his chest. 'Officer down!' he cried. 'Back-up! Back-up! Back-up!'

V

'Here, doggie, doggie,' called out Gaille, standing well to the side of the house. 'Here, boy.'

The German shepherd opened one eye, then the other. It looked wearily at her for a moment, as though this wasn't how it wanted its day to start, but then duty called and it bounded to its feet and galloped towards her, so that even though she knew she was well out of its range, she jumped backwards all the same, sending a jolt through her ankle. The dog reached the end of its tether and jerked back, though not so violently as last night, as though it was learning. Then it rose up on its rear legs and made like it was one of the four horses of the apocalypse.

Behind its back, Iain appeared round the far side of the house. Using Gaille as a distraction, he crept forwards with his rope, tied a slipknot round the dog's leash where it met the metal spike, then retreated to a safe distance. Now it was his turn to make a rumpus. The dog turned and looked back and forth between him and Gaille, torn by choice. Iain took a couple of steps towards the front door, enough to provoke it into charging. He danced easily out of range, then pulled on his rope so that the slipknot ran all the way up the dog's leash until it was tight against its collar, effectively pinning it between himself and the spike, like a wild horse being broken by two cowboys with lassos. Iain now leaned back as though abseiling down a cliff, and stepped to his left, dragging the dog after him, until he'd reached an olive tree. He looped his rope twice around its trunk then tied another knot in it, trapping the dog impotently between its two leashes.

After that, getting through the front door was a breeze. The wooden jamb had rotted; it splintered quickly before Iain's crowbar. The door opened straight into a main room, its bare-cement floor covered by scattered worn rugs. There was a tattered armchair to their left by a shuttered window, a Mauser hunting rifle leaning against it, along with a box of shells, as though Petitier had liked to sit there and shoot any wildlife that came into view. The walls above it were haphazardly decorated with framed black-and-white photographs of what appeared to be the surrounding countryside and escarpment, while the back wall was given over entirely to shelving, crammed with books, folders and magazines, more books stacked upon the sturdy oak desk in the corner.

Iain sniffed the vinegary air. 'Fish and chips,' he said. 'A man after my own heart.'

She went to the desk to see what books Petitier had been reading before leaving for Athens. A dictionary of Minoan scripts. A treatise on the Phaistos disc, along with a replica of the disc itself, as though for reference. A book on vulcanology; a copy of Plato's *Timeaus*; an article on the Late Helladic in Akrotiri. 'Hey!' she grinned. 'Seems he was working on his own "Atlantis Connection".'

'How about that,' said Iain. He went to the shelves. Two ranges were crammed with leather-bound journals, dates in black marker pen upon their spines. He plucked down *Mai-Decembre 1995*, flipped through the creamy pages, turned to show her. There were entries on each page, written in some kind of code, blocks of five hieroglyphs at a time. 'You're the expert,' he said. 'Reckon you can crack it?'

Gaille shrugged. If it was a straightforward substitution cipher using English, French or Greek, it would only be a matter of time and effort; but

351

Petitier would have known that himself, and so might well have sought to make it harder. 'I'll give it a go,' she said.

There were three doors in the right-hand wall, all closed. The first led to the kitchen. Several plates were stacked neatly in a draining rack. There was cutlery in the drawers, well-used saucepans on a shelf, a basket of logs by the wood-fired oven. The fridge was off; when she opened it up, she found nothing inside but a bad smell. The larder, by contrast, was well stocked. A smoked ham was hanging from a ceiling hook, two fat sausages and a plucked game bird. There was a sealed tub of coffee, another with a freshly harvested honey-comb inside, dripping sweet gold. Earthenware jars and screw-top bottles on the shelves held olives and olive oil, garlic, tomatoes and tomato juice, sweet-corn, onions, beetroot and other pickled vegetables. A rack of unlabelled red and white wines stood on the floor between a small sack of grain and another of rice.

The second door led to a bedroom, a discoloured sheet over the thin double mattress, a couple of bare grey pillows from which tiny feathers were protruding, like white stubble. She got down onto her knees to look under the bed, thick with dust, like winter's first sprinkling of snow, while a boot lay on its side with a hole gaping in its rubber sole. The third door led to the bathroom, its sink yellowed with age, the cast-iron bath caked with grime, its plug-hole clotted with hair. There was a shower attachment too, but its head was rusted and the curtain was all bunched up at one end, while the wall behind it was black with mildew. She gave the loo a precautionary flush before she glanced into it, then threw open the window shutters and leaned out, grateful for the fresh air. Mercifully, the dog had stopped barking, perhaps realising the futility of its efforts, or merely worn out.

'What do you say to a division of labour?' suggested Iain. 'You check out this place, try to crack that code. I'll take the valley and the hills. After all, if he's found a Minoan site, it won't be in here. And with your ankle and all . . .'

'Makes sense,' agreed Gaille.

'Good,' said Iain, rubbing his hands in anticipation. 'Then let's rustle up some breakfast and go to it.'

TWENTY-NINE

I

Alexei Nergadze dropped his cup as he saw the armoured personnel carriers charge out of the forest fringes down the hillside towards the castle. He saw them but he couldn't take them in. It wasn't possible. Not here. No way could they have driven those vehicles up here without being spotted and reported by lookouts in the villages. Not unless they'd bypassed the villages with transport helicopters.

But that would mean . . .

He heard the chunter of distant rotor blades, turned to see a pair of white swans taking off from the lake, leaving their reflections on its rippled surface, and a moment later a formation of helicopters appeared over the woods on the far bank and sped low across the water, fanning out and

354

weaving as they grew close. This couldn't be happening. It couldn't be. But it *was*. Their shit-bag president had decided to pre-empt the elections. And he, Alexei, had just given them their excuse. He looked with utter hatred down at the antiquities policeman lying at his feet. 'You're dead,' he told him. He pressed the stock of the shotgun into his shoulder and aimed down at the man's face. 'You're fucking dead.'

He didn't hear the sniper's bullet that killed him, supersonic as it was. His shotgun clattered to the ground. A moment later, he'd joined it.

II

An empty water bottle in the back of the van rolled back and forth across the floor each time they took a corner. The noise got on Edouard's nerves, but he didn't stamp on it or pick it up, because looking at it gave him an excuse not to look at Knox, lying there balled up, his wrists bound behind his back, a roll of duct-tape making a merman of his legs. His mouth was taped too, and he was breathing fast and hard through his nose, as though suffering a panic attack.

They passed through Kifissia out into the open country. Gravel crunched beneath their wheels as they turned up Mikhail's drive, then stopped outside the house. Davit came around to open the rear doors, not meeting Edouard's eyes, as though he felt just as ashamed, but didn't want to acknowledge it. He picked Knox up, slung him easily over his shoulder, then carried him inside and dropped him on the front of the settee, so that he spilled onto the floor.

Nadya was still cuffed to a downstairs radiator, just as they'd left her. 'I'm so sorry,' she wept, when she saw Knox. 'I'm so sorry.'

He paled when he saw her pulped hand. He shook his head, perhaps to tell her that it wasn't her fault; perhaps to deny the brutal reality that faced him.

Mikhail sat on the settee and smiled politely down at Knox, a surgeon meeting his next case. He ripped the tape free from Knox's mouth, scrunched it up into a ball that he tossed aside. 'I wanted you to see your friend Nadya,' he said. 'I wanted you to know she'd betrayed you. It's okay, you understand, to betray things. Unless you want to tell her differently.' Mikhail had been through Knox's pockets on the drive here. He held up his mobile phone, the photo Gaille had sent him on its display. Then he opened the red-leatherette box and showed everyone the ring inside. 'Planning to pop the question, are you?'

'Those are mine,' said Knox. 'Give them back.'

'Or perhaps you already have, and she said no.'

'Fuck you.'

'I wouldn't blame her for saying no, if this is the best you can afford. I bet that's why she fucked off to this Agia Georgio place. Or maybe she's got a hankering for a new man. I enjoyed our little tussle in the lift. I think she did too.'

'She thought you were a creep.'

Mikhail's expression tightened. He set the mobile and ring-box down on the glass table, picked up the pliers instead. 'You and I are going to spend a little quality time together now,' he said. 'If you're disrespectful to me, if you hold out on me, if you cause me excessive trouble, it won't only be you who pays. Your girlfriend will too. I'll make sure of it.'

'There's no need for this,' said Knox. 'Whatever you want, just ask.'

'What a hero! No wonder she said no.' He leaned closer. 'She'll say yes to me, all right. I bet she's already thinking about it.' With the sole of his boot, he pushed Knox onto his front, so that he could get at his hands. Then he separated his left thumb from his other fingers and took it between the jaws of his pliers. Knox braced himself for the pain, he cried out in anticipation.

It was too much for Edouard to bear. 'No!' he blurted out.

Mikhail turned and drilled Edouard with his gaze. 'I beg your pardon.'

'Think about it,' said Edouard, switching to

Georgian, lest Mikhail think he was coaching Knox on his interrogation. 'Imagine you're right about all this, I mean that this guy and his friend really stole the fleece and hid it at the airport. What if they don't have lockers? What if they have one of those left luggage places where you have to hand your stuff in then show some ID to get it back?' He nodded at Nadya. 'How will it look if his hand's like that? You know what security's like in airports these days. They'll be onto us in no time.'

Mikhail stared hard at him, trying to read the intent behind the words. But then a happy thought evidently struck him, for he smiled. 'Very well,' he said. 'I know just the thing.'

III

Nina Zdanevich had barricaded herself and her three children into her room the night before, pushing her chest of drawers across her door in case anyone tried to pay a midnight visit. But no one had. She was heaving it back into its proper place when she heard gunfire on the battlements. The Nergadzes and their friends taking pot shots at the birds upon the lake, no doubt. They liked to shoot things, the Nergadzes, particularly things that couldn't shoot back.

But this time they did shoot back.

Electrified, she rushed to the window. It wasn't easy to see, because her room looked out along the line of lake's bank, and everything was happening either to her left or to her right; but she could see a helicopter approaching so low over the water that its blades were ruffling its surface, and from the other direction armoured jeeps zigzagging down the slopes, making difficult targets of themselves. It took her a moment to understand what was going on. Because nothing had happened until now, she'd thought her husband had failed her. But he hadn't failed her. By God, he hadn't.

'What's going on?' asked Kiko.

She was about to tell him and the girls something reassuring when machine guns ripped out a different answer, and helicopters thundered over the castle walls. She heard a soft thump and some unknown instinct must have recognised it from television, for she shrieked and turned and spread her arms to protect her children, just a millisecond before she felt the explosion pulse out from the castle wall, then the window blew out and sprayed glass like shrapnel across the room, dust and plaster falling on them like soft rain; while paintings fell from the walls and slammed into the floor, their frames shattering.

'Over here,' she cried, running to the wall. 'Get down.'

Her children did as she ordered, bless them. She

grabbed the mattress off the bed and hauled it over them, began murmuring prayers that they all knew, holding each others' hands in the darkness. A boot slammed against their door and it flew open. She risked a peek. A man with an AK-47 ran to the window, knelt and fired off a succession of short bursts before his fire was finally and emphatically returned, rounds spattering the walls and ceiling, ricochets whining against the mattress. He dropped his gun and clamped both hands to his neck. The blood seeped through all the same. He caught her eye as he turned and ran, and they shared a human moment, bafflement and fear.

The bullets kept on coming. Kiko was crying, Eliso and Lila were shivering and pale. They couldn't stay here. The gunfire eased a moment. 'Follow me,' she cried. 'Keep your heads down.' She crouched as she led them into the corridor, a chain of held-hands. It was chaos outside, people running from their rooms, half of them still in their nightclothes, all fleeing in different directions, bumping into each other, no one sure what was happening or what to do. Another loud explosion; the windows overlooking the courtyard blew in, covering the floors with glinting shards. She looked down at her children's bare feet. 'Careful,' she said, sticking close to the interior wall. 'Tread where I tread.'

She saw through a window onto the courtyard

the shattered wooden gates hanging on their hinges, armoured vehicles driving over the drawbridge and into the castle. A helicopter set down in the court-yard, soldiers bulked up with bullet-proof vests charged out and took positions. Other helicopters hovered low overhead, shooting at the battlements. People began coming out of doors, arms raised in surrender, then lying face down on the ground while soldiers bound their wrists with flexi-cuffs. That was where she wanted to be, as near to safety as you got in situations like this. She reached the turret, set off down the spiral steps, met a man coming the other way, a rocket-launcher on his shoulder, his face exultant with battle fury. She reached the ground floor, stopped and looked out. Gunfire banged, splinters of stone flew. 'I'm with children!' she cried. The shooting stopped. She looked out again. A kneeling soldier in a flak jacket beckoned to her. She put up her hands and went out, her children following. The soldier pointed her to the grass, motioned for them to lie down. Kiko was wailing and crying; the girls were whey-faced, unsteady on their legs. But they did as they were told. Nina put her arms around them, protecting and comforting them as best she could. The gunfire went on and on, the crump of flash grenades, the yelling of soldiers living on their nerves; but suddenly it began to die away, and just like that it stopped.

Different noises now. Softer. Men whimpering and crying out, women sobbing, horses whinnying and crashing hooves against their stalls. People began emerging from the buildings, important people, people she recognised from the television, who she hadn't even realised were guests here. There was a look in their eyes, as though they realised how little their wealth and status counted for right now. Ilya Nergadze himself was led out to a prison van. For a moment, Nina exulted, she even contemplated shouting something triumphant; but then she saw the murderous rage upon his face, and looked away at once, praying he hadn't seen her.

A man in a shabby black police uniform walked across the grass towards her, holding a blood-stained handkerchief to his nose. He looked like nothing, except for the way everyone deferred to him. 'You must be Nina,' he said, his bloodied nose making him sound as though he had a cold. He squatted down and ruffled Kiko's hair. 'And you must be Kiko.'

'Yes,' said Kiko, wiping his nose and then his eyes. 'Who are you?'

'My name is Viktor,' he said. 'I'm a friend of your father's.'

'He called you?' asked Nina.

'Yes. He called me.'

'All this?' she asked, bewildered. 'Just because he called you?'

Viktor laughed. 'Let's say he gave us an excuse.'
He stood to his full height once more. 'Speaking
of which, I don't suppose any of you know about
some gold being melted down, do you?'

IV

Knox didn't know what the man had said to
save him from the pliers, but he was grateful, that
was for sure. But then Mikhail smiled and barked
out orders in Georgian, and the tame giant went
outside and returned with a garden bench, its
varnish sweating from a recent shower. 'Put him
on it,' said Mikhail, switching to English, presumably because he wanted Knox to know what he
was up to. 'Strap him down tight. I don't want
him moving.'

Knox tried to fight, but it was hopeless, bound
hand and foot as he was. The giant mummified him
with duct tape, pinioning him to the bench, his
wrists still tied behind him, jabbing uncomfortably
into the small of his back. Mikhail walked unhurriedly away. Knox could hear him on the stairs.
He came down a minute later holding a leather gag.
Knox held out as long as he could, clenching his
jaw tight, turning his face to the side, breathing
through his nose, but Mikhail simply pinched his
nostrils together and waited until he ran out of air,

then shoved in the leather bit, clasped it behind his head and tightened it until the strap gouged Knox's lips and gums. Then he tightened it a little further, just because he could.

'Let me go,' pleaded Knox. But the gag made mush of his words.

'Fetch me a towel, please, Davit,' said Mikhail.

'What kind of towel, sir?'

'A hand-towel. Not too big.'

'Yes, sir.' He fetched a green one from a downstairs bathroom. 'Will this do, sir?' he asked.

'Perfect, thank you, Davit,' said Mikhail. He leaned closer to Knox, the better to confide. 'All that talk of enhanced interrogation techniques while I was in the States. It makes a man curious.' He folded the towel in half and placed it over Knox's face. The fabric itched his skin. With it over his eyes, he could see nothing but the material itself, glowing faintly from the sun. Footsteps walked away from him, kitchen closets opened and closed. There was a jangling, as though someone had pulled out a nested set of saucepans, and rested them on the counter. A tap was turned on. Water sprayed on metal, a loud initial drumming that gradually quietened and deepened. Some vessel being filled, a large saucepan or a casserole dish, to judge from the time it took. The procedure was repeated with a second pan. Then the footsteps came back over.

Knox had heard about water-boarding, of course, but he hadn't paid attention to the details, had never imagined it might happen to him. He didn't know, therefore, the mechanics of it, or how to resist.

'Lift his feet,' said Mikhail. 'They need to be above his head.'

The far end of the bench was picked up and held about a foot off the ground. It was an uncomfortable sensation in itself, blood flowing towards his head; but it was nothing to his fear of what was coming next. He took and held a deep breath just before the first saucepan was tipped over the towel. Most of it splashed away, but plenty more soaked through the towel into his mouth, held open by the bit, and trickled down into his throat. He had to fight the urge to cough.

'He's holding his breath,' observed Mikhail.

A fist smashed into Knox's solar plexus, knocking the wind out of him. He heaved for air just as the second saucepan was tipped out, and so he breathed in water, triggering his gag reflex, making him buck and convulse, his whole body arching as it dedicated itself to the single ambition of air. He choked out as much water as he could, sucked in again, got only towel and more water. He couldn't breathe. He couldn't breathe. The necessity of air was extraordinary, like nothing he'd ever felt before, utterly terrifying, he tried to kick and flail, he hurled himself sideways so violently that his shoulder almost dislocated from its joint, but still he had no air, his head was pounding crazily, his heart was bucking and kicking, and he could feel the blackness coming; and it was a relief when it pulled over him like a shroud, and he was gone.

THIRTY

I

A furious barking accompanied Iain's departure, but the German shepherd must have realised its impotence, for the fury was soon replaced by a self-pitying snuffling that distracted Gaille from her efforts to decipher Petitier's code. She went to the door, stood there watching indecisively from the shadows. There was enough slack between the two leashes to allow the dog a little movement. It began to turn in circles, so that she worried it might choke itself; but it stopped in time and went the other way, unwinding itself. A fly buzzed by Gaille's ear; she flapped it away. The movement caught the dog's eye. Instantly, its whimpers turned back to yowls of fury, it started straining at the rope, trying to get at her.

She fought her instinct to retreat indoors, lest

it think it had won a victory. Instead, she took a couple of steps outside into the pleasant freshness of the morning. Sunlight glinted on a pair of steel bowls by the door, presumably food and water for the dog, empty except for a few caked-on scabs; and next to them was what looked like the thigh-bone of a goat or sheep, gnawed bare of meat. She felt a swell of irritation at Petitier, that responsibility for his wretched dog should fall onto her. But fall on her it had. And suddenly she noticed how *thin* the German shepherd was, its ribs showing, its coat patchy and speckled with sores and scabs where he – it was a he, Gaille now saw – had scratched himself against the stone walls. And he was slightly favouring his left hind leg too. And despite his still furious barking, her heart went out to him.

They hadn't finished their *conchiglie* in tomato sauce the night before. She fetched the leavings down from the roof, scraped them into one of the bowls, refreshed them with some water, then added slivers of ham from the joint hanging in the pantry. Then she filled the second bowl with water and took them both out. He raged to see her, hurled himself so violently towards her that she couldn't help but jump back and splash water over her leg. 'You stupid fucking dog!' she cried. 'I'm only trying to feed you.'

But he continued to snarl until she shrugged her

shoulders and took the bowls back inside. The barking stopped at once, the whimpering resumed. She gave a wail of exasperation and went back out. This time she defied his barking to set both bowls down on the ground as near to him as she dared. Then she went back inside and fetched the Mauser and held it by its barrel and pushed the bowls with its stock close enough to him that he could feed. He didn't even look at them, not while she was there, just continued to rage, so she returned inside and replaced the Mauser and picked her notebook once more, tried to focus on the journals.

She strongly suspected a simple substitution cipher. Petitier would surely have wanted to be able to consult them without going through elaborate decipherment every time. People who devised their own ciphers were often so familiar with them that they could read them almost as easily as though they were in plain text. No code could hope to defeat sophisticated modern decipherment techniques anyway, so all he'd have hoped to do was confound a casual visitor – and a substitution cipher would have been plenty for that.

The trick with cracking such ciphers was to find repeating sequences of symbols, which would indicate the same original word. It wasn't long before she'd identified several of these, enabling her to take some guesses at what those words might be, then applying the letters she'd broken back to the journals. But though she tried in a variety of languages, all she got was gibberish. She put it aside for the moment, took a different tack, totting up all the different symbols he'd used, hoping to discover at least what alphabet the deciphered text was in. The Greek alphabet had twenty-four symbols, for example, as opposed to the standard twenty-six of the Roman or the twenty-eight of the Arabic. But she quickly counted forty-two different symbols, suggesting his cipher included numerals and mathematical or grammatical symbols, as well as letters. She tried a third approach, noting down the relative frequency of each of the symbols and combinations of symbols; but that didn't prove much help either, for she didn't know what language she was working in.

She put her pad down in frustration. There was silence outside. Or not silence, exactly. Her ears pricked up at the sound. She rose stealthily and tiptoed to the door. The dog had his muzzle deep in the bowl of pasta, and as she watched he threw back his head to gobble a mouthful down, and the glad squelching noises of his swallowing were a kind of music to her ears.

II

Knox's ribs and chest felt as bruised as he could ever remember. His stomach too, from the punch he'd taken. His heart felt worn as perished rubber, and his throat and nostrils were chafed raw, as though sand-papered from within. He turned to one side, spat out watery mucous that ran feebly past the gag and down the side of his mouth. Time was blurring, his mind was playing tricks. He wasn't sure how many sessions of this torture he'd already endured. Four? Five?

'Ah,' said Mikhail. 'Rejoined us, I see.' He was holding the hand-towel down by his side, still wet, but twisted in a gentle spiral, as though he'd just wrung it out.

Knox shivered with Pavlovian tremors. 'What do you want?' he asked. But the gag rendered it into an incomprehensible moan.

Mikhail flapped out the hand-towel and then folded it in half, ready to lay once more over Knox's face. 'Hold his head,' he told Davit.

'Please,' wept Knox. 'No more.'

'He's ready to talk,' said Davit.

'Lift his feet,' Mikhail told Zaal.

'Please,' said Knox. 'I beg you.'

Mikhail set the folded towel back over Knox's face, turning his world dark. His heart started racing, he could hear footsteps going round and around, deliberately building his apprehension. 'Do you know what the function of torture is, Zaal?' asked Mikhail.

'To get information, sir?'

'No,' said Mikhail. 'Information is the *fruit* of torture. It's not the function.'

'I'm not sure I understand, sir.'

'Mankind is self-aware, Zaal. It's what separates us from the animals. Our minds are distinct from our bodies, our thoughts from our words. If you like, we're each puppeteers pulling our own strings. During ordinary interrogations, that gap is still there, that distance between mind and body. It allows people like Mr Knox here to *consider* their answers, to say whatever they believe is to their greatest benefit. The function of torture is to eradicate that gap, so that the subject's thoughts are no longer distinct from their words.'

'To turn people back into animals?'

'Exactly, Zaal. Very well put. The trouble is, of course, that you need a certain level of pain to eradicate that gap; but people can't talk under that level of pain. It's not physically possible. You therefore have to relieve the pain to conduct the actual interrogation. And as soon as you relieve the pain, that gap can grow again, your subject regains a little control over their own strings. So the true purpose of torture is to eliminate that gap for good, and we do that with *dread*. Not suffering itself, but the anticipation of it. Watch.' Knox's feet began to rise, he heard the swill of water, he bucked and kicked and screamed. 'See,' said Mikhail. 'I'm not doing anything to him at all. All I'm doing is lifting up his feet. But right now he'll tell me just exactly what I want to know.' He removed the towel then reached behind Knox's head and loosened the gag. 'Won't you, Mr Knox?'

'Yes,' wept Knox.

'So what am I after?'

'The fleece. You want the golden fleece.'

'Because you have it, don't you?' And he folded the towel and made to place it over his face once more.

'Yes,' screamed Knox. 'I have it! I have it! I have it!'

'You see,' said Mikhail. '*That's* how torture works.'

III

Gaille had already given Petitier's journal code her best shot in French, English, German and Greek, both modern and ancient. But perhaps she should be trying other languages still. He was almost certain to have been an accomplished linguist: archaeologists had to be, not merely because they dealt so directly with ancient languages, but also because the important literature was still divided between English, German and French.

So what other languages had Petitier known? She went along his shelves. He had a couple of works in Italian, another in Spanish. She couldn't help but notice that many of the volumes were still in pristine jackets, and she recognised several that had only recently been published. Academic texts like these didn't come cheap. Along with the solar panels on the roof, and the well-provisioned pantry, it seemed that, whatever else had motivated Petitier to announce his discoveries to the world, it wasn't the need for money. She went back to her chair, but her mind was clouded with fatigue, and she knew she'd never make any real headway unless she cleared it first. She clenched and then splayed her hands fast fifteen times, an old student trick that unfortunately seemed to have lost its potency, so she went outside instead, to get some exercise and fresh air.

The German shepherd was having a snooze. That was something. She went around the side of the house, where a pen had been put up in a clearing, presumably for the dog when it wasn't on guard outside the front door. It was a wire cube some two metres square, ugly, uncomfortable and offering no shade at all, and its corners were filthy with dusty, dried-out stools, not cleaned for months.

She continued on around the back. There was a citrus grove there, with an outbuilding beyond it, and then a chicken run with a wooden hutch, out of earshot of the house. The birds clucked and jerked in alarm at her approach, all trying to hide behind each other. There were gutters on bricks for food and water, but they were empty. Her exasperation with Petitier grew stronger. The outhouse door gave a tormented squeal when she pulled it open. A long-handled broom, a spade, a fork and some other gardening tools were slouching against the left-hand wall, a sack of chicken-feed against the right. She grabbed handfuls from it that she tossed through the wire for them to peck at, then fetched a basin of water from the house. She let herself into the run, slopped the water into the trough, then retrieved eleven eggs from the hutch.

The greenhouses were next. The wooden framed door of the first dragged on the ground, as though unopened in weeks. It was murky inside from the dirty polythene, sweltering and pungent with rotting vegetation. There were parallel beds of rich dark soil either side of the central aisle, and raised plastic guttering above, with tiny holes pricked in them, from which to sprinkle water. She went a little way along the walkway, checking out the produce, congested and in serious need of attention. Tomatoes, potatoes, eggplants, sweet-corn, broccoli, pomegranates, peppers, cucumbers. More than Petitier could possibly have needed for himself and his menagerie; presumably he sold his surplus in Agia Georgio or Anapoli in exchange for supplies. She took enough for herself and Iain, was glad to re-emerge into fresh air.

The doorway of the second greenhouse was even more overgrown, an impenetrable tangle that made it hard for her to fight inside. But the interior was surprisingly well tended, far more so than the first. She walked down the aisle with mounting astonishment. The beds were filled with crocuses, poppies, marijuana and other exotic plants. And, at the far end, a miniature forest of hallucinogenic mushrooms: the distinctive red-and-white caps of *amanita muscaria*, the muted tans of psilocybin. She laughed out loud. *How about that? The man was a stoner.* She went back to the house. The dog had woken up. She hoped that she'd earned a little credit with the food and water she'd given him. Not a bit of it. If anything, they'd restored his strength and determination to defend his territory. He snarled and snapped and strained so hard for her that she feared one or other of his leashes would give way. *Fine*, she thought. *Be like that*. She stowed her eggs and vegetables away in the pantry, then settled once more to work on Petitier's journals.

IV

Mikhail was delighted to have broken Knox so cleanly, but when he looked around at Boris for commendation, all he saw was doubt instead. 'Yes?' he asked. 'Is there something you want to say?'

Boris pulled a face, apologising in advance for any potential offence. 'It's just, I was wondering, this man you talked about the night we arrived The professor. The one who'd seen the golden fleece for himself. The one who'd *touched* it. Remember?'

'Of course I remember. What about him?'

'Did he . . . I mean, did he tell you this *freely*? Or did you have to . . . you know?'

'What does that matter?' asked Mikhail. 'He wasn't lying, if that's what you're getting at. He told me the truth.'

'Yes, I'm sure, but how can you –'

'He was telling me the truth,' bridled Mikhail. 'Or are you questioning my judgement?'

'No, sir. Of course not.'

'Good.' The question had soured his mood, however. It was time to show these people that his judgement could be trusted. He looked down at Knox. 'Tell me how it happened,' he said. 'Start at the beginning.'

'It was all Augustin's idea,' said Knox urgently. 'I didn't want anything to do with it.'

'What was his idea?'

'Petitier came to him asking for help. He thought someone was after his fleece. But Augustin wanted to turn it in. I mean it's *history*, for Christ's sake. Petitier went crazy. They got into a fight. And then . . . you know. But he was only defending himself.'

'Is that what he told you?'

'He'd never have done something like that deliberately.'

'Sure!' snorted Mikhail. It always amazed him how trusting these sheep were. 'And what happened then?'

'He called me in my room. He was in a panic. I promised to help. We were due to collect his girlfriend from the airport, so we decided to make it look as though we'd left Petitier unharmed, that he'd been attacked and robbed *after* we'd left. We took the fleece into the airport before she arrived, stashed it in one of those airport lockers.'

'And the key?'

'We knew we were likely to be searched when we got back, so we buried it out there. There are hedges all around short-term parking. We meant to go back for it when everything had settled down, but Jesus!'

Mikhail sat back on the settee. It sounded plausible enough, except that Knox seemed a little too eager to be believed. He turned to Boris. 'What do you think?'

'I don't know. Maybe.'

'Davit?'

'Don't ask me, sir. Above my pay grade.'

'That's helpful.'

'Why don't we get him to describe the fleece to Edouard,' suggested Zaal. 'He should be able to tell us whether or not it sounds authentic.'

'Good thinking,' said Mikhail. He looked around the atrium and frowned. 'And just where exactly *is* our historian friend?' he asked.

THIRTY-ONE

I

Edouard had been fighting anxiety all morning, desperate to find out what had happened to Nina and the children, yet unable to make the call. But the moment attention had focused on Knox, he'd headed up to his room, closed the door, taken the mobile into his bathroom, turned on the shower. Then he'd called Viktor for news.

Four times he'd tried his number. Four times someone else had answered, told him that Viktor was unavailable, offered to get him to call back in due course. But Edouard couldn't wait for due course. And when he tried for the fifth time, he was finally put through.

'Hang on,' said Viktor. 'I've got someone here for you.'

'Edouard?' asked Nina. 'Is that you?'

'Nina, my darling!' he said, tears springing to his eyes. 'Are you all right? Are the children all right?'

'We're fine. We're all fine. Thanks to you.'

'What happened?'

'I've never seen anything like it,' she exulted. 'The Nergadzes are finished. Ilya and Sandro were driven off in a police van. A police van! We'll never have to fear them again.'

'No,' said Edouard.

'And we got your cache back too, your Turkmeni gold.' She gave a happy laugh. 'Actually we got *two* sets, because they'd already made copies of all the pieces, so that they could have substitutes ready when they melted down the originals; but they hadn't started yet.'

'That's wonderful news. And listen, if you ever tell me not to trust someone in future, I'll take that as –' Outside the bathroom door, a shoe scuffed on carpet. His heart seemed to stop.

'Edouard,' said Nina anxiously. 'What is it? What's going on?'

The door kicked open. Mikhail stood in its frame, his shotgun in both hands, the others standing behind him. Edouard clenched the mobile tight. 'I love you, Nina,' he told her.

'Edouard!' she screamed. '*Edouard*!'

'Tell the children I love them,' he told her. 'Tell them I was thinking of them.'

'Edouard!'

'Finish the call,' said Mikhail. Edouard nodded and complied. He couldn't let Nina hear this.

'Who was that?' asked Mikhail. 'Who were you talking to?'

'Your grandfather was abusing my son,' said Edouard. 'I had no choice.'

'Your son is dead,' Mikhail told him flatly. 'All your family are dead. You've just seen to that. I'm going to slit their throats one by one, and I'm going to reach inside and pull their fucking tongues out. Now tell me who you were talking to.'

To Edouard's surprise, the imminence of his own death didn't scare him as much as he'd always anticipated. 'You're finished,' he said, looking from one to the next. 'All of you, you're all finished. And I did it. *Me*. Edouard Zdanevich.' The muzzle of the shotgun erupted; he felt for the briefest moment the astonishing force of the impact upon his chest and throat, but then he was gone.

II

The dog kept nagging at Gaille's conscience like an unwritten thank-you note. She didn't know what to do about it. She took out a jug of water and some more slivers of ham. The sun was high and fierce upon her skin, making her wonder how it felt for the dog, who had no shade at all. He just stood there with his tongue lolling out, panting hard. At least he didn't fly into a fury with her this time, perhaps out of exhaustion, perhaps because he was as uncertain about their changing relationship as she was.

She couldn't reach his bowls without putting herself within his range, so she set down the plate of ham and the jug of water just out of his reach, hoping he didn't think she was teasing him with it. Then she went back inside for the gun, used the muzzle to hook the bowls and drag them towards her. The dog watched silently as she put a few slivers of ham in his bowl, not wanting to give him too much, for she didn't know what kind of diet he'd been on and didn't want to make him sick. She refilled his water bowl too, then pushed them both back.

The dog was hungry enough that he didn't wait for her to leave this time, he gobbled up the ham while she watched, his eyes flickering her way every so often, as though he knew he was doing something shameful. But gradually he seemed to come to accept her presence, and she got the sense that she could take it a step further. She took a deep breath and walked with baby steps towards him. She could see his sinews tauten beneath his fur, but he didn't move. She stepped into his range and then just stood there, daring him to do his worst.

He set himself as if about to spring; he growled and bared his fangs. But it was all rather half-hearted, and when she didn't back away, his eyes clouded. He looked away, pretending he'd lost interest in her, waiting to see what trick she'd pull. She stayed absolutely still, she did nothing. He turned and looked at her again, and his snarl was gone, his eyes were mournful and wet. She knew how wrong it was to project human feelings onto animals, but she sensed in him at that moment a great sorrow in himself, left here to guard this place, and failing. She crouched slowly, held out her hand. And, just like that, everything changed. His head down, his tail a lowered scimitar, he sniffed her and snuffled his wet muzzle into her palm. Then he abruptly turned away and went back to his bowls, began thirstily to lap up more water.

She went slowly to him, murmuring as she did so, so that he wouldn't consider her a threat. She stroked his head and back. His coat was mangy and covered with sores and scabs; his backside was enflamed and smeared with faeces. He ate the last of his ham, looked up from his empty bowl, not demanding or expecting more, but merely enquiring hopefully. She felt an unexpected stab of affection for him as she refilled his bowl, then she went to sit with her back against an orange tree and watched with satisfaction as he scoffed it up.

III

Mikhail watched Edouard's body hurl back against the wall and then slump sideways into the shower, taking the opalescent curtain down with him, smearing it scarlet. He felt spatters of blowback on his face and hands. He checked himself in the mirror above the sink then wiped the worst of it away.

On the floor, Edouard's mobile phone started to vibrate and turn in slow circles. The ringer had been turned off, but a call was coming in. Mikhail stooped to pick it up and answer it. 'Yes?' he asked.

'I want to speak to Edouard,' said a man.

'Too late.'

'Who is this?'

'I might ask you the same question.'

'Edouard is under my protection,' said the man. 'If anything should happen to –'

'Like I said: too late.' He ended the call, scrolled through the list of recently-dialled numbers. All of them to Georgia, none of them local. That was something. They probably still had time before the Greek police got here. He turned to Boris. 'Call my father at Nikortsminda. Let him know they may have trouble coming. Then call our pilot. Tell him to prepare for departure.' He checked his watch. 'In three hours from now. We need to collect the fleece first.'

'The fleece?' asked Boris. 'Are you serious? We don't have time for that now.'

'That fleece is the key to the election,' retorted Mikhail. 'The election is the key to us getting away with this.' He beckoned for them all to follow him out through the bedroom onto the landing. 'This house is going up,' he told Zaal. 'Grab everything that will burn. Sheets, beds, chairs, curtains, carpets, everything. Heap it all up beneath the landing. Davit, we need accelerants. There's a bag of barbecue charcoal outside. Bring it in. Check the cupboards for white spirit, gas, lighter fluid, anything that will flame. Siphon fuel from the cars if you have to.'

'Yes, sir.'

'What about our guests?' asked Boris, nodding at Nadya and Knox.

'We're taking Knox with us,' said Mikhail, dancing down the steps into the atrium. 'He knows where the fleece is.'

'And the woman?'

'Baggage,' said Mikhail. He broke open his shotgun, spitting out the two spent cartridges, savouring those pungent wisps of grey smoke, their combat smell. Then he strode across the floor towards her, stuffing in fresh cartridges as he went. She opened her mouth and shrieked, her lips making a perfect circle, like the red ring of a rifle target.

'Don't do it!' yelled Knox. 'I won't give you the fleece if you do, I swear I won't.'

'You'll give it to me,' said Mikhail.

'Kill her now, it's proof you'll kill me too. Why would I give you anything?'

'You want another go on the ducking stool, is that it?'

'Sure,' said Knox. 'Let's stay here until the police turn up. Or maybe you could bring your bench and bucket in the car.'

Mikhail hesitated. The man had a point.

'I can't get hold of your father,' said Boris. 'He's not answering his mobile.'

'Then try the castle.'

'I did. The lines are dead.'

Above him, on the landing, Zaal threw a great heap of bedclothes over the balustrades, gravity winnowing out the pillows and blankets from the white sheets that fluttered to the floor like wounded ghosts. For a moment Mikhail had a blink of childhood, standing above a girl's broken motionless body, knowing he'd gone too far this time. He walked over to Knox, pressed the shotgun's muzzle against his forehead. 'You'll get the fleece for me if I let her live?'

'Yes,' said Knox.

'I have your word?'

'Yes.'

Davit came in through the front door, carrying

a bucket in each hand, each so full that the metal handles were bending with the weight, liquid slopping to the floor, the sharp smell of petrol. 'I got it from the cars,' he grunted.

'Keep it coming,' said Mikhail. 'And splash some around the Ferrari and one of the Mercs. They'll need to go up too. But leave the van and the second Merc. We'll be needing those.'

'Yes, sir.'

He looked around the house, taking his time about it, wanting his men to know that he was still in charge, not just of them, but of himself too. 'Ten minutes,' he told them, checking his watch. 'Ten minutes to finish up and pack. Then we're out of here.'

THIRTY-TWO

I

The air inside the atrium was thick with fumes, sharp enough to give Mikhail the first throb of a headache. But he didn't let it rush him. Stillness amid chaos was a virtue he admired.

'Come on, sir,' said Davit, offering him the box of long-reach barbecue matches. 'We need to get out of here.'

He looked up at Edouard's bloodied body, lying like some fallen hero atop the makeshift pyre of furniture and linen, then took the matchbox. Its side was warped and damp from having been left outside too long, making the matches difficult to strike, but finally one fizzled and caught. He nursed it into flame, crouched and touched it to the corner of a petrol-soaked sheet. The flame climbed and spread, already radiating intense heat. When it reached the pool of accelerants at its heart, it erupted in a balloon of searing flame, forcing the others back. He alone stayed where he was, gazing raptly up at it, its spreading canopy of black smoke.

He picked up the shotgun, considered it a moment. Too risky to take inside the airport with him, and if he had to ditch it anyway, best to destroy its evidentiary value. He tossed it into the flames, the remaining cartridges too. He picked up the steel briefcase with its millions of euros, then went into the kitchen for the sharpest and sturdiest carving knife he could find.

Outside, the Ferrari was glistening with fuel. Mikhail struck another match. He'd got the knack now. He threw it in and watched with satisfaction as the petrol flared and then the upholstery caught, choking black smoke pouring out and up into the sky. He enjoyed beautiful things, Mikhail; but he enjoyed destroying them too. Next he set the spare Mercedes blazing; there was less satisfaction in that. Shotgun cartridges began to detonate inside the house. Glass crashed and tinkled, the skylight sucked in by the vacuum. 'Boris,' he said, 'you and Davit take Knox to the airport in the van.'

'Yes, boss.'

'When you get there, call in. I'll be nearby with Zaal and Nadya. You don't need to know exactly where. Get Knox to retrieve the key, then collect the fleece from the locker. If everything goes smoothly, we'll meet up again at the private jet terminal.'

'And if it doesn't?'

'Then you take care of Knox. I'll take care of Nadya.' He turned to Knox, pressed the knife against his throat. 'Her blood will be on your hands. Do you understand?'

'Yes,' said Knox.

'Good,' said Mikhail. 'Then let's get out of here.'

II

Gaille couldn't keep thinking of the dog as the dog. Perhaps because of the quest she was on, the name Argo popped suddenly into her mind. She said it out loud and he turned and gave her a quizzical look, his ears folded forwards. 'Argo, it is, then,' she said.

The sun was beating down hard. She had to do something to get him shade. She could release him from the rope, but she was worried he might attack Iain when he came back. She fetched the broom from the outhouse and swept his pen as clean as she could. Then she took a drawer from the rickety pine wardrobe in Petitier's bedroom, levered out its back slat and fitted it with a blanket to create a makeshift basket that she set in the corner. She draped a couple of Petitier's old jerseys over its roof and down one wall, offering a sizeable area of shade. Then she fetched his bowls and refilled them and put them inside. Not great, but better than it had been.

She went back over to Argo, crouched, opened her arms. 'Here, boy.' She wrapped her arms around him and hugged him, wanting to re-establish their bond before moving him. A muscle started fibrillating in his leg as he accepted her embrace. There was a limit to how much close contact Gaille could stand, however, what with his fetid breath and his coat infested with all those sores.

She went to fetch the nail-scissors and anti-septic cream from her bag, but then decided to do the job properly. She filled the basin with water, took it out, set it down near Argo, then went back inside for a towel and a white T-shirt from Petitier's room. She squirted a little of her apple shampoo into the basin, stirred it with the T-shirt until she'd worked up a nice froth. Argo must have sensed what was coming, for he backed away as far as his rope pinions would allow. She picked up the basin and advanced on him and splashed about a third of it over his back, then hurried out of range. She gave him a few moments to vent his indignation, then crouched down and lowered her gaze meekly until she was confident she had his forgiveness. She went in close and sponged him with the T-shirt. He didn't like it. He clamped his tail between his legs, he whined and yelped; and, when that didn't put her off, he growled menacingly instead.

She took the hint and stepped away. Her nose was itching; she wiped it with the back of her hand. She couldn't exactly stop, for he was bedraggled and covered in suds. She picked up the basin and emptied it over him, making sure to avoid his eyes. Then she took it back inside and refilled it. He yelped and yapped and danced from side to side in an effort to get away, but she hardened her heart and drenched him with that too. Then she grabbed a towel and went in close and began to dry him; and though at first she could feel his trembles of indignation beneath, he began to enjoy that, because he stopped struggling and let her have her wicked way with him.

She cut away the worst tangles of his coat with her nail-scissors, anointed his sores with antiseptic cream. To her surprise, he didn't fight that either, he bowed his head and nuzzled her shoulder and her hand and then her cheek. The wetness of his snout and the gluey rasp of his tongue provoked in her an unexpectedly strong tug of affection. She put the towel around him again and hugged him tight, pressing her face into his shoulder, smelling the fresh scent of her own apple shampoo. And in that moment she understood that, with Petitier dead, she'd already made a commitment to this dog; and the only question really left was how Daniel would react when he learned that their household-to-be had already acquired another member.

She untied the rope from the orange tree, grabbed hold of his leash near his collar, wrapped it several times around her fist until she was confident she had him. Then she unbuckled him from the steel spike and led him around the side of the house to his refurbished pen. She'd anticipated a struggle, but he went happily enough, perhaps because he'd spotted his steel bowls. She unclipped his leash and went back out, bolting him in, then stood there wondering what else she could do.

His coat was all spiked up. He needed a brush; damned if she'd use her own. And she'd just used the broom to sweep his pen out; not much point using that. She went into the house to rummage. She checked the bedroom and bathroom and then the kitchen. A red light-bulb rolled into view as she tugged open a reluctant drawer. She frowned and held it up. A red light-bulb. What on earth would Petitier want that for? She only knew of a couple of uses for red lights: and it seemed somewhat unlikely that he'd been running a brothel out here. She looked out into the main room, at the black-and-white photographs on the facing wall. No one developed and printed black-and-whites commercially any more. There just wasn't the demand. She went over to them, looked more closely. One print had the sunlight deliberately overexposed to make it dazzle, a classic trick of DIY photographers. Her skin tingled as she reached the only logical conclusion.

Petitier had his own dark-room.

III

The best Nadya could figure it, she had half an hour left to live.

She sat in the back of the Mercedes with her wrists bound in front of her, rather than behind, the one concession Mikhail had made to her shattered hand. She didn't look at it, for it just hurt more when she did. Instead, she focused on the back of Zaal's head, his incipient bald-patch, the way his skin bunched and stretched against his collar as he glanced in his mirrors, the dark fuzz that had grown since his last haircut. Odd to think it might be the last thing she ever saw.

Her remaining half-hour broke down like this. In twenty minutes or so, Boris and Davit would arrive in short-term parking, and they'd ask Knox to show them the key. He'd bluff them for a while. Five minutes, say. But Boris would eventually lose patience. He didn't truly believe there was a key, after all, or a fleece. No one did, except Mikhail.

So in twenty-five minutes he'd call through with the bad news. And that left her last five minutes, during which Mikhail would take painful revenge before he killed her.

The Mercedes' tyres made soft drum-rolls on the patched road, sticky and then smooth. She found the rhythm strangely lulling. Sticky. Smooth. Sticky. Smooth. Tall grasses were growing in clumps beside the road, their pale stalks sharp as weapons. She glanced across at Mikhail, who was watching her with wary amusement. 'There's something that's always bothered me,' she said.

'What's that?'

'The night you killed my husband: why didn't you kill me too?'

'You were a babe,' he said. 'I never kill a babe. Not unless I've fucked her first.'

'You still haven't fucked me,' she pointed out. 'Does that mean I'm safe?'

'You're not a babe any longer.'

She snorted softly as she looked away, assessing the Mercedes' interior for fight or flight. The doors were all locked and the windows sufficiently tinted to prevent anyone seeing much inside. And there was nothing for her to wield, save possibly the steel briefcase stuffed with all that cash lying upon the front passenger seat, too cumbersome for so enclosed a space, except perhaps as a shield. Perhaps she could hurl herself at Zaal, twist the wheel, force a crash. Or simply unlock the door and throw herself out. A broken leg, a broken arm, a fractured skull. Small prices to pay.

Mikhail must have read her mind, for he leaned forward to double-check that her door was locked, then he smiled and showed her a glint of his kitchen knife. She realised something then. Her own life was already lost. But play this right and she could still take this man down with her, and avenge her beloved husband at last. The thought made her smile, and the smile caught his eye. 'What?' he asked.

'I was just thinking how trusting you are,' she told him.

'Trusting?'

'Yes,' she said. 'Trusting.'

He was silent a moment or two, trying to work it out. But he failed, and the curiosity proved too much for him. 'In what way?' he asked.

The tyres accelerated their snare-drum whispers, the rhythm meshing with her heart, fast, loud, and urgent. Her mangled knuckles began to throb even more violently, her mouth grew sticky with apprehension, letting her know that this was her moment. 'The Greek police are bound to tie this all back to you.'

'We'll be long gone before they do.'

'They'll seek to charge you with Edouard's murder. They'll start extradition proceedings.'

'They can try all they like. I'm a Nergadze.'

'But that's the point,' said Nadya. 'You'll be fine, I agree, though maybe it'll mean lying low for a while. But what about Boris? What about Davit? They must realise your family will have to throw the Greeks a sop. And who better than one of them? I'll bet they're wondering right now which one of them is the most expendable. I'll bet they're wondering whether it wouldn't be wiser to look out for themselves. I mean, think about it: you've just sent them to collect an artefact worth millions, even on the black market, certainly enough to buy them a new identity and set them up for life.'

'Boris has been with my family for twenty years,' said Mikhail tightly. 'He'd never dream of betraying us.'

'Ah. That's okay, then.'

'He wouldn't dare. And he handpicked Davit himself.'

'Good. Then you've nothing to worry about. But I have to ask: what would *you* do in their situation?'

Mikhail sat back. A pensive glaze came over his eye. It was perhaps ten seconds before he reached forward and tapped Zaal's shoulder. 'Call Boris,' he said. 'Tell him to pull over and wait. We're going into the airport in convoy.'

THIRTY-THREE

I

A man in a wheelchair outside the entrance to Evangelismos Hospital watched amiably as Nico Chavakis laboured up the front steps. 'Crazy, isn't it?' said the man. 'Putting steps this steep in front of a hospital, of all places?'

Nico was wheezing too hard to answer, so he smiled and nodded instead as he walked on inside, feeling obscurely aggrieved, wishing he'd followed his first instinct of giving this DVD of Knox's talk to a courier to deliver, rather than coming all this way himself. But Augustin was only in Greece – and thus in hospital – because he'd accepted Nico's invitation to address his conference, so Nico felt a certain responsibility for him, however much he disliked such places. A visit was the least he could do.

He dabbed his brow and the corners of his lips, giving himself a chance to catch his breath, before putting his handkerchief back in his pocket and going to the information desk. The woman gave him directions to intensive care, but warned that he wouldn't be allowed in. His heart was still pounding erratically as he made his way along the corridor, so that he began to fear he might make it into Intensive Care the hard way, and he allowed himself a gallows chuckle at the thought.

The woman was right: the two policemen wouldn't let him through, no matter how he pleaded; but they did at least send for Claire. She came out a minute or so later, a stern expression on her face, as though time away from Augustin was time wasted. 'Forgive me,' he said hurriedly. 'I didn't mean to cause any trouble. My name's Nico Chavakis. I organised the conference.' He gave a little shrug, to let her know how sorry he was that things had turned out this way. 'I wanted to see how Augustin was doing. But they won't let me in.'

She gave the two policemen a glare. 'They won't let anyone in,' she said.

'How is he?'

'Not good.' She shook her head as though scolding herself for her low spirits, then forced a smile. 'It could be worse, though.'

400

'I'm glad.'

She took him by the elbow and led him a little way along the corridor, then began telling him in great detail about the injuries Augustin had sustained, the care he was getting, the changing prognosis. She spoke quickly, and her accent was hard for him, and she used technical language more suited for medical personnel speaking amongst themselves, placing it far beyond the grasp of Nico's English; but he understood intuitively that his role here wasn't to understand so much as to listen sympathetically. He nodded and sighed and clucked his tongue as appropriate, and let her talk her heart out.

It was a good fifteen minutes before she was done. She glanced around at the ICU doors, as if wondering whether something might not have happened with Augustin while she'd been away. Recognising his cue, Nico gave her the DVD and the spare DVD player he'd borrowed from a colleague at the university, explaining that Knox had wanted her to know how well Augustin's talk had gone. Her eyes began to well; she wiped them with a paper tissue. He watched her return to her lonely vigil, and he felt again a deep yearning for someone in his own life who'd feel that strongly about him.

The man in the wheelchair was still sitting outside the front doors. He'd lit himself a cigarette that he cupped in his hand like he was throwing a dart. 'Good visit?' he asked.

'Yes,' answered Nico, rather to his own surprise. 'It was.'

II

Mikhail could feel the adrenaline build as they caught up with the van a mile or two shy of the airport, then headed on in. It was an invigorating rather than unpleasant feeling, like a good workout. He smiled across at Nadya. 'Don't do it,' he told her.

'Don't do what?'

'Whatever it is you're planning.'

'I'm not planning anything.'

He grabbed her by her hair and pulled her face down onto his lap, her cheek against his prick. He unbuckled his belt and pulled it free, made a noose of it that he tightened around her throat. 'Keep it that way,' he advised.

Traffic began to congeal. Some men in uniform with their weapons holstered were chatting jovially among themselves. He heard the canned thunder of a take-off, and then an Olympic Airways jet appeared over the main terminal building, hurtling upwards into the cloudless blue sky. Another summer coming. It would be nice to spend one in Georgia for a change. He felt a little swell of resentment towards his father and grandfather, the way they'd made him live in exile for all these years. But that time was nearly over. And he'd be going home in triumph too, bringing the fleece with him to ensure his grandfather's victory. He'd be a national hero, able to pick his ministry. Defence was lucrative, sure, but he had a hankering for education. There was just something so rewarding about working with children.

They drove through the shadow of an overpass, then by a long line of parked bikes and motorcycles. Short-term parking was to their left; they followed the van in. There were berths for perhaps a hundred and fifty cars, but it was nearly full. The sheep were flying home for Easter. The van slowed ahead of them, found a place to park. Zaal pulled in nearby. When he'd put on the handbrake, Mikhail passed him Nadya's noose. 'You know what to do if she makes trouble?' he asked, as he made to get out.

Zaal nodded confidently. 'You know it, boss,' he assured him.

III

The afternoon was drawing on, so Gaille began her search for Petitier's darkroom outside, taking advantage of what daylight remained; but the greenhouses and outbuildings all leaked far too much moisture and light, and she couldn't find any trace of photographic supplies.

Her ankle was throbbing badly from all the walking she'd done. She didn't want to exacerbate the injury, so she decided to give it a rest, maybe run the idea past Iain when he returned, see what he thought. But going back into the house, she caught a faint reprise of the vinegary smell she and Iain had both noticed that morning. Vinegar was used as a fixing agent in photographic dark-rooms, Gaille knew. Or acetic acid was, at least. Surely that meant the darkroom was somewhere in this house. She checked the kitchen and larder for vinegar, just in case, then went room by room, searching cavities and closets, pulling books from the shelves to look behind them, tapping the walls for hidden spaces. Nothing. Her puzzlement grew. She stood in the middle of the main room with her hands on her hips and stared around her.

Her ankle was still throbbing. She sighed and sat down in the armchair. It was only then that she took proper notice of the rugs thrown negligently around, particularly the largest of them, the one beneath her feet, with its flamboyant if faded motif of Theseus and Ariadne standing at either end of a fiendish labyrinth, and the golden thread that connected them through it.

IV

Lying on his side in the rear of the van, his wrists tied behind his back, Knox heard the roar of a take-off, and knew they'd reached the airport. A speed-bump was like a jab in his ribs, still aching from the water-boarding. They stopped and then reversed, presumably into a parking bay. He didn't have the first idea how to play this. He looked up at the big man; his arms folded, he stared implacably down. He'd get no joy there.

The passenger door opened and Mikhail climbed inside. He knelt on the passenger seat and reached back, grabbing Knox by his hair and pulling him towards him, then up onto his knees. 'I'm going to take off your gag now,' he said, touching his knife against his throat. 'You're not going to make a sound. What you are going to do is tell me *exactly* where this key is. Do you understand?' He waited for Knox to nod, then he loosened the gag, allowing him to spit it from his mouth, so that it dangled around his neck like some macabre medallion.

'Well?' asked Mikhail.

The corners of Knox's mouth were dry and sore. He licked some saliva balm onto them. 'I need to be able to see,' he said. Mikhail swayed back out of his way. He leaned forward. The Metro and railway lines were to Knox's left, the gleaming terminal building was to his right, and directly ahead and above was the enclosed walkway connecting the two. And, around the lot itself, a wide but well-trimmed hedge, much as he'd remembered.

'Well?' asked Mikhail.

'We were over the other side,' he said, nodding at a stretch entirely taken up by parked cars. It was just his bad luck that a 4x4 chose that moment to pull out, leaving a slot free for Boris to drive in to.

'Well?' asked Mikhail, once they were parked again.

'I can't see from in here. Let me out and I'll get it for you.'

'Sure,' scoffed Mikhail. He increased the pressure on his blade. 'I'd advise you to start remembering.'

'Augustin hid it, not me,' said Knox.

'But you were with him?'

'Yes.'

'Well, then.'

'It's about two thirds of the way along this side,' Knox told him. 'It's by the base of one of the shrubs. He scratched his initials in the bark.'

'And his initials are?'

'AGP.'

Mikhail nodded. 'Go,' he told Davit and Boris.

'Yes, sir.'

Knox watched with a sinking heart as they walked off on their futile search, while Mikhail's knife pressed cold as ice against his throat.

THIRTY-FOUR

I

Gaille dragged the armchair back against the wall, then pulled the rug aside. And there it was, a wooden trap-door embedded in the cement. The wood had warped and swollen over the years, so that she had to give the rope handle a hard tug to open it on its hinges. It threw up a soft fog of dust and detritus as it came, then released a gentle but reassuringly vinegary aroma.

She rested the trapdoor all the way on its back and looked down the narrow flight of steep bare steps, cobwebs and motes of dust and gloomy shadows at the bottom vanishing into pure darkness. Something scuttled. A rodent in the basement or a bird upon the roof; she knew which she'd prefer. She shook her head at her hesitation. The house had electric lights powered by the solar cells:

presumably the basement did too, though she couldn't see any from here. She made her way down, one step at a time, her palms pressed against the cold rough walls on either side. There was a corridor leading to her right at the foot of the stairs, going back along the spine of the house, and there were three doors leading from it, two to Gaille's left, one to her right. She tried the first left-hand one, fumbling in the darkness until her wrist touched a string that she grabbed and pulled. A single dangling bulb came alight, revealing a small room with a plumbed-in sink and wooden tables against two of its walls. An enlarger stood on one of the tables, surrounded by all the paraphernalia of a darkroom: colour-coded developing trays and tanks, an assortment of light filters, chemical containers, tongs, thermometers, a magnifying glass, boxes of photographic paper. Three lengths of washing-line cord were strung from wall to wall, fitted with clips for hanging photographs up to dry, though there weren't any there at the moment.

She went back out and through the second left-hand door, found the light-switch. It was a little larger than the first room, and also fitted with a sink, as well as a worktable and a desk and chair too. Beakers, flasks and test tubes lounged indolently in wooden racks. A kaleidoscope of chemicals in glass jars stood on the shelves. And she noted a gas burner too, an oven and digital scales and filters and what looked to her laywoman's eye like a centrifuge. A home chemistry lab.

Photographs were pinned or taped against the walls, new ones put up wherever there'd been gaps, so that their corners overlapped, enabling Gaille to deduce the order in which they had been put up, like stratification in an archaeological dig. Some had been there years, to judge from their fading homogeneous greys and the crackled yellow of the sticky tape from which all adhesiveness had long-since gone, so that it clung to the wall by mere force of habit.

Each photograph depicted a different plant or fungus, some in the wild, others in Petitier's greenhouse, or harvested and in his kitchen. Many of them had handwritten notes attached with a paperclip, instructions on preparation along with scrawled additional information on dosages, experiences and antidotes.

There was a shelf of books, too. A directory of psychoactive mushrooms; a pamphlet on African ethnobotany. Pagan shamanistic cults. Aldous Huxley's *The Doors of Perception*. Wasson. Ruck. Other half-familiar names. She pulled out and flipped through a field guide to hallucinogens, stopped at an evocative watercolour of *myristica fragrans,* then again at a gorgeous picture of *galbulimima Belgraveana*, a dream-inducing narcotic used by native Papuans.

She went back out and through the facing door into the third room. It was significantly larger, this one, with multiple lights. Most of it was given over to metal shelving on which stood grey archival boxes and racks of folders, dates going back well over a decade written on their outside edges, along with some of Petitier's incomprehensible hiero-glyphics. She opened one up at random, found four seal-stone fragments inside, each individually wrapped in tissue paper, each inscribed with Linear A symbols. She returned the box to its place, continued along the shelves, pulling out another every couple of paces: shards of painted pottery decorated with plants and wildlife; a crude earth-enware figurine of a heavily pregnant woman; a small but exquisite polychrome vase; fragments of marble and other stoneware; a bronze dagger with designs wrought upon both blade and handle.

She took this last to the work-table, where the light was better. Her hands trembled a little as she turned it around, her thrill at all these treas-ures spiced with anger that Petitier had kept them to himself. A dozen or so photographs were pinned in a snaking pattern to the wall above the table. Each was taken outdoors, each showed a different slab of rock, and each rock had at least two symbols chiselled into it. She remembered the symbols she'd seen herself, atop the escarp-ment. She looked for them among the photographs, and there they were. A thought came to her: she hobbled upstairs for the replica Phaistos disc on Petitier's desk, brought it back down. Yes. The symbols on it were similar to those in the photographs, though they formed different clusters. But then she turned it over and felt shivers scurry up her spine.

II

Zaal sat sideways in the driver's seat with his back against the door, the better to keep an eye on Nadya. Late afternoon sunlight refracted through the tinted glass and laid a blurred rainbow on the steel briefcase. All that money! He let his mind drift off on a fine daydream: strutting in expensive clothes down some Riviera waterfront to the larger of his yachts, while beautiful women ignored their men to throw him admiring glances.

'How much is in there?' asked Nadya.

Zaal returned reluctantly from his reverie. 'None of your business.'

'He must trust you a great deal.'

'Yes. Because he can.'

'Still. It's an awful lot of money.'

Zaal laughed and shook his head. 'You think I'm crazy? Do you have any idea what he'd do to me?'

Nadya shrugged. 'He wouldn't be able to do anything to anyone, not from gaol.'

'If they ever put him there.'

'They'll put him there, all right,' replied Nadya. 'Don't you get it yet? Your friend Edouard blabbed. The police are going to be waiting for you when you board your plane. This is the last bit of freedom you'll enjoy for thirty years.'

He gave the noose a little admonitory tug. 'Be quiet.'

'Mikhail murdered Edouard,' insisted Nadya. 'You didn't. Your friends didn't. *He* did. But when he goes down, he'll have all the money in the world for expensive lawyers, to bribe judges and intimidate jurors. He'll make it seem he's the innocent one, that you guys pulled the trigger. The police won't care. The more the merrier, as far as they're concerned. Think about it. You're risking the rest of your life for a psycho. You think he'd do the same for you?'

Zaal licked his lips. There was truth in what she said. But Mikhail scared the hell out of him. All the Nergadzes did. 'They'd come after me,' he said.

'Not from where they'll be. Our president has been praying for the Nergadzes to screw up this badly. You really think he'll let this chance go? He'll stamp down hard and keep on stamping until there's nothing left.'

413

'I'll believe that when I see it!' scoffed Zaal, giving her noose another little reminder. 'Even if they *could* put the whole family away, it wouldn't stop them having money, it wouldn't stop them from having influence, it wouldn't keep them from their revenge.' He gave a dry laugh. 'Believe me, I know what they're like.'

'They can't take revenge unless they find you first. And they won't, not if you're smart. There must be millions in that briefcase. You can buy yourself a new identity, a new life. Live like a king, or rot in a six-foot cell. It's just a question of whether you've got the balls.'

'I'd be dead before I got out of the parking lot.'

'Not necessarily,' said Nadya. 'Not if you had some way of distracting him. Something that he'd have absolutely no choice but to take care of first.'

'Like what?' asked Zaal.

'Like me,' said Nadya.

III

Knox sat absolutely still as he waited for Boris and Davit to return, for Mikhail kept teasing beneath his chin with his knife, like a barber with a cutthroat razor. It was five minutes before they reappeared. 'He's full of shit,' said Boris, climbing in. 'There's nothing there.'

'Nothing there?' echoed Mikhail. He turned to Knox with a frosty smile. 'Could you explain that to me, please.'

'They missed it,' said Knox. 'They must have missed it.'

'Of course.'

'It's there,' insisted Knox. 'Take me and I'll show you.'

'We looked everywhere,' said Boris. 'It's not there.'

'You lied to me,' said Mikhail, pushing Knox back down onto the floor of the van, switching around his grip on the knife, the better to cut rather than stab. 'I warned you what the penalty for lying would be.'

'I didn't lie,' insisted Knox. 'Your men missed it, that's all.'

'No,' stated Mikhail. 'You lied.'

'I thought the fleece mattered to you,' said Knox. 'Are you going to give it up so easily, just because your guys can't find the right fucking bush?'

'There is no right bush,' said Boris.

'Let me show you,' pleaded Knox. 'For Christ's sake, what harm can I do while I'm trussed up like this?'

Mikhail nodded, to himself more than to Knox. 'I want you to understand something,' he said. 'If you're lying to me, you'll die and the woman Nadya will die. You already know that. So let me add this: your girlfriend Gaille will die too.'

415

'No,' said Knox weakly.

'Yes,' said Mikhail. 'I'll find her and then I'll fuck her and then I'll kill her. You have my word on it.'

'She has nothing to do with this,' protested Knox.

'She does now,' stated Mikhail. 'You just made sure of it. Unless, of course, you want to change your mind and admit there is no key.'

A moment of silence, as Knox struggled against his fear; but the instinct for self-preservation was too strong for him. It seemed it hadn't been an aberration, him standing by while Augustin had been attacked; it was who he was. 'It's there,' he said. 'I swear it is.'

'Very well.' Mikhail turned to Davit. 'Untie his legs. Put your jacket over his shoulders. I don't want anyone seeing his cuffs.'

'Yes, sir.'

Mikhail and Boris got out and came round to the back, opened the doors. Davit kept his hand on Knox's shoulder as they climbed out. He was surprised that so much of the day had passed that dusk was already falling. All around them, lights were coming on. Mikhail pressed his knife hard into the soft flesh beneath Knox's ribcage, angled upwards at his heart. 'Don't even think about calling for help,' he warned. 'You'll be dead before you can fill your lungs.'

They walked along a narrow strip of grass between the parked vehicles and the waist-high hedge, the Georgians interposing themselves between Knox and the few people around. Not that they were looking his way, all too focused on their own business. A man kissed his sweetheart farewell. Another heaved suitcases into his boot. Mikhail kept his knife-tip pressed so hard against Knox's stomach that he could feel the blood trickling. And still he walked. All those documentaries he'd watched over the years, grainy footage of half-naked starving prisoners being herded into trees: it had bewildered and frustrated him that they'd gone so quiescently to their death. Fight, run, spit in their guards' faces. Something, anything. How much worse could it get? Now, here he was, doing the same. And, to make matters worse, he'd betrayed Gaille first, just for this wretched extra minute. The thought was brutal and bitter. His pace faltered, he drifted to a halt.

'Well?' asked Mikhail. 'Is this the place?'

THIRTY-FIVE

I

The symbols chiselled into the various rocks matched clusters on the reverse of the Phaistos disc. There was no question. At least, the only question was what it signified. Gaille brooded on it for a minute or so, but without coming to any firm conclusions. Perhaps Iain would have some ideas. She set the disc aside, went back to the shelves, chose a folder at random from one of the many wire racks. It proved to contain photographs taken inside a cave, of several niches filled with crude votive offerings; pre-Minoan from the look of them, though she was no expert. A second folder chronicled the excavation of a pit perhaps a metre long by half a metre wide. It included standard archaeological photographs of various finds in situ, with a wooden ruler next to them to show scale, and a file-card with a date and reference number, presumably cross-referenced to the boxes.

She looked through several more of the folders, found one with pictures of the escarpment face. She was about to put it back when she noticed something incongruous, and so she took it into better light. Yes. There was a man in a dark shirt and jeans crouching in the dappled shade of a tree halfway up. She squinted more closely, but he was too distant from the camera to be recognisable. But one thing was clear: Petitier had been under surveillance, and he'd known himself to be. No wonder he'd got spooked. No wonder he'd tried to pre-empt discovery by coming clean.

She put the folder back. It seemed they were in date order, so she decided to start with the most recent. One of the first folders she opened contained another set of pictures of the man hunkering down, though in different clothes and on another part of the escarpment. But these were of a different order of clarity, focused and sharp, almost as though Petitier had been sufficiently spooked to invest in a telephoto lens. In the first shot, the intruder was looking through his field-glasses, so she couldn't see his face. But in the second his features were all too easily recognisable. Her legs went a little weak on her, she had to reach out for the shelving to steady herself.

It was Iain.

II

It wasn't premeditated. It wasn't planned. Something simply switched inside Zaal as he watched Mikhail and the others shepherding Knox along the verge, none of them even looking his way. Four million euros on the passenger seat. *Four million!* His mouth began to water and just like that he knew he was going to do it.

Nadya must have sensed it; there was exhortation in her eyes when he turned to her, willing him on. He gave her a sheepish grin, feeling something akin to gratitude. He let go of the belt so that it hung loose around her neck. 'Go on, then,' he said, unlocking the door for her.

'Good luck,' she said, shuffling along the seat, opening it.

'You too.' He turned on his ignition and his headlights, then waited until she was out before setting sedately off towards the exit, not wanting to draw attention to himself, willing Mikhail and the others to keep looking the other way long enough for him to complete his getaway.

He might have made it, too, had Nadya not begun to scream.

III

Mikhail read the truth in Knox's eyes. There was no key. There never had been. He felt the serene rage he often felt before a kill. He clamped his left hand over Knox's mouth to prevent noise, then drew back his knife-hand and was about to stab him when a woman behind him began to shriek. He turned to see Nadya screeching and pointing, while behind her a black Mercedes headed for the exit. Knowledge of Zaal's betrayal filled him instantly; he understood it all. Nadya paused to take in a deep breath, then screamed again. All around, people started looking towards her, then following her finger. Two security guards hurried from the main terminal building. For the shortest moment, Mikhail almost succumbed to the urge to kill Knox, just to release his anger; but the security guards were already too close. Personal experience had taught him that there was always a window of confusion in situations like these. The key was having the nerve to seize it. He turned the knife around so that its blade was flat against his wrist, then made as if he was tearing himself free and ran towards the guards, waving and pointing back at Boris, Davit and Knox. 'They've got guns,' he shrieked. 'They're armed. Terrorists! Terrorists!'

All around him, people heard the dread word

and scampered for cover. The two guards unbuttoned their holsters and yelled at Davit, Knox
and Boris to put up their hands. Mikhail ran past
them, making out he was too petrified to do anything but flee; then he dropped the pretence and
began sprinting across the car park after the
Mercedes. Zaal saw him coming; he surged towards
the exit. But two cars were already queuing to
leave, and a third was coming in. He tooted then
drove down the narrow lane between them, his
side-mirrors folding back as they caught, the screech
of metal on metal as he forced the Mercedes through
and then turned left into the one-way stream of
traffic. Mikhail caught up with him at that moment,
tried to open the passenger door, but it was locked.
Zaal put in a little spurt, but there was too much
traffic and confusion for him to get away clean.
Mikhail caught up with him and tried the hatch-
back. It was unlocked and it lifted up and he threw
himself inside as the Mercedes lurched off again.
Zaal looked in his mirror and his complexion turned
to white when he saw Mikhail kneeling there. He
tried to open his door but too late, Mikhail leapt
over the back seats and grabbed his chin from
behind and hauled it back, sawing his knife across
his throat, cutting through his windpipe and carotid,
blood spraying over the wheel and dashboard and
the inside of the windscreen, Zaal's feet sliding
off the pedals, the Mercedes drifting to a halt.

He heaved Zaal aside then took the wheel and gathered his bearings. Thankfully the tinted windows seemed to have prevented any of the few bystanders from seeing what he'd done. But he didn't have long. The windscreen was splattered with blood, so he wiped it with his sleeve, but only succeeded in smearing it all the worse. He felt the indignity of it all. Someone was going to pay for this.

Panic had blocked the exit ahead. There was no way through. He pulled a U-turn, put his hand upon his horn and kept it there as he drove back against the traffic. A lorry was hurtling towards him; he had no choice but to wrench his wheel around and head the wrong way up an access ramp. He made it unscathed to the top, reached an overpass, sped by the air traffic control tower then through a pair of half-open gates along a small access road. He turned off his headlights, lest they give the police a target, and raced on until he reached what looked like a freight area under construction, some nearly-completed offices and warehouses set around a huge parking lot. There was equipment and materials everywhere, but no sign of workers; the site had evidently closed down for Easter. He drove a lap of the parking lot looking for a way out; but the only way out was back the way he'd arrived, and headlights were already approaching down that, swinging slowly back and forth, searching for him and blocking off his retreat.

An aircraft took off from a runway just the other side of the warehouses. Perhaps he could get to his plane. But Knox would surely be blabbing his mouth off right now, and the police would get to him before he could take off. He felt a spike of hatred for him, and his hand drifted to his groin as he thought of the revenge he'd take upon his girlfriend. What was the name of the place she'd sent those pictures from again? Agia Georgio, wasn't it?

The headlights were getting closer. There were three containers parked against the fringe of the lot. He drove over to them, hoping to hide behind one or other of them, but two were parked so close to the fence that he couldn't fit behind, and the third was jacked up a metre or so off the ground, so that his Mercedes would instantly be spotted beneath it. He was running out of time. He drove along the line of newly-built offices and warehousing. A steel shutter was three-quarters up on one of the lock-ups; they were painting the inside. He drove inside, got out to pull the shutter down after him, then bolted it on either end.

A car arrived outside. Its engine turned off. He stood there quietly, wondering if they'd spotted him. A minute passed. He heard two men talking, and their footsteps. Someone tried to lift up the steel door, but the bolts held and they moved along. The engine started again. He listened to it leave. He went to the Mercedes, turned on its interior light, checked himself in the rear-view. His face was caked red with Zaal's blood. For such a small man, he'd certainly proved a gusher. He stripped naked, squirted wiper fluid onto the windscreen that he mopped up with his shirt and used to wash himself and his trench-coat clean. He put on some clean clothes from his suitcase, tucked his knife into his belt, grabbed the money. He went over to the shutter, listened for a minute, then unbolted it and lifted it just enough to check that the lot was clear. He lifted it a little higher, ducked beneath it, then pulled it down behind him, and stood up tall.

Rather to his surprise, he discovered that he was enjoying himself.

THIRTY-SIX

I

Knox stood helpless as security guards and police converged upon him, handguns and automatic weapons aimed at his chest and face, yelling at him to do as Davit and Boris had already done, and put his hands above his head. But Knox couldn't put his hands above his head, they were cuffed behind his back; and if he shrugged off Davit's jacket to show them, they might well think he was going for a weapon, and kill him just in case. 'Don't shoot!' he pleaded. But he could see fear in their eyes, how close they were to the edge.

Nadya ran across him just in time. 'No!' she shouted. 'His hands are cuffed. His hands are cuffed.' She had her own arms raised as she came over to him, but she lowered one to knock Davit's jacket from his shoulders and turn him around for the police to see.

Tension decreased instantly. Weapons lowered; someone cracked a joke and earned laughter. 'What's going on?' one of them asked Nadya. 'What the hell happened to your hand?'

But Nadya ignored the question. She worked some saliva up into her mouth instead, then turned to Boris and spat it shotgun at his face.

II

Gaille stared numbly down at the photograph. Iain.

So he'd been here before. At least twice. Which meant he'd known about this place long before Knox had telephoned him. All that nonsense about knowing Petitier as Roly, about his Belgian archaeologist friend, about asking directions at that shop in Anopoli! He'd been stalking Petitier for . . . she checked the date on the first folder of photographs – for at least six months.

It took a few moments for the barking to register. Argo was going berserk outside. It could only mean Iain was on his way back. She froze a moment, wondering what to do. But she couldn't let him find her here, not with these photos. She hurried out, switching lights off as she went, then ran up the steps and closed the trap door behind her even as she heard his boots outside. She laid the rug back out, pulled the chair across it, then stood there attempting negligence as the door opened and Iain came in. 'Fuck me!' he said, throwing himself down into the armchair. 'My *feet*!'

'Long day?' she asked.

'I hadn't realised there'd be so much to search.'

'Any luck?'

'Some. I found his Minoan site.'

'But that's brilliant!' she exclaimed, trying her hardest to sound suitably impressed. 'Where?'

Iain nodded south. 'Most of it is covered up with earth, but there's enough still exposed to get an idea. A small palace or temple dating from Early Minoan II, I'd say, though there are obvious signs of destruction and a rebuild in the Mycenaean. But he can't have been doing anything there for at least five years, probably longer. So if he's found anything recently, it must be from somewhere else.' He looked up at the racks of journals. 'I'll bet those are his excavation notes. You make any progress on them?'

She shook her head. 'His code's too difficult for me. I did make friends with his dog, though.'

'Yeah. I saw he was in his pen. How did you manage that?'

'Bribery. Petitier hadn't left him any food or water. I gave him a bath too. He was really filthy.'

'I'm feeling pretty filthy myself,' grinned Iain. 'Do I get a bath too?'

'I scavenged some eggs and peppers and things,' she told him, ignoring him. 'What would you say to an omelette and a glass of chateau Petitier?'

'Now you're talking.' He leaned forward to undo his laces then kicked off his boots. He stretched out his legs, wriggled his toes. She limped through to the kitchen, swinging her bad ankle out wide, instinctively wanting him to think she was more badly injured than in fact she was. She opened a dusty bottle of wine, splashed ruby liquid into a pair of tumblers, took them and the bottle back out.

'Cheers,' said Iain, offering his glass in a toast, before slurping down a full third of it.

'Cheers,' agreed Gaille, taking a more modest sip, struggling to keep the smile on her face, suspicion from her eyes.

III

Theofanis and Angelos were going through a folder of stills from the CCTV in the hotel lobby when the call came through. Theofanis listened for thirty seconds or so then turned to his boss. 'Trouble at the airport,' he said.

'What's it got to do with us?'

'They've arrested a bunch of Georgians. And that guy Daniel Knox too.'

Angelos grunted like he'd been punched in the gut. 'Knox,' he said, as though it were a swear word.

'Apparently he's been asking for us,' said Theofanis. 'Apparently he thinks we'll vouch for him.'

'*Us*?' asked Angelos incredulously. 'Vouch for *him*?'

'That's what they're saying. What do you want to do?'

Angelos checked his watch. 'How long do you reckon to get out there?'

'Forty minutes, I'd say. This time of night.'

Angelos grabbed his jacket in one hand, the file of photographs in the other, then strode towards the door. 'Tonight let's make it twenty.'

THIRTY-SEVEN

I

Night had fallen while Mikhail had been in the lock-up. Lamps had come on around the parking lot, casting pools of yellow light. Away in the distance, he could hear sirens. The police, as ever, were searching in the wrong places.

The runway lay the other side of these buildings, but it held little attraction for him. Open spaces and high security were the last things he needed. He headed the other way instead, across the parking lot, then over the low fence and through a thin line of trees, until he found himself on the top of a grass bank, looking down at the airport road, on which traffic was moving tantalisingly freely. Getting to it, however, meant crossing a well-lit security fence topped by strands of obliquely-set barbed wire, monitored by security

431

cameras. Hard, but nothing he couldn't handle. He was on his way down the slope when a truck rolled into view on the road beyond. It slowed down just enough for an armed police officer to jump down and take up position by the fence, then it drove on a couple of hundred metres, before dropping off another man. The bastards were securing the perimeter.

He cursed and headed back to the cover of the trees, got out his mobile and began trying to call in assistance. No one answered. Not his father, not his grandfather, nor any of his brothers. No one. It seemed incredible to him that a nothing of a man like Edouard could have inflicted a serious wound upon his family, yet he could see no other explanation. He had a sudden suffocating memory of gaol, and an unfamiliar sensation rippled through him, like a breeze through a field of grain. He made calls further and further afield. Only when he tried Cyprus did anyone finally answer: Rafiel, their Cypriot chief-of-staff. 'Who is this?' he asked.

'It's me. Mikhail. What's going on? Where is everyone?'

'Haven't you heard?'

'Heard what?'

'There was a massive raid on Nikortsminda. Police and army. I spoke to Iakob. He managed to get away, he wouldn't say how. He says there was shooting, there were helicopters. He says your grandfather has been arrested, your father and your brothers too. But that's not the worst. Your brother Alexei; he was killed.'

'It's not possible,' said Mikhail. 'They wouldn't dare.'

'The TV stations are apparently showing footage of him head-butting a policeman and then aiming a shotgun down at his face,' said Rafiel. 'People don't like families who put themselves above the law.'

'It's a stitch up,' said Mikhail. 'The people will never accept it.'

'I don't know,' said Rafiel. 'There are reports from all over Georgia of people coming out onto the streets, of scuffles and gunfire, but it's all too sporadic. There's no one to organise it, no one to *lead* it, not with your family all under arrest. All except you, of course.'

Mikhail blinked. That aspect of it hadn't occurred to him. The arrests had left him *de facto* head of the family, *de facto* head of the entire Nergadze-led opposition, indeed head of all resistance to Georgia's fascist government. Others might have shrunk from such a responsibility, but not Mikhail. 'Listen to me,' he told Rafiel. 'I'm boss now. Is that clear?'

'Yes, sir.' The relief in Rafiel's voice was palpable. Orders. Structure. Hierarchy. 'What do you need?'

Mikhail paused. The president had declared war upon his family; he had to realise he couldn't risk leaving a single Nergadze on the loose. Fly home now, the authorities would arrest him on the spot. Stay here, they'd pile pressure on the Greeks to hunt him down. And until he was neutralised, one way or another, they'd keep looking. So his first job was to buy himself time and space. 'Move out to the boat,' he told Rafiel. 'Take everything I'll need to run our family's operations, then sail her out into international waters.'

'Yes, sir. Then what?'

'Stand by. I'll call back with a rendezvous point.'

He jogged along the tree-line until he reached the back of a car rental lot. He was still cut off from it by the security fence, but at least here it was partly shielded by trees. He drew the knife from his belt and fitted it through the wire, so that it dropped onto the grass the other side. He checked that the briefcase was locked and tossed it over the top. It landed with a loud thump on the other side; but there was no one around to hear. He took off his trench-coat and draped it over his shoulder and then began to climb. The mesh cut into his fingers, leaving red welts. It was hard to get purchase with his feet, they kept slipping and scraping, but he made it to the top in the end.

The triple strands of barbed wire leaned away from him, designed to keep people out of the airport's secure area, not inside. He grabbed his coat from his shoulder and spread it out over the wire, then clambered over it, safe from the barbs. He took a firm grip of his coat then dropped down the other side, pulling it after him, the barbs acting like a brake upon the leather. He stayed low for a moment or two, then crouched to collect his knife and the briefcase, and went to the nearest car. Its door was unlocked, but there were no keys in the ignition. He considered trying to hotwire it, but these new models were a bitch, their alarms went off at the slightest provocation.

Headlights swung his way. He ducked down, fearing it was police. But it was just a minibus dropping off customers. A family of four got off first. Father, mother and two sweet-looking girls. The idea came to him instantly: take the two girls hostage in the boot and make their parents drive him to safety. It went against his better nature to trust his fate to someone else, but he couldn't see a better alternative.

He watched them to their car, exchanging banter with another passenger, a businessman in a pearl-grey suit, trying to look younger than his forty-odd years with his hair swept back and down to his shoulders. Mikhail silently willed him to leave them alone; but they kept chatting as the husband stowed their luggage in the back of the Mazda, while the wife strapped in her children.

Then they were away, waving cheerfully to the businessman, who walked on along the line of cars, looking for his own. He pressed his key-fob and the corner-lights of a sleek Citroen soft-top flashed orange.

The new plan came to Mikhail as suddenly and completely as the first. But this appealed to his nature far more, for it meant he had to rely on no one but himself. He pictured in his mind how it would go. A high-risk strategy, of course, but then everything was high risk in such situations. And if he could pull it off, he'd be clean away. He bowed his head and walked towards the businessman, already climbing behind the wheel. 'Excuse me,' he said, keeping a good distance back, so that the man wouldn't think him a threat. 'You don't have the time, by any chance?'

'Of course,' grunted the man. Belgian or Dutch, to judge from his accent, but an EU passport for sure, which was the main thing. 'Seven twenty-five.'

'Thanks so much,' smiled Mikhail. He nodded at the car. 'I like your taste. Nothing beats a good soft-top.'

The man grinned. 'I have five kids. All I ever get to drive back home is my wife's damned people-carrier. Makes a change to get in one of these from time to time, remember what a proper car feels like.'

'I'm the same with my own kids,' said Mikhail, reaching behind him for his knife. 'Until I've been away from the little bastards for a day or two, that is. Then all I can think of is getting home to see him.'

'Yes, well,' shrugged the man, buckling himself in, inserting his keys into the ignition. 'That's fatherhood for you.'

'Indeed, it is,' agreed Mikhail, walking towards him. 'Indeed it is.'

II

Pandemonium had settled down into mere chaos at the airport, not helped by the fact that flights were still arriving and departing, the Easter weekend too important to disrupt. Police and antiterrorist units had arrived in huge numbers, and were now checking everyone leaving or entering the terminal buildings, while also going meticulously through the parking lots and public areas before sealing them off, gradually cutting down the space in which Mikhail could move. They'd also set up a roadblock at the airport exit, to check all departing vehicles, but the tailback had quickly reached the terminal building itself, threatening to wreak havoc. The police had there-fore thrown numbers at the problem, and cut their searches to an inspection of ID and a quick look in the boot, and the queues had shrunk back down.

Knox watched an ambulance leave, its blue light flashing but its siren silent, taking Nadya into Athens for treatment on her pulverised hand. She should have left long before, but she'd insisted on giving her statement first, to help exonerate Knox. He'd tried to convince her there was no need, for although Boris had zipped his lips, Davit had cracked like an old jug, and was spilling everything. Chatter on the police radio seemed to corroborate Knox's story too: a mansion north of Athens had been found blazing, along with the husks of two expensive cars. So, from almost being shot as a suspected terrorist, Knox had rapidly found himself demoted to a mere object of curiosity, passed into the safekeeping of a kindly policewoman, who at least took the trouble to find keys for his handcuffs. She unlocked and removed them now. His wrists were sore and swollen, and his fingers throbbed painfully with returning blood, but his spirits still lifted. 'Is that it?' he asked. 'Can I go?'

'The boss wants to have you looked over by a police doctor,' she told him. 'After all, if you've been tortured as you say you have . . .'

He gave a little snort. 'You mean he wants to make sure that my injuries match my account. Where's this doctor, then?'

'On his way. You don't mind waiting, do you?'

'Do I have a choice?'

He leaned against the parking-lot booth while he killed time; a police car pulled up alongside him, but it was Angelos and Theofanis in the front seats, not the doctor. 'What are you two doing here?' he asked.

'You're the one who wanted vouching for.'

'I only said you knew who I was. I didn't expect you to drive out here.'

'Yes, well, we still have some questions.' Angelos nodded at the back seat. 'Get in.'

'I'm waiting for a doctor.'

'Just get in.'

Theofanis turned in his seat as he climbed in. 'We're trying to fit everything together,' he said. 'Petitier. Your friend Augustin. This man Antonius we found hanged. Mikhail Nergadze. Whatever happened here earlier –' He didn't have time to complete his thought, however, interrupted by commotion on the airport exit road. They all looked across to see a car roaring against the traffic towards them, its headlights flashing and horn blaring to warn other cars out of its way, as though it had taken fright at the police roadblocks.

Knox caught a bare glimpse of the driver's face as he sped by, but it was enough. 'It's him,' he said numbly. 'It's Nergadze.'

Angelos didn't hesitate. He turned on his ignition, thrust it into first and then span a U-turn.

A train of police cars was already in pursuit, and they joined its tail, hurtling the wrong way up a slip-road to an overpass, past the control tower, then through open gates down a track to a vast parking lot around which some offices were being built. Even in the darkness, it was obvious that there was no way out for Mikhail, other than the way he'd come in. 'We've got him,' muttered Theofanis.

Mikhail must have realised this too. He slowed and came to a stop. The police cars slowed likewise, blocking off his escape. They had their man; there was no need for heroics.

Angelos lowered his window. 'Give yourself up,' he shouted.

'Fuck you,' cried Mikhail. 'Fuck all of you. I'm not going back to gaol. I'm never going back.'

'You can have a lawyer. You can have a trial.'

'A trial?' he scoffed. 'I'm Mikhail Nergadze. You hear me? Mikhail fucking Nergadze! And who the fuck are you?' He stamped down his foot and began to accelerate across the open prairie of the tarmac, then turned in a long sweeping curve, hurtling almost flat out towards a container parked against the edge. Knox flinched as the Citroen's low bonnet passed beneath the container's high fuselage, then its windscreen and bracing struts hit in a shriek of metal and glass, and the soft-top squeezed up on itself like a concertina, before being hurled high in the air and landing some way back upon the tarmac, while the shorn bottom sped on beneath the container in a shower of friction sparks, before crashing through the wire fence and out into the trees beyond.

It was several moments before anyone reacted. They were all too stunned. But then flames started licking around the base of the container, while the broken Citroen groaned and hissed and screeched from its wounds. The police cars fanned out and drove warily across, none wanting to be first, hardened to horrors though they were. They reached the perimeter fence, stopped, got out. The air beyond the container was filled with banknotes, as though a bomb had gone off in the steel briefcase. They fluttered down all around them, and several of the policemen were already gathering them up in handfuls, stuffing them in their pockets, careless of their evidentiary value.

Knox and Angelos pushed past them. The topless Citroen had burst through the wire fence beyond, before coming to a halt in a tangle of brambles. The steel briefcase was open in the rear, obscene amounts of cash lying loose in and around it. Both its air-bags had deployed, though they hadn't done much good for Nergadze, still belted into the passenger seat, his left arm dangling down by his side, his gold watch still on his wrist, yet with his right arm and everything from his chest on up sheared clean off, along with the car's windscreen and roof, by the giant guillotine of the container trailer.

THIRTY-EIGHT

I

Gaille pleaded exhaustion and a headache shortly after they'd eaten, then asked about sleeping arrangements. Iain told her to take Petitier's bed, insisting he'd be fine in his sleeping bag on the living room floor. She didn't argue: chivalry had its benefits. She prepared for bed then covered the mattress with the cleanest blankets she could find, and climbed between them. Moonlight slipped into the room down the side of the curtains, throwing a pale blue tint upon the wall. She stared up the ceiling and wondered what to do in the morning, torn between checking out the rest of the basement and getting out of here altogether.

She tensed at soft footsteps outside her room. There was a gentle double rap upon the door and then it opened and Iain was standing there, his

443

sleeping bag over his shoulder. 'Are you awake?' he asked. She said nothing. 'Gaille,' he said more loudly, taking a step towards her. 'Are you awake?'

'Why? What is it?'

He came fully into the room, closed the door behind him. 'Shift up,' he said.

She rose up on her elbow. 'What are you doing?'

'The floor's like rock in there. I can't sleep, honest I can't. My legs are killing me from all that walking. I need something soft. Please, Gaille.'

'I don't know,' she said.

'Don't be such a prude,' he said. 'You can trust me, you know. I mean we shared a sleeping bag last night, for Christ's sake.'

She shifted across, not sure how else to handle it. At least the mattress was wide enough for two. He flapped the sleeping bag out beside her, clambered into it, gave her a smile that she could just about see in the darkness, then turned onto his side and put an arm around her waist. 'Stop it,' she said.

'Only teasing,' he sighed, taking his arm away. 'So you and Danny Boy, huh? Was this his idea of a romantic holiday, or something? A conference on Eleusis?'

'We were hoping to visit the islands too,' she said defensively. 'I've always wanted to see Ithaca.'

'You should visit Cephalonia while you're there. It's just a short ferry ride away, and it's absolutely stunning. Everything Athens isn't.'

'Don't you like Athens?'

'I *hate* Athens. The worst thing about my job, I spend half my life shuttling back and forth.' He let out a slightly forced laugh. 'One thing's for sure, if I was trying to make an impression on a beautiful woman, I wouldn't take her there.' He grabbed a pillow, turned it to its cool side. 'Just as well I no longer have one, I suppose.'

Gaille didn't quite know how to respond to that. 'Good night,' she said.

'Yes,' he agreed. 'Good night.'

II

The airport had its own medical centre, but after the police doctor had listened to Knox's account of being water-boarded and beaten, he insisted on taking him to a nearby hospital instead, where they had the equipment to check for internal damage. He was sitting up on the examination table, waiting for the results, when the swing doors pushed open and Theofanis came in, carrying a manila folder and a plastic bag. 'There you are,' he said. 'I've been looking for you.'

'And now you've found me.'

He ignored Knox's tone, held out the bag. 'We found some things of yours in Nergadze's van,' he said. 'Angelos wanted you to have them back.'

'Angelos did?' asked Knox in surprise.

'He's a good man,' said Theofanis. 'He just has a tough job sometimes.'

Knox looked inside the bag, saw his wallet, mobile and the red-leatherette ring box. 'Thanks,' he said. It was a crude peace-offering, but welcome nonetheless. He checked the ring before he put it away in his pocket. It made him think of Gaille, of the threats Mikhail had made. He took out his mobile, and remembered how Mikhail had seen Gaille's photos and text message, all the information he needed to track her down.

'What is it?' asked Theofanis, noticing his unease.

'Nergadze,' said Knox. 'He vowed he'd make Gaille pay if I betrayed him.'

'The man's dead.'

'Yes, but who knows what he did before he died?'

'While running for his life?'

'You didn't meet him. I did. He wasn't the kind to make empty threats, or to forget about them just because he had other matters to attend to. And he's connected, too. His family are incredibly powerful. If he'd given orders –'

'Don't worry about it,' said Theofanis. 'The Nergadzes are finished. The whole family's been taken down by the Georgian government.'

'You're sure?'

446

'I spoke to one of their agents myself. I had to tell him about the poor bastard that Mikhail shot and burned.'

'Even so,' said Knox. 'I need to speak to Gaille. I need to know she's okay.'

'Why don't you just call her?'

He shook his head. He'd tried from a payphone in the hospital lobby. 'She's not answering.'

'I could send a car.'

'She's two hours' walk from the nearest village.'

'Oh.' Theofanis pulled a face. 'Maybe not, then. Not on Easter weekend. Not with the case tied up.'

'Tied up?' snorted Knox.

'Sure. This guy Nergadze and his gang wanted the fleece. They murdered Petitier and Antonius for it. Then they abducted you and this woman Nadya.'

Knox shook his head. 'Nergadze killed Antonius, I'll give you that. But not Petitier. He only abducted me because he believed I'd killed Petitier myself for the fleece. How could he possibly believe that if he'd done it himself?'

Theofanis frowned and held out his manila folder. 'Then have a look at this,' he said.

Knox took it from him. It contained grainy stills from a CCTV camera, of a man in photographer's trousers and a T-shirt, the peak of a baseball cap pulled down over his eyes, masking

447

his face almost entirely from view. 'What are these?' he asked.

'Your lawyer friend Charissa suggested we check the CCTV footage for the hotel lobby the afternoon Petitier was killed. This man arrived there an hour before Petitier. He ordered coffee from the bar then took a table and watched the door. You can see he doesn't even touch his drink. But after Petitier checks in, he waits fifteen more seconds then goes after him to the lifts. I'll bet anything he was waiting for Petitier.'

'Yes,' agreed Knox. 'Do you know where he went?'

Theofanis shook his head. 'We're still looking through the other tapes.'

'And you think he could be the killer?'

'Let's just say we'd like to talk to him. Do you recognise him?'

Knox looked again at the photo. It wasn't Nergadze or any of the other Georgians, that was for sure. And it didn't look like anyone from the conference. Yet he looked familiar all the same, though Knox couldn't work out why. 'I don't know,' he said, passing the folder back. 'But I assume this means Augustin is no longer a suspect.'

'We still have some questions for him,' replied Theofanis. 'For example, what was in that canvas bag he took into the airport?'

The answer came so suddenly to Knox, he couldn't help but laugh. 'Roses,' he said.

'I beg your pardon.'

'When Claire came out of the terminal, she was carrying a huge bunch of white roses. That's what was in the bag.'

'He could have bought them at the airport.'

'Sure, he could,' said Knox. 'After all, he'd only been fretting for a week about making things nice for her, so of course he'd have left it to chance that they'd have flowers on sale.' He'd had enough of Theofanis suddenly, enough of this interminable suspicion, of this determination to find guilt. He jumped down from the examination table, winced as he landed. 'I'm off,' he said. 'I need to get to Crete.'

'You're not going anywhere until you've got clearance.'

'Then you'd better give it to me, hadn't you? Or would you rather fetch one of your colleagues to put me in the bed next to Augustin?'

Theofanis met his stare for a second or two, then sighed and backed down. 'You won't get anywhere tonight,' he said. 'You've already missed the last flight. But I'll drive you back to Athens if you like, and you can fly out in the morning.'

THIRTY-NINE

I

Gaille woke abruptly to a dawn chorus outside her bedroom window, Iain's rhythmic exhalations upon her neck and shoulder, his arm around her waist; but it wasn't any of those which had disturbed her, and which now made her stiffen. It was her belated realisation of something he'd said just before they'd drifted to sleep the night before. 'I *hate* Athens. The worst thing about my job, I spend half my life shuttling back and forth.' Innocuous enough, except for that hollow laugh he'd followed it with. She hadn't picked it up at the time, but it was as though he'd realised too late that he'd said something stupid, and was trying to cover.

She turned slowly onto her back, tipped her head to the side to watch him lying there, his mouth fractionally open, the golden glitter of his stubble, the swell and fall of his chest. The one person who'd known what Petitier looked like, what he'd been up to these past twenty years. A man who, beneath his self-deprecating jokes, yearned for a great discovery. As quietly as she could, she lifted his arm off her. He stirred but didn't wake. She got to her feet, tiptoed out of the room, closed the door softly behind her.

His backpack was resting against the wall by the front door. Her breath came a little faster as she put her hand on it. The fabric felt faintly charged, as though lightly dusted with electricity. It ran against her nature, looking through other people's belongings, but she couldn't stop herself. She unzipped a side-pocket, checked the contents: a lighter and a box of waterproof matches, a torch, a multipurpose penknife, tattered maps of Crete and a handheld GPS. She went through the other pockets, equally stuffed with hiking supplies. The main body of his backpack was filled with clothes. She came across his photographer's trousers, scrunched the cotton for anything in the multitude of pockets. She found his wallet, checked it briskly, put it back. She felt something else, pulled it out. An Athens metro ticket. She turned it to the light, squinted down, went a little numb. It had been validated on the same afternoon that Petitier had –

'What the hell are you doing?'

Her heart skipped a beat. She looked around to see Iain in the bedroom doorway, wearing only his boxer shorts. 'You're up,' she said, stuffing the ticket back in the pocket, the trousers back in the pack.

'Yes. I'm up. Now what the hell are you doing?'

She didn't know what to say. She just squatted there, waiting for inspiration. 'I was only . . .' she began.

He began walking towards her, fists down by his side. 'Yes. You were only what?'

'I was looking for your first-aid kit.'

'Oh.' He stopped short. 'What for?'

'My ankle,' she said. 'I wanted some new bandage. This one's getting dirty and stretched. You don't mind, do you?'

'Of course not,' he said, though warily, as though he didn't quite buy her story. He crouched and unzipped the lower compartment, pulled out the kit.

'I didn't want to wake you,' she said. 'You had such a brutal day yesterday. I wanted to be gone and back by the time you woke.'

'Gone and back?'

'I have to find out what's happening with Daniel and Augustin,' she nodded. 'I *have* to. It's driving me crazy. I thought I could climb high enough to get a signal on my mobile.'

'On your own? With your ankle still crocked? Are you *mad*?'

'I wouldn't take any risks.'

'What do you mean? Just climbing that path is a risk.'

'It's my choice.'

'Really? And who would have to rescue you if something went wrong?'

She hung her head. 'I'm sorry,' she said. 'I guess I wasn't thinking. But I just . . . I *need* to know.'

He sighed and put his hand on her shoulder. 'You shouldn't even be thinking of climbing on that ankle, not for another day at least. Tell you what, why don't I head back up myself. I'll call Knox, tell him what we've been up to, pick up his news. And we can make plans for getting you safely out of here. How does that sound?'

'Terrific,' she said, forcing a smile. 'And thank you so much.'

'My pleasure,' he told her; but there was still something in his eye. His gaze drifted to the Mauser leaning against the wall. 'And maybe I'll take that with me,' he said. 'See if I can't bag us something fresh for tonight's pot.'

II

All the early flights to Heraklion were full, but there was room on the first departure for Chania, a port in north-western Crete. Knox landed a few minutes before six-thirty; with no luggage to collect, he breezed through arrivals. There was only one car-hire booth open, manned by an unshaven middle-aged man in sunglasses who kept pushing the sleeves of his rumpled linen suit up past his elbows. He tried to scare Knox into taking additional insurance against the deductible. 'Nasty roads,' he told him. 'Terrible drivers.'

'Don't worry about me,' Knox assured him, as he took the keys to a Hyundai. 'I live in Egypt.'

It was still early, the roads were empty and good, gorgeous shrubs in full bloom either side, like an extended fairway at Augusta. Bugs tapped the windscreen every few minutes, leaving little smears of themselves. He made excellent time to Vrises, cut south and headed up into the White Mountains. Black nets hung from the steep hillsides like widows' veils. There was a haze in the air, as though someone had lit bonfires. He passed through Petres, then had the road entirely to himself. At first he enjoyed it, taking the hairpins a little faster than was prudent, but gradually the complete quietness began to alarm him. Even this early on a Saturday, it shouldn't be *this* quiet. He was nearing the top of a high pass when he saw the first sign of trouble, road so freshly laid that the glistening tarmac slurped stickily at his tyres. He'd only gone another quarter mile when he saw a pair of huge grey pipes by the side of the road ahead, supports for a tunnel being bored in the cliff. A thin slurry sprayed against his under-carriage as he drove over it, and then the surface disintegrated even further, just raw bedrock in places, scattered with weeds and grasses. He went down into first gear, crested the peak and then wound back and forth on the descent, half expecting to meet some impassable obstacle. It wasn't that great a surprise, therefore, when he saw the two red-and-white barriers across the road, and the bulldozers and earth-movers parked nose-to-tail beyond them, along with huge hummocks of hardcore and tarmac waiting to be laid.

He pulled to a stop, clenched his steering wheel. At another time, he might rather have savoured the righteousness of his indignation that no one had seen fit to put out warning signs thirty miles back, but all he felt at this moment was a dreadful foreboding, an irrational yet overpowering sense that Gaille was in terrible danger. He grabbed his car-rental map. His choices were awful: a massive detour through the mountains or returning all the way to the north coast, then east to Rethymno and south from there. Either option would cost him at least three hours. He got out of the car, slammed his door in frustration, then walked between the barriers to go study the road ahead.

III

Gaille let herself into Argo's pen to refill his emptied bowls. He danced in joyful circles and snuffled and put his paws up on her, smearing her shirt, his tongue like sodden sandpaper on her cheek, his rapture at seeing her extraordinary, more akin to a reprieve from bereavement than a reunion after a night apart. She couldn't help but be touched by it, by mattering so much to another creature, and she hugged him warmly, while wishing his breath wasn't quite so pungent.

Iain called out farewell as he vanished through the orange trees, the Mauser over his shoulder. She didn't buy his story about wanting to bag some game; they had plenty of food in the pantry. He'd simply wanted the rifle for himself, or to deprive her of it. The thought sobered her. She watched him until he'd vanished into the walnut grove then went back inside, uncertain what to do. A decent mobile signal was the best part of an hour's climb away, even for Iain. Add in time talking, she probably had two hours before he got back. She needed to use that time well, which meant learning more about Petitier's finds and Iain's incursions. She went back into the house, pushed aside the armchair, rolled up the rug, lifted the trap-door and limped down the steep steps into the darkness, fumbling for the lights. She started by double-checking that it had truly been Iain in the photographs, that her imagination hadn't been playing tricks.

It was him all right. No question.

Boots scuffed behind her. For the second time that morning, she looked around to see Iain standing there, the Mauser still slung over his shoulder. 'I knew it,' he said. 'I knew you'd found something.'

'But I only just did a moment ago,' she blustered. 'It was all those photos on his wall. I mean, how on earth could he have had them developed? No one does black-and-whites any more. So he had to have his own darkroom. Don't you see?' She spread her hands, aware she was blathering, unable to stop. 'And it had to be somewhere in the house, because of that vinegar we smelled. Acetic acid, you know. Developers use it as a fixing agent.'

Iain wasn't listening. He was staring in astonishment around the basement. Then he looked back at her, at the folder she was holding. 'What's that?' he asked.

'Nothing.'

He walked over and snatched it from her, throwing her a superior stare as he opened it. 'What the . . . ?' he muttered, when he saw the photographs of himself. His complexion paled as he flipped through them, quickly at first, then more slowly, buying himself time to come up with some kind of story. But he must have realised it was useless. He let the folder and the pictures drop to the floor, then shook his head sadly at her, as though she only had herself to blame for anything that happened now.

FORTY

I

Knox stood on the edge of the hillside and stared down. He could follow the grey ribbon of road through countless tortuous hairpins to the valley far beneath, where it straightened out and ran for miles before vanishing over the distant horizon; yet he couldn't see a single vehicle upon it. He'd hoped that someone might be coming the other way, that he could hitch a ride with them when they were forced to turn around. No chance. He got out his mobile instead, to try Gaille's number again or see if he couldn't somehow summon a taxi. But he was too high and too remote to pick up a signal.

Those options closed to him, he studied the road again. The irony was that he could probably make it past the road-works and the parked vehicles, but a landslide, presumably triggered by all this heavy machinery, had bitten a great chomp out of the road's underpinning just a little further on, leaving only a precarious slab of rock like a bridge to the other side, but with virtually nothing beneath to support it.

Knox stepped carefully out onto it. Even under his own modest weight, it seemed to bow a little. He measured its width at its narrowest point, then went back to the Hyundai. The road was perhaps a foot wider than the car; if it held, at least. He pulled a face, unhappy with his options. Apart from anything else, the car wasn't his, and he was puritanical about respecting other people's property. Besides, Theofanis was surely right: Mikhail was dead, and it was only paranoia to think he'd have arranged something malevolent before he died. And, even if he had, it wasn't as though Gaille was alone. Iain was with her, and he was no pushover. People often underestimated him, because of his boyish looks and fair hair, but –

Knox went cold. Belatedly, he realised why the figure in the hotel CCTV had looked so familiar. It had been Iain. He was sure of it.

It made up his mind for him, at least. He needed to get to Gaille now. He moved the barriers aside, got back in his Hyundai, put it into first gear and edged forwards, driving with painful slowness up and over a heap of hardcore, his undercarriage scraping rock, though too slowly to do any damage. He rode his brakes down the far side, letting gravity do the work. There was a pile of tarmac next, dumped against the cliff-face. It crunched beneath his tyres, setting off small cascades, tilting him at so steep an angle that he had to lean against his door. But finally he was over that too. He passed the earth-moving equipment more easily, his tyres still crunching from the accreted tarmac, then reached the narrow bridge.

He put on his handbrake and got out to inspect it once more. Even if it held, it was going to be incredibly tight. He got back in, steered as far away from the drop as he could, until his passenger side scraped the cliff-side. He hated causing such wilful damage, but he steeled himself and pressed on. He heard something crack beneath him and then the whole section of road he was on lurched perceptibly and began slowly to tip sideways like a ship being launched into the sea. It was too late to reverse back out, so he stamped his foot down and surged forwards. His front tyres bumped the far side and rode up it even as his back wheels sank behind him, his undercarriage scraping along the torn edge of the road. He stamped down even harder and his wheels span furiously, but then somehow they gained traction again and he spurted forwards onto the other side as the road fell away behind him in a furious avalanche of rock; but now he was hurtling too fast at the upcoming hairpin, he slammed on his brakes and hauled on his steering wheel with all his weight, throwing the Hyundai into a skid that brought him to a halt less than a metre from the edge, his engine stalling, the sweat pouring off him, fully aware of how close a call he'd just had.

He sat there a few moments to compose himself, then got out. The next stretch of road was scattered with debris from the landslide he'd just caused, but there was nothing he couldn't clear away or steer around. He took a tour of the Hyundai. His driver-side front tyre was buckled and flat, and the offside wing looked as though it had been shredded by some vengeful harpy; but he didn't need it looking good, he only needed for it to run.

There was no point wasting time changing his tyre or clearing the road until he'd found out the answer to that question, so he got back into the driver's seat, his heart in his mouth, and tested the ignition. Unknown things rattled, clanked and whirred within the bonnet, then died away again. He tried it a second and then a third time, without success.

But on the fourth it came reluctantly to life.

II

There was something uncomfortably vault-like about this basement, Gaille suddenly realised. If someone should die down here, and the trap door was sealed, their body might never be found.

'So I've been here before,' said Iain. 'So what?'

'You might have told me,' she said.

'Yes,' admitted Iain. 'Perhaps I should have. But it would only have made you suspicious, when there was nothing to be suspicious about. I mean, look at it from my point of view. When I started doing the research for my book, I found I was consulting the exact same materials as Petitier had already consulted. The *exact* same ones.'

'You got curious?' suggested Gaille, shuffling fractionally to her right, trying to open up a line to the doorway.

'*Of course* I got curious,' agreed Iain, stepping sideways to block her. 'Why wouldn't I have done? So the next time he turned up, I kept an eye on him. You should have seen him. Clapping his hands all the time. Cackling. I knew he must have found something good. It was obvious. What was I supposed to do?'

'Inform the authorities.'

'Of what? It's not illegal to do research, you know.'

'So you followed him?'

'He didn't make it easy,' nodded Iain. 'He was paranoid as hell. He kept stopping and getting out and glaring at the traffic behind him. It took me three goes, and I had to use a different car each time. Do you really expect me to have told you that straight out? I'd never even met you before. What if you'd got all holier-than-thou on me and insisted on going to the authorities? It could have killed my career.'

'I gave you the perfect cover, didn't I? A chance to come here and check this out, then blame me if it went wrong.'

'This is absurd, Gaille. You're being absurd. I didn't have to bring you here at all. I could have kept it to myself. You'd never have found out. No one would. But your friend was in trouble, and I thought I could help. Was that really so wicked? Anyway, how come it's okay for you to investigate, but not me? You think you're so special, don't you, you and Knox? You make a couple of lucky finds, and now you think you're *entitled*. Well I'm a Minoan scholar, I've spent my whole life studying places like these. What's your reason for being here?'

'Augustin.'

'Sure! Nothing to do with coveting glory, I suppose. Do you two even realise the harm you've done to archaeology? I had to suffer through that bloody Alexander press conference with my wife sitting next to me. You and Knox and that fat bastard from the SCA. *Knox!* This zero of a guy I was at university with; this *also-ran*! And suddenly he's a global superstar. You should have seen the way the little darling looked at me after that.'

'You're not blaming us for your failed marriage, are you?'

'It should have been me,' he said, his eyes blazing. 'I was always ahead of Knox at university. I was always the destined one. Ask him, if you don't believe me. He was *nothing*. He was *a nobody*. I was the one! It was *me!*'

'You got angry,' murmured Gaille.

'Too bloody right I got angry.'

'That's why your wife left you. She became afraid.'

'That's it! Take *her* side.'

'You hit her. She was pregnant and you hit her.'

'Don't say that!' said Iain, taking a step towards her. 'Don't you dare say that! I never hit her. I never laid a fucking finger on her.'

'Yes, you did.'

'She was going to take away my son,' he yelled. 'What the hell was I supposed to do?'

'And this was your way to win her back, was it?' asked Gaille. 'To prove you were a somebody after all. That was why you couldn't let Petitier give his speech, wasn't it? You couldn't have him going public before your book came out. So you followed him to Athens.'

He took half a step back in surprise. 'What are you talking about?'

'You're always travelling there. That's what you told me last night.'

'It was a figure of speech.'

'Sure! And that Athens Metro ticket in your backpack. Is that a figure of speech too?'

He stared numbly at her. Too late, Gaille realised how reckless she'd just been. She nodded twice, as if she were the one in charge, then walked for the stairs, hoping he'd be too dazed to stop her. But he came after her when she was barely halfway up, pushed past her and turned to block her escape. 'We're going to talk this out,' he said.

'Talk what out?' She tried to get by him, but he was too strong. They jostled a moment, his forearm accidentally pressing against her breast. His throat coloured; he scowled and shoved her tumbling to the bottom. She landed on her side and winded herself on the point of her elbow. He began walking down towards her, a disturbing mix of resentment, fear and lust in his eyes. She scrambled into the chemistry lab, slammed its door behind her, grabbed the chair and leaned it at an angle beneath the handle.

'Let me in,' he demanded. 'Let me in.'

'Leave me alone.'

'This is crazy, Gaille. You're acting like a crazy person.' He pounded on the door so hard that the wood trembled and the chair ceded a few millimetres. He hit it again and the chair fell away altogether. She threw her shoulder against it and tried to hold him back, but he was far too strong for her, pushing her slithering backwards. She retreated against the work table. He advanced upon her, reached out and touched her breast again, purposefully this time. She crossed her arms in front of her and turned her shoulder. The shelf of chemicals snagged her eye as she did so, all those skull and crossbones labels. She reached out and grabbed a bottle of sodium hydroxide, twisted off its lid and discharged it at his face. He cried out and closed his eyes and flapped wildly at the white powder.

She broke away and ran to the steps and up, slamming the trap door down after her. There was no lock, so she tried to shift the armchair back over it. He was too quick for her, however; the trap-door flew up and slammed onto its back and then he was out, fumbling like some horror-movie zombie. She fled outside, where Argo was barking and jumping against the wire of his pen, sensing she was in trouble. She unbolted the door, went inside, grabbed his leash and tried to buckle it to his collar; but he was too excited to stay still, he kept dancing in wild circles, snatching the buckle from her fingers.

'Come out of there,' demanded Iain, his face reddened by the caustic soda, tears streaming from his eyes.

'Stay away.' She finally clipped on the leash, wrapped it around her fist, then opened the door. Argo lunged at Iain; it was all Gaille could do to hold him.

'Keep him back,' yelled Iain, taking hold of the Mauser by its barrel, wielding it like a club.

She hauled Argo away to her right. It was a battle at first, but then he abruptly conceded and forged ahead instead, snuffling intoxicating scents in the grass, dragging her flailing helplessly in his wake like some out-of-control water-skier. She tried to steer him towards the escarpment, but he was too strong and determined, he wanted to go north.

'Come back,' said Iain.

'Leave me alone.'

'Okay,' he said. 'You're right. I *was* in Athens. I admit it. I heard Petitier was going to give a talk, and I got angry. I don't know why. I suppose I'd come to think of this place as mine. I went to Athens hoping to talk him out of it. I waited for him in the lobby. When he checked in, I overheard his room number, so I went up to talk to him. But he never showed. He must have spotted me. And, anyway, all those archaeologists there made me realise what a dick I was being. Whatever he's found here doesn't belong to me *or* to him. It belongs to everyone. He was doing the right thing. So I took the first flight back to Crete. That's when Knox left all his messages and I found out what had happened. Of course I kept my mouth shut. If I'd owned up to being there, the police would have jumped to all kinds of conclusions. You don't know what the Greek police are like. The last thing on earth you want is to be caught up in a murder enquiry here.'

Argo had dragged Gaille to the edge of the yellow gorse, was now following it around. He suddenly turned and plunged into the gorse itself, forcing Gaille to follow. There was a path of sorts, wending this way and that through the prickly labyrinth, but it was so narrow that she had to turn sideways to follow it, doing her best to cushion her sore ankle each time she landed. Argo never hesitated, the scent strong in his nostrils. But it was only when Gaille saw a dried crust of orange peel on the ground that she realised it wasn't just *any* scent Argo was following.

It was Petitier's.

III

The Hyundai's engine was gurgling and clattering, but somehow Knox made it down to the coast. He passed the port of Hora Sfakion, headed

inland again, up a steep and zigzagging road. He
put the gear-stick into second for a tight corner
and then couldn't get it out again. He reached the
top, then passed through the small town of
Anapoli. Men were sitting at two tables outside a
café in the square; they got to their feet when they
saw him bunny-hopping along, and started clapping and whooping him on, like he was a cyclist
in the Tour de France. He followed signs to Agia
Georgio. His mobile began to ring as he rattled
across a gorge on a timber bridge, but it fell off
the passenger seat when he fumbled for it, and slid
beyond his reach. He didn't dare stop to retrieve
it, lest the car wouldn't restart.

The landscape was as calm as his nerves were
jangled. Hills, woods and meadows, untended
flocks of sheep and goats. A flight of finches took
off ahead of him and fled down a narrow tunnel
of trees. He reached Agia Georgio to find a gate
barring the road, leaving him no choice but to
stop. His engine stalled at once, as he'd feared it
would, and wouldn't restart. His mobile began
ringing again. He grabbed it from beneath the seat.
'Yes?'

'It's me,' said Angelos. 'Now I want you to
listen. I don't want you getting alarmed.'

'Alarmed?' asked Knox, getting out of the car
and letting himself through the gate. 'What's
happened?' A Doberman leashed to a fencepost

started barking so furiously that he had to clamp a hand over his ear to hear.

'It's just, there's some confusion about the body we recovered from the wreckage last night,' said Angelos. 'It may not have been Mikhail Nergadze after all.'

Somehow, it wasn't the shock to Knox it might have been. Somehow, he'd almost expected it. 'Tell me,' he said, giving the Doberman a wide berth.

'The Citroen was rented to a Belgian businessman named Josef Jannsen. He flew in from Bruges to check out a nightclub down in Varkiza he was thinking of buying. He was due to meet the owners there last night, but he never showed.'

Knox jogged up a narrow cobbled road to a village square. A mountain spring was splashing into a carved stone drinking fountain. He scooped a mouthful of the icy melt-water before continuing on up. 'You're saying it was this guy Jannsen in the car, not Nergadze?'

'That's how it looks. According to one of the Georgians, Nergadze had a bunch of tattoos; but there weren't any on the body we found. Nergadze must have realised there'd be a major manhunt for him. This must have been his way of stopping it before it could get started. We think he waited in car-hire until this poor bastard Jannsen turned up. He killed him and cut off his hair and then traded clothes with him. Then he set the driver's seat as low and as far back as it would go, belted Jannsen in and sat on top of him.' A stout woman dressed all in black watched suspiciously from the shadows of her porch. 'Maybe he genuinely hoped to drive out,' continued Angelos. 'I can't say. But he certainly had a contingency plan. We know he'd been to that industrial area before. We found the second Mercedes in a lock-up there, along with the body of one of his men, the one who tried to steal his cash. So it looks as though he deliberately led us there, yelled out his name so we'd be certain it was him, then drove at that container.'

Knox nodded, picturing how it would have happened. 'He'd have waited till the last moment, then dived down passenger side.'

'Maybe that's why he chose a convertible, because the roof would shear off more cleanly. Or maybe that was just luck. And that's why it was raining cash. It looked like a lot of money, but it was only a fraction of what was in the case. We reckon he scattered it around precisely so that the first policeman to get to the car would be watching it, rather than the trees. Meanwhile, he'd have hidden the rest of the money along with some clean clothes and Jannsen's passport and wallet; I'll bet once he was out of the car and away, he collected them, cleaned himself up, then went calm as you like into the terminal. Only a crazy man would even contemplate such a thing, of course. But from everything you've told us . . .'

'Into the terminal?' asked Knox. The road deteriorated into an unsealed track. He jogged along it, his breath coming faster. A mule munched grass as it watched him pass. 'You're not saying he just flew out of there?'

'It looks like it,' admitted Angelos. 'At least, someone flew out last night, using Jannsen's name and credit card.'

'Nergadze,' said Knox. 'Where did he go?'

'This is why I don't want you getting alarmed,' said Angelos.

'Oh, Christ!' said Knox. 'He flew to Crete, didn't he? He's going for Gaille.'

'He can't be *that* crazy. He's on the run, remember. He must know we'll work it out eventually. He's certain to go to ground.'

'No,' said Knox. 'He's going for Gaille.'

A shout at the other end of the line. 'Bear with me,' said Angelos. Knox could hear angry voices, recriminations. He kept running, the phone clamped against his ear. The track grew worse. He saw a roadblock of boulders ahead, and two cars parked side-by-side in the trees. 'Okay,' said Angelos. 'Here's the very latest. Heraklion Airport has confirmed that Jannsen landed late last night. He hired himself a rental. A Mazda.'

'Don't tell me,' said Knox. 'Licence plate: HKN 1447.'

'How the hell did you know that?'

'Because he's here,' said Knox numbly. 'He got here before me.'

FORTY-ONE

I

Argo surged irrepressibly through the gorse, cutting beneath the worst of the thorns, with Gaille, still hanging onto his leash, taking numerous scratches on her hands and arms. She half stumbled on a stone and cried out and hauled him back so violently that he stopped at last, if only in surprise, allowing her to recover her balance and glance back.

Iain was striding through the gorse behind her, but that wasn't what shocked her. What shocked her was that a third person had appeared, a man wearing jeans and a green sweatshirt and a plain blue baseball cap tugged down over his eyes, who'd also found the mouth of the path and was following them along it.

Iain must have seen the surprise on Gaille's face,

for he whirled around. 'Who the fuck are you?' he demanded.

The man held up his hands to allay suspicion. 'Don't be alarmed,' he said. 'I'm a friend.'

Iain grabbed his Mauser from his shoulder, levelled it at the man's chest. 'I'll be the judge of that,' he said. 'What's your name? What are you doing here?'

'My name's Mikhail,' replied the man, spreading his arms as wide as crucifixion, but still walking towards Iain. He nodded pleasantly at Gaille. 'Your friend Daniel sent me. He's worried sick about you. You should have called him.'

'We can't get a signal,' she said.

'Ah,' he said. 'Is that all it was?'

'Stay where you are,' ordered Iain.

'Please lower that thing,' said Mikhail. 'I hate guns.'

'I said stay where you are.'

'I'm one of the good guys,' said Mikhail, continuing his advance. 'I can prove it.' He extended his left palm forward, like a policeman stopping traffic, then reached behind him with his right hand, and drew a hunting knife from his belt.

'What the fuck . . . ?' muttered Iain, taking off the Mauser's safety-catch. 'Stay back!'

But it was too late, Mikhail was already on him. He swatted away the Mauser barrel with his left hand, then thrust the knife hard up beneath Iain's ribcage, lifting him off his feet for a moment, giving the blade a sharp, vindictive twist. The Mauser discharged with a futile crack, clattered to the ground. Mikhail pulled out the knife, allowing Iain to slump to his knees and onto his back, making ghastly keening and sucking sounds. 'Guns don't kill people,' Mikhail told him piously, as he wiped the blade on his sleeve and put it back in his belt. '*People* kill people.' Then he picked up the Mauser and turned it on Gaille.

It was only now that she recognised him from the lift. He saw it in her eyes and grinned. 'I told you I had a good memory for faces,' he said.

II

The Mazda was locked, but Knox could see discarded packaging on the passenger seat. 'He's armed,' he told Angelos bleakly. 'He's got himself a hunting knife.'

'Don't do anything stupid. I'll send cars.'

'Cars?' asked Knox. 'How long before they get here? How long before they can get to Gaille?'

'A helicopter, then. I'll call the army.'

'It'll still be hours,' said Knox. 'I can't wait. Gaille can't wait.' The track zigzagged upwards towards the pass between two high peaks high above him, but he picked a more direct line and set off up it, as fast as he could without exhausting himself. A bell tolled on a distant slope, and monks began to chant. It sounded almost like a funeral. The ground was thick with purple lavender that buzzed with insects. He passed through a collar of scorched pines out onto steeper slopes of gaunt rock. It took all his strength of will to maintain his pace until he'd made it up to the mouth of the pass.

It grew easier at once, the flatter terrain and a cooling wind blowing in his face. He ran as fast as his weariness and the treacherous footing would allow. Gaille must have come this way with Iain. The thought reminded him of his earlier suspicions about his university friend. He'd forgotten them completely in the shock of Angelos' news about Mikhail, but surely they were worth reporting. He checked his mobile. He still had enough signal to make a call.

'I'm getting your helicopter,' Angelos promised. 'You have to give me time.'

'It's not about that,' panted Knox. 'I think I know who that man in the CCTV is.'

'And?'

'His name's Iain Parkes.' He came to a wire fence, its stakes topped by animal skulls. He pushed down the top strand and straddled it. 'He's an archaeologist at Knossos. And he's with Gaille right now.'

'Okay,' said Angelos.

'Okay?' protested Knox, as he continued along the pass. 'She's stuck on her own with two killers, and you're telling me it's okay?'

'I didn't mean it like that. It's just the coroner sent over his toxicology report earlier. He now thinks our initial assessment was wrong, that Petitier wasn't killed by a blow to his head, after all.'

'What?'

'It was a heart attack, almost certainly brought about by an overdose. His system was flooded with drugs. Cocaine. Opium. Speed. Acid. You name it. I've never seen levels this high. You could boil down his blood and sell it on the street for millions.'

'An overdose,' muttered Knox in disbelief, as he recalled Augustin lying in intensive care.

'Theofanis thinks it happened like this,' said Angelos quickly. 'Petitier was an addict, that much is clear. Mixing with other people is hard after twenty years on your own. Not to mention giving a talk to a large conference. He'd have wanted a big stash close to hand.'

'That's why he was protecting his bag? Because it was filled with drugs?'

'It makes sense. I mean, we've been trying to find out what flight he came in on, but none of the airlines have any record of him. So now we're thinking maybe he came by boat instead, because he couldn't risk his bag being searched. Anyway, he gets to the hotel, Augustin lets him in, then leaves. He's confused, he's stressed, he thinks he's being followed. He takes something. Then something else. A real cocktail, uppers, downers, whatever he's got. He begins to feel unwell. He feels *unclean*. People often do with hallucinogens; their skin crawls. He takes a shower. He has his first cardiac event, not fatal but severe enough to make him fall. He hits his head against the taps. His scalp splits open, he's disoriented. He knows he needs a doctor, but he can't risk anyone finding his drugs or it could mean years in gaol, so he struggles out of the bathroom, dripping blood, and takes his overnight bag out onto the balcony. He rips it open, flings his drugs over the railing, then goes back inside for the phone. But he doesn't make it in time, he has his second heart attack, and it cripples him. And then he just lies there dying, unable to do anything until you and Augustin come in.'

'LSM,' muttered Knox.

'I beg your pardon?'

'His last word to me. Not Elysium. LSM. It's a variant of LSD that he experimented with. He was trying to tell me what drugs he'd taken. And his final croak. Cocaine.'

'I've suspended Grigorias,' said Angelos. 'I want you to know that. And we'll hold a full and independent investigation. You have my word. I've already sent a team to look in the alley beneath the balcony, see if we can find those drugs.'

'The hotel keeps its trash there,' Knox told him. 'I heard them collecting it yester –' A gunshot cracked out ahead, echoed ominously off the pass walls. 'Jesus,' said Knox. 'Did you hear that?'

'I'll get you your helicopter,' promised Angelos.

Knox stuffed the mobile back in his pocket as he ran. Two more shots sounded, giving strength to his heavy legs. The pass suddenly dropped away ahead of him and he reached the precipitous brim of a massive caldera. He scanned the plain at its foot, the fields, the house, the high surrounding cliffs. His eye was snagged by movement in a sea of yellow gorse far away to his right, where a figure shrunk by distance advanced upon another huddled in a clearing. Even from this distance, he knew it was Gaille. He yelled as loudly as he could, but the wind threw his shouts back uselessly in his face. He looked down at the excuse for a path beneath him: however recklessly he took it, he couldn't hope to get to Gaille in time to help her. But there was a track of sorts leading around the rim of the escarpment, and maybe if he got to the cliffs above her . . .

His legs were already aching and weak, but he steeled himself for one last effort, and set off.

III

Gaille flung herself to the ground as Mikhail turned the Mauser on her, hiding beneath the canopy of gorse. Beside her, Argo was going crazy; he danced in circles, tangling up his leash, then broke away from her and raced back along the path. 'Argo!' she cried. 'Come back!' But he didn't listen, he charged on. She braced herself; a single shot cracked. Her heart twisted. She heard Argo fall, his piteous yelps and whines. A second shot, then only silence.

Hatred, grief, anger, terror. Too many emotions to process. She heard rustling: Mikhail was coming for her. She scrambled through the gorse on her hands and knees, the gorse's secret life revealed, beetles and lizards and butterflies, sunlight dappled by the tangle of branches. A bird whirred from its nest almost beneath her face, startling her so that she raised her head above cover, ducking back down again before Mikhail could shoot.

She emerged into a small clearing, the last thing she needed. She crept around its edge, looking around for a way out, not seeing one. The escarpment rose to her left, though it wasn't a sheer wall like elsewhere, but rather a shale-covered slope. She leapt to her feet and ran along it with her head ducked, hoping to put distance between herself and Mikhail, but the shale gave way beneath her, she stumbled and fell almost at once into the yellow tangle. To her surprise, branches of gorse fell away with her, and she saw that their bases had been sawn-through, and that they'd been deliberately stacked against the foot of the hill, as if someone had been trying to hide something.

Mikhail was still bulling his way towards her. She pulled more branches away, revealing symbols chiselled into the rock-face, a triangle and a wavy band, and then the small low black mouth of a cave opening. She dropped down onto her hands and knees to crawl along it, grit and earth sprinkling on her face and hair, before it abruptly opened up. It was too dark to see inside, yet the echoes of her own heavy breathing gave her the impression of cavernous space. She got out of the way of the mouth, allowing in enough light to see a pickaxe and a sledgehammer resting against the wall. The sledgehammer was too heavy for her, so she took the pickaxe instead. The thought of using it against anything living made her feel queasy, but she reminded herself of what Mikhail had just done to Iain and Argo, and it gave her strength. She could hear him approaching outside; she hid herself out of view. The faint light dimmed further as he found the mouth. 'Are you in there?' he teased. 'Are you *waiting* for me?'

'Go away,' she told him.

'I won't hurt you if you come out. You have my word.'

'I said go away.'

It went even darker, she heard him grunting his way through the cave's tight mouth. She lifted the pickaxe, readied herself to strike. Perhaps he heard her, or glimpsed her foot, but he must have realised his vulnerability, for he stopped and then retreated. The cave grew a little lighter again. She rested the pickaxe back down on the ground, keeping a firm grip upon its shaft, certain it wouldn't be long before he tried again.

FORTY-TWO

I

Nico held his phone in both hands for the best part of a minute, as though it were a talisman, as though it had the power to answer prayers. And maybe it did.

All people's lives were set as children, Nico believed. Formative years, they called them, and they were right. The first time you ate a food that astonished you with its exquisite taste. Your first love, your first applause. Magical moments that made you so yearn for a reprise that you'd structure your whole life around them.

For Nico, the defining moment had come during a family holiday in the Peloponnese. His brother had been the class swot; he'd persuaded his father to take them on a tour of Mycenae, Epidaurus, Corinth and the other great sites. Nico had suffered from a boredom so intense that it had been a kind of torture. Then they'd visited Olympia, site of the ancient games. This had been long before the tourist boom, of course; they'd been the only ones there. *More damned ruins! What did people see in the things?* He'd mooched off by himself, had come across a tall grassed bank, a short arched passageway cut into it. He'd walked through it and had emerged shockingly into the ancient stadium. He could remember that moment still, the dazzle of the rising sun, the grassed banks for the crowds, the whole arena infused with a spirit of celebration, competition, achievement. Of *greatness*. He'd never really understood until that moment what people had meant by atmosphere. He'd never believed in ghosts. But all that had changed in a single heartbeat. His dream of becoming an Olympic athlete had been born at that moment; and when that dream had failed him, he'd turned to archaeology instead, because his love of ancient Greece had been born that day too.

He owed that love to his parents.

The ringing, when finally it began, seemed longer and deeper than usual, as though time itself were being distended. He almost hung up on the fifth ring, but then it was picked up and it was too late. A man's voice. 'Hello?' he said.

'Hello, father,' said Nico, his mouth sticky and dry. 'It's me.'

A silence ensued; an incredulous silence, if silence can have such a quality. Then: '*Nico*?'

'Yes.' The silence grew and grew. Too much time had passed. This had been a mistake. 'I'm sorry,' he blurted out. 'I shouldn't have —'

'No!' said his father. 'Don't hang up. Please. I beg you.'

'I wanted to talk to you,' said Nico. 'I wanted to see you. I thought maybe lunch.'

'Of course. Your mother and I . . . that is, we were having friends over. The Milonas. You remember them?'

'Yes.'

'We'll put them off. They won't mind.'

'Not on my account. But maybe I could join you. I'd like to see them. It's been a long time.'

'Of course. Of course. I'll go tell your mother now. She'll want to make sure we have enough. And Nico . . .'

'Yes?' He waited, but his father said no more. It took Nico several seconds to realise it was because he couldn't speak without betraying himself. It was strange and rather shocking to hear his father weep. He'd always seemed the embodiment of strength. 'It's okay,' he told him.

'It's not okay,' sobbed his father. 'It's not. It's not. Forgive me, Nico. You have to forgive me.'

'I forgive you, father. And I'll see you for lunch. Ask mother to do some of her *spanakopites*. I can't tell you how I've missed them.' He put the phone down then stared down at his hands in surprise, the way they were shaking. Then something splashed into his palm, and he realised he was weeping too.

II

Inside the cave, Gaille waited for Mikhail; but moments stretched into minutes and still he didn't come. Her adrenal surge ebbed; her arms and shoulders began to ache from the tension and from gripping the pickaxe handle too tight. She tried to loosen her grip, only to discover that her palms had glued to the wood with congealed blood. She must have torn them open on the thorns or the shale. She pulled them free one at a time, the reopened cuts stinging like lashes.

She risked a glance along the throat of the cave to its mouth. Motes danced with midges in the circle of sunshine, but there was no sign of Mikhail. She felt a flutter of hope. Perhaps he'd given up, realising that her position was impregnable. Perhaps rescue had arrived. Or perhaps he was simply waiting for curiosity to get the better of her. Her eyes had adjusted a little to the gloom. She could see things now that had previously been hidden. A generator with its pearly white plastic tank; an orange electrical cable snaking off it; a wooden crate on the floor beside it. She took another glance to make sure Mikhail hadn't returned, then hurried to the crate and rummaged through it for anything useful. Old water bottles filled with fuel that left their distinctive stench on her hands. A torch, heavy with batteries. She turned it on, found another replica Phaistos disc in the crate, reminding her of the triangle and wavy line she'd seen carved in the rock. She looked for those symbols now and found them at the very centre of one of the spirals, suggesting the disc was a map of some kind, one side of which led here. She looked at the spiral on the obverse side. There was a rosette at its heart, symbol of Minoan royalty. She set the disc back down and shone the torch upon the nearest wall, where faint traces of ancient paintings showed upon the rock, then up at the high jagged ceiling and finally at the rear of the cave, where a passage vanished into the darkness. She considered going to look for somewhere to hide, but decided against. The cave mouth was defensible, but once Mikhail got inside, she'd be lost.

The torch beam started to dim, the batteries evidently weak, for all their weight. She turned it off again, its light too valuable to squander, then put it back in the crate and returned to her post. Her hopes began to rise as the minutes passed and there was still no sign of Mikhail. But then she heard noises outside, and those hopes came crashing back to earth. The cave grew darker again. 'Getting lonely yet?' he asked.

'Leave me alone.'

'It's lovely out here. Lots of nice moss for you to lie on.'

'Go away.'

'I have to do this, you know. I gave your boyfriend my word. I always keep my word.'

His assault was coming. She could tell it from the excitement in his voice. She tightened her grip on the pickaxe, lifted it above her head, prepared herself to bring it down. *One shot,* she prayed silently. *That's all I ask.*

Scuffling in the passage, then a glimpse of his head beneath his baseball cap. She didn't hesitate, she smashed the pickaxe down. But to her horror his head simply tumbled away across the cave, coming to rest on its side, and it was Iain looking up at her, not Mikhail. She shrieked and dropped the pickaxe just as Mikhail appeared, his blood-smeared knife in his hand. She turned and fled blindly into the cave. The floor was slick; her feet flew from beneath her, she careened down a short abrasive chute, her elbow and knee banging, her head hitting rock. She staggered up, fumbled her way along a wall, small pools of drip-water on the floor seeping through the thin canvas of her shoes, cold as fear upon her soles.

Behind her, she heard the rip and stutter of Mikhail hauling at the generator's starter-rope. The engine caught first time and lamps began to glow all around, robbing her of the sanctuary of darkness, and leaving her at Mikhail's mercy.

III

Knox's legs were jellied with fatigue, his ankles turning with painful regularity on the loose rocks that he used as stepping stones to cross the thick tangle of thorny shrubs. It felt like he'd been circling the escarpment for hours, though it could only in truth have been twenty minutes. The terrain near the cliff edge was so difficult that it forced him out wide, denying him the chance to monitor what was going on below. But eventually he reached the marker he'd given himself – an outcrop of rock like a pine-cone lying on its side – and he cut back to the escarpment rim to find himself high above the yellow sea of gorse, the clearing visible a little to his below, though without any sign of life.

What now?

His breath was whistling in his throat; a stitch jabbed in his side and at his bruised ribs. He got down onto his knees then lay on his front and leaned out over the edge to examine the cliff-face beneath him for a manageable way down. What he saw could have been better, but it could have been worse too. The top third was almost sheer, but it was craggy enough to offer plentiful holds, even for an inexperienced climber like himself. Beneath that, it grew incrementally less steep to a slope of loose earth and shale that fed straight into the gorse.

He gave his legs a few moments more to recover, then he lay on his belly and grabbed some roots with either hand and swung his legs out over the edge, searching with his toes until they found crags and ledges strong enough to take his weight. He let go of one of the roots and took a grip of the cliff edge, then lowered himself further. He kept at it, not looking down, his progress frustratingly slow. But finally he reached the end of the first section, where the gradient relented a little. The face was still steep, but seemed to consist of bands of limestone that had weathered at different speeds, creating a series of giant steps cut by time and nature. It was an opportunity to make up some time. He turned around until he was facing outwards, then jumped down onto the ledge several feet beneath him, legs bent to cushion his landing. He stumbled a little but made sure to fall against the face and away from danger. He picked himself up, wiped the grit from his palms, then looked down for another ledge to jump down to. This time, however, his ankle turned beneath him, and he stumbled the wrong way, forcing him straight into a third leap, then a fourth, his arms now flailing wildly for balance. He hit the lower slopes at such speed that it would have been suicide to try to stop, so he went with it instead, trusting to gravity and the skill of his quick feet, his legs pumping crazily, soil and loose grey stones cascading all around him, until finally he stumbled and tumbled and crashed like a bowling ball into the gorse, the thorns ripping his shirt to shreds, but acting like a safety net too, slowing and then stopping him.

He lay there for a moment, face down in the tangles, gathering his breath, assessing himself for injury. Every inch of him throbbed and stung and ached, but nothing felt broken or ruptured. He got gingerly to his feet, fought his way through the gorse and the creepers to the clearing. There was a gash in the rock-face. Light was coming from inside, along with the low chunter of a generator. He breathed in deep to steel himself, then got down onto his hands and knees and crawled inside.

FORTY-THREE

I

The lamps were each connected by a short white flex to the main cable, noted Gaille, the junctions wrapped in balls of duct-tape to keep out moisture. They made eerie pockets of light in the darkness, coaxing ghosts and monsters from the walls, so that she suffered a sudden brief flashback to a forgotten childhood trauma, losing hold of her mother's hand while walking with her through a fairground haunted house, giving her a horror of the darkness that had lasted for months.

She reached a new gallery, sparkling with seams of quartz and calcium, glanced almost instinctively upwards to see how high the chamber's ceiling was; but the footing was too slick for such liberties, and her feet went from beneath her, so that she had to grab the wall and cling on. The moment she let go again, however, she slipped once more, clapping her ankle against rock, grazing her skin, feeling the sharp pulse of drawn blood.

There were chalk-marks scrawled in French upon the wall. *Plumed head*, read one. *Ox-hide*, read another. Symbols from the Phaistos disc, discovered and marked up by Petitier, more evidence that the disc was a map designed to find and navigate through this place. But navigate to what? A low overhang forced her down onto hands and knees. She crawled through a cobweb veil, gossamer, flies and grit congealing in her hair.

A lamp was wasting its light by lying face-down against the left-hand wall. She turned it around to illuminate a large chamber with a ribbed roof and several shallow pits dug in the dirt floor. Several boxes of artefacts were stacked against the walls, votive offerings and what looked like fragments of bone. Caves had often been used as cemeteries by the ancients, one reason why so many of them had become sacred ancestral sites. An albino insect scurried for the darkness as she set the lamp back down, giving hints of a closed ecosystem in which everything fed off everything else.

She followed the orange cable up a hummock of loose rubble, an ancient rock-fall through which Petitier had burrowed a tunnel several metres long. She hoped that the far side would prove defensible, like the cave mouth had been, but the new gallery opened up too gradually for an ambush. Again, Petitier had left abundant evidence of his excavations; despite everything, Gaille couldn't help but notice how meticulous he'd been. He hadn't simply charged around with a spade, looking for plunder, as she'd half expected. He'd taken great pains to –

Mikhail suddenly grunted behind her. She whirled around, heart in her mouth, expecting to see him almost upon her; but she was alone. Nothing but cave acoustics. The fright spurred her on, however. The cave forked in two ahead, with symbols carved into the rock above either passage, circled and chalked by Petitier. The orange cable led away down the left-hand passage, offering her a very Manichaean choice between light and dark. She was about to choose darkness, the better to hide, when it occurred to her that if Mikhail had taken the torch, he'd have too great an advantage. She headed left instead, came to a high rock shelf against which a wooden ladder was strapped with frayed white rope. She climbed it quickly, knelt down to untie it and pull it up after her, but the knots were damp and pulled so tight that she couldn't work her fingernails into them, and then she heard Mikhail coming and it was too late.

She fled deeper into the caves, reaching the top of a sloped shelf of rock, so smooth it looked almost polished. She got onto her backside and used her palms and heels as brakes as she slithered down to the foot, finding herself at the opening of a very different kind of passage, one that had been deliberately excavated out of the rock: its floor was level, its ceiling arched, and its walls were smoothed and inlaid with fragments of marble and precious stones. There were even substantial sections of surviving plaster, the paint upon them recently revived by Petitier, to judge from the basket of cleaning equipment upon the floor. To her left, a young man vaulted over a bull. To her right, three goddesses held up poppies, grapes, mushrooms and other gifts of the earth, while snakes weaved about their feet.

She walked along this corridor to the top of a staircase. But it didn't lead her far. A great section of the roof and side-wall had collapsed, laying an impassable barrier of rubble across it. Petitier had leaned a short wooden ladder against the leftmost section of this accidental wall, and had dug a hole in its top corner, through which he'd fed the orange cable, so that a little light glowed weakly from the other side. She climbed the ladder, hoping she might somehow be able to squeeze and wriggle through, but the hole was too small – no bigger than was necessary to reach a camera and its flash attachment through, and take photographs. And again she realised that perhaps she'd misjudged Petitier: he hadn't sought to address the conference from fear of being caught, but because he was an archaeologist at heart, and he'd considered whatever lay behind this wall too important for him to tackle by himself. And so he'd stopped.

Scuffling and heavy breathing behind her. She turned to see Mikhail arriving at the far end of the passage, his shirt shredded, his powerful upper body revealed, the patchwork of crude tattoos, the Mauser slung over his shoulder, his hunting knife in his hand. She climbed back down the ladder, but there was nowhere left to run or hide. He must have realised she was trapped, for he came unhurriedly towards her, almost with a swagger. She stooped for a sharp and heavy stone, held it behind her back. He reached the top of the steps then sauntered down them, tucking his knife into his belt as he came. She waited until he was close and then swung the stone hard at his temple; but he must have been expecting it, for he caught her wrist easily and twisted it until she cried out and dropped the stone. He grabbed a fistful of her hair and pulled her sharply sideways until she was off-balance, then he hauled her by it back up to the passage floor, where he threw her down and kicked her onto her back and stood astride her, pinning her wrists beneath his feet.

'Please,' she begged. 'Let me go.'

He laughed at that, as though she'd only meant it as a joke. 'I've been looking forward to this,' he told her, kneading the sideways bulge of his erection through his trousers. 'I gave your boyfriend my word. I always keep my word.'

The lamplight stuttered a moment, as though the generator was running out of fuel. There was noise back along the way they'd come. Gaille turned her head sideways just in time to see a third person arrive at the far end of the passage, sledgehammer in his hand.

'You!' scowled Mikhail.

'Yes,' agreed Knox. 'Me.'

II

It had been a mixed morning for the Intensive Care team. One of their charges had died; another had been returned to a general ward. As a result, the unit was empty except for Augustin and two nurses, so Claire felt free to unplug the headphones from the DVD player Nico had brought the day before.

She hadn't watched it the night before; she'd had too much else on her mind. But this morning she'd already played it through twice. There was something compelling about it, though she wasn't sure what. Not the words themselves, for even though they'd been written by Augustin, the technical language and obscure references mostly went over her head. It was more to do with the way Knox had somehow captured Augustin's qualities of voice, despite their different accents: his cadence, his metre, his trick of making listeners wait, the mischievous delivery of his punch-lines.

When this calamity had befallen Augustin, a treasonous internal voice had whispered to Claire that protocol didn't compel her to stick by him, as she'd stuck by her father. He wasn't blood, after all; they weren't yet married. She could simply fly back to America and pretend this episode had never happened. But she knew now that wasn't possible. When you gave your heart this completely to another person, it was no longer yours to take back.

On the DVD, Knox was nearing the end of his talk. She turned the volume up. It was a real comfort to listen to Augustin's words, but this was what she truly enjoyed, the extraordinary ovation that would shortly greet its conclusion, the tribute it so clearly represented to the man she loved. Each time she played it, it made her heart swell.

Augustin's left eyelash fluttered, delicate as a fly's wing. Though it was one of the few times she'd seen him show even that much sign of life, she didn't let it get her spirits up. His doctors had taken him off the barbiturates the night before, in the hopes that he might come out of the induced coma; but she was experienced enough with ICU patients to know that such tics happened all the time.

She leaned closer, just in case, murmured his name and squeezed his hand. His eyelash fluttered again, then opened for a blink before closing once more. She watched transfixed, simultaneously terrified and charged with hope. Then both his eyes sprang open, bloodshot and perplexed, even alarmed. She stood and leaned over him so that he'd know she was there, that he was safe and loved and cared for. But it didn't seem to do any good. His agitation increased, he slid his eyes to the side, he tried to speak.

'Don't talk,' she pleaded, anxiety battling euphoria. 'Just try to rest.'

He didn't listen, his lips moved again, he muttered something that she couldn't hear, because the applause had just started on the DVD, all that splendid thunder. She jabbed the button to silence it, put her ear back to Augustin's mouth, and finally made out his words. 'What's that bastard Knox doing,' he murmured, 'delivering *my* talk?'

III

Gaille's euphoria at seeing Knox was almost instantly extinguished as Mikhail grabbed his Mauser and turned it on him. Knox had no time to reach him or even flee, so Gaille twisted her wrist free from beneath Mikhail's foot, reached up and grabbed the Mauser's strap and tugged down hard just as he fired, the bullet crashing into the rock floor and then ricocheting harmlessly away.

Knox seized the moment she'd bought him, charging down the passage with a full-throated roar, swinging the sledgehammer in a wild arc at Mikhail's head, forcing him to use the Mauser as a staff to defend himself. It cracked and splintered in his hands, the barrel coming loose from the stock, yet still holding sufficiently to save him from the sledge, though his knees buckled and he stumbled backwards. He threw away the broken gun and grabbed the sledgehammer's head instead, wrestling Knox for it, using his greater strength to swing Knox around and against the wall of rubble, tearing the hammer from him as he do so.

Mikhail took it by the shaft and went straight after him, swinging like a baseball batter aiming for the bleachers. Knox ducked in time and it slammed into the rubble behind him, dislodging some of the smaller stones that cascaded away down the other side, making Petitier's hole a fraction bigger. Mikhail cursed and briefly let go of the shaft, his hands fizzing from the impact, then swung a second time. Knox tried to duck beneath it again, but Mikhail was expecting it and lowered his arc just enough for the head to clip Knox's temple as it passed, before smashing like a wrecking ball into the rock behind, sending more stones crashing, creating a thin but distinct gap at the top. With Knox dazed and down, Mikhail raised the sledgehammer for the kill, but Gaille thrust the Mauser's splintered stock at his face, making him lose his footing on the scattered stone marbles, and fall backwards. She grabbed Knox's hand and dragged him up and over the shrunken mound, then they were fighting their way through the rubble, pushing it aside as they went, scrambling down the other side, coughing and blinking from the thick dust.

They found themselves near the top of a wide flight of steps, looking out over the floor of a huge gallery, vast and dark as a night-time cathedral. The only thing Gaille could see clearly was the thin crevice in its high domed roof, its jagged edges overgrown with vegetation, the walls beneath black with dirt and guano. A few bats, disturbed from their roosts, flapped around so high above them they looked like specks of dust. On the wall beneath the crevice, a little weak sunlight glittered on waterfalls of quartz that fell in frozen cascades, and threw shadows on ridges of stalactites and stalagmites, so that they looked for all the world like the pipes of some grotesque church organ.

There was grunting and cursing behind, as

Mikhail came after them. Knox still looked disoriented; she led him briskly down the steps to the cavern floor. A narrow flight of steps led up to a circular dais on which sat a marble throne, glowing palely in the darkness. A pair of golden rings set with rough-cut stones lay in the thick dust upon the throne's seat, while a golden headband with two gilded horns lay beside it, along with a golden goblet; and just for a blink Gaille had the strongest image of a man sitting here millennia before, and perhaps even dying here.

Something on the throne's high back caught her eye. A sheepskin robe, only woven from the finest imaginable thread that gleamed beneath its coat of dust as only one metal could. Her breath caught in her throat as she touched it. 'Jesus!' muttered Knox groggily. 'Is that . . .'

'The golden fleece,' whispered Gaille. 'So he found it after all.'

Footsteps on the cavern floor. Mikhail was coming. A narrow walkway led away from the dais along a colonnade of double axes. They fled down it to a second, larger platform. Her eyes had adjusted a little to the intense gloom, and she could see that this new platform was shaped like a giant rosette, with the largest stalagmite that Gaille had ever seen at its heart, thrusting almost obscenely upwards. It had a shallow basin at its foot for libations and sacrifices, as though it had once been worshipped as some great deity come to earth; and now she drew close enough that with a shock she realised what deity it was, for it looked just like a gigantic bull rearing up on its hind legs above her; and it wasn't merely imagination playing tricks, but a deliberate likeness of a bull sculpted from an original accident of rock. Elephant tusks had been set upon its head, and its shoulders had been smoothed and shaped, and the limestone ridging of its torso had been exaggerated to create the impression of a coat, creating a Minotaur to stand immortal guardian at the heart of this natural labyrinth. Only its base had been left unshaped, perhaps out of reverence, or perhaps because the whole stalagmite stood at a slight angle, and they'd feared to weaken it, lest it topple and shatter.

And that wasn't the end of it. On the platform at either side of the massive column, and behind, an extraordinary array of artefacts had been gathered. Most were rendered unrecognisable by thick coverings of dust and debris, though others had been sheltered by chance or the topography of this great chamber. They'd evidently once been arranged in groups divided by a grid of lanes, but so many of them had fallen over or disintegrated over the millennia that they'd made an obstacle course of themselves. Bowls of gems and semi-precious stones had scattered on the floor. A pink marble statue of a goddess, her arms raised in benediction, lay aslant across their path. A golden pendant of bees circling the sun lay in the dust. There was ancient weaponry too, shields and swords and axes; but all too pitted and fragile to be of use. She stooped for an ivory figurine of a young woman with an almond-shaped skull, cousins to the ones she and Knox had recently discovered in Akhenaten's tomb. She slapped it against her palm, but it was too light to do any proper damage, so she set it back down.

They ventured deeper and deeper into the treasures, putting distance between themselves and Mikhail, and it was then that they came across their most astonishing discovery yet: a towering golden statue of a bearded charioteer being drawn up into the sky by six winged horses. And her heart twisted with sadness for Iain, despite everything he'd done, that he'd not lived long enough to see it.

'What?' asked Knox, sensing something in her manner.

'Atlantis,' she told him.

FORTY-FOUR

I

All his life, Mikhail had known in his heart he was destined for greatness. All his life, he'd known his time would come. That was what they didn't understand, the little people who sought to hold him back and subject him to their petty rules. But it hadn't been until this very moment that he'd understood exactly what form his greatness would take.

The golden fleece. *His* golden fleece.

He reached out reverently and touched it. It was made from exquisitely fine threads of gold twisted together into amazingly lifelike tufts that rippled as he brushed them. He set the sledgehammer down on the rock floor, then picked up the fleece with both hands, expecting it to be so heavy that it would take all his strength to lift. But not only was it an artefact of indescribable beauty, it proved an astonishing achievement of craft too, for it was little heavier than the rucksack full of rocks he'd sometimes take on his runs whenever he feared he was growing unfit. He swung it around onto his shoulders in the almost certain knowledge that it would fit perfectly, as though it had been made for him; and it did. It had a chain and buckle for clasping around the neck. He fitted them together and laughed exultantly when they locked. Then he stood there for a moment, his chest swelling with pride as he imagined how he'd look on the world's television screens when he wore it on his return to Georgia.

A Nergadze would be Georgia's next leader after all. Nothing could stop him, not now that he had this. And fuck the elections; fuck the ballot box. Popularity had always been his grandfather's conceit. But their president had declared war, and Mikhail was the man to give it to him.

He looked along the avenue of double-headed axes down which Knox and Gaille had fled. They couldn't be allowed out of here, lest they blab and ruin his triumph. He tried to unbuckle the fleece, but its clasp had jammed, and its collar was too tight around his throat for him to pull it off over his head. He reached for his hunting knife, to cut through one of the links, then hesitated. It felt too like sacrilege. He put his knife away again. He was

Mikhail Nergadze, after all. He could take out Knox and the girl by himself, hampered by a thousand fleeces.

He picked up his sledgehammer once more, then set off along the walkway.

II

Knox still felt nauseous and unsteady from the glancing sledgehammer blow he'd taken. He felt strangely powerless, too. Mikhail had shown even in their brief tussle that he was far too strong for him at the best of times, let alone armed as he was with a sledgehammer, a hunting knife and a boundless willingness to inflict pain. Gaille's cheeks were glazed with tears and she kept shuddering. He put his arms around her and hugged her. 'This is the last time I ever send you away to keep you safe,' he whispered in her ear.

Somehow she managed a laugh. 'Is that a promise?'

'It's a promise.'

'Thank Christ. But what do we do now?'

'The police are on their way,' he assured her. 'We just need to find a way out of here.' Easier said than done. The crevice in the roof was far too difficult a climb. And the floor surrounding the rosette platform was impassable with huge boulders and jagged rock. Which left only the way they'd come, back along the colonnade of axes and then through the cave.

But first they had to get by Mikhail.

He looked back past the stalagmite. His stomach clenched as he saw the faint aura of the golden fleece around Mikhail's shoulders as he advanced towards them.

III

Mikhail reached the base of the stalagmite then the edge of the gallery of treasures. The narrow lanes between them were too constricted to allow a good swing of his sledgehammer. He considered leaving it behind or even throwing it out into the surrounding rocks, but he didn't want to give Knox or Gaille even the slightest opportunity to arm themselves, so he gripped it by its throat to shorten its shaft, then pressed on.

He walked slowly, scouring the darkness as he went, half expecting an ambush at every step. It didn't come. He paused to listen, but heard only his own breathing; and just for the briefest moment he had a flashback to that Fort Lauderdale gaol just three weeks before, pressing that psychologist against the interview room wall with his body, the way her breathing had fused with his, the feel of her pussy as he'd cupped it with his hand. He didn't know how he'd come to understand her game, other than he'd always had a sixth sense for duplicity. Luring him on so that she could cry rape and have him banged up for years; or even perhaps wearing a second recording device, hoping to trick him into an indiscretion. It didn't matter which. All that mattered was that she'd thought to betray him and bring him down, and so she'd had to pay, just as Knox and Gaille were about to.

He saw a flutter in the shadows ahead, but pretended he hadn't. If they thought they could ambush him or even outflank him and so get back to the walkway, they had another think coming. It was just a question now of waiting for his chance.

FORTY-FIVE

I

Knox and Gaille backed cautiously away from Mikhail's advance, trying to loop around the stalagmite to the walkway. But Knox trod on a loose rock and instinctively grabbed Gaille's forearm to stop himself from falling, pulling her off-balance too. It was only a moment, but it was enough. With a terrifying war-cry, Mikhail charged out of the darkness, the sledgehammer raised like an executioner's axe, swinging it lethally down at Knox's head. Knox had no time to get out of range; he leapt inside the blow instead, slamming his shoulder into Mikhail's chest, dumping him onto his backside, the hammer passing harmlessly behind his back. Mikhail let go of its shaft, drew his knife and in a single fluid movement slashed up at Knox's face.

'Run!' yelled Gaille.

Knox didn't hesitate. He turned and fled with her out of the gallery of treasures down the colonnade of axes then over to the steps and clambering breathlessly back over the rubble mound. The generator must have run out of fuel, for the lamps had gone out in the passage, leaving it dark as blindness. He crouched and felt for the electrical cable. 'Grab my shirt,' he told Gaille. 'Don't let go.' He waited till she had a firm grip, then set off up the passage, using the cable like Ariadne's thread to guide him back out of this labyrinth. Aware Mikhail would be able to use it too, he pulled it after him as he went; but a loop of it snagged on a rock and he couldn't tug it free. And then he heard Mikhail, and it was too late. They scrambled up the ramp of rock, picked up the flex again. The blackness had settled around them so completely he could see nothing at all, making it hard to know how much distance they were covering. He held out his free hand defensively, lest he crack his head on an overhang. They'd soon come to the top of a high rock shelf; he remembered that much. He got down onto hands and knees and crept along until he felt its edge, then he found the top of the ladder and climbed briskly down. He waited for Gaille at the foot then they tried to rip the ladder from the wall, but again Mikhail was on them before they could finish, and they turned and hurried on, Mikhail cursing and muttering behind as they passed through tunnels and galleries. Gaille was struggling to keep up, so Knox slowed as far as he dared. Then finally there was a lessening of the darkness and he glimpsed greyness ahead, and suddenly they were at the cave mouth, blinking at the light, flinching at the horrific sight of Iain's head lying on its side. They got back onto their hands and knees and crawled along the throat of the cave until they were outside.

There was no way to defend the mouth, not against Mikhail and his knife. Knox thought he could see a pathway through the gorse out into the main body of the plain, so he charged straight into it. Passage proved easy enough for the first few metres, but it grew increasingly tangled and hard. He held up his forearms to protect his chest from the spines as he fought his way past the tough stubby branches, creating a path for Gaille to follow. His legs tired, he began to falter; but then he heard an engine, rising then briefly fading away, before a black wasp appeared over the southern escarpment face. His spirits soared: Angelos had delivered his promised helicopter. He looked around as Mikhail emerged from the cave, the golden fleece still clasped around his throat, gleaming gloriously in the sunlight. He strode into the gorse after them, taking advantage of their wake to close rapidly.

Knox waved his arms to attract the pilot's attention. He feared he'd be too far away to be seen, but the helicopter abruptly changed course towards him. Fighting through the gorse was like wading through deep mud; he couldn't sustain his pace much longer. Gaille must have sensed it, for she pushed past him, taking her own turn at forcing them a path, looking back every few moments to make sure he was following.

The copter made a fierce noise as it drew close, blasting them with its downdraft as it made to set down by the edge of the gorse. Its door slid open even as it was still landing, and two men jumped out. Knox glanced exultantly back at Mikhail, expecting him to flee while he still had the chance. But Mikhail was not only still following, he was waving to the men, gesturing instructions. And only now did Knox notice their lack of uniforms; only now did he recognise the helicopter from the Internet photograph of Ilya Nergadze's yacht.

He yelled at Gaille to stop, but she didn't hear him over the din of rotor-blades. She fought her way through the last of the gorse and ran out; but one of the two men drew his handgun and aimed at her chest. She stopped uncertainly and looked back at Knox, still tangled in the gorse. The fear in her eyes twisted at his heart, but there was nothing he could do. The second man now drew

his own gun; he aimed at Knox and fired twice.
Knox dived for cover then scrambled away beneath
the yellow canopy, putting distance between
himself and where he'd been. Then he lay there
panting hard, remembering with a dreadful foreboding the cruelties Mikhail had inflicted on
Nadya, and wondering what horrors now awaited
the woman he loved.

II

The look on Rafiel's face was all the confirmation Mikhail needed that the fleece was his ticket
to the presidential palace.

'Is that . . . ?' he asked in awe, reaching out to
touch it.

'Keep your hands to yourself.' The helicopter
blades were slowing down, but he still had to shout
to make himself heard. He nodded to the second
man, who was holding Gaille with his arm around
her throat and his gun against her side. 'Who are
you?'

'Nukri, sir,' replied the man, clicking his heels
as best he could.

'You're a soldier?'

'Yes, sir.'

'Good.' He turned back to Rafiel. 'Where's the
boat?'

Rafiel gestured south. 'We were about twenty-five knots southeast when we set off. She'll be closer now. But we need to get moving. There were police on the slopes when we were coming in.'

'We're dealing with Knox first.'

'Yes, but if they call in their Air Force –'

Mikhail turned to him. 'Don't ever question my orders again,' he said. 'Do you understand?'

'Yes, sir. I'm sorry, sir.'

Mikhail nodded emphatically; but the man was right, they needed to be quick. He grabbed Gaille by her hair, pressed his knife against her throat and dragged her over to the gorse. 'Give yourself up,' he shouted out to Knox. 'Give yourself up now or she dies. You have five seconds. Four. Three.' He watched intently for movement as he finished the countdown, but saw nothing. *What a coward that man was!* He turned his knife around in his hand to make it easier to slash her throat, but then he paused, inspired by a better idea.

III

The rotor blades had been slowing down, but now they started speeding up once more, the copter preparing for take off. Knox crept closer to the edge of the gorse and peered out. To his exquisite relief, he saw Gaille standing on this side of the helicopter; and he could also see, through the cabin window, the pilot and Mikhail and the two other Georgians all safely inside. They were about to take off, and they were leaving Gaille behind.

The helicopter began to rise; it was only a couple of metres off the ground when Gaille began to rise with it, kicking and thrashing like a fish on a hook. Only now did Knox understand. Mikhail hadn't let her go after all; he was hanging her instead from a black cord like a dog's leash he'd slung out the cabin window. Her face was already red, her mouth gaping as though screaming, though he couldn't hear a thing over the din of the copter as it hovered there just above the ground. The cabin window now slid open, and Mikhail showed himself, the fleece still buckled around his throat. He reached out his hand, waved his hunting knife back and forth for Knox to see, then he tossed it down onto the ground in a clear challenge: cut down your woman or watch her hang.

Fear welled in Knox, but love did too. He jumped to his feet and burst out of the gorse and sprinted towards her, weaving left and right, keeping his eyes on the fallen knife. He heard the expected cracks of gunfire even over the roar of the blades, dived into a roll, snatching for the knife as he came up, but missing. And now the helicopter was turning away and beginning to rise, taking Gaille with it. He had no time. He leapt for and grabbed one of the sled-skis of its landing gear. The downdraft from the rotor-blades, the slickness of the black composite material, it took everything he had to hold on. But he tightened his grip and swung a leg up and over the sled-ski, then the other, hauling himself up, grabbing one of the struts holding the sled-ski to the copter's undercarriage. They were rising fast now, Gaille dangling from its other side, her face purple, her legs thrashing, her tongue protruding. He anchored himself as best he could, then reached out beneath the copter's belly to the other sled-ski. His finger-tips brushed it. He tried again, straining every bone and sinew, caught enough of it to commit himself to the transfer. The helicopter tipped as he swung from one side to the other, then hauled himself up. He put an arm around Gaille's hips and lifted her to relieve the pressure on her throat. She was still thrashing, desperate for something to stand on. Her heel clipped the sled-ski but then she had her feet upon it. He held her there as best he could while picking loose the knots around her wrists with his fingernails. She pulled a hand free and then the other, the coil of rope dropping away to the earth far below as she frantically loosened the noose around her throat and gulped in breath. But, even at that moment, she started to topple and fall outwards. It took Knox a bare microsecond to realise that Mikhail had let go of the leash, the only thing that had been anchoring her against the helicopter's side. She looked up at him as she fell, reaching for him with her freed hands, imploring him with her eyes. Without thinking, he wrapped his legs around the strut and crossed his ankles and let himself drop, catching her by her calf, her cotton trousers slithering through his fingers, but grabbing her ankle and holding it tight as they surged even higher, the rocky plain now a good two or three hundred metres below, far too far for her to survive a fall.

He tried to lift her back up, but he wasn't strong enough, it was all he could do to hang on. She reached up for him from her waist in an effort to grab his forearm, but she couldn't quite manage that either, beaten back by the downdraft of the rotor-blades. They crested the escarpment, headed south towards the sea. Still he clung on, but he was tiring fast, his joints screaming. He looked up, praying that someone inside the helicopter would take pity on them, only to see Mikhail leaning out the cabin window, watching raptly as he waited for Knox to drop her.

FORTY-SIX

I

The land plunged away beneath the helicopter, a series of cliffs and bluffs almost sheer down to the coast two thousand feet below, where waves broke white against the rocks. Knox felt Gaille slipping from him; he cried out in his effort to hold her. She must have realised her time was short, for she swung a couple of times then gave it everything, bending upwards from her waist, grabbing his wrist for a moment but unable to hold on, dislodged by the juddering of the helicopter and the blast of its blades. She tried again, and clung on this time, then climbed her hands up his arms to his hair and his nostrils and chin, grabbing his shirt and trousers and then hauling herself up him and back onto the sled-ski, taking the weight gloriously off him, allowing him to lift himself up to safety too.

Mikhail had been watching all this from the cabin window. He smiled as he reached out his handgun and aimed down at Gaille. From point blank range, he pulled the trigger three times. The first round caught Gaille in her forehead, the second in her chest as she was already falling. But there was no third shot, his clip was already empty.

Knox watched in disbelief as Gaille fell, her outflung limbs describing silent slow spirals, passing through a wisp of cloud before vanishing from view. Then he looked up at Mikhail, who was still leaning out the cabin window, watching him rather than Gaille, savouring every detail of his pain. Then he turned his gun on him and pulled the trigger twice more, evidently unaware that he'd run out of bullets. He shrugged indifferently when he realised, withdrew back inside the cabin, and closed the window.

Knox sat slumped on the sled-ski in numb despair, his heart and guts ripped out, taken by Gaille as she'd fallen. He didn't know how long he sat there before the rage began, lapping at him at first, but then coming in giant waves. He stood up on the sled-ski, holding himself against the cabin door by its outside latch, trying to open it; but it was locked from inside, as was the window. He glared in through the glass, but Mikhail only winked at him, relishing Knox's powerlessness and grief, while the others looked away, pretending to themselves that this wasn't happening, that they hadn't just abetted in the murder of an innocent young woman. He pounded on the glass, but it did no good; and it was galling to have his rage so impotent, to have it *sneered* at like this, and his fingers grew cold from the wind and altitude, making his hold on the door-latch uncertain, so he sat back down upon the sled-ski before he fell. He anchored an arm around the strut, and the red mist gradually dissipated, leaving only the most exquisite anguish and the dull necessity of revenge.

The coast was shrinking fast behind them. A black dot on the horizon grew large and then took shape. Nergadze's yacht. They circled around to its stern, where the helipad was swarming with crew. The pilot drew them closer and closer, the downdraft ruffling the deckhands' hair, making spinnakers of their shirts. One of them drew a handgun and took aim at Knox, but someone in the copter must have waved them off, perhaps worried about their accuracy from the yacht's lurching deck. A second deckhand fetched a long boathook instead. The helicopter edged close enough for him to swing it at Knox, catching him a painful blow on the calf. He swung again and caught his knee. Knox had no way to protect himself, nowhere to hide. The sea beneath was a maelstrom, chopped up by the downdraft. Jump, and he'd be easy pickings, unless they simply left him there to drown.

He grabbed the other sled-ski, swung across. The helicopter lurched; deckhands yelled and scattered. The pilot swung around to bring Knox back into their range. The rage returned to Knox: he remembered Gaille. Sitting upon the sled-ski, he unbuttoned his jeans, then peeled them off leg by leg and stood up. Mikhail watched curiously from inside the cabin. Holding his jeans by one leg, Knox tried to throw the other leg upwards like a length of rope, hoping they'd catch in the blades, but the fury of the downdraft made that impossible. He bit the fabric between his teeth instead, then shimmied along the sled-ski towards the rear, where the copter's roof was lower. He clawed his fingernails into the rubber seals at the top of the cabin window as he hauled himself up, the ferocious downdraft making it feel like climbing against a waterfall. But his anger gave him strength and somehow he fought his way up onto the roof, then crawled on his belly to the place where the Jesus nut held the blades to the top of the copter. The downdraft was still fierce, but not as bad as he'd feared, as though he'd reached the eye of the storm. He fed his jeans into the whirling blur of metal, and they were snatched from his grasp and instantly shredded, but some of the threads wrapped around the Jesus nut, choking it and making it cough, and the helicopter momentarily lost power, dropping and lurching violently sideways, the rotor blades sawing wickedly across the yacht's deck. A deafening crack as they hit and shattered, lethal shards flying like shrapnel, giving Knox a harrowing glimpse of deckhands screaming and holding bloodied stumps.

One of the helicopter's sled-skis caught in the deck-rail. It hung for a moment on the side of the yacht, then broke free and plunged down into the sea, taking Knox with it. A fuel-tank split open; the water stank and seared his eyes. Sparks flew and the surface around him burst into gouts of flame that he felt searing at his back and shoulder, so he dived underwater until they were out. He resurfaced to see one of Mikhail's men wrestle open the copter door from the inside and leap out into the sea, flailing as though he couldn't swim. A second man followed. Knox let them both go, then pulled himself in through the open door before it could close again from the force of water. The cabin itself was still buoyant with trapped air, but the tail was sinking fast, the floor already sloped backwards at a forty-five degree angle, more water gushing in all the time. The pilot was strapped in his seat, his mouth and eyes open, his neck broken from the crash. Mikhail was still inside too, very much alive but trapped by the fleece, jammed between the side of his seat and the helicopter's buckled frame. He was working furiously to undo the clasp around his throat, but when he saw Knox he must have known he had no more time, for he hurled his shoulder against the cabin wall, bending the metal back just far enough to pull the fleece out and so free himself.

The cabin now sank beneath the surface, leaving only a pocket of air trapped against the helicopter's windscreen. Mikhail made for the door, but Knox dragged him back. He was a diver; water gave him his only edge. Mikhail turned and put his hands on Knox's shoulders and pushed him under. Knox wrapped his arms around Mikhail's waist and dragged him down with him. They wrestled furiously, turning this way and that. Mikhail got his hands around Knox's throat and began to throttle him. Knox tried to pull him off, but he was too strong for him, the man was pure muscle; but damned if he'd let him beat him. He drew his knees up beneath his chin, put his feet in Mikhail's chest and kicked himself free. Then he splashed up to the small pocket of air still trapped against the windscreen, coughed and spluttered out water, breathed thankfully in.

Through the glass, he could see how far they'd already sunk, sunlight sparkling on the surface fifteen or twenty metres above, the black whale of the yacht's underbelly. Mikhail bobbed up beside him, gasping for air, fighting to keep his head above water, still weighted down by the fleece. Knox didn't hesitate: he threw himself upon Mikhail's shoulders as he was breathing in, made him suck water exactly as he'd forced Knox to the day before, while he'd had him strapped to his water-torture bench. The memory gave Knox strength and steel; while Mikhail was still spluttering, he pulled him beneath the surface and held him there, wrapping his legs around the base of one of the seats, ignoring the depth-gauge protests of his own sinuses, the punches and slaps and clawing; vengeance was all that mattered, he owed it to Gaille, and finally he got it, as Mikhail's struggles slackened and then went still.

Knox's own lungs were screaming for relief. He pulled himself upwards but the windscreen had buckled just enough that all the air had bubbled away. The cabin door had closed again and now was almost impossible to open against the wall of water; but he managed it in the end, kicked for the surface high above, keeping his body stream-lined as he surged upwards, fighting the urge to open his mouth, using his will as never before to suppress his natural reflexes until finally he breached the surface and sucked in the glorious air, letting it flood and circulate back through his system.

Around him, the detritus of the crash. Life-jackets and broken lengths of plastic, and things on fire. He couldn't see anyone in the water, but people were wailing in anguish and agony on the deck above him, sounds to gladden the heart. The adrenaline of combat started to subside; he felt the full sear of the burns he'd taken on his back.

A fighter jet marked with Greek insignia roared so low over the yacht that he flinched from it, its vapour trail making strange contortions of the sky. Then he looked north towards the coast, and saw two helicopters sweeping across the sea, and all he felt was a terrible anger that now they were coming, now when it was too late.

EPILOGUE

The man from the British Embassy wore a black suit and tie, as though he'd come to a funeral. As in a sense he had. He settled himself primly beside Knox's hospital bed, his discomfort with such places evident from his efforts to look at ease.

'Who are you?' asked Knox.

'You've caused quite a stir, you know,' the man told him, smoothing down his trouser leg. 'You've had all kinds of important people flying back and forth.'

'Is that right?'

'It is, it is,' he beamed. 'You're the toast of the Foreign Office. The way the Greeks have treated you and your friends . . .' he shook his head with mock reproach. 'A very nursable grievance, that. We'll be able to leverage it for years.'

'I'm glad to have been of use.'

The man seemed to realise that his levity was

inappropriate, for he assumed a more sober countenance. 'That's not why I'm here, of course.'

'Is it not?' asked Knox, turning his head towards the window. He could see the perfect blue sky outside. Sometimes there were gulls, but not right now.

'How much do you know about what's been happening?' asked the man. 'With the Nergadzes, I mean?'

'Nothing.' Nico had been in, but mostly he'd talked about the ongoing excavation of Petitier's cave and the successful decryption of his journals, the manic personality they'd revealed. '*I have found the lost labyrinth*,' one entry had run. '*I have found the golden fleece. I have found Atlantis.*' And Iain's book, being published early to seize the moment, looked set to make a fortune for his widow and son, even though – or perhaps because – it was becoming clearer and clearer just how closely he'd modelled his own theories upon Petitier's research. But Knox was indifferent to it all; it meant nothing.

'Ilya is going to be released, you see,' said the man. 'He's reached an accommodation with the president. That's how it works, with men like that. They reach accommodations. He's pleading guilty to some minor infractions, he'll spend a little time in gaol. No great punishment, all things considered, but it'll mean the end of his political aspirations, and of his family's too. And when powerful people are humiliated and crippled like this, they tend to look for scapegoats.'

That caught Knox's attention. '*Me?*' he asked incredulously.

The man nodded. 'He blames you for his grandson's death. Or he claims to, at least, which isn't quite the same thing, not with these people. He's not exactly shedding many tears over Mikhail, believe me; but he was family, so he has to be seen to care. More to the point, he has to be seen to do something. He needs people to know that there'll be the gravest possible consequences for anyone who crosses him.'

'You're not saying he's put a price on my head?'

'A *huge* price,' said the man, with evident satisfaction. 'Five million euros, to be exact. Complete overkill, if you'll pardon the expression. These days, you can commission a hit for a couple of grand. Hit-men are feeling the pinch just like everybody else. But of course it's not really about you. Nergadze is using you as a way to warn his enemies not to take him lightly, just because he looks weakened. Not that that's much consolation, I imagine. It's no fun, having a price on one's head.'

'You've had one yourself, have you?'

He shook his head. 'No. But I've worked with people who have. You might say that protection is a specialty of mine. Which is why I was asked to come here and talk to you, of course.' He made a steeple of his hands. 'The thing is, protection isn't easy. Even in the United Kingdom, it isn't easy.'

'That's okay, then. I live in Egypt.'

'Not any more, you don't. Our Egyptian friends won't take you back. You wouldn't last a week there, anyway. Not with that kind of price on your head. No, it's back to Britain with you, and you'll just have to get used to living in a security cocoon. Not much fun. And *very* expensive for our poor old taxpayers.'

Ah! thought Knox. *Now we get to it.* 'Unless . . . ?' he asked.

'You do have an option, as it happens,' smiled the man, as though he'd only just thought of it. 'I wouldn't normally raise this, not while you're recovering; but these are extraordinary circumstances, and if we're to do it, this is our moment.'

'Do what?'

'You suffered extensive burns, you see. Not life-threatening, not any more. Though your being a rare blood-type didn't help. You might want to get yourself a bracelet in the future, or one of those medallion jobbies. Save everyone a lot of grief. But the point is this: the world believes you're still perilously sick. So imagine if we were to arrange for a Medevac plane to fly you back to England. Imagine you were to have a setback. Acute renal failure, say. It often happens to burn victims. Imagine you were to go onto life support, but despite the heroic efforts of our very best doctors . . .'

'And then what?' asked Knox. 'Plastic surgery? A new identity?'

'Maybe a tweak here, an injection there. But nothing major. You may be a household name, but you're not a household face at all. You've kept an admirably low profile for someone in your position. My colleagues have already taken the liberty of releasing some photos of you, tweaked just enough to give a false impression. Throw in some three-day stubble, tinted contact lenses, highlights for your hair . . . Trust me. We're good at this kind of thing. It would give you a whole new start. Think of that. Half the people I know would give their right arms for a whole new start. And it wouldn't be forever, not if you don't fancy it: just until old man Nergadze dies, and the family implodes, which it will. They always do in the end. Maybe you could teach. Not Egyptology, of course. That'll be out for a while. History, say. Or diving. Didn't you work as an instructor once? I have a friend from my service days who runs a marine salvage business down in Hove. He's always moaning about how hard it is to find high-quality underwater archaeologists. Shipwreck sites are so regulated these days, people like you are in great demand. Think about that. You could travel overseas again. I know how much you like to travel.'

'Yes,' said Knox. He understood something now, something that had been puzzling him. Augustin had come by earlier, pushing himself in his wheel-chair, recuperating from his own injuries. 'What a pair we make,' he'd grunted, as he'd helped himself to Knox's fruit.

'Yes.'

'I watched that pig's ear you made of my lecture.'

'The best I could do with the material I had.'

Silence had fallen, then grown heavy. Augustin had covered Knox's hand with his own. 'I'm so sorry about Gaille,' he'd said. 'I don't know what to say.'

'Forget it.'

'I want you to know something. Whatever decision you make, you'll have my complete and unquestioning support. Claire's too. You do realise that, don't you?'

Knox hadn't understood what he was getting at, not at the time; but now it seemed clear that this man had been scouting for their opinions.

'Well?' he asked. 'What do you say?'

'This would save you a lot of money, would it?'

'That's not the only reason,' he replied. 'Your quality of life will be better, I promise.'

'May I think about it?'

'Of course. But we can't wait forever. How about I come by again in the morning?'

'Fine,' said Knox. He turned his head to the side until he heard the door close. Sometimes, he could sense a great black pit opening up in the world, he'd be confronted again by the loss of Gaille, by the completeness of his failure as a man. He could feel it opening now. His breath grew faster as he braced himself. It started as it always did with a reprise of that helpless terror he'd felt when Mikhail had had him strapped down to his bench and then poured water into his mouth and made him drown. It would be haunting him for months, he knew, if not years. And the knowledge provoked in him an intense rage, not just at Mikhail, who he'd held responsible until now, but at Mikhail's father and his grandfather too; particularly at his grandfather. He'd known Mikhail was a psychopath, yet he'd sent him to Athens all the same, surely aware of the carnage he was likely to wreak. And instead of feeling remorse at what he'd done, all he could do was use his death as an excuse for more of his wretched power-games.

Rather to Knox's surprise, his rage felt good. Or, more accurately, it felt better than despair had done.

He hadn't listened closely to the man from the embassy. He already knew he'd accept his offer, if only because he lacked the will to refuse. But, as he lay there, a new thought came suddenly to him. Personal experience had taught him how hard it was to attack extreme wealth head-on. So long as the Nergadzes knew he was alive, they'd find it easy to protect themselves from him, or perhaps even succeed in getting rid of him altogether. But should they believe him dead . . .

He let the idea take rough shape in his mind. A new identity, a new look, a new passport. A year or two to recuperate and let the Nergadzes think they'd got away with it. And then some way to get undetected onto their home turf. And the man from the embassy had even given him an idea for that. For a moment, Knox envisaged himself working on some marine salvage job near the Black Sea coast, where all the oligarchs had their summer houses. Then in a room alone with Ilya Nergadze. How he'd get from one to the other he didn't yet know; but he had all the time in the world to work out the details.

He relaxed back into his mattress, his pillow, looked up at his window, that parallelogram of perfect blue. A gull swooped into view, lit silver-white by the sun, hovering like the holy ghost upon a thermal before drifting slowly out of sight. For the first time in days, he began to feel a little better, a little stronger.

What was it Nico had said that night at the restaurant? Having a purpose, that's the key.

Yes. Having a purpose.